'Akhtar used to … think in English. Tran… …nce: taking up someth… …written in Urdu, and then … …glish. It's a very good example of true … …psi … and in Tanweer's very capable hands this is one happy and safe journey – but a rollercoaster nonetheless' Mohammed Hanif

'Reading Bilal Tanweer's almost seamless translation of Muhammad Khalid Akhtar's novella *Love in Chakiwara and Other Misadventures,* one is reminded afresh of the role of translators in opening windows into new and exciting worlds, worlds that would regrettably be closed for a great many due to the picket fences of script and literary cultures. Tanweer's translation brings to life a world that is hard to believe, but actually exists in Urdu' Rakshanda Jalil

'Urdu is … a language of many linguistic nuances and stylistic curlicues. Despite this … Tanweer's version strikes the English reader as hilarious in parts, and never less than captivating. One turns the pages of this book with always a smile, and sometimes a loud guffaw' Tabish Khair

'Faiz Ahmed Faiz … considered Muhammad Khalid Akhtar's *Love in Chakiwara and Other Misadventures* "the greatest novel in the Urdu language". Its greatness will now not be lost on subsequent generations that think and speak in English thanks to Pakistani writer Bilal Tanweer' *Catch News*

'In novelist Bilal Tanweer's elegant translation, Muhammad Khalid Akhtar's reputation as a writer of great distinction in modern Urdu literature comes through vividly. Steeped in irony, wit and an impish sense of humour, his voice is strikingly contemporary, even though the copiousness with which he tells his stories harks back to another era' *Huffington Post India*

'*Love in Chakiwara* [...] has certainly become a wonderful novel in this rebirth, which will take the English reader to the world of post-independence Karachi and introduce them to its characters, possibly in one of the evening gatherings in Changezi's bakery' *Mid-Day*

'*Love in Chakiwara and Other Misadventures* ... is a lovely contribution to the world of Urdu literature, not least because of its profoundly humanist ethos' *Newsline*

'*Chakiwara* ... a rather colourful, even if decrepit part of Karachi ... In Akhtar's depiction, through this accessible translation, it appears a vibrant and lively place, with never a dull moment' *Scroll.in*

'Bilal Tanweer has done the non-Urdu speaking world a great favour by translating the works of Akhtar into the English language' *The Book Review*

'Tanweer has managed to produce a translation that is a joy to read; fresh and funny but also fully accessible to an English audience' *Friday Times*

LOVE IN CHAKIWARA

and

other misadventures

Muhammad Khalid Akhtar was born in 1920 in Bahawalpur, to a family of scholars. An engineer by training, he began writing in his early twenties. Khalid Akhtar produced numerous stories, essays and travelogues, many of which were published in the Urdu magazine *Sawera*. *Love in Chakiwara and Other Misadventures* (*Chakiwara mein Visaal*), one of his best-known works, was written in 1964, and won the Adamjee Literary Award. Khalid Akhtar died in Karachi in 2002.

Bilal Tanweer is the author of the novel T*he Scatter Here Is Too Great*, which won the Shakti Bhatt First Book Prize and was shortlisted for the DSC Prize for South Asian Literature. He has translated works by Sa'adat Hasan Manto and novels by Ibn-e-Safi. His writings have appeared in various publications, including the *New York Times*, *Caravan*, *Granta* and *Words without Borders*.

LOVE IN CHAKIWARA

and

other misadventures

Muhammad Khalid Akhtar

Translated from the Urdu by

Bilal Tanweer

PICADOR INDIA

First published in English 2016 by Picador India

First published in paperback 2017 by Picador India
an imprint of Pan Macmillan Publishing India Private Limited
707, Kailash Building
26, K. G. Marg, New Delhi – 110 001
www.panmacmillan.co.in

Pan Macmillan, 20 New Wharf Road, London N1 9RR
Basingstoke and Oxford
Associated companies throughout the world
www.panmacmillan.com

ISBN 978-93-86215-21-5

'The Love Meter' first published in Urdu as 'Miqyas-ul Mohabbat' in
Khoya Hua Ufaq, Sang-e-Meel Publications, Lahore, 1986
'Love in Chakiwara and Other Misadventures' first published in Urdu as
Chakiwara mein Visaal, Lark Publishers, Karachi, 1964
'The Smiling Buddha' ('Muskurata Hua Buddha'), 'The Love Meter',
'The Downfall of Seth Tanwari' ('Seth Tanwari ki Tabahi'), and
'Love in Chakiwara and Other Misadventures' first collected in
Majmu'a-e Muhammad Khalid Akhtar, Oxford University Press, Karachi, 2011

1 3 5 7 9 8 6 4 2

Typeset by SÜRYA, New Delhi
Printed and bound in India by
Replika Press Pvt. Ltd.

Contents

The Smiling Buddha

(Excerpted from the *Chakiwara Chronicles* of Mr Iqbal Changezi, Proprietor, Allah Tawakkul Bakery)

These bizarre, tragic and somewhat preposterous series of events (yes, every tragedy has a smattering of comedy after all) that I witnessed in Chakiwara and in which I had a minor role, all began on the morning of 17 July, 1952.

The reason I remember the date is because I keep a diary, a chronicle of sorts, where I record important events or stories every day. On days when nothing interesting happens, I write, 'Nothing interesting happened' under the date. This chronicle has now spread to over seven thousand pages and it could even be turned into a book of eight or nine volumes. In these times of sluggish markets and a general indifference to literature, I don't think any sane publisher would even touch this manuscript with a bargepole. I don't care. I only write it to feed my habit – or addiction – and my friends, Muhammad Deen Asp, Qurban Ali Kattar and others have assured me that the manuscript will certainly be published under their supervision after my death with great ceremony and fanfare. Why they should wish to preserve my personal treasure for the coming generations is beyond me. The chronicle, naturally, is full of bilge and drivel, much like myself. As far as its writing is concerned, I hope that readers who understand me will forgive my nonsensical banter.

I have not used any specific method or care in selecting or structuring the events of this chronicle. I have tried to shape them into a story, even though many would argue rather uselessly with me over calling this a 'story'. They can go to the devil for all I care.

I will call this 'The Story of the Smiling Buddha'. It could also be named 'The Chinese Dentist' or 'The Last Act' but I think 'The Smiling Buddha' is most appropriate because whether one agrees or not, the Buddha played a crucial role in giving a twist to these thrilling events. I am convinced of this.

❁

On the aforementioned morning, I was standing outside Allah Tawakkul Bakery on a ladder with a paintbrush in my hand, painting the bakery's signboard. All businessmen know that the first principle of success is keeping up the appearance of the shop: it must be clean, shiny, and overall in a tip-top condition. It had occurred to me that morning that perhaps the declining sales of bread could be shored up by repainting the dirty and faded letters of the bakery signboard. Painting signboards is not easy; it is far more demanding than writing a three-hundred page novel. I have seen painters who ended up painting themselves while trying to paint a signboard. The painter, who is not in the most comfortable position, grapples with the looming hazard of toppling from the ladder on the passersby below. And yet, painting is not without its pleasures. My colours were coming out bright and fine, and I whistled away as a heady rush of happiness overcame me.

Then out of nowhere I heard something that sounded like an agonized whimper; a long, drawn-out 'HAAEY'. I looked below. Near the foot of the ladder stood my friend Qurban Ali Kattar dressed in the coat-pant that I had lent him last week. His mouth was covered with a handkerchief and there was an anguished expression on his face, which sported an imperial beard. He was staring at me. The sudden, unexpected appearance of this ghost-like figure startled me and I staggered. The bucket slipped from my hand and a large dollop of thick green paint splashed straight on his face and soaked his clothes and a part of his beard. Without paying much attention to his grumbling laments (I couldn't even hear them properly), I asked him what made him quit his soft, warm bed so early in the morning. I reminded him that the bakery didn't open before 8 a.m.

'Changezi yaar! Come down,' he said impatiently. 'You have toppled the paint bucket on me as revenge but I won't say anything. You will regret this later. In any case, I am very ill and if you don't wish your friend an early death then I need to be taken to a doctor urgently.'

'Why should I take you? Why don't you walk there yourself?' I said.

'With illnesses such as mine, the moral support and care of friends is extremely important,' Kattar said. 'I don't want to go alone. What if I collapse on the way to the doctor?'

'What has happened to you?' I asked.

'Changezi yaar, really, I am extremely ill,' Kattar said. 'If something happens to me, imagine the terrible vacuum that would be left in the world of literature. You think this whole thing is just a joke?'

'I am only asking you what the illness is, and why are you holding that handkerchief to your mouth?'

'My gums hurt so much. I couldn't sleep all night. Aaeye! Haaey!' Kattar groaned. 'I have a shooting pain in my head and body. Changezi! I think the recent nuclear tests have made the atmosphere toxic and given rise to radioactivity. I think I have become radioactive.'

I sent Qurban Ali Kattar towards a water tap and calmly finished the work at hand. When I came down he was sitting on the steps of the bakery with a long face. Even after rubbing and scrubbing his face with water, the paint was still stuck to his beard and nose.

I unlocked the door of the bakery and settled him in an armchair.

'Changezi yaar!' he said. 'Get me a steaming hot cup of tea. It might reduce the pain.'

I made tea. Meanwhile, he put his hand in the jar and ate two or three small cakes because he claimed he was unable to chew buns or biscuits.

'When will you take me to the doctor?' he asked. He actually appeared to be in great pain.

'Not taking you to the doctor,' I said. 'Wait for the shops to open up. I'll take you to a dentist. You'll be fine once your jaw tooth is pulled out. He'll probably charge four or five rupees to remove it. If you don't have the money with you, run home and get it first.'

He said he wasn't in a condition to go to his flat so I lent him five rupees. It was about 9 a.m. and Muhammad Deen Asp had also arrived. We helped the weeping, moaning Qurban Ali Kattar to a Chinese dentist's shop on Marriot Road. Let me tell you, it was a very interesting scene. A few people came to sympathize with the unfortunate patient, asking what had happened to him. Some even thought we had kidnapped the novelist but they did not intervene to help him, thinking it must be for a good cause. On our way, we encountered ex-comedian Chakori in his excessively tight hat, who decided to accompany us for moral support. By the time we reached the Chinese dentist Ah Fung's shop, the patient was wailing and kicking like a suckling baby and we had to almost lift and carry him. Finally, we succeeded in offloading him on an empty chair inside. We tried to silence him with words of consolation and even appealed to his manhood but this only made him wail even louder.

When we reached his shop, Ah Fung was busy fixing an old woman's mouth. He looked at the new patient a bit oddly and I think he even gave us a faint smile.

'What happened to the young gentleman?' he asked.

'His jaw hurts,' I explained.

'Okay, he wants it removed?'

We did not know the young gentleman's intentions but we nodded in agreement.

'Bas, I will take one more minute,' said Ah Fung.

The dentist's one minute was indeed one minute. The old woman vacated the revolving chair and we got hold of Qurban Ali Kattar and firmly lodged him in it, ignoring his protests.

Qurban Ali Kattar said he didn't want to lose his jaw tooth but the old dentist asked him to open his mouth wide and with his deft fingers, located the aching tooth. He made a knocking sound and shook his head.

'The young gentleman has very, very severe pyorrhoea,' he addressed us as the guardians of the patient. 'My advice would be to have all the teeth removed. For now I'll remove the jaw tooth.'

The novelist tried to get up and run from the dentist's chair but Chakori and I held him down by his shoulders. Ah Fung started working the moment I gave him the signal. He thrust a syringe into the aching gum and handed Kattar a medicated cotton ball to place on it.

Meanwhile, the novelist who had penned countless romantic tales and death-defying adventures was hanging on to his chair like a terrified child. He gave us the look that a sacrificial goat gives the butcher right before getting butchered. He still seemed inclined to run off but our merciless stares left him affixed to his chair.

Ah Fung was an artist when it came to his work. He first cracked a few jokes, then talked about the weather, and then his pincers made a swift leap into the novelist's mouth. Next thing we knew, the aching tooth had been plucked out.

'Help! Help!' Qurban Ali Kattar shouted. 'I don't want my tooth removed.'

'Sit quietly, Kattar,' I said. 'It's already removed. No need to make a fuss. Everyone's looking.'

Ah Fung showed the novelist his bloody tooth. But only after great difficulty did Kattar believe that it was actually his own tooth. I was about to suggest that he save it as a souvenir but the dentist threw it away in the basin next to his chair. The novelist sat slumped as if he had lost all will to walk after losing one tooth and a few drops of blood. In fact, he was probably expecting us to carry him home on a stretcher. Ah Fung put a medicated cotton ball on the aching gum and gave Kattar a few sulphide tablets. He looked truly amazed when his terrible pain vanished. We thanked Ah Fung for saving our friend and asked our novelist to pay him five rupees. He shuffled in his pocket for the note.

'Changezi yaar! I cannot find it!' he said. 'Are you sure you gave me five rupees?'

Ah Fung was looking at us, so I quickly paid his five rupees and asked the novelist to vacate his chair because other patients were waiting. When we were leaving, Ah Fung bent down and said, 'Young gentleman's teeth are in a terrible state. He must immediately have all teeth removed. I will make him a brand new set. A very good one, first class!'

And just like that, we started visiting the dentist two or three times a week. It wasn't easy to convince the novelist to get all his precious teeth removed. It took Asp and me whole days and many hours of argument to achieve this feat. He was reminded of the consequences of not having his teeth removed. We made it clear to him that his pyorrhoea was in a highly advanced stage and if he didn't get his teeth removed his chances of death were fairly obvious.

'Who cares about poor Qurban Ali Kattar,' he said, testing the loyalty of his friends. 'What difference does it make to you if I die?'

'It would make a huge difference,' I said. 'Who will borrow my shirts and ties? Who will come for breakfast at the bakery every morning?'

'Changezi, you are such a scrubby miser! Do you really value these silly things more than the friendship of someone like me?'

Clearly, Kattar's sense of humour had nearly gone extinct and he didn't appreciate my cheeriness.

So we offered him some more arguments to convince him against dying too early, which seemed to appeal to him. We told him that if he died an early death, Urdu literature would go bankrupt and it would be impossible to fill the tremendous void he would leave. We pleaded with him in the name of Urdu literature itself to please allow us to have his teeth removed. Muhammed Deen Asp took a different approach. He explained to Kattar that with his current set of teeth, further success in his romantic ventures was highly doubtful, but if he got a sparkling new set installed then he would look many years younger and that way, half of Chakiwara's female populace would be in his pursuit wherever he went. And so, just like that, the novelist finally conceded to the advantages of having his teeth removed, and since the dentist's fee and the cost of the new set was going to fall entirely on Iqbal Changezi's head, this free makeover didn't seem like a bad deal to him. 'I did not know,' he said, 'that my friends were so devoted and cared so deeply for my welfare. I am proud of you, friends.'

After that, it became routine for us to visit Ah Fung's shop. The novelist had agreed to have all his teeth removed and get a new set installed in their place. He often reiterated that he was doing this only to make his friends happy. Ah Fung, noticing Qurban Ali Kattar's generally decrepit state, would remove one tooth every three or four days. Asp or I would always be present for support during these visits since Kattar didn't have the courage to go there alone. Sometimes, even Chakori accompanied us on our trips. He was one of those people who never worked and yet somehow managed to get by. A short, skinny man with Mongolian features, he was an interesting fool who babbled at random and recounted funny anecdotes from his Bombay days. His brown penetrating eyes would stay fixed on the dentist; he observed his movements with singular concentration as if he wanted to learn dentistry. As we discovered later, this was exactly what he was doing. Sometimes, he'd fetch poor Ah Fung's instruments and would try to win his approval with fawning banter. Ah Fung also looked pleased with him and laughed at his jokes. Asp and I however, were always wary of the actor despite his easy and jocular manners. We were never completely enamoured of him and could see that his eyes gleamed with a certain cunning.

Due to our regular visits to Ah Fung's shop, everything there became familiar to us – the tooth and gum charts, images of gigantic, coiling heads of fire-spouting dragons, the medicine bottles in the open cupboard behind the corner table. From beneath the blue curtain peeped two steps that went up to the room where the dentist lived. There might be many dentists in this city with similar arrangements but what was unique to Ah Fung's place was a bronze statue of the Buddha, seated in repose, performing religious penance. It was on a shelf just above the dentist's chair from where it used to catch our attention and quicken our blood. This Buddha was different from others – it was a heavy, ungainly Buddha whose ugly features created an aura of depravity and wickedness rather than of peace and serenity. On top of his head was a sculpted cone-shaped tower, some nine inches high. Whenever I saw it, I felt a cold shiver run down my spine, as if this vile Buddha was alive and watching me. We got used to seeing him but this feeling of unease never left us, and we never understood why the dentist had placed it right in front of his chair. Maybe to render his patients numb with terror so that they wouldn't pay much attention to their freshly pulled-out teeth.

Ah Fung was himself a gentle and benign Chinese man whose face showed no signs of wickedness and whose crooked brown eyes often started sparkling with glee on hearing Chakori's wisecracks. In his white dentist's robe, this emaciated man of nearly fifty, fifty-one years, wearing golden-rimmed spectacles, looked more like a Chinese philosopher than a dentist – a bit like Confucius – who bore no inner resemblance to the hideous and chilling statue on the shelf. We usually collect only those pictures and decorative items that resonate with us even if we are oblivious of them. But who can say what turbulent emotions rage like waves in the deep, silent ocean of a human heart? On the left arm of that gentle Chinese man, a fire-spewing dragon was tattooed – a savage symbol of his race – but the tattoo and that statue bore no resemblance to his genial personality.

One day, I finally asked Ah Fung about the Buddha; where did he find it and why was it so different from other Buddhas and if he had placed it there in order to frighten his customers. (Often while we were on our way to the shop, the novelist Qurban Ali Kattar would complain that this statue had not let him sleep the previous night, and in his nightmares it had chased him with outstretched arms.)

Ah Fung gave me a quizzical look as if he was not at all expecting such a question from me. It is likely that no one had ever asked him about it before.

'Mr Iqbal! This is a Buddha from the Ming era. Some two thousand years old. Made by one of the emperor's famous statue-makers, Hunsha. A friend who knows a lot about statues has told us. When the Red Army was entering Shanghai, I saw this statue while escaping. It was lying in a heap of junk outside the Hall of Justice. I liked it and picked it up. I don't know much else myself…'

He said this while working on one of Chakiwara's hookers, a slightly chubby girl who was getting a filling in her teeth (because all sorts of people in Chakiwara visit his shop). She rolled her eyes flirtatiously and said, 'I also like it. I like it, bas. I am going to take it sometime.'

'You are not going to take it, little madame,' Ah Fung said with feigned seriousness. His eyes gleamed flirtatiously.

'Oh, you just watch, Ah Fung-ji.' She pressed his nose between her fingers playfully.

'Madame, sit still,' Ah Fung said, doing his work. 'This Buddha has been with me since ... It was with me when I went to Hong Kong, it was with me when I went to Siam. It was with me when I went to Malaya. A curio merchant offered five thousand dollars for it. I told him, "Nothing doing, my friend." Now it's with me in Karachi. Mr Changezi, the thing is, I have developed an association with it. I feel that if this stays with me then everything will be all right for Ah Fung. There will be no danger for Ah Fung. And if it's not with me then some disaster will befall. This is my superstition.'

We laughed at Ah Fung's ridiculous superstition; the chubby girl laughed the most and she repeated that she would pinch it someday. But Ah Fung was now deeply serious and I began to understand his superstition a bit. If we think about it, all of us are superstitious about something or the other. I have an oil lamp in the bakery with a large crimson globe. It's useless, it hasn't been lit in years but I never feel like parting with it and I wouldn't sell it to anyone even for thousands of rupees. I feel that the destiny of Allah Tawakkul Bakery and my own are somehow mysteriously linked to this lamp, and without it, things would not be the same.

I am of the opinion that men who live alone – that is, ones without wives and children – often fall prey to such superstitions. And Ah Fung was a very lonely man. He had neither child nor wife. He was a stranger in an alien land. All kinds of people visited his shop. Quite often they were women of all types and ages – some were housewives, some hookers. He was a master of his work and his rates were reasonable.

His demeanour towards his female patients was made of professional good humour, and he indulged in the occasional teasing, which his clients enjoyed; he was quite popular among them. I believe that he occasionally spent a night or two with a call girl in his room right above his shop, but these things don't cure loneliness. There are many Chinese restaurants in Karachi and many Chinese are also dentists, many are in other businesses, but as far as I know, Ah Fung did not find friends even among his compatriots. Very few ever visited him and he didn't go out to meet them either. However, despite his aloofness, he kept a tab on their news and state of affairs. Quite possibly this reticence in him was out of tight-fistedness, a common trait in the Chinese people. He was quite cautious with his money. But at the same time, it could also have been out of his natural shyness.

It took me about a month and a half to get the novelist's teeth removed one by one. During this period, Qurban Ali Kattar managed to write at least two novels – *The Comforting Beauty* and *The Secret of the Terrifying Statue* – and fell in love with nearly all the good-looking women between the ages of fourteen and thirty that visited Ah Fung's shop in his presence. Our beloved novelist, like most creative artists, posesses a sensitive, compassionate heart, and he is perpetually in a state of passionate love. (During those days he'd visit me at the bakery and read out his day's work, meaning two or three chapters of his novel, and sigh and pine in the absence of the women he had last seen in Ah Fung's shop.) But there were no limits to his ingratitude. Everything that we – Asp and I – were doing to keep literature alive by getting his teeth extracted, all the things we did to encourage and support him in his love affairs, he showed no appreciation for any of it. In fact, he repeatedly complained that his friends didn't help him and for that reason none of his romantic exploits were ever successful.

We tried to assure him that the bakery would continue to provide the milk, rusk and biscuits to keep his soul and dilapidated body together (it wasn't possible for him to chew solid food given the condition of his teeth) and that his occupation as a lover would receive a tremendous boost from his new set of teeth. But attempting anything beforehand would be useless because any girl in her right mind would not cast even a glance towards a man with that floppy a mouth – and that too, a novelist.

Now the issue was to get the new set of teeth for the novelist. Ah Fung's charges were four hundred but he was willing to accept three-fifty from us. Due to a shortage of money, we kept delaying the matter. Qurban Ali Kattar went to his publisher to collect the royalties of his previous books and the payment for the new ones. The publisher took both novels and handed him a hundred rupees for each manuscript, saying that the demand for his novels had declined greatly because some 'smart' young men had entered the arena and they didn't hesitate even one bit in revealing the complete details of human 'ennui' in their writing.

One morning we were actually talking about the new set (Qurban Ali Kattar was talking and I was helping Asp load bread and pastries into his van) when ex-comedian Chakori dropped by. He looked flamboyant in his pleated jacket and blue trousers. He was wearing a felt hat and carried a stick in his hand. We knew he was a dandy but we had no idea where he found all the money for these flashy excesses.

'Good morning, gentlemen! Kattar sahib, are you feeling well? What is this talk of new teeth?' Chakori always spoke to us in a particularly amiable manner. And although we had known each other for over a year now, we could not reach a level of comfort and familiarity with him that would allow us to communicate with each other in a more informal manner. Despite spending so much time together, Asp and I didn't know much about him. He never told us anything about what he did, where he lived or where he found those fine hats and clothes. He was around forty, forty-five years of age. Crooked, brown eyes, large ears, a broad forehead. Even at this age, his body was flexible and skinny. It had a kind of restless energy that was neither particularly attractive nor repulsive. There were glimpses of the old comedian in him still. But he wasn't a funny man; it would be difficult for someone who didn't know him to say that he was a comedian by simply looking at him. I know a few things about his previous life – even if not much. (I've met many people who still remember Chakori's films and antics, and they still beam if you mention his name.)

Fifteen years ago, Chakori was a well-known name in the Indian film industry. He appeared with Siddhu Pandey – who was a rotund fellow with a baby face – they both appeared together like Laurel and Hardy, and their silly antics and clownish buffoonery were greatly entertaining. Millions grew fond of them. Usually they performed in action films, doing minor roles as the hero's comic friends or accomplices, or in the role of lovers who get fooled by the girls. Then, I think, Siddhu Pandey died. Chakori appeared in a few films after that but didn't get very far. He disappeared from the world of cinema and nobody knew what had happened to him – if he was even alive or not. He simply vanished. And now, a few years after Partition, he had surfaced in Chakiwara's Ghareeb Nawaz Hotel in the company of Shahsawar Khan – the inventor of the Magic Ring. That's where we met him and it was only after three or four months that it dawned upon us that this man was the same famous comedian, Chakori, who was celebrated everywhere and the mere mention of whose name caused people to break into smiles.

Chakori said good morning to the novelist and asked how he was doing.

'Chakori yaar! Don't ask how I am doing. Sometimes I think you're the only friend I have left in this world,' he said, making a despondent face. 'I have been asking these people to get me a new set of teeth… They all conspired to get my teeth extracted. Now how can a renowned novelist, author of over fifty novels, face his fans or other people with a flabby face? Even my publishers have turned their backs on me and, what is more, Mr Chakori, I cannot eat anything other than milk biscuits without my teeth!'

'You come with me,' Chakori consoled him. 'I will go to your publisher with you. I will teach him a lesson.'

'No, I don't want to see that bastard's face,' Kattar said. 'He wants me to write bilge that he can sell under the counter. He tells me to write that! Tells me! Qurban Ali Kattar! Who sacrificed his personal ambitions so selflessly to serve Urdu literature!'

'You are right, Kattar sahib,' Chakori said. 'You are the pride of Urdu literature.'

After loading the van, Asp drove away in it and I joined their conversation.

Chakori said, 'Kattar sahib is right. His new teeth should be fixed soon. I remember that in Bombay, at the Pradhap Cine Toon where I used to work, there used to be a beautiful, noble Parsi actor, T. Karanjiya. You must have heard of him. The actress Madhbali was madly in love with him and really wanted to marry him. Karanjiya agreed because Madhbali was very beautiful and also very wealthy. Their wedding date was fixed. One day before the wedding, Madhbali went to Karanjiya's room in the studio where he was putting on some make-up. He had put his dentures in a glass of water for them to get cleaned. You know how repulsive a man looks without his teeth, so when Madhbali saw Karanjiya, she screamed and ran out the door. Forget about marrying him, she refused to even appear alongside him as a heroine anymore. Very few people know that the sparkle on the pearl-white teeth of T. Karanjiya – that heartthrob of millions of women – was completely fake.'

Chakori's pointless anecdote had nothing to do with the matter at hand but still Qurban Ali Kattar whimpered and threw a murderous glance towards me as if I was solely responsible for his revolting appearance and black fortune.

'Kattar yaar, you will get the set. Let some money come in,' I said, consoling him.

'Let's go to Ah Fung right now and place an order for a new set,' Chakori said. 'Actually I have some business with him too. I came here so that I could take you along. Changezi sahib, he thinks highly of you, please intercede on my behalf. I want to work with him as an apprentice for a while. It won't take me long to learn dentistry. In fact, I have learnt a lot already just by observing him. Dentistry is a good vocation, if nothing else, at least one can lead a respectable life. I have never told you about my financial affairs. What's the point of worrying one's friends? I don't have a job right now. I will only help Ah Fung at his shop and he won't have to pay me anything.'

I didn't expect Chakori to say something like this. For a moment I was nonplussed because what he said was completely 'out of tune'. It wouldn't have surprised me if the novelist had said this because such fancy schemes often spring from his creative, introspective mind and, to be honest, there could've been good reason for a novelist to do such a thing. For instance, making a dentist the protagonist of his novel or to have the good fortune of extracting the teeth of beautiful women might help further his own romantic interests.

But what do we know about other people's difficulties? Chakori was already a penniless loafer. Maybe he wanted to earn an honest living with this profession. And if he just wanted to live a respectable life, then why not? Shouldn't he be allowed to do so? Why not? But in my heart of hearts, I thought it unlikely that Ah Fung would take anyone on as his apprentice.

'And,' Chakori added, 'I will personally arrange to get Kattar's sahib's set made for cheap.'

We got on the tram and got off at Ah Fung's shop on Marriot Road. He was occupied with an old Makrani woman's teeth. There were two or three other customers in the shop too. We ordered a new set for Qurban Ali Kattar, whose measurements were already with Ah Fung. Then I asked Kattar to pay a hundred-rupee advance from what the publisher had given him. At first, Kattar made an unhappy face but then quietly handed the hundred-rupee note to Ah Fung.

'Mister Changezi,' he said, 'there wasn't any need for this!' but then quickly pocketed the money. He seemed happy about the advance.

I said to him, 'Your friend, Mr Chakori, would like to learn dentistry.'

Ah Fung thought I was joking. 'And why does our friend Mr Chakori want to learn dentistry?'

'He says he'd be able to earn a decent living. Can you keep him as your apprentice for two or three months? He will only observe the work and help you out.'

'Apprentice, Mr Changezi?' He lowered his eyes.

'As I said, he will only observe and help out.'

For the first time he looked at Chakori. 'Mr Chakori, are you serious?'

'Mr Ah Fung, I really want to learn this work,' Chakori said. 'I already understand it a little bit and would be able to assist you.'

'We had a boy who was my assistant but he left. I do need an assistant, but an apprentice...' His voice trailed off.

'Mr Chakori will work like an assistant boy and will work without a salary.'

'Look, Mr Changezi, you are my friend. I can't say no to you. But I want to do some thinking to see if Mr Chakori will be able to work here or not,' said Ah Fung. 'Why don't you come here at six o'clock when I finish up, and then we'll talk.'

When we – Chakori, Asp and I (Kattar had left us immediately after drinking his milk at five in the evening, saying the creative mood was upon him, and he wanted to prepare the structure of his novel using the latest techniques that his publisher had told him about) – reached Ah Fung's shop at 8 p.m., he was closing for the night. He was waiting just for us. After shutting the shop, he led us to the small alley next to it where a door opened to a flight of stairs leading to his flat. This flat remained padlocked during his work hours. There was a direct way to this place from inside the clinic where a set of stairs went through his workshop.

Climbing the narrow flight of stairs, we crossed a gallery and reached a long room adjacent to the workshop, some fourteen by eight feet. At the centre was a large, low table; next to the wall stood two tall wardrobes. On the other side of the room was Ah Fung's tiny kitchen. There wasn't any furniture except for a large fridge and a small ladder. What the purpose of the ladder was, we didn't find out. From here, we entered Ah Fung's bedroom. In the corner was a single bed with a foam mattress. On the side table was a Chinese table lamp and a transistor. There were lanterns hanging on the walls, emblazoned with dragons and other patterns. And on the floor there was a red rug while a couple of comfortable armchairs were placed next to the wall. It was a cosy room but without too many frills and trappings.

Ah Fung turned the lights and ceiling fan on. We settled on the chairs and he on his bed.

'You will have tea, right?' Ah Fung said. 'I'll just put some water in the kettle to boil.'

We started making small talk when he returned. I asked, 'Ah Fung, you didn't marry?'

'Ah marriage! Whom will I marry, Mr Changezi? No woman loves poor Ah Fung!'

Then we asked him when and how he had come to settle in Karachi. He told us that his father was a government doctor in General Chiang Kai-shek's regime, and that they lived in Canton. Ah Fung was the youngest among four brothers and was very weak when it came to studies. His father often beat him. He escaped from home to Shanghai when he was fourteen.

He starved there for many days and spent many nights on the streets. He also worked as a coolie and, for two years, polished shoes outside Shanghai Bank.

'But I, Mr Changezi, wanted to learn a skill that would help me eke out a living. Then it so happened that I got a job as a tableboy with an Englishman who was a dentist. He was very kind to me and when he saw that I had an interest in his work, he kept me as an assistant boy. Mr Changezi, when a man has a passion for something, he learns to do it too. I learnt the work with him for four years and also saved up some money. I fell in love with a girl, Ling Fi. She was the daughter of a hotel-keeper – a tall girl with golden hair. She had beautiful eyes. For her sake, I left my English master and bought a small shop near the Shanghai waterfront and started my own dentistry work. Shanghai at that time was a noble city and a young, hardworking person could earn a lot of money and become rich. In the rest of China, however, due to General Chiang Kai-shek and his generals, there was severe inflation. The currency was totally devalued. To go half a mile in a rickshaw cost four thousand dollars and the price of a shoe was fifteen thousand. On the streets and bazaars people were dying of starvation – that's why the communists came to power. Yes, so I asked Ling Fi to become my wife and she gave me her word. But then later she said, my father doesn't like you. And a month later she married a well-to-do clerk. She broke my heart. I went to the sea to commit suicide and even jumped but a lifeguard saved me…'

A shadow flitted over his face and I felt there was perhaps a horrific aspect of this story that he could not share with anyone. '… and Mr Changezi, I really loved Ling Fi very much. My customers were mostly sailors, they paid whatever I demanded.

During this period I did not speak with my family. They did not even know if I was dead or alive. Then, as you know, when Mao's Red Army invaded Shanghai, thousands fled the city. I could have stayed back; the Red Army wouldn't have said anything to Ah Fung – General Chiang wasn't my personal friend, you know. But Mr Changezi, by then Shanghai felt like a prison to me – a vast prison. I couldn't bear living there anymore.'

'Was it because of Ling Fi?' I asked, smiling. 'The city where your love was rejected.'

I saw the same shadow fall over Ah Fung's face – it was enveloped by a pale yellow cloud and his greenish eyes turned cold. His heavy eyelids now reflected fear and cunning. Oh God, I thought, Ling Fi and her husband – did he really ... ? He was hiding something. Quite possibly, my suspicions were unfounded but to leave Shanghai just because of the Revolution made no sense. The communists would not have said anything to a proletarian dentist.

'So Mr Changezi, I escaped Shanghai with the sailors in a junk boat. I had some savings and some clothes. And this Buddha statue, that I found in the garbage in front of the Shanghai Bank. I spent a month in the junk on the Sea of China and then those people dropped me off in Hong Kong, where I spent one horrific month. I didn't know anyone and Hong Kong has a cold heart for the poor. There I found some space in a Japanese cargo boat among local sailors who washed the decks. They were transporting some toys, textiles and watches to Malaya. But I abandoned that boat at Singapore ... it's a long story, Mr Changezi. I spent the Second World War in Singapore – and with the help of a friend, opened a little dentist's shop there, but then I got tired of that place as well. Six months before your country came into existence, I arrived in Karachi, and now it has been six years since I started working here, and I feel that I'll stay. The city is good for business and I am not so young anymore.'

'And your mother, father, brothers and sisters? Any news of them?' I asked.

'No, Mr Changezi, I don't know what became of them. They must have forgotten me. It's been some twenty-five, thirty years since I left my father's house. I do know that my father was killed in the Revolution but my brother and mother are alive and one of my brothers is a colonel in the Red Army. I have never written to them and they don't know where I am.'

I was very surprised. Ah Fung was an odd Chinese. He had deliberately distanced himself from his family as if they were dead to him. I believe there must be some other reason. Maybe he did something so damaging and humiliating in Shanghai that his family couldn't forgive him and he was afraid of reappearing in their lives like a bad dream they had forgotten. Or maybe there was another reason. Or perhaps there was no reason at all because there are in fact people who temperamentally and out of their choice isolate and fortify themselves in their own tiny worlds.

Suddenly he said, 'Oh Mr Changezi! I forgot about the tea! The water must have boiled dry by now.'

He got up and came back with three cups on a tea tray that had no milk pot. We began drinking the tea.

'I have given this some thought, Mr Changezi,' he said, 'and I cannot refuse you, but I cannot keep Mr Chakori as an apprentice. He can work as my assistant but for a month or two months only. When I don't need him I'll just say it. There shouldn't be any bad feeling about this.'

'Why should there be any bad feeling, Ah Fung?' I said. 'It is your business. When you don't need an assistant or you find the kind you need, you can ask Chakori to leave without any obligations.'

We thanked him and were about to leave when a fat, middle-aged woman with unpleasant features entered the room. Her face was covered with a thick layer of cosmetics. She had certainly come from the bazaar.

'Ah Fung!' she said. 'Give me some brandy.'

Ah Fung, without any hesitation or confusion, said, 'Madame! I don't have any brandy! Why do you need it?'

'Then please get it for me,' she said flirtatiously. 'I have a cold and fever and there's a lot of phlegm in my chest. I am losing my voice too. I can't even speak.'

'You can't have brandy.'

'Please have a look; you'll find it,' she glanced at us hopefully as if we were brandy drinkers. 'I am feeling sick. I gave money to that scoundrel Imama and asked him to get me brandy but the bastard came back empty-handed. He never finds anything.'

'I am telling you there is no brandy, there is a little gin… but gin…' Ah Fung said.

'Okay, give me gin at least. Gin is also good for the phlegm.' She sat on the edge of Ah Fung's bed. Ah Fung opened the closet and pulled out a quarter bottle of Booth's Gin and handed it to the fat woman.

'This is so little,' she said, seizing the bottle and hugging it to her blouse. 'It won't even wet my throat. Okay, give me twenty rupees? I will send Imama again for some brandy.'

'Now go, go away,' Ah Fung said cheerily. 'No twenty rupees! This gin will fix your bronchitis. Tomorrow you'll be healthy as a horse.'

'Give me twenty rupees,' she extended her hands. Then she started telling us stories of her establishment. 'Parveen and Mehwish have both left for Hyderabad with Shaddu Khan this morning. The magistrate's son came and took her away in his Mazda motorcar. They will stay there for four days. The magistrate's son has promised her that her brother will be released on bail.'

I noticed that Ah Fung was not flustered by her presence. Clearly she visited often and, using some excuse, filched money from the dentist. It gave us a glimpse of Ah Fung's sex life. We came down the stairs, leaving the woman in the flat. Ah Fung must have been right behind us because as soon as we exited, the door clicked shut and the latch snapped into place.

So that's how ex-comedian Chakori started working with Ah Fung as a dentist. Whenever Asp or I passed the shop in a van or a tram, we found him busy with something or the other. If nothing else, he'd be adding a fresh coat of paint to the signboards or filling out the bottles to be handed out to the customers. If he was facing the street and we'd wave at him, he answered by waving his hand too. But we were busy with our own work; we got a chance to visit Ah Fung only very rarely. And there was no need to disturb him because he was the only competent dentist in the area and was always occupied with customers.

I admit that I couldn't fully understand why Chakori wanted to learn dentistry. Sometimes I had suspicions about whether he was really serious about learning dentistry and if he, after learning, would actually start a dentist's shop. I had got him this job on my personal recommendation. Imagine my position if he did something stupid, pulled some stunt. I wouldn't be able to look Ah Fung in the eye. Once I expressed my misgiving to Muhammad Deen Asp. He said to me, 'Changezi, don't worry. Chakori's working with great enthusiasm. Ah Fung is very happy with him. He has found an assistant that he doesn't have to pay too much. Have you seen the shop lately? It looks like a completely different place. New paint, pots and plants and flowers.'

Asp was right. When I passed by the shop a couple of days later, it looked unrecognizable – freshly painted, sparkling bright with delicate Chinese letters and designs. Its shutters and panels were glittering like silver and one could see floral designs and arabesques that weren't there earlier. The entire shop seemed drenched in a festive mood. And it wasn't just the exterior; the walls inside were shimmering with a cream distemper too. All this was Chakori's handiwork and I was impressed with his artistic hand. But was Ah Fung happy with the enthusiasm of his assistant? Was he fond of these new colours? And who was paying for the paints? It must have been a costly undertaking ...

One Sunday when Chakori arrived with Qurban Ali Kattar's new set of teeth, he looked all flashy in his dandy double-breasted suit. We asked him about the new look of the shop.

'Changezi sahib!' he said. 'Dirty and unkempt environments disturb me, so I thought I should clean and paint Ah Fung's shop and make it more pleasant. I know a lot about colours. When I mentioned it to Ah Fung, he said there wasn't any need. The shop was all right as it was. Then he said that he rented the shop and didn't wish to spend on its decoration. I told him he didn't need to spend a single paisa. I got some paints and brushes from a friend who is a construction contractor –

thank God I have wonderful friends – and I repainted it within three, four days. And now it feels completely different. Have you seen it? Ah Fung is very happy now. Without spending a paisa, he has a new shop which feels a delight to work in. It also attracts more customers. Do you know that since I have started working there, his income has multiplied one and a half times over?'

'Chakori yaar!' Asp said. 'You are a man of qualities, not just a plain actor. Now tell us, how are your dentistry skills coming along? Have you learnt anything or not?'

'Ah Fung does everything himself,' he said. 'But I keep my eyes open and observe each and everything. I have a sharp mind and I pick up on things quickly. Ah Fung doesn't want me to learn. You know how some people are miserly when it comes to teaching others their trade.'

'How long will it take you to learn this work?' I asked.

'A month or two months at the most,' he said. 'I've already grasped about fifty per cent of it. Removing teeth or doing the fillings is straightforward work. I am now learning to construct dentures according to given measurements, just by watching Ah Fung. Do you know that in Qurban Ali Kattar sahib's set, I have constructed these two teeth next to the molars?'

By this time, Qurban Ali Kattar had arrived. Thanks to his floppy face, his chin was brushing against the curve of his nose. In his dark gown (his shirt had gone to be laundered) he resembled one of the three witches in *Macbeth*. He was holding a fountain pen in his hand.

'Changezi yaar!' he said as soon as he entered. 'I am here just for my glasses of milk. I have to return immediately to complete the fifth chapter of my novel, *The Long and Helpless Scream of Love*.

I am in the middle of writing an especially violent scene where the heroine, whose name is Marjana Shaheed, takes off her clothes and ...' he paused.

'And ... ?!' Muhammad Deen Asp asked eagerly.

'And jumps into the Lyari river but the hero – his name is Umar Bakhsh, and he's a novelist – saves her. I'm not going to give away the plot. But you'll be smacking your lips when you read it. I am writing this novel according to my publisher's guidelines. To be perfectly honest with you, I am stunned at my own imaginative and creative powers. Changezi, my friend, this novel-writing really is a divine gift.'

We were all very impressed and readily agreed that these things are indeed God-given and cannot be attained otherwise.

'Bring the milk quick! If it gets late, I'm afraid I'll lose my moment of inspiration. I haven't eaten since morning.'

I sent Asp to fetch the glass of milk and gave Kattar the good news that the set of teeth had just arrived.

His delight and anticipation were worth watching. He looked at Chakori's hand and insisted that it should be fitted in his mouth there and then. He opened his mouth as wide as possible – which created an opening not bigger than a sparrow's mouth.

Right after getting the teeth fitted, he wanted to eat rusk and samosas with his milk but Chakori explained that it would hurt at first but gradually he'd be able to chew everything. He drank two cups of milk (with his new set put in) and no doubt started feeling spirited and handsome like his novel's hero, Umar Bakhsh. He dashed towards his cramped, dark flat on Corporation Street, where the fifth chapter of *The Long and Helpless Scream of Love* awaited its culmination.

Chakori said, 'Kattar sahib paid a hundred rupees for his set and one-fifty is still due. Please give it to me; I will take it to Ah Fung.'

I did not have the money at that moment. But a vague thought also crossed my mind that perhaps Chakori couldn't be trusted with even this little amount. 'I will personally deliver the money to Ah Fung tomorrow,' I said. 'You don't have to worry; I also want to meet him.'

Now I want to reproduce two incidents as they were inscribed in my chronicle, written under two different dates. (My readers probably know that I have been writing the *Chakiwara Chronicles,* which to date has reached seven thousand pages and won't ever be published.) This is probably not a good writing technique because it disrupts the flow of the story, but I don't profess to be a novelist like Qurban Ali Kattar. These two incidents, to a certain extent, could be inserted into the story because they shed light on a certain character, and his ways and habits.

✾

9 September, 1953

Tonight at the Ghareeb Nawaz Hotel, a tribute event was organized for Qurban Ali Kattar for receiving a new set of teeth and for the completion of his novel, *The Long and Helpless Scream of Love.* All of the novelist's friends, including Haji Bhalay Deeno; barons of Chakiwara and members of the National Assembly, Dr Ghareeb Muhammad, Jam Qadir Bakhsh Lashari; the master of spirituality and the man of miracles, Shahsawar Khan (accompanied by his she-goat and bear cub) had all gathered to celebrate this occasion.

The novel had been accepted for publication and the publisher had awarded the novelist five hundred rupees for it. The novelist had agreed to bear the cost of this ceremony himself – something that everyone appreciated greatly, mainly because it was the first event of its kind.

The novelist was wearing a flaming red tie that I had given him that very morning. He sat between Haji Bhalay Deeno and Shahsawar Khan looking quite ruddy and a bit pompous. He laughed boisterously and revealed his teeth at the slightest hint of amusement to show off his new pearly whites. The conversation, as expected, was extremely sophisticated and intellectual and wise. Bhalay Deeno and Shahsawar Khan were in their element (so were the she-goat and the bear cub).

Muhammad Deen Asp had just risen to deliver the welcome address when we saw Professor G. I. Baz, one of Karachi's well-known personalities, a psychologist who writes for a women's magazine (where he gives people bad advice on their mental ailments), coming towards us. Along with him was a strange-looking creature, an old man, wearing a dirty-looking white achkan and churidar-pajamas. White from brow to beard, he leaned on his walking stick and walked slowly. We had not seen him before at our Ghareeb Nawaz Hotel events. Professor G. I. Baz introduced his companion as follows: 'This is Hazrat Farsh Langoori, the famous poet of India and Pakistan. He is the special disciple of Dagh Dehlvi. He has published some six or seven collections of poems and has just arrived from India; otherwise he doesn't travel anywhere.' And then he read a famous verse of his:

Yaadgar-e-zamana hain hum log...
Mere memorials of time are we...

When G. I. Baz and Farsh Langoori settled down, a silence fell upon everybody. We all felt blessed seeing such an eminent poet at Ghareeb Nawaz Hotel. With Farsh Langoori's presence, the mood of the gathering changed, and everyone turned his attention to him and forgot about poor Qurban Ali Kattar.

After tea – I noticed how despite his age, Farsh Langoori's appetite was better than our youngsters', and how he and G. I. Baz led the assault on the biscuits and bananas – G. I. Baz stood up to add a few more words of praise for Farsh Langoori and humbly requested him to regale the audience with his verse.

It had been accepted by then that it wasn't Qurban Ali Kattar's ceremony anymore and we had gathered to listen to Farsh Langoori. After all, it was not every day that such a celebrated poet of the Indian subcontinent graced Ghareeb Nawaz Hotel.

Farsh Langoori, affecting the mannerism of a truly great poet, feigned reluctance at first. 'I didn't come here to recite poems and, besides, I don't even have my notebook.' But then he relented due to the audience's appeals (G. I. Baz's voice was the loudest amongst these) and agreed to recite his fresh ghazal and nazm. And then, swooning to his own verse, he began reciting his couplets. I am not sure if his poems entertained the audience but his style certainly did. While reciting, he emitted a voice from the lower throat and swung his head and hands like a puppet. For every couplet, G. I. Baz cried, 'Wah wah' and 'Subhanallah Hazrat,' and writhed as if from a stomach cramp. Bhalay Deeno and Shahsawar Khan didn't understand a thing. At first they nodded to keep up appearances but then Shahsawar Khan placed his head on Qurban Ali Kattar's shoulder and went to sleep and Bhalay Deeno folded his arms across his chest and started staring at the ceiling. Some poems sounded familiar – as if I had read them before.

'That is Dagh's ghazal! That Chunni Bai was singing it on the radio the other day,' Asp whispered in my ear. Then I realized that Farsh Langoori was a fake and we were being fooled. Finally, Asp couldn't resist any longer.

'Sir, pardon my presumptuousness, but this ghazal happens to be by Dagh.'

'When did we say it is not Dagh's?' Farsh Langoori said and then let out a thunderous laugh and started peeling off his brows and beard and sat up straight to fix the hunch on his back, and suddenly, in front of me was a man who looked like M. A. Chakori, the comedian.

We were all in fits for a long time – except for Qurban Ali Kattar, whose ceremony had been wrecked. Chakori's impersonation of the old Indian poet was so complete that it would have deceived anybody. He had learnt a great deal from his films and was a natural artist.

When we stopped laughing, Asp stood up and completed the welcome address but when Kattar rose to read a chapter from his novel, *The Long and Helpless Scream of Love*, Shahsawar Khan said to his animals, 'Come on, children, let's go!' So Shahsawar Khan left with his animals without even saying goodbye and Bhalay Deeno called Chakori over and began talking to him. Nobody paid attention to poor Kattar's mumblings and I am not sure whether he even managed to finish reading his chapter.

1 October, 1953

Last night I was at a party at the Beach Luxury. You will ask how I happened to be at a party in such a grand hotel. Actually, an importer-exporter friend of mine, Muhammad Muneer Tanveer, had invited me to this party that he had thrown for his friend, Lord Tudor, an industrialist dealing in English motorcars. He said I could bring one or two friends too, if I wanted. 'Evening suit is compulsory,' he said, 'and the time, 7 p.m. sharp, okay?'

I took along Asp and Qurban Ali Kattar. I owned a much-loved evening suit from my college days that I happened to have worn only once or twice. We borrowed another suit from Bhalay Deeno, which he had got stitched by a famous tailor on Elphinstone Street very recently on the occasion of him being elected as Member of the National Assembly. It fit Muhammad Deen Asp perfectly, who in just a couple of years had put on weight and now looked plump and portly. The third suit we bought for just eighteen rupees in a used-clothes store in Soldier Bazaar. This suit was loose on Qurban Ali Kattar's frame, and he looked more like a scarecrow in it. So I took it and gave him mine which was now one size too small for me. It fitted Kattar fine – that is, to the extent that anything could fit Kattar fine. We only had to get the sleeves shortened so that his hands could come out of the coat. We also had to get the pants folded a bit. And we made him wear a thick waistcoat on top of his undershirt so that the coat looked smart and didn't hang. In our dark bowties, stiff, starched shirt collars and shining black shoes, we looked quite the night birds on the prowl.

After dusting and polishing ourselves, we stepped out of the bakery, measuring each step carefully (my black patent shoes were a bit tight on my feet). We bought three roses from Lee Market and pinned them to our buttonholes and then set out for Beach Luxury on a nimble-footed Victoria. The air was a little humid and the leisurely journey through the McLeod Road traffic was very pleasant. We felt on top of the world.

We reached Beach Luxury a little before seven. I had been to this hotel a few times but it was the first time for Kattar and Asp, and they were a bit nervous. I tried to pep them up.

We waited in the reception lounge. After a while, Muhammad Muneer Tanveer staggered in with his guests. I couldn't help but notice the remarkable dignity and self-confidence that the black-marketing of import licences and its consequent wealth had produced in him, and how his once-emaciated face now glistened with layers of fat. The sprawl of his body was quite impressive and one could hardly identify the rotten, scrawny young man that he had once been who read other people's poems as if they were his own at poetry recitals and mostly got by on the praise of his friends.

At first he did not recognize me but when he did, he smiled as if he was delighted and overwhelmed to see me. However, when he saw my companions, his smile lost some of its lustre. Sure he'd suggested that I could bring a friend or two along, but he didn't expect that I would actually do such a thing and test the strings of his hospitality to that degree by lugging along two freaks in borrowed evening suits. But when I whispered in his ear about Kattar, he was satisfied. Even though he hadn't read any of Kattar's books, he had heard the name. And once upon a time, before he had entered the world of import-export, he too had harboured the desire to make a name for himself in the world of literature.

Lord Todd was a short, friendly and easygoing man of around fifty–fifty-five years. Muhammad Muneer Tanveer flagrantly exaggerated us in his introduction. I was presented as the chairman of a large company whose bakeries and confectionery products reached all corners of Pakistan. Qurban Ali Kattar was introduced as a famous novelist whose books sold in the thousands and who was the Charles Dickens of Urdu Literature. Asp was presented as a bright and able advocate who had never lost a single case and who was about to be nominated as a judge of the High Court in a couple of years.

I think that Lord Todd did not believe everything his host told him because there was a wicked gleam in his eyes and he pressed a bit too hard when he shook our hands. It was also possible that he was fake too – perhaps he was an ordinary salesman in his company who had, in order to have a good time in a foreign country, assumed the title for himself. Apart from Lord Todd, there was a lady there as well. A woman of luscious but fading beauty. She had an expansive bosom and wore a pearl necklace around her neck. She completely stunned Qurban Ali Kattar and he kept staring at her. I thought her face looked familiar and then finally, I recognized her as Miss Wharton, who was Muhammad Muneer Tanveer's stenographer, and remembered that I had seen her typing in his office many times.

We proceeded to the dinner on the terrace. It was a dinner-and-dance night and the terrace bustled with men glittering in evening suits and women shimmering in warm, sparkly dresses. Everyone was cheerful and chatty. A band on a platform was playing Western tunes.

At dinner, Lord Todd, in his jovial way, cracked a few jokes. He was one of those whose conversations were easy and interesting. After dinner, people stood up to dance and the music picked up. A kind of frenzy overtook everybody and people started getting up in pairs.

Lord Todd danced many numbers with Miss Wharton. He was an inch or two below even her shoulder. She, on the other hand, was a broad, imposing woman. His hand, instead of being around her back, kept touching her buttocks and he looked like Miss Wharton's naughty little fat baby. Lord Todd enjoyed his dance very much. Muhammad Muneer Tanveer also danced a couple of numbers with Miss Wharton. She danced as well as she typed. Then he found a dancing partner from among the wives of his businessmen and officer friends who either didn't know how to dance or were happy simply watching their wives dance with others. I noticed that their wives, when approached by someone, did not hesitate even for a moment. They left the side of their insipid husbands and immediately embraced their partners. Whenever Muhammad Muneer Tanveer returned a hot, breathless, intoxicated wife to a husband, he never forgot to say 'Thank you.' The husbands accepted the 'thank you' and immediately resumed their conversations about horse racing, new motorcars and latest stocks with their friends.

We, the Chakiwara group, could only cast longing looks at this funfair. It was all out of our league because none of us knew how to dance. This was a completely different world – the world of the carefree rich folks.

Qurban Ali Kattar asked longingly if there was a dancing school in Karachi. I replied that he shouldn't be thinking about such things at his age and should focus all his attention on writing novels.

Lord Todd was drunk and happy. He wanted us to have a good time too. When we said we didn't know how to dance, he said, 'It's very easy!' and then forced Miss Wharton to dance with me. We danced to one number, but it was very awkward and I kept stepping on the poor woman's toes. She kept laughing.

After a while, we caught sight of a foreign lady who was sitting alone on the terrace. She seemed lost and sad and melancholic. She must have been around forty-five; heavy-set with pencilled brows, a thickly powdered face, her hair was coloured platinum and she wore a glittering white dress and a lot of jewellery. There was a glass in front of her from which she sipped occasionally. Her eyes had a hunger, a greediness. I imagined that she was a rich widow looking for a good time but there was nobody around to give her that.

Lord Todd, having returned after another song, also noticed her. 'Good God! That's Mary Harris, owner of Harris Chain of Stores. She's a millionaire. That necklace she's wearing is made of real pearls. It costs almost 30,000 pounds. She must be on a world tour.'

'She appears quite unhappy and frustrated,' I said.

'She wants a lover,' said Lord Todd. 'She looks hard in all her rouge but her body is still soft and voluptuous. Not bad, Mr Changezi! Why don't you give her a good time? She can give you a nice jigjig.' I laughed.

'Don't laugh,' said Lord Todd. 'Mind you, you Pakistanis are not really chivalrous yet. If Mary Harris in her fading charms and her jewellery was in Italy somewhere, she would have been crowded by lovers and could have easily picked her young man. You Pakistanis – no good!' He guffawed loudly.

We were chatting like this, occasionally glancing at the American millionaire, when a slim-looking man came to her table. His back faced us and his suit was stretched tight over his slim figure and buttocks. He said hello to her and we saw the widow's pale face break into a smile. She stood up and gave her hand to the young man, who placed it with great panache on his shoulder.

'It's good,' Lord Todd said, 'that even in Pakistan, you now find gigolos.'

'Gigolo?' Muhammad Muneer Tanveer and I asked together.

'You don't know? It's a very old profession in the West. Many young men earn their keep this way – in fact, live in luxury. You know, Casanova was a gigolo. They go to bars and hotels and look for prey. When they see a rich, middle-aged widow, they ensnare her. They are professionals and know how to say all the things these women want to hear. The women also know that they are gigolos. They don't see anything wrong in having a bit of a good time.'

'Do these people earn decent money?' Qurban Ali Kattar asked. He was probably planning his next novel with a gigolo as the protagonist or maybe considering this line of work for himself.

'These people are not capable of doing anything else. Now this gigolo is easily going to extract thirty or forty pounds for dancing two or three numbers with Miss Harris, plus four or five drinks. If she wants to spend the night with him – and I think that she does – then the gigolo might make two or three hundred pounds. As long as she is here, he might even stay with her, take her around. Quite often, an old lady completely loses her head for her gigolo but Miss Harris seems shrewd and keeps her wits about her. Regardless, the gigolo earns whatever he pleases, and he also gets gifts of his choice – new suits, gold cigarette cases, precious watches, etc.'

Lord Todd amused us with more stories about gigolos. All this time, our eyes followed Miss Harris and her gigolo on the dance floor. They were at some distance from us and often disappeared amidst the groups of dancing couples. I saw in her eyes that she was drunk and her face beamed with delight. Her young man had her clutched tightly in his arms and she looked happy dancing with him.

They danced to four or five more songs. Miss Harris was an indefatigable dancer. The smiling face of the gigolo was in front of us now. M. A. Chakori. He did not see us. His eyes were glued to the white folds of Miss Harris's neck and the necklace of pearls around it.

Miss Harris returned to her table afterwards.. Chakori was with her and when we got up (it was 12:30 at night by then); they were still sitting there talking. Miss Harris was smiling and batting her eyelids.

That night I figured out Chakori's mysterious means of livelihood, and also the source of his dandy clothes, cufflinks and cigarette lighters.

❁

Now as I think about it, I feel certain that Chakori saw us that evening at Beach Luxury and understood that we now knew of his real, despicable profession – that of a gigolo – because after that he avoided meeting us and came to the bakery only very rarely. After the first of October, my journal has only a few entries about him. He even stopped coming to the weekly meetings at Ghareeb Nawaz, where he was a regular participant in the literary arguments. Regardless, it was certain that he now felt guilty in our presence. A couple of times when he visited the bakery, there was a certain formality in his manner and he hesitated making eye contact. Then he told us that he had learnt eighty per cent dentistry just by observing Ah Fung. It really wasn't much more difficult than hairdressing. He said he was about to leave Ah Fung and start his own dental shop on George Street.

'I have already told Ah Fung of my plans,' he said, 'but he doesn't pay attention to such talk. He says: Chakori, what's the hurry? We will turn you into the finest dentist in all of Karachi!'

'But didn't you say he doesn't teach you anything?' I asked.

'Mr Changezi, who teaches anyone anything? I don't blame him. One has to teach oneself. Nobody taught me how to be a comedian. I just watched two or three films by Charlie Chaplin and became one. Director Karsaz agreed to give me the part of a donkey-driver in a scene in the bazaar. For ten rupees. I only had to pass by driving my donkeys. But I performed such antics on the set and put such life into the role that Karsaz broke into laughter on the set itself, called off the shoot and immediately gave me the role of the aide-de-camp to the Emperor, which was being played by Siddhu Pandey. Jamal Machlipuri had to rewrite the script because of my role.'

'You really were a star comedian,' I said. 'But why did you quit the film industry? Why did you suddenly vanish?'

'Actually, after Siddhu Pandey's death I lost interest in the industry. We were a pair. Maybe things would have continued as they were if I had carried on, but it wasn't fun anymore.'

After he left, Asp and I fell into thinking. Perhaps Chakori wasn't such a bad person after all. We were strangely affected by the story of his quitting the film industry after Siddhu Pandey's death and were ready to somewhat forgive his profession as a gigolo. Was Chakori's profession really as despicable as we thought it was?

One day Qurban Ali Kattar dropped by to eat his lunch and to read to us the latest chapter of his novel and hear some words of praise. In this new novel, the hero, Karim, in order to feed his family of four younger sisters and two brothers, is forced to adopt the profession of a gigolo. We felt that our novelist's vision was finally showing some hints of originality and turning revolutionary, and his art was now pulling away from the hackneyed subject of an oppressive society to embrace newer and uncharted heights of realism.

'Look here, Changezi my friend,' he said. 'It is vital for a man to be realistic. I have not been realistic in life and that's why I get slapped about no matter what I do. I have been deceived by my closest friends. Now in this chapter, after emotionally satisfying two wealthy widows, Karim becomes pragmatic. Keeping my publisher's advice in mind, I have written these scenes in reasonable detail and in an extremely blunt manner, and you will forget your – what's his name – that Henry Miller Esquire – what was I was saying? Did I finish my thought?'

'I guess not.'

'Yes, so I was saying, that after satisfying those wealthy widows, Karim receives from them two thousand dollars, apart from valuable rings, suits, a radio, etc., with which he rents himself a little bungalow on Drig Road and gets Samina, Farkhanda and Rubaba – they are his younger sisters – admitted into an English-medium school. He arranges for his brother to enter school too. To pick them up and drop them off at school and for evening recreation at Clifton, he buys a small second-hand car. His beloved, Ruqaiya, had refused to marry him earlier. Now her parents look at his newly acquired wealth and agree to marry their daughter to him – but now it is his turn to refuse. Therefore, he marries a lonely Jewish lady who is a millionaire.'

'All of this is in this one chapter?' I asked.

'No – this is a general outline of the novel,' Kattar said.

'So this chapter only talks about the satisfaction of wealthy widows?'

Asp cut in – 'But the hero is a gigolo? Kattar sahib, it won't work. Readers will not accept it.'

'What's wrong with being a gigolo?' Kattar was curt. 'If there is no problem in being a lawyer or government officer or contractor or minister, then why is being a gigolo objectionable? All of them aim for worldly success and to make money for themselves. I have shown Karim avenging an oppressive society. The oppressive society oppresses precisely those people – people like Kattar – who have no money –'

Asp and I exchanged glances. The novelist was a completely changed person. Furious with society and willing to take it head on. The likelihood of his novel being banned was quite high. Or, perhaps, his publisher wanted to sell it as one of those under-the-counter titles.

'And where is my food?' Kattar asked. 'Bring it immediately. I have yet to finish this chapter. My time is extremely precious.'

After two or three days, when I visited Ah Fung's shop to clear the dues for Qurban Ali Kattar's teeth, I did not find Chakori there. I asked the dentist, 'Is Chakori not around?'

'Oh, Chakori sahib?' he said, inserting a syringe into the neck of an old woman. 'He has gone out on an errand for me – to Habib Bank – to deposit some money. He should be back anytime now.'

I was a bit taken aback, and was about to say that he shouldn't have sent him to deposit the money or trusted him to that extent, but then I thought it better to keep quiet. Ah Fung's face was completely calm and I couldn't help but realize that Chakori had won this man over completely with his amiability and warm-heartedness and it probably wasn't the first time he had been sent on a task of this nature. I felt certain that this Chinese man also trusted him with other similar tasks where money was involved – like encashing cheques, paying taxes or utility bills – that a busy person like him was unable to do. There was no doubt that Ah Fung had found his assistant's honesty and integrity to be exceptional.

'Do I caution him to be wary of Chakori?' I wondered. What right did I have to raise suspicions about someone's loyalty? Chakori had given Ah Fung no reason to doubt him regarding anything. Why should Chakori do such a thing now? But still, I was somewhat worried because I had recommended him to Ah Fung personally, who had agreed to keep him only on my insistence. If something ever happened and Chakori deceived him, I would feel morally responsible. How would I ever look Ah Fung in the eye again?

'Is Chakori learning some work? Are you satisfied with him?'

'He's a very clever man,' Ah Fung said. 'A fine gentleman. He's like a brother to me – a young brother. Why such a fine gentleman wishes to learn dentistry I can't understand. He wants to leave this place. I told him, you stay here and in two months I will make you such a good dentist that you won't find a third such dentist – like Ah Fung and Chakori – on this side of the Suez!'

The manner in which Ah Fung praised his assistant suggested that Chakori had won his heart and the dentist was anxious about him leaving. Chakori had a special talent for making friends and for making them feel special. But to me and Asp, his charm always felt superficial and insincere, like a performance. But it was entirely possible that we were unable to develop a closeness with him due to our contrasting sensibilities and manners.

Ah Fung had a good many reasons to be happy with his assistant. I glanced around his shop. It looked quite different from the place where we used to bring our novelist to get his teeth extracted. In fact, it had undergone a transformation – the walls had been brightened with new colours and the roof was a fresh sea-green and crimson. The earlier decay and disorder had disappeared. The shop felt more expansive, perhaps because everything had been put into its proper place and all the junk had been moved to a room upstairs.

And then my eyes fell upon the smiling Buddha and immediately that wretched statue sent a shiver down my spine. It stood fixed in its old place and looked every bit as malicious and wicked as before. I am a considerably rational and normal human being and unaffected by superstition, but this statue always left me sweating. Was it just my imagination? Was he not staring at me with his crooked white eyes? Did his smile look so menacing only to me? I thought that, just like snakes, lizards and grasshoppers disgust some people, perhaps this had something to do with my subconscious too. I was about to say to Ah Fung that he should remove this statue from his shop and put it somewhere else but I was afraid that this smiling Buddha was listening with his long, pointed ears with rings, to every word that I uttered. He'd laugh at me, shaking his fat, wicked belly and consider me a mortal enemy and take his revenge on me. I felt as if the statue was a carrier of an evil spirit that was alive.

I do not exaggerate – I felt like running out of Ah Fung's shop that very moment – away from those gazing eyes, from that ferociously poisonous smile, far, far away. That statue had that effect on me every time but that day it was particularly intense, and I am unable to give a rational explanation for it. There is a saying that between heaven and earth there are many invisible things and feelings that are beyond human comprehension or consciousness but they exert an influence that is greater than the things of which one is aware. That day I experienced something of that sort. I was about to leave when Chakori arrived in a red floral silk bush shirt and white duck pants. On his fingers he was wearing two jewel-encrusted gold rings – Miss Harris' gift to him, perhaps. In his felt hat there was a feather that looked so outlandish that I couldn't help smiling. In his presence, my terror lessened (and the smile of the Buddha also started to feel relatively insignificant). He probably was not expecting to see me and looked a bit embarrassed.

'I was about to leave,' I said. 'I came to clear the dues for that set of teeth.'

He placed the bank slip in front of Ah Fung.

'It was quite a scene at the bank today. When I reached there I saw that a bank clerk – his name is Majid, he sits at the token counter – had come to work without his shoes, wearing just his underwear. When the bank manager admonished him, there was a verbal exchange between them and the entire bank staff gathered. Changezi sahib, the whole thing turned into a scuffle. The manager was at the receiving end of two or three slaps. Then the staff got hold of the clerk. He kept kicking them and even tore up a couple of ledgers. They say he's lost his mind and have taken him to a mental hospital. Changezi sahib, he's the only bread-earner in his house. He got married just last month. Until yesterday, he was an attentive, hard-working clerk and perfectly normal. Nobody could imagine he would go crazy. This human brain is a strange thing!'

I do not know why but I immediately wondered whether he was telling the truth – because why would he need to lie here?

Ah Fung said, 'Yes, many go crazy but it is difficult to tell some crazies from the rest. We say Hitler was crazy, but that man who dropped an atom bomb on Hiroshima, wasn't he crazy as well?'

'They should have stopped him when he was entering the bank in his underwear and without shoes,' Chakori said. 'They should have understood that something was wrong. Once in Bombay, we were working on a film, *The Woman with a Gun*, by Mahabharat Movie Toon – you must have seen this film, it was a box office hit, Siddhu Pandey played a gang leader of some dacoits. We were about to shoot the scene but Siddhu Pandey was still in the make-up room. Charan Jeet Lal was the director. He called out, 'Oye Pandey, what happened? Come here this minute, you bastard!' Siddhu Pandey had not yet worn his breeches but he got so confused that he ran onto the set holding his breeches in his hands, stark naked! Everybody made fun of him and had quite a laugh. It affected him deeply. Siddhu Pandey was an exceptionally sensitive man. He fell ill after that and died. The human brain is such a delicate thing.'

This anecdote had no real link to the bank clerk incident, but that's how Chakori often talked. He connected things in such a way that they became more interesting.

'Oh, it's one already!' Chakori said. 'Ah Fung ji, sir, I need to take care of lunch. Worship the belly before all else. Sir, would a two-egg omelette, fried fish and onion curry be okay? Coffee?'

'Right, Chakori sahib! Take these slip-books with you. Keep them in the drawer. I will come up in a bit.'

So that was it! Chakori wasn't just an assistant. He was also Ah Fung's cook and God knows what else. Who would want to let go of such a man!

I left the shop, but instead of heading towards the bakery I began walking towards the bank. My account was also with the same branch of Habib Bank. However, I had no cheque to cash and I only wanted to verify Chakori's story.

One of Bhalay Deeno's nephews worked there. I went to him directly and asked him about the aforementioned incident at the bank. But he knew nothing about it. He also said there was no token clerk called Majid.

'Who told you?' he asked.

'Nobody ... It's not important anyway.'

He smiled and resumed typing, thinking that the heat was getting to my brain.

After that incident, I did not visit Ah Fung's shop for a long time. Work at Allah Tawakkul Bakery kept me occupied. We were busy wrangling with the Food Department over raw sugar and flour quotas. Finally, one officer at the Food Department approved our quota on the condition that we would deliver two large loaves of bread, a four-ounce pack of butter, and a quarter pound of naan khatai before his children left for school every morning. (He lived ten miles away in Lalu Khet.) And although no business in this world is easy, still I would like to advise people who wish to start a bakery business to not even think about it until and unless they have relatives or well-wishers in the Food Department and in the Police.

Then our van broke down. Muhammad Deen Asp was driving it to deliver bread and other goods to a store near the Lyari river on Muhammad bin Qasim Street when the steering wheel failed and the van nearly fell into the river. In this accident, two donkeys were injured and we ended up paying six hundred rupees to their owner. Despite this, he insisted on registering a complaint against us. Without the van we couldn't deliver the goods to our clients and patrons, which caused further losses. Finally, when the van got repaired (the workshop bill was one thousand rupees), Muhammad Deen Asp's paternal grandfather, who lived in Wazirabad, died, and he had to leave for about a week. It's true what they say that when it rains it pours.

During this period, whenever I passed through Marriot Road and glanced at Ah Fung's shop, I always saw Chakori standing there with the dentist. So he was still working as Ah Fung's assistant and had not left. I would have been happier if he had left him. I was still ill at ease with my friend.

Amidst our own troubles, news about Ah Fung and his business somehow kept reaching our ears. His reputation was being damaged in Chakiwara now. Someone reported at Ghareeb Nawaz Hotel the other day that women of bad character were brought to the Chinese dentist's flat each night and, quite often, his mouth smelled of alcohol during the day. His hand sometimes shivered while working and didn't work as efficiently as before. Bhalay Deeno's daughter had gone to him for pyorrhoea. Ah Fung gave her an injection and scraped off the infected outer skin. But either the syringe wasn't sterilized or his hand shook while injecting and the girl's gums turned septic and she fell so ill that she nearly died. This had never happened before. It's quite possible that some other things we had heard from various places had been exaggerated by those who narrated these stories. But there is no smoke without fire.

A few days after Asp's return, I had a terrifying dream (I have devoted three pages to it in my journal) from which I woke up soaked in sweat, my heart thudding loudly. (It was with this nightmare that my nervous issues began; they grip me occasionally even now. Even Dr Ghareeb Muhammad's death-defying medicines haven't been able to cure it completely.)

I dreamt that I was standing alone under Lee Market Tower on a dark night. There was nobody around. Somehow I knew that the water level of the Lyari river was rising and having sunk nearby homes and neighbourhoods, it was now rolling towards Lee Market and Chakiwara. I hear the hissing of its dark, raging waters. But I am helpless. There is no use running either. I am waiting for someone who suddenly emerges out of the darkness. That man, in a high-collared Chinese coat and moccasins, is very tall. When I look up at him I am petrified. It is the face of the smiling Buddha. His eyes are still red but his lips don't reveal that menacing laugh. This man comes skipping and bouncing towards me the same way I would to school. Then we begin to walk side by side, like old friends. He says, 'Have you seen Ah Fung?' I tell him he must be at home. He says, 'I have looked for him; he's not there.' Then he says, 'You see, Mr Changezi, we are each other's guiding lights. I am his and he is mine.' And then he turns into my school headmaster who taught us History. He also has a wooden leg just like him. 'So now we're about to drown. Look, water!' he says. Suddenly I see a terrifying wall of water just four yards away from me, about to break on us. I scream and wake up and thank Allah that it was a dream.

Asp supported me with his arms and gave me a glass of water but the effect of the dream lingered for a long time. I don't remember most of my dreams but that dream, just like some from my childhood, remains clear and distinct in my memory.

After that, I started having those nervous attacks I mentioned. For hours at end I would lie flat on my back and stare at the wall – I was unable to think. I don't think it was related to business because the affairs at the bakery had improved considerably, thanks to Asp's untiring efforts. I felt listless after these fits. They had no fixed time or trigger. One minute I would be sitting healthy and happy, and suddenly my hands and feet would grow cold, my heart would begin thudding and an intense weariness and fatigue would overcome my body. After which I was not able to speak and it felt as if any moment my breath would fail me. Asp took me to a doctor in Chakiwara, who wrote me a prescription for some tablets and some patented medicines but nothing worked; instead my condition deteriorated. Asp had to be away from the bakery for many hours on end due to work. Kattar visited every day for lunch and read out the latest excerpt of his novel. When I would excuse myself, he felt hurt. He probably thought I was just pretending to be ill.

When my fits did not abate, Asp became really worried and one morning he drove me in his van to Dr Ghareeb Muhammad of Corporation Street. Most of Chakiwara's residents visit Dr Ghareeb Muhammad when they fall ill. Without a doubt, he is an able and generous fellow. His list of accomplishments includes numerous medical and scientific discoveries. Apart from curing physical ailments, he also cures spiritual maladies, and often writes prescriptions that strike at the root of the illnesses with the precision of an arrow.

When we reached his shop, we found him engrossed in work, looking at a slide through an old microscope (while his small, well-trimmed pointy beard grazed the table). A couple of patients were there too, amongst whom was that saucy and loudmouthed chubby girl, Saji. Her small, firm frame in a golden-rimmed, maroon shalwar kameez made her look even smaller and petite; her head was covered like a pure maiden's. The doctor, on the other hand, was not paying much attention to his clients, no doubt because he was busy devoting himself to the larger cause of human welfare. It's quite likely that he wasn't even aware of their presence even though they all craved his attention. Finding him occupied, I started chatting with Saji. I asked her what had brought her to the doctor. 'Haye! I have a splitting headache. It's been four days now. Doctor sahib, now please stop your work for a bit!' She said the last part of her sentence in a stifled voice, so the doctor would not overhear her, and giggled mischievously.

Then she said, 'That friend of yours, what's his name, sissy Kattar, that guy who you brought to Ah Fung for teeth removal – I ran into him three or four days back. He now roams around with a new set of teeth but he still looks the same old sissy. He wanted to sleep with me. I said, "Do you have four hundred in your pocket?" What does he do anyway?'

'He writes novels,' I said.

'That explains his shape. Tell him to do something else. Useless loafer! You are so nice but what's wrong with all your friends? That Chakori Pakori – what does he do at Ah Fung's shop? Just looking at him makes me nauseous. That cross-dresser! Cheat, scammer! He will ruin Ah Fung's good name. There's something not right about him.'

'Saji, when did you meet him?' I asked.

'The day before I visited Ah Fung's flat. This friend of yours, Chakori Pakori, came in a taxi to pick me up. I told him straight up, 'Oye mister! I don't know you. Who knows where you'll take me? And how do I know that Ah Fung has sent you? Go back in your taxi. I know where Ah Fung lives, I will get there myself. He handed the money to Amma and told her: "Send Saji with me." I didn't agree to it. What do I know of that fraud? Anyway, he went back to his taxi cursing me. I grabbed my burqa, took Bhai Gaman along and went to Ah Fung's place on foot.'

She paused and said, 'I actually feel sorry for poor Ah Fung. Your friend has turned him into an alcoholic. That poor fellow, his hands shake now and ...' She made a lewd gesture. 'He plays in Chakori's hands like a suckling baby. I stayed there the whole night. Ah Fung lost his consciousness after a single trip, but that Chakori started to get fresh with me. I slapped him in the face. I told him, "Get away from me, you eunuch! I did not come from my mother's womb if I don't break your bones! Don't you touch me!" You know what he said? "You got four hundred for the entire night." I said, "It was to spend the night with Ah Fung." I can't stand him. I got up at four o'clock, washed my face and left.'

'And why can't you stand Chakori?' I probed.

That's when she said something strange. 'I can't really say. I just dislike him. Look at these bottles. I like one of them and can't say why. I want to throw and smash the other one. Bas, one doesn't like what one doesn't.'

How do you respond to such logic? We have a bad feeling about certain people and it is often correct.

'And you are all dressed up yourself,' I said.

'Amma bought us new clothes,' she said.

'We are going to Dubai tomorrow. There's a supplier. She lives in Bath Island. She's taking me along with a few other girls to Dubai. There's a lot of money there. If I manage to put in three or four months, I'll make fifty, sixty thousand. Then I'll be able to get my brother into a good school and take my mother to a good hospital. She has a blister in her intestines.'

'Have you got your passport made?'

'The woman who is taking me has arranged everything. She has a lot of fake passports. We only need to stick my photo in one. I will travel under Durr-e-Shahwar's name ... Doctor sahib! Haye Allah. I am in such pain.'

Dr Ghareeb Muhammad finally turned away from his microscope and towards his patients. He examined each one of them carefully and gave them a prescription after a thorough diagnosis. Once Saji or Durr-e-Shahwar left with her pills, it was our turn. Doctor heard my story attentively and then shook his head with dismay.

'Iqbal sahib! I understand your illness,' he said 'This isn't a physical ailment. It's spiritual. You are under an evil shadow.'

'Shadow?' Asp and I asked with a sudden gasp.

'Yes, a shadow,' Dr Ghareeb Muhammad said. 'I know very well that today's modern, educated people don't believe in such things and think all this business about shadows-vadows is nonsense. But my own research in the occult sciences has definitely proved that demons, witches, djinns, ghouls, all exist. Often they enter the minds of humans and cause numerous diseases of which there is no cure in modern medicine or medical pharmacopoeia. This is exactly what I was researching just now.' He pointed towards the microscope. 'And I have reached some definitive and startling conclusions.'

'So this shadow can be cured?' I asked.

'Why not?' Dr Ghareeb Muhammad replied. 'Earlier, spiritual maladies were cured using charms, talismans and spells, and we know that they have proved effective in certain cases too. But as far as I know, nobody has studied this phenomenon scientifically. It has entirely been under the domain of African witch doctors, maulvis, pundits and quacks who didn't even know what they were doing, and why a demon possessed a particular man or woman. And besides, there are many different types of occult species and a remedy that works against one is utterly useless against another.'

Then we listened to the doctor's lecture about the occult sciences, which was quite interesting. He assured me that I would be cured and asked me to lie under a machine which looked similar to an x-ray machine. He had invented it himself. It had a few wooden logs whose function I couldn't decipher, and a round drum which could be turned using a handle. It did not even need electricity to run. I kept lying in it motionless while the doctor made some observations in his little notebook. Then he asked me to get up.

'It is an evil spirit, different from a normal demon or djinn, which is disturbing you,' he said. 'It has been wandering around for two thousand years and according to the machine, right now it is trapped in some sort of a bronze object.'

This diagnosis by Dr Ghareeb Muhammad caused a strange sensation in me and suddenly I thought of Ah Fung's smiling Buddha.

'But there's nothing to worry about,' Dr Ghareeb Muhammad said. 'I will give you some holy powder. Drink it every two hours with warm water or sherbet and don't step out of your house for three days.'

We paid twelve rupees as donation to the doctor and left with pouches of the powder. I don't know if it was merely psychological, but after three days I was actually feeling better. During this entire period, I did not get a single fit. On 3 December (this is the date in my journal), I left the bakery at around ten o'clock. I had to appear as a witness in the Small Causes Court at the trial of Chand Muhammad, proprietor of Ghareeb Nawaz Hotel, who had been stopped and beaten up by a few Makrani thugs on William Street a couple of nights back. On Marriot Road, I turned back after having passed by Ah Fung's shop. It had been ages since I had last seen the Chinese dentist – over a month. It occurred to me that I should ask after him, and also find out if Chakori still worked with him or if he had left.

There were no customers in the shop. Chakori was not to be seen anywhere. Ah Fung was sitting in his white dentist's robe at the medicine desk, fitting some teeth into a frame. He was facing the wall and his back was towards the street. He had seen me coming inside. He said with his back to me, 'Come on in, Mr Changezi! You well? You haven't come to see me in a while.' His voice sounded choked as if he was hoarse.

'I was just passing by; thought I should drop in and ask how you were doing. I don't see your assistant Chakori anywhere.'

'He left a couple of days back, God knows to where.'

'Why?'

'He said, "Ah Fung, please give me permission. I will do my own work now."'

'He did not leave an address? Didn't say where he was going?'

'No, Mr Changezi!'

Ah Fung didn't turn around to face me even once during our conversation. This struck me as odd and a little cold. He stayed occupied with the teeth. He also looked weaker and more tired than before. So I left.

On my way back from the Small Causes Court, I passed by Ah Fung's shop once again. This time he was bent over a burqa-clad woman but his back still faced the street. There was something odd about the manner in which he was leaning over his patient. Why was he so rude when I went to see him an hour back? He acted as if he didn't even know me and wanted to get rid of me. Forget about standing up to greet me, he didn't even bother to acknowledge my presence with a smile. Was there something – a fear or an unfamiliar terror – residing in him and eating him up, sucking his powdered cheeks deeper into his face? There was certainly something unusual and uncanny about all this. Now I can't say for sure if it was at that moment or at some other point, but a speck of fear lodged itself in my mind and by the time I reached the bakery, it grew into something larger and stronger. It was outrageous and terrifying at the same time.

I didn't mention any of this to Asp, who was at the bakery. I imagined he would find it funny. Besides, he was busy with his account book, happily painting tiny, handsome numerals, adding and dividing them as if everything was well with the world and the world he was in was the best of all possible worlds. That's when the novelist arrived, sobbing and sullen-faced. He complained that his new set of teeth had become loose and now hurt him. He had to remove it before eating. But despite this, he had completed another twenty-to-twenty-five-page chapter of his novel. Then for the next hour, I was forced to listen to the awe-inspiring adventures of his gigolo leaping in and out of various beds.

In the evening, he took me to his publisher and introduced me as his literary agent so that I could convince the latter of the novel's qualities and negotiate a higher payment for him. The publisher was a wry, sultry middle-aged man. He listened to our stance patiently but there was no oil to be pressed from his seeds. So we left his office and Kattar took me along to show me a house on George Street, where his latest beloved lived. A beauty with luscious hair and bewitching eyes. She was the daughter of a dockyard worker. I instructed him to finish his novel first. By then, hopefully, the financial situation at the bakery would also improve, and I would be able to attend to his needs.

When we returned to the bakery, Asp informed me that Chakori had visited in my absence and looked disturbed and nervy.

'What did he say?' I asked.

'He's left Ah Fung's job,' Asp told me. 'He wanted to borrow our van for a night.'

'Van? For what?'

'He said he needed the van for a friend who is shifting houses. I said our van isn't working well and our driver isn't here either. He said that wasn't a problem; he'll drive it himself and return the van to the bakery by morning.'

'And?'

'I told him that nobody knows how to drive this van except me. If he wants I could drive and help his friend with the shifting. He said he didn't wish to give me any trouble since shifting is quite a hassle and it could take a good four to five hours.

Then he started insisting that he was a really good driver and mechanic himself and would be able to drive it somehow. And that if any serious problems arose, he would get it fixed. But I did not agree. He tried to convince me quite a bit that no damage would come to the van but when I refused, he went away with a drawn face, saying he'd try to get a van from somewhere else.'

'You did the right thing,' I said. 'We cannot lend the van to anybody. We have yet to clear the workshop bill. But who is this friend he was talking about?'

'He didn't say, I didn't ask either.'

'Did he say why he left Ah Fung?'

'Yes. He said, "I have learnt dentistry quite well, and I want to set up my own shop now." He also said that Ah Fung had been acting distant lately and even spoke to him rudely a few times. Then he said he might go to Saudi Arabia. A dentist had asked him to come along with him. And besides, Ah Fung has been planning for some days to go to Hong Kong himself. He has been able to trace his family and they have sent a letter saying his mother is on her deathbed.'

'So much news!'

'I couldn't trust everything he was saying,' Asp said. 'You know Chakori. He's like a container without a bottom.'

'In any case, I am happy you didn't give him the van.'

'I was ready to go with him but he refused.'

That night I thought for a long time about Chakori. Why did he ask for the van when he avoided visiting the bakery altogether? And why did he need the van anyway? I couldn't believe his story. And if Muhammad Deen Asp was ready to go with him, why didn't he accept his offer?

I thought about this for a long time and decided to take certain steps. It was too early to involve Asp. But I fell asleep and in my dream I saw the smiling Buddha somehow going around my head in circles. And then the novelist also turned up in there and pointed to the statue, 'Look, yaar Changezi! Even he has a new set of teeth.' And then I woke up. I was drenched in sweat.

I had some plans for the next day. I washed, showered, and by 8:30, was ready to go out. I waited for Asp, who was out on his morning round in the delivery van. He arrived and before I could explain to him where I was going, the novelist was standing on top of our heads. He wanted me to accompany him to Ah Fung's about the new set of teeth which was causing him a lot of pain. I was forced to go along. I couldn't take the van because only Asp knew how to drive it well. Only he was privy to the secrets of its gears and brakes. I thought it was a good opportunity to visit and spend some time at Ah Fung's shop. By the time we reached it was 9:30 but the shutters were still down. Nobody was even present downstairs. I went to the door which led to the stairs to his house but there was a padlock.

When we asked around we found out that Chakori had told everybody that Ah Fung had received news of his mother's illness and was planning to leave for Hong Kong. Had he left already? Going by his daily routine, the shop should have opened by now, and if he was ill, then the stairway to his flat should have been open. Why was there a padlock outside?

Kattar had to go back to work on his novel. So I went to Habib Bank myself. My bakery's account was also in the same branch. Inside, there weren't too many people. The light clicks of the typewriters sounded pleasant to my ears. I went inside the booth to my friend Assistant Manager Sarfaraz's office and planted myself upon his luxurious black leather sofa. He was not there at the time, but arrived four to five minutes later.

'Changezi, my friend, where have you been? You don't come over often enough,' he said warmly. 'Where are you these days?' He ordered coffee.

After some small talk, I said, 'Sarfaraz, can you help me with something?'

His face changed colour for a moment but he maintained his pleasant demeanour. He probably thought I would ask about an overdraft or some big loan.

'What's the problem?'

'Sarfaraz, rest assured I am not here to ask for an overdraft. The thing is that I am well aware that it is an unethical practice for a bank to disclose the account details of one of its customers, and I shouldn't ask you for such things, but Sarfaraz, can you tell me the balance in Ah Fung the Chinese dentist's account, the one who lives on Marriott Road?'

'The bank is not allowed to disclose this information. It is unethical indeed. What if I say no?'

'Then the matter will stand closed. I will finish this coffee, say thank you and leave.'

'Why do you ask? Does he owe you any money?'

'No, he doesn't owe me anything and this isn't needless curiosity either. This information could be important.'

For a while, he kept puffing his pipe and looking through his golden glasses.

'Do you have his account number?' he asked.

'Account number? No.'

'Then how would we find out without the account number?'

Then wrinkles showed on his face as he broke into a smile.

'See what an efficient banker I am? I know Ah Fung's case by heart. His cash balance is only ten rupees. The minimum account balance required to keep an account open.'

'Only ten rupees?'

'Sixty-five, seventy thousand in cash was withdrawn from his account yesterday. Mr Ah Fung is an old client of ours. Everyone in the bank knows him.'

'Did he present the cheque himself?'

'Yes, he came himself. He said he wanted to thank the bank. He was leaving for Hong Kong and he direly needed the money. He assured us that when he returns from Hong Kong, he will have money deposited in this very same branch, which has always provided him with very good service.' The coffee arrived at that point.

'What are you thinking?' Sarfaraz asked.

'Did he really come himself to get the cheque cashed? Are you sure?'

'Yes, he came here himself. I know him very well. He sat in the same sofa you are in right now.'

Then he called in the cashier at the counter who verified what he had said.

'Yes, Mr Fung came personally. The last couple of months he had been sending his assistant for depositing and withdrawing cash but yesterday he came personally.'

'Did you notice anything odd or unusual in his behaviour?'

'He was completely normal. He looked a little thinner than before and there were dark circles around his eyes, as if he was very worried about something.

I stood up.

'Thank you,' I said. 'Sarfaraz, you should ask your clerk to re-verify the signatures.'

'Are you thinking of a fraud? What have you got yourself into, yaar? And what is your relation to Ah Fung anyway?'

I left after this. But as I was leaving I heard Sarfaraz calling out to a clerk asking him to bring yesterday's cheque of seventy thousand cash.

I took a taxi and reached the airport. There I made inquiries at the ticket counter of PIA and of other airlines to find out whether a Chinese gentleman had travelled to Hong Kong on one of their flights in the past two days. They checked their passenger lists and told me nobody had travelled under the name Ah Fung on those dates. However, there was somebody called Wang Lu who had taken the midnight Air France flight to Hong Kong via Bangkok.

On my way back, I found the Chinese dentist's shutter still down and wondered at the series of bizarre events that had taken place recently. Marriot Road was bustling with traffic and pedestrians. The sun was soft and beautiful at that time of day. To my right was a green garden where schoolchildren were running around with little flags. Despite this, I felt that all manner of evil spirits, witches and demons had been unleashed upon this city. My inexplicable nervous illness began to bother me again and in the bustle I felt agitated, terrified and alone.

When I reached the bakery, I was in no condition to share my suspicions and anxieties with Asp. But when he saw my condition, that good man ran to give me his shoulder. A few moments later, I was lying flat on my bed with a warm water bottle and a massage poultice. He mixed Dr Ghareeb Muhammad's powder in some water and started rubbing my feet. Very soon I was in the tender arms of sleep. My eyes began closing and I sank deep into the embrace of a merciful slumber.

Whatever happened that night, I realize now, was a fateful accident; a cycle of coincidences because things happen the way they are meant to happen. When one mentions the word 'accident', people raise their eyebrows, their expressions reveal worry, but isn't it true that people are born accidentally, live by accidents, stumble to their place in the world through a series of accidents and finally return to meet their Creator through accidents? One day you'll see a man happy and healthy, engaged in lively banter, and you envy him for his high spirits and good fortune; the next day you'll read in the paper that he was found dead in his room. Isn't that an accident? It is quite possible that I may not have woken up from my sleep that night, but I did wake up and when I did, I felt completely refreshed and healthy. (Was it Dr Ghareeb Muhammad's powder?) I glanced at the clock. It was 11:30. Moonlight streamed into the room from the little glass ceiling window.

Suddenly, I was gripped by the urge to wander around Chakiwara's streets. Just like the ghazal poets. As soon as this occurred to me, I stood up from the bed, changed my clothes and left the house, leaving the door slightly ajar.

Lee Market Tower stood tall in the moonlight. Everything below was silent, desolate and dead. Occasionally, one spotted a man walking.

Was it just a coincidence that my feet started moving towards Marriot Road? After passing through that narrow bazaar, which is usually so packed with crowds that during the day it is a pain to go through it, I reached the broad, open Marriot Road. On my right were three- and four-storeyed concrete buildings and on my left, behind the iron railing, an open ground and some scattered bungalows. A few cafés were still open. A giddy Victoria clattered through the night's silence.

I was a few steps away from Ah Fung's shop when I saw a van approaching. Its headlights were turned off. I don't know why but on an impulse I hid behind a lamppost. The van slowed down and turned into Ah Fung's lane. As the van turned, I also caught a glimpse of the driver's face. For a moment I was shocked. It was M. A. Chakori. I kept looking at the van from behind a shop but it drove straight on. It must be somebody else, I thought. I was probably mistaken. Then suddenly the headlights came on. It was the same van. I watched from my cover. This time it stopped in front of the stairs that led to Ah Fung's flat. The headlights switched off. The driver's door opened and Chakori stepped out. He was wearing a well-ironed grey suit. He walked to the rear end of the van and started searching for something. He was muttering something under his breath. Then he locked the van carefully and checked each door to make sure it was locked. He pulled out a key from his pocket and unlocked the door to the staircase of the flat. As soon as he went in, I entered the lane. I was sure he must have locked the door from inside but it flew open when I kicked it. He probably hadn't locked it because he was planning to leave quickly once was his work was done.

I quietly climbed up the stairs and reached the gallery in Ah Fung's flat and through that entered his living room where somebody had just turned on the light. I was feeling very scared but somehow I controlled my fear. I looked carefully and saw Chakori standing with a metallic object in his hand. It's impossible for me to explain the expressions that flitted through his face during those moments when he saw me. He probably took me for a ghost at first. For a second, it looked like a shiver ran through him, striking with fear and shock, as if his soul had been sucked in. There was a smile on my face even though I felt a force saying to me, 'You idiot! This man is dangerous! You won't be able to leave this place alone.'

'You, Changezi sahib!' he said finally. 'You here? At this time? I came here to see my old friend Ah Fung.'

'But Chakori, where is Ah Fung?' I said, looking into his eyes.

His brown feline eyes lit up with an indescribably treacherous look and he said in his typical nonchalant manner. 'Ah Fung? He's not here. He received a letter from Hong Kong. His mother is very unwell. So he's probably already left.'

'Oh really?' I smiled. 'And he has handed his keys to an assistant who left him three to four days back?'

'When did I leave Ah Fung? Who told you that?'

'Ah Fung himself,' I said. 'He told me you don't stay with him any longer.'

'Oh, so you were indeed fooled, Changezi sahib!' he said laughing. 'I was about to tell you that it wasn't Ah Fung but your humble servant Chakori and it was just a prank. I felt that the business shouldn't be affected due to Ah Fung's departure and the customers should be kept under the impression that he is still around.'

'So who was the Ah Fung who cashed seventy thousand from the bank yesterday?'

'Seventy thousand!' His face turned pale and he immediately realized that I knew a lot – perhaps not everything, but quite a lot – and that I wasn't fooled by his performance. He began trembling. Feeling defeated and realizing that his plan had failed, a dangerous spark flashed in his eyes. He ground his teeth and swore loudly. The next thing I knew, we were circling around the table, alert, watching each other with unblinking eyes. Every single one of our veins was as taut as the strings of a sitar. Chakori was holding a long fruit knife in his hand.

In that moment I knew he had decided to kill me. I wished for something to defend myself. In terms of physique, I was heavier and more muscular than Chakori and if it were a bare-handed contest I would have taken him out; but right now he was armed with a lethal weapon and a ruthlessness like that of a cornered tiger. In this state, he could be extremely dangerous. Our movements around the table were deliberate and carefully measured. Our eyes were fixed on each other. Not a single sound in the room except the sound of our breathing.

Those five or ten minutes we spent chasing around the table felt like hours. Both of us were out of breath. Neither of us uttered a word. I was facing the workshop when suddenly my eyes fell on the smiling Buddha. It was lying on the low table next to my elbow, still with his nasty venomous smile plastered on his face, like a vile presence that was relishing this contest.

Suddenly it struck me as to how this thing had landed here in this room. Perhaps Chakori had brought it here to take with him, thinking it was worth something.

Chakori had now reached the wardrobe. His movements were telling me that he was now tiring of this game and would attack me with his knife at any moment. I imagined the knife piercing my chest. For a moment, darkness filled my eyes and then, instinctively, my hand fell upon the smiling Buddha. I lifted it by the pointed lock of hair, and as if in a dreamlike state, flung it with all my strength towards Chakori, who was poised to jump at me with his knife. I remember he ducked and saved his head, but that heavy statue clanged loudly against the big wardrobe. The doors of the wardrobe flung open from the impact and the erect, bloodied corpse of Ah Fung fell with a thud upon Chakori, who was getting up, and took him down under its weight. I heard an agonizing cry, followed by silence.

The police reached the spot half an hour later and took both the corpses to the morgue for a postmortem.

When I returned from the police station, it was already morning and Muhammad Deen Asp was trying to start the engine of the van.

The Love Meter

1

You must have read the tragic news regarding the death of Dr Ghareeb Muhammad a few days ago. You probably glossed over it in the same cursory manner as you did any other piece of news relating to daily suicides, robberies and kidnappings, and probably forgot all about it immediately. In which case, you would certainly be unaware of the odd and saddening chain of events that eventually culminated in that painful and horrific tragedy. I mean, how many of you would actually know that this doctor from Chakiwara, whose medical practice was not indebted to any academic degree, was Pakistan's first original scientist, and had he lived a bit longer, would have been the pride of his nation? However, owing to his untimely death, this newborn nation was unfortunately deprived of the services of a scientist and inventor whose equal this era might never see again.

I was his friend – his only friend in any event, who had completed his middle-school education – and therefore the only one capable of writing complete sentences in Urdu with subject, object and verb. So it is my duty to reveal to the residents of Chakiwara, first and foremost, then to Pakistan at large, and then to the world, regarding the tremendous loss that has been inflicted on science by my friend's death, and how his astonishing invention – the love meter – became the cause of his death, and led him to plunge and drown himself in the raging waters of the Lyari river.

Everyone who lives in Chakiwara knows Corporation Street well. It is Chakiwara's most fashionable street, and this part of town has the same significance for us as Elphinstone Street does for Saddar. What is Corporation Street? A bunch of crooked houses made of mud, and small shops that shy away from the main road and face the other way. Halfway through Corporation Street, there is a water pump where jasmine-faced women crowd together and fill water all day long. The width of the street increases or decreases with every ten steps you take. Often the municipal lampposts along the edges suddenly appear in the middle of the street like unexpected, protruding arms. In short, Corporation Street is another name for romance. My friend Manzar Kamali, who is also a progressive writer, calls it 'the lane of tender beauties', and I think it is hard to come up with a better name for this street. On Corporation Street, about two furlongs up from Fazal Muhammad Tea Shop was Dr Ghareeb Muhammad's shop. He was a bespectacled man with a pointed beard and a generously domed forehead. Just a glance at him would be enough to convince anyone that if the word 'genius' could be applied to anybody, it would have to be to this doctor from Chakiwara.

As a doctor – I have to say this with much dismay – he was among those thousands of doctors who, upon examining a patient, ruefully shake their heads and tell the relations that the patient could have been saved had they brought him in a month or two earlier. Some conspiring elements in Chakiwara have routinely insinuated that the doctor played a major part in populating the Lyari graveyard. This is a vile and pathetic accusation. The fact of the matter is that Dr Ghareeb Muhammad was usually called upon only at a juncture where there was no chance of the patient's survival.

About a month before his suicide, a mysterious change came over Dr Ghareeb Muhammad. He appeared silent and somewhat lost. I visited his shop several times but when I saw the terrifying anguish and sublime awe on his face, I couldn't muster the courage to voice my opinion. He had reduced his visits to patients. Only once did he hint that his mind was occupied with grave matters: 'Asp! I am expending all my days and nights on an invention that will wreak havoc in the world. Compared to it, all earlier inventions – the radio, the atom bomb, et cetera – will look like toys. When this invention makes its entry, all the theories of German psychologists will look ridiculous, and the coming generations will refer to the time before Dr Ghareeb Muhammad as the Dark Ages of Humanity.'

2

I AM SURE THAT IT WAS DURING THOSE DAYS THAT Dr Ghareeb Muhammad first thought of inventing a device that could be used to measure love. Actually, it wasn't a product of his mind alone – Hakim Allah Lok Sanyasi also played a part in bringing this scheme to its completion. They debated the need for this instrument for many, many hours in Chakiwara's kind and gracious restaurants, which, by the by, even in these inflationary times, continue to serve their customers with raw-sugary tea and rubbery buns for only two aanas, maintaining their traditions of magnanimity and hospitality. If we ever showed up during these discussions, it seemed as if a natural calamity had struck and they would start looking right and left as if searching for their shoes and immediately change the subject. At first we all assumed that they were plotting some dangerous move such as blowing up Chakiwara with explosives in the dead of the night, but we had to relinquish this idea, considering their past record of patriotism and personal sacrifice. We concluded that this pair of Socrates and Plato – these two great dome-like heads – were certainly devising an eccentric formula, an invention that would revolutionize the lives of the residents of Chakiwara. But once I did hear them say, '... a barometer of that love meter!'

So one morning last July I was walking towards Yaqoob Makrani to borrow five rupees when I paused in front of Dr Ghareeb Muhammad's shop. 'Why shouldn't one nick five rupees from Dr Ghareeb Muhammad instead?' I thought to myself. 'After all, a friend in need is a friend indeed.'

Doctor sat with his feet on a chair and his back towards the lane. He was playing with a watch-like instrument on the table. There were other instruments lying on the table – instruments that, as far as I know, doctors do not use – a hammer, half a dozen nails and cogs, and two screwdrivers. I thought the doctor was fixing his watch, and it was no surprise to me since the doctor was a multi-talented man. I went inside the shop and before he could turn around and notice me or hide his watch-like thing, I was already upon his head and caressing his baldness with my fingers.

He abruptly flipped the watch-like device around as if he was just toying with it, but his face betrayed the look of a little devil caught red-handed.

I hazarded a guess, 'Isn't this the love meter?'

He was so surprised that he jumped in his chair. 'How do you know! Who told you! Only two men in the entire world know about this – this ignorant man and Hakim Allah Lok Sanyasi!'

'Who told me?' I said in a low voice, trying to impress him with my lies. 'Why wouldn't I know about it? I have been researching the love meter for many years now, but my formula has some flaws. Actually, the key chemical ingredient that's required for this device – the flesh heart of a mountain bat – is extremely rare in Pakistan.'

'Really?' the doctor said in an authoritative tone a – one that a senior, more successful scientist employs with his novice colleague. 'So you are a fellow-scientist? I am glad to know this.' Then he gave me a condescending look and shook his large frightful head and said, 'But I am afraid you have gone in the wrong direction. Using the heart of a mountain bat for the love meter? Ha ha ha. I know why you didn't succeed. You lacked the correct scientific approach. For such an invention, the first condition is the correct scientific approach. Take the thermometer, for example. For this you don't need any special – in fact – *any* scientific approach. Any idiot can invent it. It is a simple, straightforward device that measures the temperature of the body. But ah, the love meter! Measuring love in correct degrees is not as simple as measuring the temperature of the body. Along with physical laws, it is essential for its inventor to have complete mastery over spiritual laws as well. And to bring spiritual laws within the dominion of the correct scientific approach is no walk in the park. If not for the aid of the Great Master of Spirituality, Hakim Allah Lok Sanyasi, I too would be stumbling in the dark like you. This is precisely where all of you go wrong. You want to invent the love meter according to the same physical laws that underlie the thermometer – that mercury expands under heat. But love is not subject only to physical laws. Hahaha! Hehehe!' he laughed arrogantly, which displeased me very much.

I controlled myself and asked, 'But is this love-measuring device of yours, the love meter, completely finished?'

'Yes, completely finished! What were you thinking? What have I been doing for so many days?' Dr Ghareeb Muhammad replied, giving me a conciliatory look. 'My love meter works with the precision and beauty of the formula "two plus two equals to four"!' Then he said with a start, and in a harassed tone, 'Asp, my friend!' (Actually, my real name is something else. My friends and relations call me Asp out of love. That's also the nom de plume I use while writing ghazals.) 'These inventions have to be patented too. Do you know anything about this patenting business?'

'Leave that to me,' I said, offering myself as a rock of support to my friend. 'I am a specialist in these things. Just recently I have patented a new method of making bread. But why are you so eager to get the love meter registered?'

'Why shouldn't I be eager! Imagine if somebody else brought this invention to the market first – then what?'

'Who could invent this other than you?' I said, encouraging him. 'I mean, I had a chance, but due to the lack of the correct scientific approach, it's now out of the question. And besides, I am your best friend. How could you even expect your friend to act so unscrupulously?'

'No!' he said. 'I don't doubt you. If I fear somebody, it is that one man who is privy to many secrets to do with this invention. You know, one can never be completely sure about somebody's intentions.' He brought his face close to me as if to tell me a secret – so close that some of the hair from his pointed beard poked their way into my mouth and tickled my tongue. 'Now what do I have to hide from you? You are my best friend. Asp, my friend, I cannot forget the troubles you took to find the nightingales for my love compound. I am afraid of Hakim Allah Lok Sanyasi. He knows the secrets of the mechanical parts and the machinery; besides, the device also contains some talismans supplied by the learned man.'

'Talisman!' I cried out. 'You mean your love meter works with talismans?'

'Not just talismans. They come later. Before all that, there is an extremely complex mechanism of parts, cogs and springs. It is similar to the mechanism of a wristwatch – only much more complicated. This strap that you see here, it's made of a special material that is hollow from the inside, and even the English, German and American chemists and materials scientists are unaware of its chemical properties.'

He didn't want to share any further details, so I took another route. 'Doctor, you already know that I am your best friend. Please don't forget the time when I spent four or five days without food or drink searching for your nightingales in deserts and gardens everywhere; and when I finally brought them to you in a basket, everyone was jealous and insinuated that these were not nightingales but wild wagtails – and you agreed with them and I had to call upon novelist Sheikh Fazal Ali in the middle of the night to act as my witness. Please reflect on these things for a moment, and explain to me in detail how this device works.'

He hesitated briefly but then fully explained the mechanism of the device to me. There was a little strap or bracelet attached to the watch that could be worn around the wrist. A crystal-like piece was fixed on the other end of the bracelet – it was not actually made of crystal but of some other mysterious material that can never be discovered by Western materials scientists and chemists until they give birth to someone who can simultaneously be a scientist as well as an accomplished saint. The special property of this crystal was that normal physical temperatures had no effect on it but the waves of love, which travelled in the air like radio waves, upon collision with the crystal, unleashed corresponding waves in the springs and bracelet of the watch. The spring got magnetized and turned the hands of the watch clockwise or anticlockwise. Numbers ranging from +1 till +6 ran on one half of the dial, while the other half was labelled from -1 to -6. These indicated the degree of love or hatred (the negative numbers showed hatred). It looked like this:

After explaining thus far, Doctor said, 'I will tell you how it works. Imagine a beautiful woman walking in your direction, and you want to find out to what degree she loves you or how intensely she's attracted to you. You wear the watch on your hand, like this, and you bring the crystal in front of your face so that it blocks her direct, piercing gaze. As soon as the love waves strike the crystal, the hand will move right or left. So, suppose the hand points to +1, it means the girl likes you, but only moderately and casually. If it stops somewhere between +1 to +3 or +5, it means she loves you with enough intensity to run away with you. +6 means she's ready to marry you – provided that her father agrees, of course.'

'And these ... what do these show?'

'Ha! You really are just a kid! You can't even understand this much. What could -1 degree of love mean? Just that it is +1 degree of hatred. If the hand moves in an anticlockwise direction and stops at -1, it means the woman hates you, and the last and most extreme degree of this hate is -6. It indicates hatred to a degree that could get you a serious thrashing from her brothers.'

When I heard 'thrashing', I did not even blink before shooting a completely irrelevant question: 'One more thing, O great chemist! Does this watch ... err ... would the love meter be reserved only for the lucky residents of Chakiwara?'

'No,' Dr Ghareeb Muhammad replied, adopting the demeanour of a great scientist. 'I am a real scientist, and a real scientist doesn't think in the limited terms of nations, countries or territories. The entire human race shall benefit from this invention – even Sikhs.'

'So generous! Even for Sikhs!' I looked at him admiringly, but then I began yelling. 'You don't wish to deprive even Sikhs from the benefits of this invention! But benefits?! Honestly, this love meter has no real benefit. You have invented an amazing device but there is no benefit in it. It will ruin households and shatter the hearts of thousands of lovers who thrive under the illusion of their beloved's chaste and pure love.'

'Even then it is a great invention,' Dr Ghareeb Muhammad replied. 'Everything has its advantages and disadvantages. I can't deny the fact that it might make the lives of its creators unbearable. Perhaps, many people who believed in their beloved's faithfulness, when they discover the truth on the love meter, will feel so hopeless that they might commit suicide – but I think overall this invention will benefit humanity. It will facilitate young people enormously in choosing their spouses.'

'Regardless, this invention is of no use to me at least. For some reason, God knows why, when women see me, their radioactive waves, that you have described so elegantly just now, simply come to a halt. I am pretty sure that if I wear your love meter on my wrist, the pointer will stay at zero. Women neither hate nor love me.'

In the end, I promised the doctor that I would keep my mouth shut about this invention and not utter a word to anybody. After this, with Doctor's permission, I wore the love meter on my wrist and measured the degree of love that various living things harboured for this humble subject. The results were as follows:

A woman walking towards me carrying a pot of water: pointer at zero.

A camel standing around the corner of Corporation Street looking at me: +4

Two donkeys coming towards me: +6 (probably +3 per donkey)

Yaqoob Makrani, the red-bearded Jew of Chakiwara, to whom I owed a hundred rupees and who had five of my ties as a security deposit: -6

The moment I saw Yaqoob Makrani's love at -6, I immediately ran inside Dr Ghareeb Muhammad's dispensary – basically a suffocating dark closet, but referred to as a dispensary, and kept myself stowed in there until the doctor gave me an 'all clear' signal that suggested Yaqoob Makrani had indeed passed by the shop.

'Really, Doctor,' I said coming out of the dispensary, brushing cobwebs off my clothes, 'Today your love meter really saved my life and honour. It informed me that today my creditor was out to break my head with his boots – the rascal was even wearing shiny new boots with spikes.'

'Okay, now give me back the meter. I have to tighten a couple of screws and a talisman still needs to go in. I will get this patented by tomorrow. But Hakim Allah Lok Sanyasi …'

'I will help you get this patented,' I said, coming to my friend's aid in this difficult situation. 'Don't worry. The clerk of the Administrator's office is my friend. Okay, I will go now …' Then suddenly, I remembered something and turned around. 'Dr Ghareeb Muhammad! Can you lend me five rupees and three-and-a-half aanas by tonight?'

He looked a bit hesitant. I subtly reminded him once again that I was his best friend. I also brought up the nightingales. Finally, he pulled out five rupees and three-and-a-half aanas from his bag and placed them on my palm.

'What is five rupees for a friend!' After giving away the money he did not hesitate to play the role of the mythical hero Hatim Ta'i, famous for his generosity. 'Here! Five rupees for my best friend! And besides, I am about to earn millions from this invention,' he consoled himself.

3

THREE DAYS LATER, WHEN I ENTERED DR GHAREEB Muhammad's clinic to find shelter from the rain, I found our serious and promising genius so completely engrossed in such a delightful activity that he did not even notice my arrival. Squatting on his toes on the floor, he was closely examining every inch of a fine white feminine leg. The owner of this leg was sitting on the chair. She was holding the edge of her long floral-patterned cloak above her knees with one hand. She was bent delightfully like a fruit-laden branch that was about to give away under its own weight. If you reside in Chakiwara, you too must have seen her. Raqiba was the name of this riotous beauty. Many young poets of Chakiwara had written furnace-hot verse addressed to her, and a number of suicides by young men were associated with her. Among the melting beauties of Corporation Street, she was without a doubt the number one. Actually, she was not that beautiful; she might be considered one of those girls who after the age of twenty turn into withered, interfering women, their noses crooked like a parrot's beak, the type of women about whom it is difficult to imagine that they once had admirers too.

This is an incident from a year ago, when the humble writer of these lines was not yet an official member of The Association of Chakiwara Bachelors. Once while passing by Raqiba's lane, he had attempted to address her with tender words of love as she stood on her balcony. But after being splashed with two bucketfuls of cold water, he quickly reached the conclusion that the beginnings of this love were not encouraging. The gentle scribe of these words has never been a persistent lover. He gets disappointed if he is discouraged at an early stage, and sets out to test his luck on other paths of love.

Ah, yes, those were the days!

I did not wish to interfere in Dr Ghareeb Muhammad's love session but I was helpless. It was raining heavily outside –

Karachi had never seen such a downpour. Finally, Raqiba lifted her eyes, and as soon as she saw me, dropped her cloak. At that moment, Raqiba's eyes were brimming with venom and I am sure if I had the love meter, its reading would have hovered between -5 and -6. The doctor gave me a murderous look, as if he wanted to eat me alive. Without bothering to reply to my greeting, he returned his attention to his patient, 'Dogs after all – they do end up biting sometimes. No need to worry, and don't be concerned about the dog being mad. I've known that dog for three years now. He's a saintly dog. The wound is light too. Show me your leg once every day.'

Raqiba picked up the box of balm that Dr Ghareeb Muhammad had prescribed for her and tenderly walked out of the shop. Watching her seriously tested the oath that I had recently undertaken at The Association of Chakiwara Bachelors in the presence of many eminent personalities.

'Phooh!' Dr Ghareeb Muhammad said, wiping sweat off his forehead. 'Phooh! I say, what a beautiful leg! What a glowing white calf!'

'That's what I am saying! What a beautiful leg, what a glowing white calf! It seems like the dog had quite a discerning taste.'

'What nonsense!' the doctor said. 'Asp, your jokes are not funny. I don't understand them. I have only seen one other woman whose legs could compete with Raqiba's. And she was Marlene Dietrich, the film actress. And that mindblowing beauty has just had her legs insured for many thousands of dollars.'

'Where did you meet her? As far as I know you've never even been to Kot Radha Kishan – forget Hollywood.'

'Ah, but I have seen her … her legs … on the silver screen. To see a beautiful feminine leg is like seeing one of the wonders of the world, and for the aesthetically gifted, a great spiritual experience. Keats wrote that famous line after seeing such a leg: "A thing of beauty is joy forever."'

'Who is Keats?'

Before the doctor could deliver a brainy lecture on Keats and English literature, a middle-aged man with glittering eyes, a kind beard, and wearing a Peshawari turban, walked in with a stick in his hand. He was Raqiba's uncle and guardian, Haji Bhalay Deeno. Doctor leapt forward and touched his feet, kissed him on his right cheek, and brought the padded chair out from the dispensary to seat him. I was thinking of leaving but when the doctor called out Fazal Tea Shop's server and ordered their special tea, I realized that I had nothing going on that was as urgent. So I stayed.

'These days, Asp sahib, you have to leave for work early in the morning,' Dr Ghareeb Muhammad reminded me courteously, gently hinting that I should be on my way.

'No,' I said in a buoyant tone. 'I have left that job and now my work has no fixed time.'

The man with the kind beard asked me, 'Did Raqiba come here?'

'Yes, she was here,' the doctor said, using the royal Urdu pronoun to refer to the queen of his heart. 'I have assured her that it's just a little wound. She would only have to come for a few days for check-ups.'

'Hunh,' said Haji Bhalay Deeno, as he slurped some tea. 'Opium is getting more expensive these days and the official suppliers are selling it on the black market.'

'You should have asked this humble servant of yours,' the doctor swooped down to offer proof of his obliging nature and his readiness to serve. 'Why else is one here anyway?'

'Okay – hunh. Arrange six tolas of opium by tonight. I will pay when my son the elder Deeno's money order arrives from Iraq. Dr Ghareeb Muhammad, you are among Chakiwara's most pious men. So many widows and orphans pray for you. I am writing a biographical study in the Makrani language with pictures of all the famous and respectable people of Chakiwara. This would be Chakiwara's "kaun-kaun", meaning who's who. In the respectable people's list, I would write your name at number two. The first name would be my own. Please provide me with a biographical note, a block of your photo, and a list of your selected works as soon as possible. The donation for getting published in *Who's Who* is only forty rupees – opium is getting more expensive and Raqiba too is now nineteen years old.'

All this time I had been unsuccessfully trying to eat a leathery bun that I suddenly swallowed. It got stuck in my throat and I had to run outside.

In the evening I saw a girl who turned out to be Raqiba. She stood modishly in front of the doctor's shop under the municipality lantern. She moved away when she saw me. Women often think of me as toxic. The doctor was in his shop, trying to smile through his beard.

I said, 'Why, you look very happy today!'

'There is a lot to be happy about,' he said. 'The old baboon has finally agreed.'

'Old baboon? Who? And agreed to what?'

'You are a kid. I have to explain everything to you. The old baboon – Haji Bhalay Deeno, who else? The man who was sitting here in the morning. You got the hell out of here but he stayed on for three more hours. Also had lunch with me. I've finally won him over. He's agreed to give me Raqiba's hand in marriage.'

'Come to your senses!' I cried out. 'You are the secretary of The Association of Chakiwara Bachelors! Recall your promises, your oath, your resolutions!'

'I am resigning from the post of secretary. Believe me, Asp, if Raqiba hadn't come into my life I would never have abandoned my best and closest friends like this. Despite all this, my sympathies and good wishes are with you and the other bachelors. I will always be marching with you shoulder to shoulder in spirit.'

'Raqiba,' I said, seething with envy. 'You are ready to abandon your oath of fidelity and your friends for a woman and take such a dangerous and foolish step, whose outcome I shudder to imagine. There is still time, Dr Ghareeb Muhammad! Turn back! Stay put!'

'Ah, that leg,' the doctor was revelling in an ecstatic trance. 'What a beautiful leg!'

'But how do you know that she ... Raqiba, also loves you. You know you are thirty-six, thirty-seven now, and not exactly the Yusuf that ladies will die for.'

'But Raqiba certainly dies for me. Her eyes clearly offer me her message of love. Her lips invite me to kiss her. In each of her gestures, hints, and moves, there is only love – love and invitation.'

When I heard the word 'invitation' I said, 'I am feeling a bit hungry. What are your thoughts regarding tea?' I looked at him with hopeful eyes. 'And as far as love is concerned, I can tell you that you are wrong. Nothing can be deduced from her manners and her lethal glances. Women are mysterious creatures.' I was speaking as if I had spent my entire life studying female psychology. 'For instance, that camel that passed here the day before and appeared so agitated, obviously it is inconceivable to even imagine that he had any sort of feelings for me, but when I put on the love meter I saw he had +4 degree love for me. My friendly advice to you is that tomorrow you should check the degree of her love using the love meter. Then consider other things.'

Now I regret giving him this advice. In a sense, it was what led to his horrific death four days later. You'd say I shouldn't have given him this advice. But I thought this reality would have dawned on him in any case – if not today, then tomorrow, if not tomorrow, then the day after tomorrow.

I started to walk out but then a thought suddenly struck me and I turned around. 'Dr Ghareeb Muhammad, can you lend me ten rupees and eight aanas until tomorrow? There is a General Working Meeting of Bread Manufacturers and this humble man is presiding over the proceedings. Out of the many president's duties, one is to entertain the members with chai and cigarettes. Only until tomorrow. You know I am your best friend. Remember those nightingales! To have a close friend by your side in Chakiwara in good times and bad, especially one who is unrivalled in giving good advice, is among life's greatest blessings.'

But I didn't even need to make such a long speech that day. Dr Ghareeb Muhammad was already imagining he was Hatim Ta'i.

He pulled out ten rupees and eight aanas from his bag and handed them to me. They were promptly snatched by Yaqoob

Makrani, who was waiting to pounce on me upon my exit from the shop.

And then I, beautifully broke and destitute as ever, walked off, whistling away in the silver evening.

My master had once said to me: Never lose heart.

4

THE HAVOC AND MAYHEM WREAKED BY THE RAINS THAT JULY will always be remembered in Karachi's history. Immediately after the rains, the gods of weather in the government predicted that a fearsome cyclone was fast approaching. However, due to some reasons known only to the cyclone, it turned around before it could reach Karachi and left the overhasty gods of weather looking embarrassed. A few others who had been eagerly awaiting the cyclone were deeply disappointed as well. Nevertheless, it would have been difficult for the cyclone to do more than what had already been done by the rains, so it probably did not feel the need to descend upon us anymore.

The conditions in Chakiwara after the rains could only be described as 'mashallah', that is, 'May Allah be praised.' Potholes had turned into ponds, and ponds into lakes. In some places, people were swimming through their lanes. The Lyari river, which in itself did not have the strength of even an ordinary stream, had now swelled into a mad, raging river, posing a hazard to nearby settlements.

This was the second day after the rains had ended. Around two o'clock at Ghareeb Nawaz Hotel, I was presiding over an extraordinary meeting of The Association of Bread Manufacturers of Chakiwara. Besides us, many other famous and revered people were present in the hotel, all searching for cures to their own maladies by consuming tea. Mr M. A. Chakori – bald and bird-like, former film actor, now unknown and forgotten and somewhat frayed – so sick of the world that now even he had stopped laughing at his own jokes. He had just one principle now, like most visitors to Ghareeb Nawaz Hotel – never to pay for his own tea. Sheikh Fazal Ali Dingvi, Munshi-e-Fazil, author of numerous sensational and spell-binding detective thrillers that played an instrumental role in turning many a schoolboy into courageous lovers and cunning sleuths. In real life, he was a chicken-hearted man, who had the habit of continuously turning around to look over his shoulder while walking. In Chakiwara, his creditors were everywhere. I was one of them too. Because of this, his own life had turned into a detective novel. Hakim Shahsawar Khan, learned diviner, doctor of physical and spiritual maladies, was also present there. If he, who was among the brightest students of Hakim Allah Lok Sanyasi, were to believed, then within two years, holy men and guardian saints would rise to take the reins of power in Pakistan after which, thanks to some special spells and charms, India would automatically surrender and Jawaharlal Nehru would request these holy men and guardian saints to rule over India too. In three years the entire population of India would convert to Islam and disbelief would be obliterated from the face of this planet. After this political commentary, Hakim Shahsawar Khan also clarified that he was preparing a scheme to melt all stone-hearted beloveds and bring them to the feet of their lovers who were pining for them. Once he accomplished this, in his view, there would be only one worthy task left: to convince the djinns, who were badly smitten with the females of Chakiwara, to leave and migrate to the other side of the Lyari river.

Besides these figures, the editor of Chakiwara's *Who's Who*, Haji Bhalay Deeno, was also at the venue. He sat in a corner, innocently slurping his tea. At that moment, with his gentle beard he appeared so full of kindness that anybody could have gone and asked for his daughter's hand without any fear. And if somebody had actually gone to him, he would have given him an affectionate, paternal look, his gentle beard would have smiled, he would have brought up the matter of his *Who's Who* and the forty-rupee donation, and when the suitor would have paid for his tea and cakes, Bhalay Deeno would have got up and gone to sleep. The next morning, he would have forgotten everything. That was Haji Bhalay Deeno for you, Chakiwara's number one resident, according to himself.

All of a sudden, through the door, I saw that right in the middle of the road there was a man in a dark gown and spectacles with a stethoscope hanging around his neck, running madly with his hands up in the air.

Novelist Sheikh Fazal Ali said, 'That looks like Dr Ghareeb Muhammad.'

It certainly was the doctor. Running at such mad speed. What had happened?

Hakim Shahsawar Khan said in an awe-inspiring tone, 'A djinn has got into him.'

'I think he's gone crazy,' one of my bread-making colleagues said, who a few months back had also gone crazy, to such a degree that he had climbed onto the branches of a tree near City Post Office and had started telling every passerby that he was resting in his nest.

Sheikh Fazal Ali said, 'The doctor cannot get crazier than he already is.'

We all appreciated the weight of this phrase and his sense of humour. Actor M. A. Chakori also felt that he should say something. 'It seems to me that Dr Ghareeb Muhammad is going to see a patient. He's in a hurry because he's probably afraid that the Angel of Death might snatch his prey before he gets there.'

We did not appreciate the joke because M. A. Chakori had not yet been granted residency in Chakiwara. He was an outsider, an alien, and outsiders have no right to make fun of original residents. This phrase was a cheap attack on our most talented scientist.

The kind-bearded Haji Bhalay Deeno came close to me and asked, 'Who was that man who was running?'

'Dr Ghareeb Muhammad – didn't you recognize your soon-to-be son-in-law?'

'Dr Ghareeb Muhammad who? I have a weak memory. I didn't have my dose of opium today. Do you have a rupee and four aanas?' And then suddenly he locked his arms around my neck and started shouting, 'This man stole one rupee and four-and-a-half aanas from me! I have been looking for him for two months!'

When I saw the situation getting out of hand, I shoved Bhalay Deeno aside, freed my neck and, lurching over the benches, got out onto the street. And there I yelled, 'Allah'o Akbar!' and scorning several hawkers and leaping clean over a donkey cart, left my followers in the dust. Dr Ghareeb Muhammad was running in front of me frantically, as if the spirits of all his dead patients were chasing after him.

'Doctor! Doctor!' I hollered after him.

Still running, he turned around to look at me and called out, 'Asp! Go to my shop and look under the tablecloth – you will understand everything!' And saying this, he increased his speed. His face was so terribly contorted with anguish and insanity that it was difficult to recognize him. I understood that he had some dangerous plan up his sleeve. He was on the promenade now, which is basically a solid embankment on the Lyari river. It presents a delightful view of women slapping dung patties into shape and of buffaloes lazing in the mud below. Behind the golden mud and the buffaloes, the sunset looks very beautiful. The residents of Chakiwara often visit the promenade for this enchanting view. But at that moment, the Lyari looked a real river and in front of me there was only water. The doctor climbed onto the edge of the embankment, a silhouette against the rosy background of the evening – a strange, forlorn image. He had his hands in the air. I started calling out to him. He loudly cried out, 'Ya Ali!' once and disappeared from my view.

Dr Ghareeb Muhammad had dived into the Lyari river. That was the end of the great scientist. But who was responsible for his death? His instrument – the love meter? Raqiba? His own increasing insanity? In any case, I knew that Pakistan had just been deprived of the talents and research of an inventor whose parallel could hardly be found in this century.

5

BOTH THE DOORS OF THE DOCTOR'S DISPENSARY WERE open. Nobody was inside and it felt as if he had just gone out for something and would return any minute. I knew he would never return – never. I moved the tablecloth. There was a sealed envelope with my name and on top of it was the love meter. The hand of the meter showed -6.

I opened the envelope. This was the body of the letter:

I, Dr Ghareeb Muhammad, the original inventor of the love meter (only two talismans in this device are the work of Hakim Allah Lok Sanyasi), am going out to put an end to my futile life, in its thirty-seventh year. Due to the rains, the Lyari river is swollen and such golden opportunities to commit suicide do not arise every day for the residents of Chakiwara. You will ask why such a successful doctor like myself, the inventor of so many marvellous inventions, the one who invented the amazing love meter, wishes to reject his worldly fame and reputation and lose his life? The reason is failure in love. Today, the woman about whose love I was absolutely sure, came to me. The moment in which she moved her tender lips forward to place on mine, I measured her love for me. Sadly, her love was a lie. Her vows and promises were a lie. The sweet intoxication of her eyes was a lie. The reading on the love meter was -6. It meant that her love was only superficial and in reality, she hated me.

You will agree that now it was pointless for me to continue living in this world.

'I hand over this shop, which is the best private clinic in Chakiwara, to my friend Asp. I don't have any offspring (I didn't get married and so this is out of the question), neither do I have any relatives who acknowledged that they were my relatives during my lifetime. Asp is my best friend. He took great risks with his life for the preparation of many wonderful medicines available in this clinic and for a long time wandered the deserts and the wilderness in search of nightingales, among other things. I hope that Asp will find a doctor's profession easier and more profitable than the bread-manufacturing business.

I also hand my invention, the love meter, to him and with that, I entreat him to never ever use it and to not make it public. The consequences of using it could be extremely dangerous, as in my own case. Surely it cannot benefit the world. Yes, if I had lived I had plans to make certain innovations whereby hate could be turned into love. But God the Magnificent had other plans for me. Now I will head out towards the Lyari river because I fear the waters might recede.'

6

THE LOVE METER IS WITH ME, ALONG WITH THE DOCTOR'S will. Even though the government has gone against the will of the deceased and has decided against allotting the clinic to me, I will still stand by the late doctor's testament. The love meter will never enter the market. I don't wish to spread unhappiness and hopelessness in Chakiwara or the world in general. If young lovers spend some years of their lives harbouring bright, colourful illusions, why should I be the one to introduce misgivings into their lives? They should be left alone, happy with their delusions.

I have the love meter in my possession but I am a very unhappy man. I tried it again today on my wrist and measured the degree of love of various objects. The results were as disappointing as before:

Camel: +4

A woman with a pot on her head: -3

A woman without a pot on her head: -3

The results are getting worse. The zero of women has turned into a -3. The camel's love however still stands as before. Maybe during next year's rains, I too ...

The Downfall of Seth Tanwari

1

I do not know Seth Tanwari's full name and have no wish to find out either. He's among those crown players in the Karachi stock exchange who roll around in millions, and whose wealth causes great fluctuations in the stock market. The world of finance remains evergreen thanks to such people and can never be grateful enough to them. However, there must be a realm beyond this one – a spiritual realm, perhaps – otherwise, one can only wonder as to how Tanwari and his financial empire collapsed so spectacularly, so suddenly. The punishment he received was much harsher than his crime (although as far as I am concerned, I have completely forgiven him).

Everybody knows that when spirits begin to hound somebody, they don't leave easily and don't listen to anybody either, no matter how much one begs or pleads. In this particular case, as will be made clear to you in the course of this account, I am utterly innocent. I did everything in my power. Two months back I was not even familiar with Seth Tanwari's face, although I cannot say with any certainty because there are so many that resemble him and his manners in this part of Karachi. (But how could he ever cross paths with an ordinary and lowly hakim!)

The thing is that Chakiwara's famous (late) Dr Ghareeb Muhammad, before diving into the Lyari river, left his will behind in a sealed envelope in his shop. While penning this will, the deceased remembered some of my services to him and bequeathed his shop – including all furniture, bottles, etc. – to me, Muhammad Deen Asp (I have his will with me as a token of the master's blessing.) The deceased did not have any family and he was free of worldly contaminations. During his last days, he loved me as a son, in fact, took my advice with regards to the invention of many of his scientific and spiritual gadgets. To sum up, the deceased was a man of many qualities.

So, in direct accord with his wishes, I took over his property and started practising medicine. This was a completely new occupation for me, but in my experience if a man throws himself blindly into his work, after a while he inevitably gains some sense of it. And besides, I already had knowledge of many mixtures and their effects because I had spent time in the late doctor's company, and I had arranged for many of the ingredients that were used in the doctor's prescriptions (birds, animal horns, etc.). Secondly, I had discovered some papers in Dr Ghareeb Muhammad's notebook that I spotted behind some large jars on the top shelf of his shop. This notebook had been in the works for a very long time, and Dr Ghareeb Muhammad had plans of publishing it once it was completed. When I scanned it, I found in there the recipes for his medicines. Basically, this notebook contained the distilled extracts of Doctor's great mind and I found it invaluable for my own medical practice.

I took a few more measures to improve my practice further (if the late doctor were alive, he would have approved). I left the board outside the shop – 'Doctor Ghareeb Muhammad' – as it was, and only added the word 'late' at the end of his name and added the following words at the bottom: Distinguished successor: Doctor Muhammad Deen Asp.

Initially, my friends and relatives made fun of me: 'When did you become a doctor?!' But after a while, everybody started referring to me as Dr Asp and the word 'doctor' became associated with my name. Following in the footsteps of the late doctor, I grew a little pointed beard too. Before leaving for his suicide, the late doctor had forgotten his spectacles in his desk drawer (or maybe left them behind intentionally). I got their broken stems fixed and started using them. The strange thing is that they were made exactly to my blindness (or short-sightedness), and after a while I was unable to see anything without them. During this period, I got married to Haji Bhalay Deeno's blessed daughter, even though the old Haji gave in after much reluctance. With this marriage, I not only settled my home but also fulfilled the life-long desire of the late doctor. I am sure that this action of mine brought peace and consolation to his pure soul.

It was either Doctor's affectionate invisible hand assisting me or it could be that Raqiba had brought me luck, but my business prospered and I usually didn't even have the time to scratch my head. My prescriptions were pointed arrows that hit their targets each time as if God had given me the powers of healing. But I understood very well that it did not have much to do with my own aptitude or performance; it was all because of Dr Ghareeb Muhammad. A couple of times he appeared in my dreams and told me what to prescribe to some of my patients whom I was unable to diagnose properly. Once he even said, 'My timepiece is lying with Haji Bhalay Deeno; go get it from him.' The timepiece was indeed with my father-in-law but it was broken. He sold it to me for four rupees and I brought it and kept it with me in the shop as a token of the late doctor's blessing.

One day I was sitting in the shop scanning the doctor's notebook when I saw in it a design for a strange kind of device.

Just below it was written, 'Device to Summon Spirits.' On the next page, Doctor sahib had listed the details of its components. Just underneath it was a cautionary note stating that this device was in experimental stages and would be dangerous to use until a way was found to send the spirits back. I assembled the device in a few days. It was a planchet-like device with one compartment containing some talismans and one-and-a-half maasha camphor, while on top was a small beauty mirror. I put it together and set it aside and decided to consult the accomplished and learned Hakim Lok Sanyasi for ways to send the spirits back. I knew very well about the outcome of Doctor's other inventions, so I had absolutely no intention of using this device until the above-mentioned defect had been corrected. But as the poet Insha says:

Whoever has been left in peace by the movement of the
Spheres, Insha

Novelist Fazal Ali often sings this verse.

So one day I had just entered my shop when two men came in. One was older than the other. The older man cut a beefy figure with a hard leathery face and wore a round black cap and a kurta-pajama. The other one was a pale-complexioned young man with cheeks set in; his rabbit-like head was not covered. Both of them were chewing paan and began walking around the shop as if it belonged to them.

The man was Tanwari and the skinny boy was his son, although I did not know this at the time. I was surprised and wondered who these people were and why they looked so interested in the floors and ceiling of the shop. I was about to ask when the older Tanwari turned to me.

'Since when have you been squatting here?' he asked.

I replied, 'What do you mean by 'squatting here'?'

'This shop has been allotted to us. You will have to vacate it by tomorrow,' he said.

'Vacate! What do you mean? Seth, this shop is mine.'

He laughed in a disgusting manner, '*Your* shop! Has the government written a lease in your name? How did this become your shop? This is evacuee property. The custodian has allotted it to us. We have paid him the rent for the last twelve months. Tomorrow you vacate it quietly, understand? Take your bottles and stuff with you. We don't wish to fight.'

I said some words to Tanwari and told both father and son to get the hell out of the shop.

He threatened me, 'We are going to call the police. We have court orders,' and waved a piece of paper in front of my eyes.

After they left, I thought carefully about the matter and the whole thing did indeed appear slightly crooked. While it was true that Dr Ghareeb Muhammad in his will had handed his property to me, it was also a fact that it wasn't Dr Ghareeb Muhammad's personal property to begin with. As Tanwari had said, it was evacuee property that Doctor himself had seized somehow. I did not even know if this shop was actually allotted to the doctor or if he had ever paid the rent for it. Another question popped up in my mind: Was it possible to bequeath allotted property to somebody else? What was the legal implication of my occupation of this property? If I tried to prove my ownership of this property using the doctor's will, would anybody take me seriously?

For suggestions and resolutions to these problems, I went to the novelist Fazal Ali. Since he wrote popular detective novels, I assumed he would be somewhat of a lawyer too, but he proved useless. I went back home and related my travails to Raqiba and my father-in-law Bhalay Deeno. He assured me that as long as he was in Chakiwara, nobody could snatch the shop from me. Tomorrow, he'd meet Khan Bahadur Khokru and get me a stay order.

The next day Bhalay Deeno had severe inflammation in his joints and decided to postpone his meeting with Khokru. As usual, I reached the shop and started examining my patients, although I was worried and kept looking towards the bazaar every ten–fifteen minutes.

Tanwari wasn't somebody you could evade easily. True to his word, he was there like the Angel of Death, along with two police constables and four or five other men. They told me to vacate the shop. A large crowd gathered around us. The truth is that a poor man has no life. They started tossing my things out on the street. I was enraged but at the same time unable to control my tears at the shop being snatched from me. In the midst of this dilemma, my eyes fell on the gadget for summoning spirits. It was lying in a corner. I picked it up and followed the instruction laid down in Dr Ghareeb Muhammad's book and called out: 'Help me, Dr Ghareeb Muhammad! Your shop is being siezed!' As soon as I said this, an electric current passed through my hand and in the mirror appeared something with a pointed beard, which somewhat resembled the doctor (okay, it probably looked like my face too). But I cannot say for sure, because the mirror, which was fastened to the wooden frame with hinges, shook and the face disappeared in a flash. It did, however, send a shiver down my spine and I felt as if Dr Ghareeb Muhammad had descended from the heavens and was now walking around in the shop. (Given that we were dealing with a wise and learned man such as the doctor, it was not improbable either.) Right then, a constable's foot fell somewhat awkwardly on the stairs as he was moving the table out of the shop, and he fell flat on his face as if somebody had tripped him over. That was the moment I was convinced that Dr Ghareeb Muhammad had indeed come to my aid.

But whether he had come at that point or later, the shop was emptied out nevertheless, and to be honest, I do not wish to have anything on record about his exact time of arrival. One has to be cautious when discussing the comings and goings of spirits. The thing is, even if the doctor had indeed arrived at that moment, he did not participate in any activity following the tripping of the constable.

After the constables (who were performing Seth Tanwari's duties with so much fervour it seemed they were his personal servants) had put out all my possessions out on the street, the seth said to me, 'Baba, it is a legal matter. We do not want to cause any loss to you. Check all your things carefully.' For this show of sympathy, I wanted to punch his face, but then I thought about jail and Raqiba and my unborn children and kept quiet.

With a weeping heart, I took hold of Doctor's notebook, stethoscope, and a couple of other things lying within my reach. On the wall was a photo of Dr Ghareeb Muhammad and me that was taken by a friend in Chakiwara; I took that with me as well.

'And baba, here, take this too,' Tanwari pointed towards the device to summon spirits.

But I did not take it. I left it on a shelf and told him that I would collect it later.

He said, 'Don't worry, we don't keep anybody's things. Tomorrow or day after, come and collect it at whatever time.'

Raqiba had arrived at the shop after hearing the commotion. We placed all our possessions in a cart. Tanwari was willing to pay us the fare, but I refused. As I was leaving, I warned Seth Tanwari, 'Remember seth, this shop will cost you a lot.'

'We are sorry, hakim sahib, but this is a legal matter.'

Pushing our belongings, we headed home with our bleeding hearts but somewhere deep down, I did not feel good at all about leaving the device in the shop. I related the incident to Bhalay Deeno when I reached home, who claimed that had it not been for his weak joints, he would've taught Seth Tanwari a lesson about what it means to steal somebody's shop. He was very sad that he had not been not around at that time. Besides this and a few curses, he did not say anything else and made no mention of Khan Bahadur Khokru.

2

I SPENT THE NEXT THREE OR FOUR DAYS FEELING ANGRY and frustrated over the loss of my shop and listening to Bhalay Deeno's inane stories. Finally, Raqiba advised me: 'Why don't you set up a shop on the footpath like other hakims in the city?' Her advice made sense to me, and I decided to work on it. I chose a spot at the end of the tram tracks, and met Yaqoob Makrani, who is the Don of Chakiwara and rents out footpath spaces to all sorts of peddlers, astrologers and kohl-sellers. He decided to give it to me for ten rupees a month and promised that he would not allow another doctor to run a business around my area. Yaqoob Makrani is a man of his word and a friend of friends.

There I set up my base. I nailed the signboard from the old shop that I had brought with me, and elaborated further in red letters:

FAMOUS DOCTOR MUHAMMAD DEEN ASP
SUCCESSOR TO THE LATE DR GHAREEB MUHAMMAD
CORVENTION STREET #1
NOW SITS HERE FOR EVERYONE'S BENEFIT
2 AANAS FOR MEDICINES. ALL DISEASES. FREE DIAGNOSIS.

Each morning, Raqiba and I would put the medicine jars and bottles, large boxes of mixtures and compounds and anatomy charts of humans and lizards in a large trunk and transport it to my footpath shop on a donkey cart (that belonged to Raqiba's brother). She would help me set up the bottles and jars and return home on it.

My wife is a highly courageous and dignified woman, and is the biggest blessing that God has bestowed on me. Daily at dusk, she'd come to collect me because I closed shop early and we'd return to our house, swaying in the twilight with our trunk. (Both the donkeys were quick and the cart had large rubber tyres.) In those moments, the fatigue of my entire day would disappear and I would feel as joyous as a king in his four-horse landau carriage. On our return journey, we'd pass by my first shop. At first I used to feel a burning anguish and I'd think lots of bitter thoughts about Seth Tanwari, but as time went on, I began seeing this loss in a more philosophical light.

Next to the shop, just around the corner, there is an Iranian restaurant, The Royal Corvention Restaurant, whose owner Pervez Milli is a great friend of mine. Pervez Milli is a round, rotund man of buttery plumpness and lavish moustaches. The late Dr Ghareeb Muhammad treated him once when he had colic. He was deeply sad about the snatching of my shop and showed me genuine sympathy. On our way back, we'd often stop at The Royal Corvention Restaurant for a chat and single-chai with Pervez Milli.

Sitting in the restaurant, my wife would look wistfully at my shop at the end of the lane and assure me that if her father wasn't handicapped from the inflammation of his joints, this shop would have never been taken away from me. Now the board hanging outside the shop read Tanwari & Co. instead of Dr Ghareeb Muhammad. Pervez Milli told me that Tanwari visited the shop only once in the morning; his son was there the rest of the day. They were turning it into a warehouse and the renovations were in full swing. The walls inside the shop had been whitewashed and in the restaurant mirrors we could see a half-bald carpenter with a scanty beard constantly busy with his work. Tanwari's son would be sitting inside on a footstool, supervising. He'd be chewing betel leaf and smoking beedi. The son appeared a skinny, rotten young man beaten up with weakness. There wasn't a drop of blood in his face. Often we'd feel a bit sorry for this young man.

But despite knowing all this, I expected the unexpected. I knew somehow that Dr Ghareeb Muhammad would not remain silent and would eventually take his revenge.

One shiny afternoon, I was returning home with Raqiba, who had come to fetch me early from work because there was some chore at home with which she needed my help. We had just turned onto Corvention Street when we saw Tanwari's pale-faced son heading fast towards us. His forehead was bandaged with a blood-stained dressing and his terrified face looked inhuman. We got scared. Something horrible must have happened. Periodically he threw frightened glances behind him as if he sensed somebody was pursuing him. Raqiba pulled the reins of our donkey cart and both of us stood staring at this spectre of a man in complete astonishment. Then something strange happened. He screamed loudly and dashed forth like a rabbit from a bush. He passed us by with his hands raised, screaming out to a horse carriage that was crossing the tram tracks as if he was afraid that the thing following him would pounce before he reached it. We saw him jump into the carriage, waving his hands madly before it quickly disappeared with him.

Everybody knows that when a Bohra or a Memon climbs into a taxi or horse carriage instead of taking the tram, it's either an emergency or he has completely lost his mind.

Raqiba and I exchanged frightened looks and moved forward. A crowd of five or six men had gathered in front of the shop. Other than the suave and mustachioed Pervez Milli, everyone else was distinctly working-class. The carpenter with the scanty beard stood holding a hammer and a roll, a pencil stuck behind his ear, looking like a little demon, swearing continually, and a little scared too. We noticed some red splotches on the hammer.

'Two days back,' he was saying, 'I told Seth that this place was haunted by a ghost. Yesterday my tools disappeared several times and then kept reappearing by themselves. I spent two hours looking for the cupboard hinges and then I found them under the saw even though I had not put them there.'

Another labourer who, like a Sikh sardar, had a densely tangled moustache and beard and lots of hair on his chest, said, 'I did not mention it because I thought everybody would think I have gone mad, but even I have seen him. Day before yesterday, I was working on a closet. I was alone at the time. My friend Noor Muhammad had gone to get some bread. I saw a man sitting with his back towards me near the door on the east side, lighting a fire. I did not pay much attention then because I assumed it must be another labourer.'

'Did he have a beard?' I asked. 'What did he look like?'

'I did not notice. He had his back towards me.'

We went inside Pervez Milli's restaurant and the story that he related went something like this: Tanwari's son had seen a ghost. He was sitting in his shop smoking beedi when something moved towards him from the corner. He screamed loudly and fell unconscious. The carpenter, who was hammering in the planks of the cupboard, rose up in a panic and the hammer fell out of his hand and hit Tanwari's son on the head. The wound wasn't deep because the hammer wasn't heavy and hadn't fallen from a great height. The carpenter quickly bandaged his head. For a while Tanwari's son was delirious. Then somebody sprinkled water on his face and Pervez Milli brought some tea from his restaurant and made him drink it (God knows if it was a single or a double). When he regained consciousness, he started running as if somebody was chasing him.

As we were leaving that place, my heart was full of gratitude for Dr Ghareeb Muhammad. Surely he had come to my aid. And even though no light could be shed on the ghost's appearance, there was no doubt in my mind that it was Dr Ghareeb Muhammad.

When I woke up in the morning I felt, other than grateful, a little anxious and fearful too. It wasn't appropriate for Dr Ghareeb Muhammad to have come into this world to help me and neither was it necessary. I believe whatever assistance spirits and ghosts have to give us, they should give while remaining in the other world and without going to the trouble of coming down here.

I said to Raqiba, 'I think Dr Ghareeb Muhammad has returned to his shop.' I said this as a joke, and both of us laughed, but our laughter was hollow and unsatisfying.

For the next three or four days, no work was done at the shop. The younger Seth Tanwari was nowhere to be seen during this period. The labourers ran away and the news that this shop was haunted was published among *Chakiwara Gazette*'s leading headlines. Pervez Milli told me that the older Seth Tanwari had come to his restaurant a couple of times for single chai. He was now planning to rent out the shop. Tanwari also kept inquiring from Pervez Milli about the shop: who were the occupants before him, and what sort of man was Dr Ghareeb Muhammad, what were his habits and daily routine like. Tanwari also told Pervez Milli that the man his son had seen emerging from around the corner was a man of average height and had a small, pointed beard and wore a turban. In one of his hands he held a surgical lancet and, grinding his bony jaws, he rushed towards his son. Later, he followed his son too. The young Seth Tanwari was now in a mental hospital, under the supervision of a psychiatrist.

Four or five days after this incident, I ran into Seth Tanwari myself. I was carrying some groceries for my house just as he was padlocking his store.

'Assalam'u alaikum, Seth,' I said. 'Do you recognize me?'

He got startled when he saw me. 'Yes, baba, how could I not recognize you? We took that shop from you. We never feel happy when we have to hurt a Muslim brother. We took it legally. We have no personal enmity with you.'

'Yes, completely legal!' I said. 'The receipt you got for paying the rent for the last twelve months and used as proof that this shop had been under your occupation for the period – you think it legal?'

'Look baba, don't be angry. We are ready to give you this shop again. We are brothers. We will not even ask for security. Just pay us twenty-two rupees rent per month. Tell me, do we have an agreement?'

'Because you are leaving it yourself … it is haunted.'

'Haunted, ha!' he laughed. 'Great! That's just superstition. We don't believe in ghosts and spirits.'

Suddenly I recalled the device to summon spirits. I said, 'Seth, I had left something of mine in your shop. I couldn't take it at the time. Can you give it to me now?'

'What thing?' his puffy face gleamed with a sly expression.

'It is a little mirror with a frame on four legs.'

'Oh,' he said a little hesitantly. 'We have kept your device safe. We don't misplace items left with us for safekeeping. I told my son, "Son, this belongs to brother Asp – keep it safe."'

He slowly unbuttoned his long coat and slid his hand into some corner to produce the device, wrapped in a handkerchief. He did not know what it was and did not even ask, perhaps assuming that it was a weird kind of mirror used by barbers. But I did sense that he was not happy parting with it, as if it was a personal loss to him. This was clear from the expression on his face.

He insisted again that I should rent the shop from him and for once even invited me to have tea with him at the restaurant. I don't usually reject such offers so quickly but I had no desire for his company and, knowing what a mean scoundrel he was – that this invitation wasn't without a purpose – I got rid of him.

With the device in my hand, I started walking quickly. I knew Raqiba would be waiting for me and angry with me for coming home late. The evening had grown darker and bulbs were glowing on three or four electric poles along Corvention Street. This modern residential area of Chakiwara always grows desolate around this time. The electricity poles do not go beyond Corvention Street. There, oil lanterns burn and glow at the corners of the lanes. I crossed one of the lanes and as I was turning I felt a strange sensation – like you have when you are a kid – as if somebody was following me. I increased my speed. The footsteps following me also sped up. On the hard surface of the lane, the crunching sound of boots on gravel was clear. Sweat broke all over my forehead. I stopped and turned around. A dim and empty street lay in front of me. A sickly dog was crossing the street but he was too far away. The footsteps died too. I started walking again and for quite a while there was no sound, but then it started again – dim at first, then gradually grew louder and clearer, as if the person following me was getting closer. This time I did not turn around and instead picked up speed. I was half expecting that my pursuer would place his cold hand on my shoulder and I felt a shiver run down my spine. Then I felt a gust of wind brush past me. Shock gripped me. I could still hear the footsteps but this time they were not behind me but in front of me, and were diminishing each passing second. I was soaked in sweat.

Once again I stopped. Around the corner of the lane where an oil lantern was hanging, I saw a short man in a lungi crossing to the other side. He was wearing a gher-dar shalwar. I froze in fear as I looked at him. This was either Dr Ghareeb Muhammad or somebody in his likeness. He was at some distance and the light was very low and I could not see if the man had a beard. In any event, I am sure this was Dr Ghareeb Muhammad's spirit that had come to fix my affairs.

I found myself standing outside an iron gate. There was a vast enclosure inside and I could see the faintly lit faces of buffaloes and the place emitted a strong stench of dung and livestock.

I had gone past this place many times but had never paid much attention to it. But six months back this stable was not here. I don't know how my eyes fell on that little faded white sign hanging outside the gate that read: TANWARI DAIRY FARM.

Tanwari … ! Tanwari was everywhere. In my haste, I tossed the device over the gate. It had started to terrify me. I had no wish of taking it home and no place was better suited for its disposal than Tanwari's Dairy Farm.

Just two furlongs on was the Bhalay Deeno Street where we lived, and I reached home without further incident. But my face must have looked really strange because Raqiba asked me the moment she saw me, 'Why, is everything all right? Why are you so pale?' – even though I had tried my best to erase all signs of my recent experience before entering the house.

3

IF THERE IS A PEACEFUL SPOT IN ALL OF CHAKIWARA, IT IS TO be found on this side of the Lyari river, near the Ghareeb Nawaz Hotel on Main Street. I used to frequent it in the evenings when I used to work in Allah Tawakkul Bakery and wasn't married. Ever since I inherited Dr Ghareeb Muhammad's shop and medical practice and especially after getting married, I had been so badly caught up in financial worries and household chores that I hadn't visited it for days on end. It is also true that Raqiba's companionship to a great degree had left me in no want of the company of friends. In spite of this, I consider it my duty to attend the weekly meeting of the Residents' Association of Chakiwara. This meeting takes place every Saturday at Ghareeb Nawaz Hotel. (I, Muhammad Deen Asp, am the secretary of this Association.)

Three or four days after the above-mentioned incident, I went to Ghareeb Nawaz Hotel to participate in the Association meeting. All my friends and acquaintances were present. Bhalay Deeno was there despite his inflammation. Saeen Allah Lok Sanyasi had returned after his forty-day prayers in seclusion at Mangho Pir and was participating in the meeting for the first time, and looked hale and hearty as always. He took so much time telling us about all the divine blessings and graces he had received during his seclusion that there was little time left for the official matters.

I was surprised to note that everybody here knew the story of young Tanwari seeing the ghost and escaping on a horse carriage. But the good people here had given it a different colour altogether, which was that Dr Ghareeb Muhammad had not only snatched the hammer from the carpenter and knocked little Tanwari's head with it but had chased him in his horse carriage too and gone with him all the way to his house in Juna Market. When little Tanwari was getting off the carriage, Dr Ghareeb Muhammad had pushed him off the carriage and he had fallen flat out in the lane.

My friends questioned me, but I preferred to stay quiet. When people inquired from Saeen Allah Lok Sanyasi – considered an authority on such matters – he limited himself to saying that certain spirits often return to the world to assist their loved ones and as such it is not a matter of great surprise. It is disagreeable to seek help from such spirits and the consequences of it are not beneficial. (Saeen Allah Lok can read people's hearts and minds. I say this from personal experience.)

At one point I said, 'This Seth Tanwari is a very smart and sly man. I have recently discovered that he also has a dairy farm business. These people are trying to take over Chakiwara with their money. The Association should put an end to his plans in good time.'

'We should declare their crossing over from Lee Market into this part of town illegal,' was the suggestion novelist Fazal Ali put forward.

A middle-aged man came and sat near us and began attentively listening to our conversation. 'I also have a little request,' he said. His tone contained enormous sadness. 'You are educated men.' Upon hearing this, novelist Fazal Ali and I took a liking to him. 'You just mentioned Tanwari Dairy Farm. I work there as a caretaker of the buffaloes. We are from Gor Gaon. There are eleven more of us there from the same village. Seth had promised us sixty rupees a month but it has been four months now and he has not given us a single rupee. When we ask him, he puts off the matter with laughter.'

'Why don't you people go on a strike?' said novelist Fazal Ali, who had communist leanings.

'What do we strike about? We are poor people. Seth is a shrewd scoundrel. He did not sign any written contract with us.' Then he laughed, 'But those buffaloes are on a strike.'

'Buffaloes?' I said.

'Yes, the buffaloes have not been giving milk for the last two days, as if their udders have dried up. Very strange. Not just one or two, all of them. Seems like somebody has cursed them. Seth is getting angry with us, says we have done some mischief.'

Two days! I suddenly realized that it had been exactly two days since I had chucked the device into the dairy farm. Dr Ghareeb Muhammad had quietly been at work. I remembered how the deceased could never sit still even when he was alive.

Fazal Ali said, 'You write a petition against him. So corrupt despite being such a wealthy seth!'

The man said, 'I'll tell you something that happened yesterday. When he came in the morning, he went straight into our quarters. There he saw a mirror that I had found behind the gate which I had dusted and kept on my trunk. Seth spotted it and asked, "Where did this come from?" I told him clearly that it was lying next to the gate since there was no need to lie. He said, 'It's mine, and must have dropped out of my pocket.' He picked it up and shamelessly pocketed it – a mean miser, that man.'

I jumped. 'So did Tanwari take away that mirror?'

'Yes, Secretary sahib. Took it away cleanly, lying to us through his teeth that it belonged to him. He's such a mean-hearted man.'

My heart was filled with misgivings. It couldn't just be a coincidence that one day I throw the mirror near the gate and the day after it lands in Seth Tanwari's pocket once again. I felt as if the mirror was in the seth's pursuit and didn't want to leave him alone. I knew that this didn't bode well for Tanwari. I was afraid.

We assured the seth's servant that we would visit the dairy farm the next day and record a petition of complaints. We would first try to meet Seth and resolve the matter by convincing him to pay the due wages. If he tried to put off the matter, the petition would be dispatched to the Labour Minister from the Association and the evil designs of Tanwari's oppression would be laid bare in front of everyone.

The aged milkman was delighted to hear all this. His dull eyes lit up, as if all his wages were already paid to him. He touched our legs as he was leaving, 'May God help you both prosper.'

4

THE NEXT DAY WE REACHED TANWARI DAIRY FARM EARLY IN the morning. It was spread over a large area. A shade made of tin sheets, supported by brick columns, covered the entire area. It had a cement floor and on both sides there were buffalo stalls and mangers. The centre of the floor was inclined where a gutter collected the buffalo excrement. The stench of fodder, dung and urine hung in the air but the place did not seem very dirty.

All the milkmen gathered around us and started grumbling against the seth. But in their complaints there was more despair than anger. Helplessness and anguish were plastered across their miserable faces. A number of times we glimpsed in their eyes the extreme hatred they had for their employer, a hatred that could be dangerous in beaten, despairing people. What's that line from that Persian poem?

Beware of forcing a cat into a corner ...

Sheikh Fazal Ali penned their petition on a foolscap sheet and it was a masterpiece of eloquence and persuasion. Fazal Ali is good when it comes to these things and if he was not adamant on becoming a novelist, he could have made a great name for himself as an extraordinary petition writer, and instead of dying of starvation and borrowing money, he would have had some money of his own and, his love affairs being one hundred per cent failures, would have been seventy or eighty per cent successful. It's an accepted reality that in these present times, a poor man's love will not go too far.

Below the petition we wrote down the workers' names and their fathers' names and got them to stamp it with their thumbs. We had planned to speak to the seth first and then proceed to another course of action if we saw that he had no plans to fulfil his promises. None of these milkmen knew the address of the seth's house. One of them said that the seth probably had a hotel in Khori Garden; we might be able to find him there. We decided to look for this hotel. We reached Main Street and got on the tram heading towards Bandar Road and, riding on the footboard, we got off in front of a building on Corporation Street. Usman, the conductor of the tram, lived in my neighbourhood and was the younger brother of the son-in-law of Raqiba's uncle, and did not ask us for our tickets. Besides, with the grace of God, I have enough familiarity with Chakiwara's tram drivers and conductors for them to usually show consideration for me. From here, we asked around and finally reached Khori Garden. This was a square area of dead, dry grass and withered plants surrounded on all four sides by seven- and four-storey buildings. A few Memon kids were playing on a see-saw and three or four pale, plump women dressed in gaudy colors and laden with jewellery were looking at them indifferently. A man with a crumpled beard, dressed in a dark coat, was walking near the fountain, swinging his walking stick and mumbling to himself. We went around the garden. We spotted a couple of hotels in the row of buildings on the east side but we didn't see Tanwari's hotel there. Then we stopped a Memon seth and asked him about Tanwari's hotel. He looked at us in astonishment as if he couldn't believe that we didn't know of such a world-famous place. He pointed his stick to a corner of the garden and said, 'There is Tanwari Hotel. There you can get single chai for two paisas. Who are you looking for?' We did not answer his question and after thanking him, proceeded to the place to which he had pointed .

There was certainly a hotel there, not in the tall buildings but within the Memons' garden. This hotel was located inside the walls of a tent with a canvas canopy on top. In other words, this was a carnivalesque or circus-like hotel. At the entrance, a sign hanging from on a wooden railing read: 'Tanwari Restaurant'. We went inside. The whole place was filled with the cheer of garrulous Memon merchants. We felt like strangers there. Everyone sat on haphazardly arranged benches. drinking single tea and talking stock markets and rates. Tanwari Restaurant did not have tables (although Ghareeb Nawaz also doesn't have any). What a shrewd man. Tanwari had figured out that his fellow nationals actually do not care about tables. Just reduce the price of single chai to two paisas and all of them will flock here.

Both Fazal Ali and I looked quite respectable. I was wearing a suit-tie that I had borrowed from Wonder Laundry Works when I used to work at Allah Tawakkul Bakery and had not yet returned. I used it only on very special occasions. It was a few sizes smaller and a bit tight around the waist, but I wore my pants low. I also had a straw hat that I got coloured white with chalk. Sheikh Fazal Ali in his tight pants and university gown looked like the ambassador from the Middle East.

We asked the yellow-faced, bespectacled young man at the counter about Seth Tanwari. He was impressed with our appearance and stood up from his seat to greet us. He probably thought we were from a government or income tax office and had come here for some give and take. He told us, 'Seth isn't here, but you should take a seat. He should be here soon.'

We sat on a bench. A limping server brought us two glasses of water and two single chais. I tried paying him but the clerk at the counter signalled to him that we shouldn't be charged. He insisted on treating us like guests. We waited half an hour for Seth Tanwari, during which we had three more single chais. The limping server brought us half a packet of beedis as well. We smoked three or four beedis and Sheikh Fazal Ali pocketed the rest.

When the seth did not arrive we went up to the clerk again. 'Even I am surprised that Seth is not here yet. Something important must have come up,' he said. 'Why don't you leave your name with me? I will pass it on to him when he comes.' I said, 'It's extremely important for us to meet him. Can you give us his home address?' He shook his head, 'You won't find Seth at home at this time.'

A skinny Memon with golden teeth, who was listening to our conversation, said: 'Oh, you ask about Seth Tanwari? I saw him in the commodities market an hour back.' He gave us directions not only to the wheat betting house but also to Seth's own house, which was on Haji Street in Juna Market. He offered us beedis. The clerk probably had some instructions. I felt as if he did not appreciate the skinny Memon giving us directions and there was some altercation between them as we were leaving.

Fortunately, when we got to the street, we saw the car that belonged to Seth Ayub's son. Its driver was a friend of my brother-in-law. Seth Ayub's son had gone upstairs to meet somebody. I told him to drop us off at Frere Road. He asked us to get in the car and zipped us down to Frere Road's Mosque Mansion. We got off and entered the commodities market. The market was a very strange place. A lot of stout and skinny Memons and other traders were gathered in a small room. Their eyes had the feverish sparkle of gamblers, and the noise of mynas filled the room. At the centre of the room was a little fenced platform where brokers stood like lawyers in black coats. Each day millions are gambled here. God knows why the government allows gambling on such a scale. If a vice is performed on a large scale by rich people it becomes respectable. We couldn't see the seth anywhere. We asked a man, 'Did Seth Tanwari come here?' He was bald and two of his teeth were made entirely of gold. He led us out of the commodities market and onto the footpath.

'Who are you looking for?'

'Seth Tanwari ...'

'Ah, Seth Tanwari,' he said. 'He was just here. Poor man's been badly done in. Betted wrong. We warned him, told him don't buy, the rate is falling. He didn't listen. Never seen anybody make such a blunder with rates. He lost a million there and then. We'd warned him. We are like brothers, one and the same. Why do you want to meet him? Here, have a beedi.'

But now I was in a hurry. In my heart I knew that his downfall was due to Dr Ghareeb Muhammad's device that was stuck to him. God knows what would befall him if it was not separated from him. Muhammad Deen Asp knows that he doesn't wish the humiliation of even his worst enemy. As far as I was concerned, in my heart of hearts, I didn't want the doctor's help. Whatever aid he had already provided was enough to gratify me, even though I did not benefit from it. But the real question now was how to stop the late doctor from helping me further.

We walked from Wood Street and reached Bandar Road. Traffic was incessant and we had to pause. Across the street a crowd was gathering around the corner bookstall and four or five trams had to stop one behind the other. A man in a suit and cap was trying to move people away.

We crossed the street. An accident had taken place. A man with an umbrella came out of the crowd and said, 'He'd be fortunate if he lives.' I tried looking over the crowd at the victim and could see lots of splattered blood. The man's round cap and stick were lying on one side, blood was gushing forth from his mouth and nose and he was mumbling something. It took me a while to realize that this was ... that man ... and something grabbed me by the throat. It was Seth Tanwari.

I immediately turned around. I felt as if I had murdered him and that it was written so clearly on my forehead that nobody could help reading it. My armpits broke into a sweat and I stood under the awning of the bookstall. The bookstall owner knew me and he asked, 'What happened? You look so pale.' I couldn't make eye contact with him.

I stood there for ten minutes. During this time, an ambulance came and I saw from the corner of my eye that they were placing his body in the vehicle. There were two or three policemen inside as well and then the ambulance moved.

Meanwhile, Sheikh Fazal Ali, whom I had forgotten about completely, placed his hand on my shoulder. 'Let's go. This Memon might not survive. The mirror in his pocket – it looked like a beauty mirror – broke when he fell and the shards pierced his chest. The man got horribly haemorrhaged.'

I looked at him blankly. He supported me with his hand and we started walking on the footpath. I didn't know what else he kept yapping about.

But this was not the end of that horrific device – nor of Dr Ghareeb Muhammad. It was yet to wreak much greater havoc and Dr Ghareeb Muhammad's ghost wandered for many days in Chakiwara and Karachi. But that's another story which I'll save for another time.

Love in Chakiwara and Other Misadventures

Author's Preface

My dear Signor Riyazeno (Riyaz Al-Rehman Esquire)!

You might remember, when this fantasy was written you were the first one to read the manuscript. And you tried your best to correct its language (alas, an impossible task!). That was some nine or ten years back when we were still not sombre and mellow middle-aged men, and still quite capable of laughing with youthful recklessness at so many sacrosanct things, including people's frivolities. During these nine or ten years, this manuscript has changed the hands of many publishers. You might even be surprised at hearing that this manuscript is, in fact, now being honoured with publication – when I have nearly forgotten that I am its author.

As you know, two things inspired this book. One was the town of Chakiwara where I spent one or two bohemian years of my life, and the second was Robert Louis Stevenson. This novel, or novella, is a botched attempt to capture the atmosphere of Chakiwara in Stevenson's colours. Its actual and real character is Chakiwara; the human characters are secondary. It's quite possible that they might not seem like real, full-blooded creatures to anyone, but I dare say that there is a certain Wodehousian vitality to them.

Sa'adat Hasan Manto read this manuscript while on his bed in the mental hospital and, in his inimitably blunt manner, told its author that this novel is utter rubbish. But

I am proud of the fact that a man like Manto read this odd satire, which has been woven from beginning to end with threads of humour and nonsense. Do you remember that poem from our B.A. English syllabus – by Hunt, I think.

Jenny kissed me when we met,
Jumping from the chair she sat in;
Time, you thief, who love to get
Sweets into your list, put that in!
Say I'm weary, say I'm sad,
Say that health and wealth have miss'd me,
Say I'm growing old, but add,
Jenny kiss'd me.

In much the same way, you can say that this 'novella', instead of being a novel, is a work of contrivance. It has countless flaws; its characters, far from being real, are fantastical wooden puppets. But you must also not forget that Manto read it in his sickbed – and for all its shoddy workmanship, it has the honour of having nursed the heart of a great artist (who is not among us now) for a brief period. For that reason, this book won't be very long – and you shouldn't feel embarrassed about being associated with it.

I will not write more – the publisher has allowed me just two sheets for the preface.

Yours,
Khalid

1

Nature has vested the potential for hero worship in just about every person, the only difference being that each one has his own special hero whom he sees through a golden haze, seated far above himself, atop the heights of Mount Olympus.

For instance, the hero of my friend, who is an ordinary clerk in the Sports Control Board, is the superintendent of his office. On many occasions, while walking through the bustling Saddar bazaar and stealing glances at the lovely faces in the glimmering shops, his fumbling hand would shake my arm, and pointing to a bald, duck-like human who would be clad in a bush shirt, he'd say to me in a subdued, deferential tone: 'That's Chaudhry Karimuddin. Our superintendent. He receives a salary of eight hundred and fifty!' When he would say this, my friend would feel proud and elated like a child, as if he had just shown me the eighth wonder of the world – a wonder that he had invented himself with his own hands. For my friend, Chaudhry Karimuddin is the god of Olympia, who has reached that summit of human success that a person like my friend is unlikely to reach even in his dreams. Usually our heroes are people we wanted to be at some point in time, but we know now we will never be able to become.

Different people have different attitudes towards their heroes and it's not necessary that they worship them either.

Heroes of C-grade clerks often produce feelings of envy in them. Ostensibly, they will belittle the successes of their superintendents and officers but their hearts are burning furnaces of envy and malice. But even they cannot help adopting a fiercely resolute posture when they talk about their heroes.

And then there are people whose heroes are politicians – no matter how many abuses they hurl at them. And for some, the heroes are religious leaders. The Hurs consider Pir Pagaro as the highest among them. Ninety per cent of the world's heroes (leaving aside the owners and directors of local offices and businesses, etc.) are political leaders occupying governmental seats – and even the most hardened among us cannot help but yield to this kind of hero-worship. A king will receive adoration and cheers from a crowd even when he's no better than an ass; and perhaps, in this world of material power, such madness from the common people – and hero-worship is indeed a kind of madness – is entirely forgivable.

My own heroes, my *real* heroes, are those who write books, and for me it's irrelevant what kind of books they write (because I will never read them). Among authors, I prefer those who have attained celebrity status or have won acclaim as 'artists of emotions', and for such reasons are well qualified for hero-worship. But aside from these literary lions, anyone who has written a book – even if he's the author of a title like *The Baked Bread* – is my hero, my veritable brother. I am even prepared to get cuffed to his chest in iron-rings and make a vow of eternal fidelity to him.

I 'collect' literary people like some people collect stamps. In my autograph book, I have signatures ranging from Sheikh

A. D. Khokhar's (author, *Now I Will Don My Pants to Go to the Dance Club*) to Chaudhry Nargis Baghdadi's (author of the famous Islamic historical novel, *The Treacherous Lion*). These autographs were inscribed with the authors' own hands (using the ink of my fountain pen), and I value it as the world's most precious treasure and keep it pressed to my chest.

I am under no illusion about my heroes. I know very well that most of them would have proved more useful to their country and themselves had they chosen not to write their masterpieces. I believe that those who polish shoes at Bolton Market Tram Station are performing a better and a far more useful function in society than these authors – because cleaning dirty, ugly boots and turning them into sparkling mirrors is a far more decent profession compared to clogging up people's minds with insipid baloney. In spite of all this, A. D. Khokhar and Chaudhry Nargis Baghdadi are heroes to me.

For me, the printed word has a charm which is impossible to resist. Whenever I see an author in the bazaar, my heartbeat escalates, and I start staring at him with smitten eyes. I want to seize him like a lover seizes his beloved. Then the autograph book comes out, and I leap towards the famous person with it in my hands. Literary people ought to know that there is at least one person in this country who is mad about them. If they are in a quandary regarding their next meal, they can knock on my door without any hesitation. They will always be welcome here. Besides meals, I also lend my shirts and ties. They should believe me when I say this: my cook is really good; I can guarantee the quality of the ghee; and I am not too parsimonious when it comes to cigarettes either. My address is: Allah Tawakkul Bakery and Restaurant, New Bus Depot, Chakiwara. I will be happy beyond reckoning to see them gulp down the stodgy and indigestible curry, because those very bellies will then produce sweet and painful romances that will keep readers awake all night rapt in suspense. There will be no mention of the bill; they will only have to take the trouble of writing four or five words in my autograph book, such as:

The food was extremely delicious. Machhli Mahigiri.

(Signature)

May God reward Mr Muhammad Iqbal, owner, Allah Tawakkul Bakery. Farsh Langoori.

(Signature)

Stuff like that.

This hero-worship of mine became the reason for my enduring friendship with Sheikh Qurban Ali Kattar, although, later on, for certain reasons, I wanted to end this friendship and I even sent out some clear and subtle signals; but this friendship, at least from Sheikh Kattar's standpoint, stands firm like ever before. He's not the kind who lets go of friends easily; he makes friends for a lifetime ...

But now I feel the need to make a fuller introduction because he is the hero of this painful romance – and besides, I've been eagerly wanting to state a few things about him as bluntly as possible. I pray to God these pages get his attention.

2

FROM A LITERARY POINT OF VIEW, SHEIKH QURBAN ALI Kattar needs no introduction. Who, after all, hasn't read his famous mystery novels, *The Decent Dacoit, Inspector Shahbaz Khan, The Rogue Beauty*? Night after night, who hasn't lost his sleep over them?

It's true that for the youth of the present generation he is just another name and they don't bother reading him; but ten years ago Sheikh Kattar's novels, without any doubt, were all the rage, and for so many – especially for the devotees of Fazal Book Depot – his name, Sheikh Qurban Ali, was the most luminous name in all of literature, and honorific titles like 'Painter of Enchantments', 'Wielder of the Magic Pen', 'Emperor of Mysteries' and so on, were often associated with it. (In those days, editors of Urdu magazines were in the habit of awarding titles to famous authors as part of the official New Year celebrations.) I remember Sheikh Kattar was capable of arousing such ardent feelings of respect and devotion in his followers that they took his name with utmost esteem and reverence, and used prefixes like Hazrat – Your Holiness – or, Allama – The Most Learned – with his name, and eagerly awaited the publication of his new books. Even though Sheikh Kattar's fame is not what it used to be earlier, even then his books are still widely read in certain circles. Just the other day,

I was surprised to find that *The Rogue Beauty* is still available in bookstores and has been reprinted for the eighth time!

Qurban Ali, according to himself, has till now written more or less fifty novels in a period of ten or eleven years, most of which are not available anymore. But these are the novels that have made it to the publication stage; there were other novels that he wrote during his student life, whose manuscripts his father, driven by vengeance, made the fuel for his hookah ... Qurban Ali never told me their exact number, but yes, he still wrings his hands with regret and often says that he doesn't rue the personal loss of the manuscripts as much as he bemoans the incredible loss that it has inflicted upon the corpus of literature. 'They were far more thrilling and mindblowing than any of my published novels.' I have heard him say this many times.

Quite remarkably, he has made only a pittance from the sales of those mystery novels. Qurban Ali is not some shrewd or wily man, but an extremely simple and guileless fellow. Cheating him is easier than cheating a child. If he was even mildly inclined towards the affairs of the world, then ten years ago, when his books used to sell, he could have earned bucketloads of money. But as I have said, he lacks business cunning, and instead of him, his publisher, Haji Qadirdad and Sons, earned those buckets of money. I once asked Qurban Ali how much he earned from his books. He avoids telling me clearly, but my estimate is that he has never made more than twenty-five to thirty rupees on average per novel. Publishers are not fools. Before the war, a publisher in Lahore, Munshi Gorbakhsh, used to pay Qurban Ali some forty-five, fifty rupees for a three-hundred-page novel, complaining about the slump in the market and assuring him that he expected to make no profit from the publication of the book. Another one of his conditions was that he would accept only one novel every two months. Perhaps, this was because he did not want to let go of other promising young novelists and didn't want to become one of those publishers who keep publishing just one author. Also, he might have thought that something available in great supply, however excellent it may be, does not remain profitable for too long, and that the patrons of the publishing house would only be able support one 'Qurban Ali' every two months. In any case, Sheikh Qurban Ali had made it clear to this bright-minded publisher that if required, he was capable of handing him a fresh thriller every four days.

One would surely agree that Gorbakhsh was mean when it came to compensating his young author's hard work. But frankly, Qurban Ali is as much at fault as Gorbakhsh. Such pure-mindedness is also inexcusable. Munshi Gorbakhsh knew the financial value of his author quite well and obviously had a very high opinion of his talent. He himself used to read Qurban Ali's novels hiding in his bed at night, utterly awestruck by the sensational stuff in there.

Remember, this was the time when Qurban Ali's creative powers were at their peak; his short stories were lapped up by magazines and his literary fame had spread far and wide. His fans had no idea that their darling author wrote these emotionally charged, sensational thrillers shut up in a small closet in Mochi Darwaza, and that he owned just one pair of pants, two shirts and a single pair of slippers, and that on most days he subsisted on just dry toast and tea.

After Munshi Gorbakhsh, Sheikh Qurban Ali fell into the clutches of publisher Haji Qadir and Sons. Haji sahib was somewhat generous, that is to say, relatively. Qurban Ali believes that he had the intention of giving him his daughter. It remains a mystery why he turned away from this proposition. Qurban Ali refuses to shed any light on the matter.

It was under Haji sahib's patronage and at his behest that he penned that famous novel, *The Rogue Beauty*, which (assuming that it still sells at bookstalls and is in its eighth edition) is certainly among Urdu's most famous novels. Anyone who has read it will bear witness to the fact that it destroys your mind's calm during the day and your sleep during the night.

In my opinion, it is in this very novel that he has rejected the established norms and conventions of the mystery novel and has attempted to break new ground in the genre. This was a revolt through knowledge (though of not a very lofty variety). To understand the nature of Qurban Ali's avant-gardism and his revolt, it is important for the reader to understand what the established conventions of the mystery novel in Urdu were, and how very strictly the writers abided by them. The novelists of Fazal Book Depot, ten years ago, had such faith in these established norms of novel-writing that all their novels had identical plots and all of them seemed to be the work of the same author.

Take any novel by Sheikh Qurban Ali Kattar (except for *The Rogue Beauty*) – by the end of it you would not only know everything there is to know about the prevailing norms of the mystery novel but the plot of ninety nine per cent of his own novels would also have ingrained itself in your head forever. Although he protests if you say it like this, the truth is that he has written the same novel over and over again. The elements are exactly the same; only their mix and order are altered.

In each one of his new novels, there is that same hero, heroine and villain, but each time under different names.

In the first chapter you are told about Mr Manzoor's ailing heart as he beholds a blazing beauty sitting in a horse carriage in the Company Gardens; how her lethal glances pierced Mr Manzoor's heart (who is our hero) and how he fell off his bicycle.

> At exactly that moment, the sound of a motorcar startles one of the horses of the carriage and it breaks into a violent dash. Immediately, Mr Manzoor delays his unconsciousness for some time, grabs his bicycle and goes in hot pursuit of the carriage and, eventually, after putting his own life at risk, saves the life of the blazing beauty by catching the reins of the horse.

At all events, quite often some accident or the other involving a veiled beauty invariably occurs in the first chapter – either her horses run amok, or she stumbles and falls, or, seeing that she's alone, some goon sets his mind on filching her wealth ... And then the hero begins his passionate love affair by saving her in the first chapter itself.

At this point, a couple of things demand our attention. One, that the hero's name is Manzoor Ali, Fazal Ali, Mehrban Ali, that is to say, some name that rhymes with the author's own name. Two, the hero always has his own conveyance; it is imperative for him to be bourgeois – occasionally he has a motorcar, but if not, a bicycle is a must. (Life's irony is that Sheikh Qurban Ali, to this day, doesn't have the means to buy even a second-hand bicycle.)

The following verse marks the opening of the second chapter:

Upon those afflicted with love, God's mercy!
Their illness worsens with remedy

This chapter contains an account of Mr Manzoor's intense illness. In a delirium he repeatedly calls out his beloved's name, unaware that his father is sitting by his bedside, hearing everything. In the third chapter, Mr Manzoor's mortally close friend, Mr Ashfaq (or Mr Sarfaraz or Mr Anwaar), arranges a rendezvous in some lonely corner through the heroine's friend Rooh Afza (or Anjum Ara or Mahpara) – who will soon, if she's not already, become the object of Mr Ashfaq's affections – and thus, fulfils the obligations of friendship. When Mr Manzoor, after overcoming his initial inhibitions, resolves to embrace his beloved, Mr Ashfaq and Rooh Afza, showing good humour, leave them alone to relish the wine of union.

The villain appears in the fourth chapter. He's on his motorcycle and wearing a black mask. He's a man of awful disposition and he's the same chap who, when all is going smoothly, throws a monkey wrench into the works. In Qurban Ali's novels, his name is something like Qadir Husain, Nadir Husain, Jabir Husain, etc. To understand his weakness for this particular rhyme for his villains' names, we would probably have to plunge into the subconscious, unconscious, etc., of Qurban Ali's previous life.

The fourth chapter contains all the sensational events – it's not necessary to recount them here – that all aficionados of mystery novels are well aware: the masked thug running away with the heroine on the motorcycle; the chase by the hero and Inspector Shahbaz Khan; the masked thug disappearing with the heroine into an enormous underground palace located in some ruins; then escape; then pursuit – *dhaz dhaz dhaz,* pistols firing, etc., etc.

The villain is eventually apprehended by Inspector Shahbaz Khan and sentenced to Kala Pani – Cellular Jail – for ten to twelve years for his horrific crimes. (This scene in the court is extremely thrilling.) These days, since Kala Pani is out of fashion in novels, villains are usually hanged to death.

In the last chapter, the novel is brought to a close with such detailed descriptions of Mr Manzoor's wedding, his moments of pleasure in the gardens of love and other such affairs, that the reader's sleep is totally and utterly destroyed.

At the end of the book is this note:

Dear Readers, We'll meet again, if God brings us together.

In Sheikh Qurban Ali's case, God does it every two months, brings him to his readers, that is.

This is the plot of an exemplary mystery novel written in accordance with the established conventions, which is how all mystery novels in Urdu were written ten years ago. But who was that oracle who had set these rules that were so stringent they did not allow anyone to wander outside their limits? Sheikh Qurban Ali ventured out of these limits just once. It was a mild and cowardly rebellion: in *The Rogue Beauty*, he has heartlessly tried to adopt a different approach – the heroine in that novel rejects all conventions, and, in an act of misunderstanding, commits suicide by swallowing the gemstone on her ring. Actually, it is the hero's fault – he doesn't reach the spot in time. In the end, with the consent of his friend, the hero marries the heroine's friend, who was actually supposed to marry the hero's friend. His friend is so heartbroken after this sacrifice that he gets on a ship to England for tourism. The veiled villain (whose name incidentally is Iqbal Husain, like mine), repents his wrongdoings and, knowing himself to be the cause of this tragedy, becomes the guardian of the graves of the heroine and the hero's friend (which are next to each other). (Here one must automatically assume that before becoming a guardian he conveniently sold or pawned off the motorcycle and veil.) In the graveyard, sitting next to the graves, he waters the jujube tree that he has planted himself, and by the time this heartbreaking, sensational and sleep-destroying novel comes to an end, Iqbal Husain is a sixty-year-old man with a foot-long white beard. And instead of being called Iqbal Husain, he's now known as Saint Jujube the King. The leaves and stalks of the jujube tree have now multiplied so much that they have started to hit and grapple each other with their hands, and the two lovers (the heroine and the hero's friend, who actually loved the heroine), who couldn't be united during their lifetime, find the joy of union in the form of trees ... Dear readers, We'll meet again, if God delivers ...

This novel was a hit. One editor of some monthly was so impressed by the astonishing portrayal of human nature and emotions in the book that he expressed his desire to kiss the author's hands. But it was this very novel which was to become the cause for the death of Haji Qadir and Sheikh Qurban Ali's business relationship. This was because of a mistake made by the printer in the first edition of the book. On its cover, instead of having the author's name as 'Qurban Ali', he went with 'Mehrban Ali'. And because there was no practice of proofreading at Haji sahib's, it got printed as it was. Incidentally, the printer's own name was also Mehrban Ali and on top of that, he happened to be Haji Qadir's own nephew! Haji Qadir corrected this error in later proofs, but after this blunder, Sheikh Qurban Ali's heart was not in it anymore and he was unable to maintain his relationship with Haji.

He felt so ill-disposed towards Lahore that he bid farewell to that city and like many other artists, headed to Karachi. He came to Karachi at the beginning of 1946. His father had already died and his relatives were as weary of him as he was of them. His age at the time was thirty years.

Everyone who is considered an artist or performer and comes to Karachi for the sake of art, will agree with me that Karachi's air is not quite suited to artists and they meet with disappointment here. Besides, there isn't much work for artists in this country anyway, and no one feels much need for it either. Lahore is still better in that respect. Sheikh Qurban Ali came to Karachi, but he must have regretted his decision later. There were no generous publishers like Munshi Gorbakhsh and Haji Qadirdad here who could get novels written upon request every two months and provide him with fifty or sixty rupees for his chai-cigarette expenses. Due to such disregard of his talent and for the lack of patrons, he started starving and realized he would have to live on the streets if things continued in the same vein. So he started knocking on businessmen's doors. He was lucky to find a vacancy for a clerk in an export firm on Bandar Road. Seventy-five rupees a month. Which wasn't bad in the sense that in his previous (literary) life, he had not earned even a fourth of that income in a month. (He tells me that he finds this income sufficient, perhaps to vex me because I know exactly how much he finds it sufficient.)

3

I FIRST MET SHEIKH QURBAN ALI WHEN HE HAD ALREADY been in Karachi for about two years. I often wonder: what if I hadn't met him that day, what if that evening I hadn't gone to meet Dr Ghareeb Muhammad on Middleway Street? I would have such immense peace and calm now. I'd probably be the world's happiest and most contented person.

Those days I used to leap out of bed early in the morning, joyous and carefree, and, seeing the Lee Market Tower turning golden in the sunlight through the window of my flat, I would say to myself, 'Look! Another blue day has arisen, Iqbal Husain! Are you going to sleep it away, as usual?'

Then, with renewed determination, I'd start shaving while humming under my breath as I listened to qawwalis and na'ats (on the incomparable Radio Pakistan) – music so affecting it makes your heart brim over with noble emotions and divine light. Then, after changing my clothes and with a stick in my hand, all the while whistling, I'd strut out into the blue day, my heart overflowing with the godliness of qawwalis and my mind resolute with the desire to conquer the world. But this was not to be: Sheikh Qurban Ali Kattar was waiting for me just around the next corner. Sheikh Kattar, the author of fifty novels, the untiring borrower of people's shirts, the man who could give himself up to his friends' care for his needs – that very Sheikh Qurban Ali Kattar stood there around life's corner, ready to ambush me!

The circumstances of our meeting were quite unique and unsuited to friendship. And if Sheikh Kattar had not been introduced to me as a writer, I wouldn't even have thought about meeting him. He was utterly unimpressive as a person. But he was a novelist, and as my readers may already know, I value novelists dearly and am not one to let them go easily once they come into my grip. Thus, it was destined that this meeting would mark the beginning of a great friendship – one of the greatest in history, according to Qurban Ali.

So, one evening I was returning home after meeting Dr Ghareeb Muhammad via Middleway Street, when smack in the middle of the road I spotted my old friend Professor Shahsawar Khan, doctor of physical and spiritual maladies, coming towards me. I hadn't seen Professor in a while; he was not a native of Chakiwara, and even though he lived here, it was his habit to occasionally disappear from Chakiwara for long periods of time. Actually, he practised all over Pakistan; he was a kind of touring doctor. Quite often, I didn't see him in Chakiwara for a full five months, and then he suddenly appeared in its lanes like some sort of djinn. He had a number of disciples in town, and the devotion and veneration they had for him in their hearts was genuine and deep. His miracles, all of which have been related by him, are indeed mind-boggling.

Professor Shahsawar Khan, with his black turban, straight, pointed moustache and Cardinal Richelieu-like beard, always looked like a real sorcerer. I, who count myself among his supplicants, had fully intended to run towards him and embrace him, but his companions forced me to change my plans.

Professor wasn't alone; accompanying him were a goat with two horns, a she-monkey wearing a red skirt, and a pre-pubescent bear cub. There was a fourth present there as well – a tall, thin and pale thirty-year-old man with a face mutilated by pox, who also seemed afflicted with some liver disease. He was so unimpressive and useless-looking that I vaguely thought him, like the goat, monkey and bear, to be among Professor's pet animals with some kind of insignificant role in his theatrical performances; for instance, lifting the she-monkey and putting her on the goat's back and taking them closer to the bear cub ... But this was a misperception on my part; a pleasant illusion, you could say. How can a man with such a sorrow-stricken face and weary heart play theatrical roles?

Dear reader, you must have guessed already: this man was Qurban Ali Kattar.

Professor had seen me, so I strengthened my resolve (it doesn't matter whether willingly or unwillingly) and, after shaking his hand, embraced him. The she-monkey started screeching, though the goat and the bear cub exhibited patience. I asked him where he had disappeared for all this time.

He raised his finger to the sky and said, 'His Lordship does not permit me to reveal this now.'

'Highness, did you go to Lahore?' I insisted.

'I can reveal this much: I wasn't in the world of mortals,' he said, to suggest he had been touring the world of djinns.

'Did they go along with you, too?' I asked, pointing to the three pets.

Shahsawar Khan gave me a burning look. 'How did you know I'd gone across to the other side of the heavens to consult Hazrat Suleiman, the emperor of the djinns, over some spiritual matters? You are not a guardian saint, are you?'

I concurred with his assessment that I was indeed a guardian saint. Professor now looked at me with considerable affection, because there was no point in hiding anything from a guardian saint, for the movements of one saint cannot be veiled from another. Now he was a little more open about things.

'Hazrat Suleiman summoned me for some urgent matters. His Djinn al-Maghrur the Arrogant conducted me to Hazrat Suleiman's palace and afterwards, the same djinn brought me back to this mortal world.' He paused. 'Hazrat Suleiman wanted to discuss a matter regarding some djinns who have rebelled against him,' he said secretively.

'Highness, you have not introduced your companions,' I pointed out.

'This is Mulla Abdul Huda,' Shahsawar Khan said, thumping his goat's flank. Upon hearing its name, Mulla Abdul Huda bleated *mein mein* to express its approval.

'This is Miss Macy,' said Professor, and made the she-monkey leap towards me by tugging its leash. 'She still follows the religion of the Nazarenes, by which I mean that she's Christian,' he said. 'I haven't named the bear yet,'

'And him – who's he?' I asked, pointing to Qurban Ali Kattar.

'I haven't asked this man for his name,' Shahsawar Khan said. 'I just found him near Lee Market Tower staring at the hands of the clock with immense sadness. I suspect he's afflicted with some spiritual disease. I am certain some malicious djinn has entered him. I felt sympathetic towards him, so I brought him here to diagnose his condition.'

'My name is Qurban Ali Kattar,' the man said, upon feeling encouraged. 'I'm –'

'Who!' I almost cried out. 'Who? Qurban Ali Kattar? Not the famous author, are you? The Thomas Hardy of Urdu literature?'

'Yes, I am Qurban Ali Kattar of Gujranwala,' he said, responding happily to my enthusiasm. 'Have you read my books?'

'You mean you are Qurban Ali Kattar, author of *The Rogue Beauty,* the most terrifying and delightful novel in Urdu literature?' I said in a frenzy. 'What a blessed day this is for me to be conversing with such a celebrated writer, the veritable Thomas Hardy of Urdu literature!'

You can well imagine that Qurban Ali Kattar had never in his life met with such rapture. Even his publisher had never told him how famous he was. For that reason, though my adulation brought colour and pride to his pale cheeks, it also left him a little flustered and embarrassed. He was already a man of weak nerves and no one in his life had ever shown such intense devotion towards him ...

'Yes, once I was known as the Thomas Hardy of Urdu literature,' he agreed, glancing wistfully at his unwashed clothes. 'It's been such a long time that I've forgotten I once was a famous writer, and so on. But even in those days when I was popular, my books couldn't pay for my expenses and my clothes were even shabbier than they are now. Famous writer! Ha!' he said, and then added with a sigh, 'Do you know what your famous writer does for a living now? He is an ordinary clerk at Sheikh Traders, working for seventy-five rupees a month.'

Bitterness of the heart often compels one to say things in front of strangers that are extremely personal and should never be said. In this regard, authors are usually made of tougher stuff than ordinary people, thanks to their habit of incessant introspection and egos that have attained alarming heights. They don't melt in front of strangers but remain cautious and sceptical in spite of their bitterness. But this one, Qurban Ali Kattar, was different from the ordinary breed of writers. There was no trace of ego in him and he was needlessly open and candid about his personal life – to such a degree that his admissions often left listeners embarrassed and perturbed.

'But your books used to sell a lot,' I said. 'In my schooldays, I used to think that you earned a lot of money. There's no reason those books wouldn't sell. See, first the books were so ... so sensational; then the author was famous; and on top of that those durable covers ...'

'Durable cover?' Sheikh Kattar misunderstood me. 'That's not true. See, my skin is becoming loose; the doctor tells me I need vitamin C.'

'I meant, with regard to the books,' I said apologetically.

'I tell you, Qurban Ali!' said Professor. 'The doctor is spewing nonsense about you needing vitamin C. What you need is my talisman, The Repellent of Calamities. No matter how malicious the djinn, no matter its size or strength, no matter how big a rascal he might be – this talisman will ward him off. You will have to make an offering of five rupees only. But since you seem to be an acquaintance of Iqbal Husain here, you are my own man; I will accept just three rupees from you.'

When he found Qurban Ali to be somewhat hesitant and apologetic, Professor Shahsawar Khan said in a casual, commanding tone, 'Come on, brothers! Let's have some tea in this restaurant here, and I will also relate to you some of my miracles.' Then he spoke softly in my ear, 'King Suleiman, while granting me leave, invited me to eat something, but I was unable to eat because of formalities and insisted that I was not hungry. It took Djinn al-Maghrur the Arrogant four hours to bring us here. Now, my dear fellow, the journey isn't a joke, being ten thousand miles as it is. I had instructions to engage in meditation and prayer for forty days. I have just completed all that and feel a bit peckish. Let's go, children.'

This 'children' was directed at the animals, who did not really need an invitation as their leashes were already in Professor's hands. And besides, Professor possessed such amazing powers by which he inspired obedience and devotion in animals that they were ever ready to follow him anywhere; this was just a restaurant.

King Edward V Restaurant is the best and most extravagant restaurant in Chakiwara. But I would never advise you to come here if you are a bourgeois from somewhere outside Chakiwara. (In that case, why would you come here anyway?) For Chakiwara's nobility and its elite, this place is very good; in fact, it is a sort of Palace of Pleasures. (Well, this last phrase is perhaps redundant.) The charm and ambience of King Edward V are a result of its collectivist spirit. Occasional cases of pickpocketing occur here, and while this is uncommon, the proprietor, an Iranian and a complete gentleman, makes no guarantees about pickpocketing on the premises. Anyone, even if he's a tramp of the worst possible kind, can come here as long as he has enough money to pay for his tea. He will be served with as much fervour as any rich merchant. No one's entry raises eyebrows, neither does the owner make faces.

When the three of us and Mulla Huda and the rest entered the restaurant, no one paid us any attention except for a few casual glances here and there – as if goats and bears were routine visitors here. I am convinced that no other restaurant in Chakiwara would have allowed us to enter so calmly. Such generosity and real freedoms are among Chakiwara's many great attractions, and for this very reason (apart from usual economic matters), I have established permanent residence in this exemplary town.

King Edward V, I can say with certainty, had no role in the construction or management of this amiable restaurant. Although, yes, his regal and affectionate face peers down approvingly from a large frame suspended above the cashier's desk upon the person paying cash. King Edward is not the only king here; other kings and queens are also present in garish and refulgent colours. This restaurant is a museum of kings. (I think Karachi's Iranian restaurant owners are the most king-adoring people. They love kings, but then who doesn't?)

We pulled up a few chairs around the table near the pillar; there were three chairs already around the table, but of course we also had Mulla Huda and company with us. Mulla Huda preferred to stand, but Miss Macy and the bear cheerfully took two seats. I had taken full care to keep at least a table-length distance between myself and them, but despite this my heart was not at ease. When I spoke or smiled, I had to observe their reactions carefully to see if they disapproved of what I was saying. Even my smile turned a little convulsive. Huda was on my right and his hirsute face was thrust between Professor and me. It was my mistake that I didn't pay much attention to Huda and thought him a benign old companion. The real threat, I suspected was from Miss Macy and the bear in front of me, but especially from the former; the bear seemed half sedated.

'Aray bhai! Hotelwaalo, chaiwaalo, bring us our tea!' Professor Shahsawar Khan cried out.

The waiter looked at us with a frown and left to bring us tea. I was eager to start a purely literary conversation with Qurban Ali Kattar to build a rapport with him, but in the presence of Professor and his companions it was impossible to find the mental and emotional composure necessary for such a conversation. Professor, who was not in the habit of staying silent for too long, started narrating his various spiritual adventures. He recounted the names of numerous defiant djinns whom he had, with the aid of spells and occasionally his shoe, kicked out of the bodies of his patients. In this connection, he also made the terrifying disclosure that Mulla Huda and company were not from among the animalia but descended from the djinns. Leaning towards me over Mulla Huda's head, he requested that I bring my ear closer to his face. When I fulfilled his request, he told me in a confidential tone (he was sharing these secrets because I was a guardian saint), 'These are rebellious djinns and I have brought them into the world of mortals as a punishment.' The news that Mulla Huda and company were djinns did not help my peace of mind in the slightest.

The hotel waiter brought our tea. He had brought three cups for the three men at the table. Professor was already impassioned. 'Can't you see there are six of us sitting here and you still bring three cups! Go now and bring three more cups of tea – less water, more milk. Don't look at me like that. If I get angry, I'll recite a spell and turn you into a baboon!'

The waiter, somewhat frightened, muttered something and brought three more cups of tea. Mulla Huda already had his mouth in my cup, and the bear had perked up as well. With his snout in Qurban Ali's cup, it began sneezing in little bursts. Professor and Miss Macy were sharing a cup.

'She's terribly addicted to tea,' Professor informed us. 'Did I mention she's a Nazarene?'

I have already stated that for the restaurant's owners, it wasn't unusual to have Mulla Huda and the likes of him visit; it was nothing more than a matter of dim interest. But the spectacle they were creating was quite dramatic and silly even for Chakiwara. Everyone in the restaurant started looking at us. And if there is anything I find utterly unnerving and unsettling, it is to become the focus of people's attention in this way. And besides, I was the only person in the group who looked like a respectable human being, one who did not seem utterly mental.

But things were about to get even more frightening. The party did not end peacefully. It was Mulla Huda who started the mischief. Despite having drunk tea from my cup, he continued to doubt my goodwill. God knows what rowdiness entered his mind but it caused him to stand on his forelegs and start sniffing my hair (he probably took it for grass). At first I tried to fend him off with gentle civility, but when he disclosed the intent to nibble at my ear, I threw him off and stood up bewildered. At that moment, ignoring Professor's 'Wait, children! Hold on!', Miss Macy snarled and leapt towards me, smashing the cups and glasses on the table. Moments later, I found myself lying on the floor of the restaurant. Professor had already pulled Miss Macy away. Everyone in the restaurant was guffawing, and out of embarrassment I turned red and was smouldering with rage. Professor was enraptured by his beasts' performance and when I stood up, he told me plainly that it was entirely my fault.

So the party ended and I had to pay for the tea and broken china because one of Professor's rules was that when he invited you to a hotel, you had to pay the bill. Qurban Ali Kattar made some symbolic gesture towards paying the bill, but at the last moment discovered he had left his wallet in some other coat pocket. In any case, we paid and took our leave and even though Professor was not ready to be separated from Qurban Ali Kattar, I grabbed the arm of the great author and, promising Professor another meeting, brought him to my flat.

There I opened my autograph book and placed it before him and ordered my servant downstairs to roast a chicken and bring it upstairs. What could be better than friendship and a fine meal? My feelings were motivated by sympathy and humanity: I had never met someone in such dire need of belly-fulfilment as Qurban Ali Kattar at that moment. Later on, he even admitted to me that he had been subsisting on tea and dry toast for quite some time.

Conversation spouted like fountains and continued late into the night. After borrowing a shirt and a tie, Qurban Ali requested my permission to leave and I accompanied him to Middleway Street. And thus began (to my misfortune), in Qurban Ali Kattar's words, one of the greatest friendships in history, and (this too according to Qurban Ali Kattar) another golden chapter was added to the *Eternal Book of True Friendship*.

4

Before I start narrating the agonizing story of Qurban Ali Kattar's meandering romantic life, I deem it necessary for the reader to know a little something about the narrator of this history as well.

I want to present a kind of general introduction about myself and Allah Tawakkul Bakery. I won't bore you with details from my early life, not just because I fear long-windedness but because they are quite painful and unpleasant to think about. This introduction exists because I feel that very often the reader wants to know who the author is, what his profession is and about his sources of income and whether he's still single.

Just behind Lee Market station, from where lorries leave for Mangho Pir, right next to the general store, a small board can be seen on which is printed in somewhat faded letters, 'Allah Tawakkul Bakery'. Just below this is another board with my name on it, which was legible just a year earlier, but now, thanks to the stains from paan-spitting, the human eye is unable to discern it.

I, Iqbal Husain Changezi, am the sole partner, proprietor and managing director of Allah Tawakkul Bakery, and by the grace of God, my bread is considered to be the best in Karachi. Actually, I am an artist in the line of baking. Those who say that my bread is flawed or inedible are simply those people whose bakeries have been defeated by mine. When my friends and I sketched out plans for our company, Allah Tawakkul, none of us could have imagined it would end up as a bakery or that it would ever have anything to do with bread. Our main reason for starting this company was to fittingly introduce Chakiwara to the world of commerce and trade, mainly for patriotic reasons, because it was disagreeable for us to see our own townspeople depending on external (that is, MacLeod Road) export-import institutions. It was an insult to Chakiwara.

The company was inaugurated with a board-mounting ceremony and an elaborate party at King Edward. The name Allah Tawakkul (Trust in Allah) was chosen because, due to lack of capital, the company's success depended largely on Allah. After running a deficit for two or three months, the directors decided to temporarily shut down the company because their fathers were being miserly when it came to providing them with more money.

How Allah Tawakkul Trading Company came to be Allah Tawakkul Bakery is in itself a long story of human resolve, hard work, perseverance and the grace of the Almighty, which I will set aside for another time. Suffice it to say that it is the fruit of fortitude and patience. But let me add quickly – lest someone misunderstand me, albeit favourably – that the person in question is not this writer: and even though, according to my friends, I may have lots of qualities, an iron resolve and patience are not among them. Actually, the bakery and restaurant were the novel ideas of my employee, Taj Ali. If there is a person with a greater heart of gold, or someone more loyal and with more business acumen – *if* such a person exits somewhere, then I at least have not met him. Before this venture, Taj Ali had worked with his father in a bakery in Delhi, where he'd already mastered the tricks of the trade. Upon the failure of the trading company, he advised his crestfallen and heartbroken master to start a bakery. At first, I was sceptical; the processes for manufacturing bread were a mystery to me – all I knew was that bread is made with flour. But Taj Ali convinced me that he would take responsibility for preparing everything in the bakery and managing it; I wouldn't have to worry about anything. I would have to keep the accounts, and that too only because I would be the proprietor of the bakery.

So that's how the bakery started. The initial capital wasn't more than a hundred and fifty rupees that I borrowed from my father because no one else would have trusted me with such a sum. The two upper rooms were reserved for living; the long room below was partitioned using a wooden board – the front for the restaurant and rear for the bakery and kitchen. Our first few days were spent in considerable anxiety and anguish but then, thanks to Taj Ali's labours, the bakery started doing well. And now, even the restaurant has started doing well. In the evenings it becomes the centre for Chakiwara's intelligentsia and luminaries; writers come here and so do their stalkers and the ensuing conversations are wonderful and of superior quality as well. Once I had the honour of hosting a dinner for the great writer Sheikh Muhammad Ijlal (author of that undying masterpiece, *The Tyrannical Society*) under this roof. Unlike other restaurants, it is not obscenely brackish, noisy or foolish. (And while I cannot tolerate gramophones and radios polluting a tranquil environment, in my opinion, these instruments also reflect the truth of society.) And there are no portraits of kings on the walls of my restaurant. I have authors here instead: from a portrait of A. D. Khokhar to photos of Hazrat Machhli Mahigiri and Chaudhry Nargis Baghdadi. I have not changed the name of my bakery either; Allah Tawakkul is a nice, comforting name, and besides, it is advantageous to shift the blame onto God in every situation, so that even if the bakery fails, I can remain free of any liability.

I shall mention another fact, after which my obligatory introduction would stand completed. I have already stated that my name is Iqbal Husain Changezi, and this perhaps might lead the reader to conjecture that I am related to Genghis Khan and Tamerlane, and so on. No, this is not the case. (It's always better to be blunt about things.) It's not just me; six years ago, no one even in my extended family was a Changezi. I was simply Iqbal Husain, when one day my grandfather, who was a toll-booth clerk in a town in Punjab (Shouldn't I just reveal the name? The town was Sialkot.), by sifting through the old family manuscripts discovered that we were Changezis. Just imagine! All this time we had been going on with our lives, not knowing we were Changezis! It was my grandfather's decision that we had descended from Hulagu Khan and were his real and legal heirs; and that if the British had not leapt in between him and us, and had allowed the stream of history to run its course, my great grandfather would have been seated on the throne of India at this very moment. I personally doubt my grandfather's research on our family history, but if by simply calling myself Changezi royal blood can rush into my veins, then what's wrong with it.

There is no need to go into the details of my friendship with Sheikh Qurban Ali here. It is a painful story of him borrowing money, going to the cinema at my expense, and using my ties and shirts. In these last two years, he has borrowed at least half a dozen shirts, one warm checked suit, one felt hat and a variety of ties. He usually requests them for half a day or a full day, because he feels the need to put his best self forward on certain special occasions. But then he happily forgets to return them.

He repeatedly comes before me wearing my shiny floral-patterned American tie and sporting my checked suit with such nonchalance and such a spotless conscience as if all these things actually belonged to him. Very few would be able to compete with him in the formidable art of adopting other people's things as their own without feeling a prick in their conscience. Too often have I heard him declare to his friends that this suit that he's wearing (that is, my suit) was stitched by Karachi's Hameed Tailor and just the cost of stitching was one hundred and twenty-five rupees (which is true). Sometimes he tells his friends (in my presence) that he likes bright American ties and that the tie that he's wearing now (that is, my tie) cost him eight rupees. There's not a furrow on his brow as he relays this information, and I find myself embarrassed instead.

Ever since his becoming my friend, the most visible change in him has to do with the way he dresses, in that, he is now generally one of the most well-dressed citizens of Chakiwara, whereas earlier he seemed to be among the most impoverished. His friends are surprised at this remarkable transformation but very few know that he owes his superficial elegance to another man's torment, or that his smart new clothes don't really belong to him. Our height and bodies are somewhat similar, and my clothes, for better or worse, fit him well. But despite being fond of bright, colourful clothes, he has no interest in taking care of them or wearing them properly. His collars are often dark and dirty, and he learned how to knot a tie only after a very long time. You might already be aware that poor Qurban Ali had never before knotted a tie; it was I who advised him that unless a man wears a tie, he cannot fully qualify as well dressed.

He did not think he could ever learn to knot a tie. When he was muddling his way through the beginning stages of his ninth or tenth love affair (his affairs never went beyond the beginning stages), I suggested to him that these days, girls (even in Chakiwara) tend to swoon over outward appearances and it was imperative for his success that he be well dressed. To that end, I made him wear my blue suit and gave him a few lessons in knotting a tie, which he could not understand completely. In the end, I knotted the tie around his neck and, praying for his luck, sent him off to his beloved. (That beloved lost to – and was replaced by – another beloved a few days later, but my checked suit and tie didn't return.) That tie would still be fitted around his neck whenever he came to visit me, and each time it would be in a more pitiable condition than before. Then the secret revealed itself to me: he had not undone that tie since I had first knotted it. He even slept with it on, probably fearing that if he untied it he wouldn't be able to put it on again. Oh yes, he certainly slept with it on: once when I went to his flat to wake him up early in the morning, he was wearing the tie. This also meant that in all this time, he had neither taken a bath nor changed his shirt. Though later on he learnt the art of knotting a tie, which resulted in the considerable shrinkage of my tie collection ...

And now, the catastrophic romance is about to begin ...

5

THIS WAS AT THE TIME WHEN SHEIKH QURBAN ALI KATTAR had just embarked on his twelfth and (hopefully) last love affair. On the bright morning of 21 December, I was standing at the door of the bakery in an extremely cheerful mood, wearing my blue striped sleeping suit and looking out at the lady in red who stood in the opposite flat enjoying the fresh morning air although I could not see her very clearly. I was humming that song from the film, *The Loafer* (which she couldn't hear):

Sometimes, oh dear, come even here
Oh sometimes, my heart's desire, sometimes!

I had no intention of attracting this lady (that is, *if* she was a lady in the first place, which she wasn't: it was her father who had donned a red blanket). I was singing simply because I felt happy for being blessed with another bright blue day and also because it was one of my darling songs. The reason for addressing someone clad in red was simply to render this hearty cheeriness fuller and more beautiful. And then I saw coming towards me someone who looked like Qurban Ali Kattar. But certainly this man so early in the morning could not be Kattar; it is very rare to see him outside his flat before nine o'clock. But then I recognized my shining American tie. This was indeed Kattar – in a terrible hurry and in his money-borrowing mood. The bright day lost its lustre; the words of the song got stuck in my throat, and I, in a terrorized state of mind, looked around for escape, but that opportunity was lost now. He had spotted me and on his repulsive face, a ghost-like expression began to dance.

'Tell me yaar Changezi,' he said, 'what are you doing standing here? Is this your sleeping suit?'

My throat emitted the sound of a gulp. Gathering some resolve, I said to him, 'Yes, this … it's the only sleeping suit I have.'

'Oh there must be another one – can you check for me?' he said. 'Come, let's go inside the bakery. I came looking just for you. (As if I had any doubts.) I have something important …'

He hooked his arm in mine and took me inside the bakery. And then, rather insolently, he lifted a cream khata'i from a tray and putting it into his mouth, he said, 'Bhai Changezi, the thing is that, would you have …'

I quickly cut him off. 'No, Sheikh Qurban Ali! The shirt I am wearing now is the only one I have left. If you don't believe me, you can come upstairs and check my wardrobe and clothes trunk.'

'I am sad to hear this,' he said, and lifted a second khata'i and savoured it with his eyes as if he had no intention of actually eating it, before placing it into his mouth. 'Even then, in my experience, I got along pretty well even with one shirt. For instance, you can stay in your flat without a shirt and during this time, you could wash it under the tap and hang it out to dry in the sun … But no, right now I've come here for something urgent. You will understand its importance from the fact that I have not even had my breakfast.'

Ignoring the obvious signal in the last part of his statement, I asked him helplessly, 'What is the important thing this time round?' If it wasn't about money, what could be *so* important that it had dragged Qurban Ali Kattar out of his bed in such a state so early in the morning? I was quite surprised and fell into thinking.

He moved towards the counter and, lifting the jar lid, grabbed a piece of cake and said, 'Changezi yaar! You have that black gown and square cap, right, that you got for your B.A. graduation? Those distinguished symbols of knowledge and learning – I desperately want them for two or three days – just two, three days. This is extremely urgent!'

You must have seen serious, intelligent people at convocation ceremonies (who would never commit such idiocy in ordinary circumstances), wearing a black gown and square cap, in which they look a bit like birds, mountain crows to be precise. I had such a black gown and tasselled square cap with me. It would not be accurate to say, however, that I got them made for the occasion of my B.A. degree conferment – after all, did I really need to spend so much money to specially get them stitched and made, when I could have easily borrowed them from one of my maternal uncles? My uncle, Maulvi Baqir Muhammad, was a professor of Arabic in a local college on sixty-five rupees a month. The college where he received his Fazil-e Ajal or some degree like that, it was compulsory for students to wear gowns. These students could be seen standing in the bazaars wearing their black gowns. Children playing in the alleys were both surprised and scared of them, and some even took them to be ghosts or evil spirits. For these students, the gown became such a habit that they wore it even after college, as they carried on with their routine lives. And it's also true that some of them used it as a coat. My uncle, who often arrived in college wrapped in his bed sheet, would never forget to wear the gown, which fitted him like a royal robe. In short, this gown and tasselled cap belonged to my uncle. I didn't return them because immediately after my graduation ceremony, he began to receive his pension and proceeded to start a grocery and cycle repair shop and had no need left for this paraphernalia in his new profession, nor did he remind me about them. The other reason was that I have a weakness for family relics, and this robe lying in my trunk was like a connection to my uncle.

'Yes, I do have them,' I admitted. I couldn't lie to Qurban Ali about the trunk's contents, and besides, once he did see it lying in my trunk (when I opened it to lend him a shirt) and he had asked me something about the use of that robe as well ... 'But how come you need this? You don't even know how to wear it.'

'Yes, I ... I want to wear it. I need it. You know ... I've found out from somewhere ... that girl has told someone that if she ever marries a man, he will have to be a college professor. Now you understand, Changezi yaar, that some girls have a literary disposition, and this girl is certainly of that type.'

'This is some new girl!' I said, terrified, because the girl he was courting just two days earlier with his silent love certainly didn't possess a literary disposition; in fact, she wasn't even literate. She was an uncut gem of the poorest class of Chakiwara – the Makranis – who had (it's possible to agree with Kattar here) a certain loutish allure. (She was probably an eleven!)

'Oh ... she ... she! I know now that I did not really love her. Besides, you do know that her brother is a complete brute.

He did not harbour good intentions towards me. Last evening, he cornered me in my lane and tried to strangle me with my tie and did not let me go until I had convinced him that my intentions towards her sister had changed. No, but this time I'm absolutely sure that I am in love.'

'Have you got any response to your love from her? I mean, has she given you a sign that makes you think that she respects your feelings too?' I said this a little disaffectedly because until now Sheikh Qurban Ali's love affairs had mostly been one-sided tragedies and the majority of his beloveds had remained uninformed of his love for them.

Actually, Sheikh Qurban Ali was an extremely chicken-hearted and cautious kind of lover. Those who have had a chance to read his thrillers are probably under the impression that their treasured novelist, just like his heroes, is also extremely brave and valiant and a handsome young man, a beguiling lover, like a rising moon behind a silver veil, someone whose mere touch would turn women to water, etc., etc. However, on the basis of my acquaintance with Qurban Ali over the past two years, I can certainly vouch for the fact that none of the views that his readers have constructed have anything to do with reality. Sheikh Kattar is the complete antithesis of his heroes. Only a psychologist would be able to explain how it is possible for a man who has never dared to even speak with a woman face-to-face to turn into a free-spirited, irresistible lover in his novels. How is it that a man who is the most gutless and timid among men, who does not even have the courage to kill a mouse, can floor four or five burly and robust thugs with a single punch?

'From that idol of mirth,' Sheikh Qurban Ali replied in a serious tone, 'certain signs have emanated, from which it can be deduced that she is not at all incognizant of Sheikh Qurban Ali Kattar's existence …' (I should mention that Sheikh Qurban Ali's conversation often has the flair and eloquence of his novels.) '… for instance, today in the evening when I passed through the alley, she was standing in her balcony, her dark tresses falling over her shoulders. She saw me but she didn't go inside, instead kept standing – what does this prove?'

'It could mean that she did not pay you any attention,' I said. 'Anyone can pass through the lane, and she can stand on her balcony all day – simply because it is *her* balcony.'

'Anyway, forget about this, Changezi yaar,' he said, shifting to the taller chair behind the counter (this showed that he had no intention of leaving anytime soon). 'You don't understand women's subtle and profound cues through which they flaunt their love for their lovers. Actually, your reading has been limited – and really, I cannot believe that you've actually read my writings (as you claim) and still remained so oblivious to the nature of women. Do you know that once the editor of the magazine, *The Quirky Imagination*, wrote before my name "The Pulse of Femininity" as an honorary title? I would advise you to study deeply all my novels once more to understand the nature of women.'

All this from a man who I was sure could not even confront a woman without trembling and who fears them as if they were beastly lions.

'All right, Changezi,' he said obstinately. 'Please ask your guy to bring a little tea – actually, coffee would be better. Coffee with cream, and then I will delineate my General Plan that I intend to put into action; I am convinced that if one acts upon it with resolve and courage, he can definitely achieve desirable results … but first, coffee. Coffee with cream.'

He sat stooped over the coffee, of which I refused to partake, in order to express my non-cooperation. He told me about his General Plan, which, in my opinion, was somewhat along the lines of the Marshall Plan, and just as obscure and incomprehensible. It was a three-month plan and differed from government plans in that the latter don't care for anything for any less than five to six years and at the end of that period they carry on for another five–six years in the same way. I could only understand the first part of Sheikh Qurban's quarterly plan which, in a nutshell, was about the first steps he would take to alert his latest beloved of his existence as forcefully as possible, and for which he urgently needed my gown and square tasselled cap. To understand the plan, you had to assume that the girl was a literary type. (For this, one had to trust Qurban Ali's dubious sense of judgment and opinions.) One would also have to assume that she had mentioned in some conversation with someone, sometime, somewhere, that she was enamoured of professors. From the face of it, the first steps for winning over the girl were absolutely clear: he would not only be making the girl aware of his existence, but would also flaunt somehow that he was Professor Qurban Ali Kattar. For that he would have to adopt the get-up of a real professor for at least a week. He'd have to walk like a professor, smile and mumble to himself like professors do, appear scatterbrained and bookish, and most importantly, wear the square cap and gown, just like a professor. (By the way, in this decadent society, professors are not what they used to be; they have more or less stopped using their brains for anything other than awarding degrees.) In short, this was the first part of the plan; the other steps, which, in Qurban Ali's view, followed from his explication of fact and reason and his incredible knowledge of the feminine nature, were a bit muddled and vague and I was unable to understand them too well. It is not important to mention them here because, as the reader will find out later, owing to various incidents and accidents some parts of the plan had to be seriously amended, and very often new circumstances led to new steps. The Qurban Ali Quarterly Plan, according to its plotter, did not support the changing circumstances (ah, the usual fate of most plans) and he eventually had to abandon it.

To me, this plan seemed to be based on sheer lunacy and, judging from Sheikh Qurban Ali's previous affairs, I had no hope of it succeeding. I thought he would turn himself into a laughing stock for not only the girl, but everyone in the lane as well – although it must be said that Qurban Ali knew everything about a woman's nature but I knew nothing!

Partly for the sake of our eternal friendship and partly because my gown and square cap were about to go down the path of my shirts (the path from which no one ever returned), I tried to keep him from this insane course of action.

'Who has put this idea in your head?' I said. 'Qurban Ali! If you walk about Chakiwara in that gown and square cap, you will become the butt of all: the jokes: little children will run to their mothers; older children will clap and chase after you … Kattar! Imagine the consequences of the gown! And even though my knowledge of women's nature is not even a hundredth of your knowledge and understanding, I can guarantee you that the girl for whom you are turning yourself into a professor, instead of falling in love, will laugh at you.'

This was it: blunt and sincere advice. It had as much an effect on him as it would have had on a brick. Instead, he imputed my sincerity to my selfishness and resentment at having to part with the gown. With a philosophical air, and his gaze held firmly towards a jar of cream buns, he said, 'Actually, in this day and age, real friends have become extinct. It's impossible to find selfless friends anymore. Changezi yaar, a friend is he who makes himself useful at the time of his friend's need, and if the occasion requires his friend's sweat, he doesn't hesitate to shed his own blood.' He extended his hand towards the jar and, taking out a large cream bun, he alleged that I was not desirous of his success in his love affair, that a gown was dearer to me than a friend like him, etc, etc.

I felt rather wounded. Whenever someone casts doubt upon the sincerity of my friendship, it infuriates me so much that I find myself willing to sacrifice everything in the manner of Hatim Ta'i. If he needs the gown and cap, then let him have it. A gown and cap are of no use to me anyway. And if Qurban Ali Kattar wants to be a laughing stock and the butt of all jokes, then that's his private business. I will give him the gown and cap. Come what may, no one should doubt this historic, eternal friendship.

'All right, Qurban Ali,' I said. 'I only gave you my opinion ...'

'Thanks for the suggestion,' he said, devouring the bun. 'But my friend Changezi, how many times have I told you – when it comes to understanding the nature of women you're just a child.'

'I will fetch the gown and cap,' I said, climbing up the stairs. 'But, I mean, these are my family relics ...'

'Didn't I say I will return them in five–six days? Going by the General Plan, I don't need to wear them beyond a week. Oh Changezi, yaar! You have those patent leather boots too, right?'

I descended with the gown and the square cap. Upon seeing Qurban Ali, I discovered how one expressed their delight using their face, even though he had no face to speak of, but whatever was there, it glowed with glee. And then his smile shrank. He had sensed the absence of the boots.

'Oh yaar, you did not get the boots,' he said.

With a tortured smile, I said, 'Oh those! I completely forgot! I'll just fetch them.' And then I climbed up the stairs and fetched the pair of boots that I wore for dancing and on which I had spent forty rupees, and knew they were now about to disappear from my life forever.

Qurban Ali was exhilarated; he wanted to wear the boots and cap there and then, but then he changed his mind. He bundled them under his arm and, standing up from his chair, shook my hand vehemently. 'Changezi! You're a true friend and my only friend! Actually, our friendship is among history's eternal friendships. Come down to my flat tonight. I will show you my beloved. She is the daughter of a Makrani chief. Ah, those piquant, gazelle-eyes; her elegant figure. She's the most beautiful and innocent girl in the whole word. This time I really feel that it is true love. The earlier affairs were consequences of my immaturity ...'

The first two sentences of his speech affected me profoundly. I wanted to sit down and shed some tears. I promised him I would certainly visit him that night in his flat (because who doesn't like to see a beautiful face). I bid him farewell and went in to change my clothes. Customers had begun to trickle in.

6

In the evening, I went to see Sheikh Qurban Ali Kattar. I always keep my promises to him because, the truth is that, despite his habit of borrowing my shirts, his company is always interesting. I find his latest stabs at love affairs, which carry the seeds of their own destruction and are destined from the beginning to be failures, tremendously thrilling and fascinating. It is a real pity that Sheikh Kattar doesn't understand that he's absolutely and completely not the kind of man for whom any woman would harbour a passion. A glance in the mirror should be enough to confirm this, but perhaps, even the ugliest of men, when they look at their faces in the mirror while shaving in the morning, see incomparable beauty and allure. His taste in ladyloves, it must be admitted though, is not that bad. Usually all his beloveds are selected based on the same standards as those of the heroines of his famous novels: all of them gazelle-eyed, tender-bodied and coquettish. Like all true artists, he certainly has an eye for beauty.

Sheikh Qurban Ali lived on Middleway Street. I and a number of my friends call it the Alley of Mourning Beauties. Here, inside the tiny dilapidated houses, behind balconies that are stocked with rotting sacks, so many comely beauties, so many invaluable gems lie wasting themselves in rags, waiting for princes who will never arrive. And when a prince does show up, he is often a coward like Sheikh Kattar. There are a few typical shops on Middleway Street: Amanullah Khan the tobacco trader (on the right while entering from Corporation Street); Abdul Haq the saddle-maker; goldsmith Fazal Muhammad; Gul Muhammad Ghareeb the shoemaker; Coleen Sean, the Chinese dentist (he can always be found at his shop along with his bulbous wife and one dozen kids); Haji Muhammad Haji Abu Bakr Soda Water Company; Mullah Haji Muhammad Abdullah the fodder supplier – all of them make up the bona fide progeny of Chakiwara's traders. The thing to note is that there are only two Hajis here but they are not as prosperous and affluent as their countless counterparts on Marriot Road and Bombay Bazaar who flaunt their Haji-ness in striking letters on huge billboards above their shops. The hotels here are shabby and filthy, extremely rundown, utterly ordinary. Horse carriages don't run around here, and if by chance one spots a Victoria, it is in such a decrepit state that one feels sorry for it and wonders who would climb into this broken, jangling piece of junk, and why this thing is still on its wheels instead of being in chunks and pieces at some junkyard. Most of the houses are skeletons erected with a combination of wooden planks, canvases of palm husk and thick mud. Further along, Middleway Street loses itself to coiling and winding alleys, where women wearing long, florid quilted cloaks and silver and bronze jewellery float along with a merry, flirtatious gait. (Chakiwara's women don't walk, they float.)

This is an area in Karachi which is a city unto itself, with its own culture, its own moral code – a flag-bearer with its own unique kind of repulsiveness. If you kept on walking straight, you would land up in that mixture of dirt and stink which is also known as the Lyari river, and which holds the same importance for Chakiwara as Thames does for London or Seine for Paris. From the recreational spot on the Lyari river embankment (now that everyone is adamant about calling it a river, let's assume for a moment that it is indeed a river), on the other side of the ground, which is laced with cow dung and populated with buffaloes wallowing in stinking mud, water and grass, you'd be able to see palm trees and barren hills. From the embankment, you are able to see the world in its last stages of decay.

But you won't have to go that far to reach Qurban Ali's flat, nor will you have to pass through any labyrinthine spaces (which is what Middleway Street looks like after it has lost its essence and its decency). You would have to go a little further past Haji Muhammad the fodder supplier's store and you will come to a water pump at the centre of the road (if you're fortunate, you'll find a few beauties filling water pots). On your right would be a little store above which is written in large white letters, 'Hasan Ali's Soda Water and Lassi are available here', which Sheikh Kattar and I have tried several times. Right in front of the building, just across the street, there is a tall building, which is among the few respectable buildings in Chakiwara. It's three-storied and made of solid concrete. In its protruding steel arms (which make all kinds of angles with the building except for the right angle) it holds billboards of three or four deceased companies. The billboards are scheming to fall upon the heads of the passersby below. However, the would-be victims have not passed by as yet. Besides the billboards, a couple of wooden plates have been wound with skeins of wire on the steel bars of the large doors. These plates provide some superficial and humbling information about the building's residents and their professions. It is quite probable that the people mentioned on the plates lived here many years ago, and are now lying in the Lyari River Graveyard and these plates are mere epitaphs now. This is likely; in fact, most likely. But among these plates, however, there is at least one, whose owner I am certain is still a resident here, and the decreasing stock of my shirts is a constant reminder that he is exceptionally alive and vigilant even now. His name (Do I even need to mention his name?) is Sheikh Qurban Ali Kattar. Right next to the plate of Phulloo Badshah, Abdul Matlub of Jaunpur the Contractor, like a neighbour, a dark green plate is tied with wires making a forty-five-degree angle to the base, upon which the following text is enshrined in white letters in a heart-warming script:

The Artist of Nature, The Pulse of Femininity,
The Emperor of Mysteries
Hazrat S. Q. Ali Kattar of Gujranwala
Here novel-writing is taught in a short period
and novels are also produced on commission.
For complete details, please come upstairs.
In flat #10 Kattar sahib awaits you eagerly!

A thick layer of dust covers the plate, and the last three–four lines are faded to the point of unreadability. Sheikh Qurban Ali Kattar is quite lucky that no one here reads Urdu, otherwise this delightful script would have surely led to practical jokes on him. Qurban Ali (like all other writers) is not entirely bereft of the passion of self-exhibitionism and like everyone else, he too occasionally dreams wondrous dreams of greatness and immortality and hears his name echoing all around the world.

But he's not as boastful and big-headed as the plate might lead you to believe. Besides, he maintains a very humble disposition when it comes to his own literature, and I have rarely seen him discuss literature, as if it were merely a pastime for him. But yes, it's a different matter that he'd be over the moon with joy if you called him the Thomas Hardy of Urdu literature, and will not admit to you that he has not read any Thomas Hardy and that he doesn't even know who he was and what kind of novels he wrote. But this is an excusable weakness.

No, the plate outside his house doesn't confirm his self-exhibitionism. The thing is that, when he first came to live in Chakiwara he needed work to fill his belly; he was qualified for only one occupation – writing detective novels, and in this art, there were only few in the whole country who could rival him. He was capable of writing a four-hundred-page novel in just four days with a mechanical sliding of his pen and had a natural flair for maintaining this speed, which he did for many years without any mental or physical exertion. Therefore, he thought of becoming a professional novel-writing instructor, or, for a fee he could write novels for aspiring writers. Someone had told him that in America and England there were courses in novel-writing on offer now and many famous novelists had agreed to teach novel-writing techniques to new hopefuls in exchange for some money. In England, there had been a slump in the novel market and famous novelists were adopting means other than selling books to eke out a living. From this, Sheikh Kattar deduced that there was nothing shameful in earning one's livelihood in this manner. It was due to his simple-mindedness that he did not realize this country was not England and here the conditions of novel writers are not exactly enviable. Nobody here wants to learn novel-writing because there are other far more interesting and easier ways to starve yourself. Since the time Qurban Ali first became a tenant in this flat (which almost coincides with his arrival in Karachi) and began his new life after putting up the board at the entrance with great expectations, not even one potential novelist has turned up.

Actually, this account is not entirely accurate, because once I made a request to Qurban Ali about learning novel-writing. He thought I was making fun of him. Forget the hopeful novelists, in the past three years, he had not written a single novel himself. The writer of detective novels writes on demand, and in a city without many book traders requesting novels, this branch of literature can never flourish. For this reason, Sheikh Qurban Ali had not been writing his books. He was living the life of his novels instead and his fecund creative powers rather than producing novels, were employed in devising quarterly General Plans.

I climbed up the stairs to the third floor where a plate affixed to the door informed me that this was indeed flat number ten. On the door, the following text was inscribed in broad, elegant letters:

Q. A. Kattar
College for Novelists

I knocked on the door. After a while, a professor-type man, clad in a dark gown and a lovely square cap, opened the door. He held a thick hardbound book with a red cover in his hand – *Oxford Dictionary*. He was also wearing rimless glasses.

'Are you the milkman?' Qurban Ali said, stumbling on his own words. 'Look, I will clear all the dues by tomorrow.'

At first I thought he was play-acting, but then I realized that he had, in fact, not recognized me at all. His spectacles had been borrowed or stolen from some severely weak-sighted old man and if any person appeared through them at all, he appeared nebulous, as if he was swimming in water. I suspect that the lenses were made of solid rocks.

'I don't understand this joke,' I said, a little hurt from his remark.

'Oh it's you, Changezi!' he said, whispering. 'Sorry, I thought it was the milkman. He's an extremely stupid and rude man and comes at this hour every day asking for past payments. I can't see anything through these glasses. Come in! She just came out to her balcony.'

I went into his room. In front of the window that opened out to Middleway Street, there was a table and chair (which I had lent him). Next to the wall was the large double-webbing bed which, too, I had given him. There was no other furniture in the room. In this room belonging to the instructor of novelists, one's eyes searched for books in vain. And except for a heap of old issues of the magazine, *The Quirky Imagination,* literature stood utterly banished from his flat. After his schooldays (when he used to devour the Fazal Book Depot novels), Sheikh Qurban Ali Kattar had not read a single word. He admitted this unapologetically but defended his inadequacy by saying that creativity was a gift from God and by reading other people's works, the artist loses the originality and freshness of his own language. Due to this dreadful lack of reading and observation, his conversations were unimaginably dull and unliterary, and his intellectual growth had probably stunted when he was still in the eighth grade. He was not even familiar with the names of authors and was irritated with them. Upon any mention of other authors, he expressed his resentment towards them by flaring his nostrils and shrivelling up his nose. On such occasions, he reminded you of a pedigree dog who, while on a walk with its master, comes across an ordinary, run-of-the-mill street dog, cocks up its snout in disgust upon seeing the latter's uncivilized face. There was a kind of 'bourgeoisness' in the way he shrivelled his nose, a kind of elitist refinement. As a writer, he imagined himself to be a bourgeois or a rich lord and thought of other writers as the proletariat, not even worthy of his contempt, deserving only the shrivelling of his nose. When it came to modern writers, especially those who called themselves 'Progressives', he was exceedingly sensitive, even though he hadn't read a single line by them. The moment he heard their names, his nostrils started to flare, his nose shrivelled, and blood rushed to his temples. Mentioning the Progressives in his presence was not without risk of injury to his nervous system. In fact, he didn't like hearing about even those writers who were not Progressives and were somewhere in Sheikh Kattar's own class and who had in many cases, become novelists by reading his own books (for example, Chaudhry Nargis Baghdadi or S. M. Jalal) – their names were just as hard on his nerves. Especially when he heard S. M. Jalal's name, all the symptoms of an epileptic fit showed on him. I can only explain this condition as an effect of envy. The world was ignoring him – the real Artist of Nature, the real Thomas Hardy of Urdu literature – and celebrating the new novelists whose novels, compared to his, weren't even one-tenth as sensational. All the titles that belonged to him – the Artist of Nature, the Emperor of Mysteries, Thomas Hardy, etc. – were now being bestowed on those new copycats, and the throne of Writer of the Nation, which was his right, had been handed to some deceitful claimant.

His envy was the envy of a forgotten genius – an acid, black envy. Despite this, my view was that he shouldn't have been so vulnerable and sensitive. He had not written a single novel in three years and, to stay in the limelight, it is crucial for a writer to get published regularly every third or fourth month in order to continually remind his fans that he has not yet retired. It is also imperative that every now and then his short stories appear in popular monthlies. The public is fickle and faithless like a woman, and if Sheikh Qurban Ali had been forgotten, it was his own fault. I mean, imagine: in a period of three years, he hadn't written a single novel, not even a short story, whereas in the same period, Hazrat S. M. Jalal averaged about two novels per month and bestowed a treasure of timeless novels upon Urdu literature – novels that were horrifying, delightful, thrilling, comical, tragic; novels soaked in the pleasures of conjugal nights, novels echoing with war cries – and crushed us forever under the weight of his favours.

'There, in front of you, the balcony with the canvas cloth curtains. That's her house,' said Qurban Ali Kattaṛ. 'She has come to the balcony four or five times already. She should be here in a few minutes again ... Have a cigarette.' He pointed with great generosity towards an empty tin on the table that had been in the same state for the past two weeks.

'Oh, is it empty?' Qurban Ali said, with a surprised expression. 'Bhai, excuse me. I guess we will have to go downstairs to get them. It is not reasonable for me to move from here. It would be a disaster if she comes and leaves the balcony in my absence. Why don't you run and grab the cigarettes from downstairs? Two Black & Whites and two paans.'

'I've forgotten the money at home,' I replied. 'Give me four aanas and I'll fetch some paan and cigarettes from downstairs.'

A spastic and painful expression appeared on Qurban Ali's face. He immediately changed the subject, 'I didn't go anywhere all day today.'

'You didn't go to the office?' I asked.

'No,' he said. 'And I am not going tomorrow either, or the day after, or the day after the day after. In fact, I am never going there again. I have already said farewell to my office.'

I was shocked to hear this. 'Not going to the office?!' I almost yelled. 'You're giving up your job? How will you survive?'

'Changezi, yaar,' he said, explaining the need for this step (he threw up his feet from his armchair upon the table; now the soles of his boots stared blankly at my face), 'the thing is I cannot go to the office dressed like this. And it has been deemed essential for me to wear this garb for a week by the General Plan. That means there is absolutely no question of me going to the office. After a week (I have calculated), I will be submerged in this passionate love affair from head to toe and I'd have to concentrate all my energies towards it. Any kind of distraction or occupation could prove fatal for me. Single-mindedness is absolutely essential for success.'

'That's all good, Qurban Ali,' I replied. 'But what will you do to fill your belly?'

'I have temporarily solved that problem,' he said. 'Iqbal, my friend, I often ponder,' here he gave me his longing-for-true-friendship look; my heart sank to my ankles, 'I often ponder – the greatest among all the blessings of this world is that of a true friend. And God has made sure I'm extraordinarily fortunate when it comes to friends. If I didn't have a true friend like you, I would never have been able to drop my job like this, all of a sudden. But now, I don't even care. For breakfast, I will come to your bakery every day at about the same time I came today, and I can even swing by in the afternoon and evening as well, but it would be so much better if your servant can deliver the food to my flat, because it is crucial for me to stay here between one and two o'clock since that's when she returns from college. And Changezi, yaar, do lend me twenty-five rupees today. That milkman is being insolent. Yesterday when I saw the laundryman coming towards me, I had to run and hide in the next alley. Now I want to clear all my accounts in Chakiwara and start a new life ...'

A whimper-like sound emanated from my throat. Sheikh Qurban Ali smiled and asked, 'Is your stomach hurting?'

'No,' I said, almost whispering. 'But still, Qurban Ali, I'd advise you as a friend to not leave your job. Jobs don't come easily these days, and besides, how long will you survive like this?'

'No,' he said. 'For at least two or three months I wish to test the loyalty of my friends. After that, once I am married to Razia and united with her, I intend to resume my novel-writing career once again. If not in Karachi, then in Lahore. You get a deposit of two thousand and five hundred for this flat which should be enough to meet the expenses of the first stages, and by that I mean the honeymoon month. In Lahore, the market for novels has greatly expanded compared to earlier times. Someone was telling me the other day that your S. M. Jalal rakes in fifteen hundred to two thousand every month from his writing, and his publisher has become a millionaire by selling his novels. And Chaudhry Nargis Baghdadi with just one novel, *Zegham: The Lion,* has earned seven thousand rupees in less than four months ...'

This time Sheikh Qurban Ali took his rivals' names with an easy condescension, without any bitterness or shrivelling of the nose; usually he never even brings their names to his lips. I think at the time he was dreaming of his success, his union with his beloved, ending years of poverty and deprivation, commencing a new life and regaining his lost reputation in the literary world – he was in a fit of delusion and overconfidence. He was even willing to forgive his rivals their successes and unauthorized imitations of his works. He did not resent their brief moments of glory. As soon as he'd reach Lahore, he would thunder down on us such riotous and sensational novels that S. M. Jalal and Nargis Baghdadi would beat a hasty retreat from the battlefield. And before fleeing off, they would hand back to him all the honorific titles they had usurped and attached to their own names, and Urdu literature's one and only Thomas Hardy would once again reclaim his throne. The editor of the monthly *The New Idea,* Maulana Taj Husain, in his characteristically eloquent and erudite style, would write a long treatise on his art and secure and consolidate his Thomas Hardy-ness forever (that same Maulana Taj Husain who is the biggest champion of literature and whose honorific titles are considered most authentic) ... Victory! Victory!

'I have also thought out the plot of my next novel,' Qurban Ali Kattar declared with a beaming face. 'But I am not ready to put my pen to paper until Razia becomes mine. Changezi yaar, now my life's success and the destiny of Urdu literature depend upon my success in this love affair. My new novel, *Inspector Shahbaz Khan,* just like *The Rogue Beauty,* will be something absolutely original.'

I was well pleased to see that after years of frustration and infertility, Sheikh Kattar was ready to resume his novel-writing career with renewed optimism and determination. He had mentioned this after a very long time, and I was amazed to see the transformation his love for Razia had brought about in this doused man. He was almost a new man now! I wanted to discuss the plot of his latest novel with him (because the truth is that it was an incurable disease), when his legs suddenly shifted and went under the table. He sat bent over his chair, opened the *Oxford Dictionary* and seemed engrossed in his studies. He appeared to be such a hardworking and brainless student that I couldn't help but smile.

'Changezi yaar, Changezi yaar,' he said, perhaps reading off the *Oxford Dictionary*. 'Changezi yaar, look at the balcony.'

I turned to look at the balcony, where canvas cloth curtains had been hung out to dry. Through the large holes in the curtains I glimpsed something red – a flash of crimson red, and my pulse started thumping. And then I saw her face clearly through a hole which was like a wide-open window in the curtain's wall. As I looked at her, I felt a noose tightening around my neck. She was breathtakingly beautiful. Never before had such a rare and lustrous pearl shone in a beggar's bowl; never in the Makranis' gardens had such a flower bloomed. O reader! Remember that it is me who is writing this; me who usually lacks the capacity to be affected by a woman's beauty.

Razia must have been in her seventeenth year. Her features were sharp and there was a pale elegance about them, as if she had been carved by some Greek sculptor out of precious stone. Her beauty also possessed a melancholic sense of fragility and it seemed as if she would instantly shatter into pieces if she fell. To pluck a flower is to smother its beauty, and she was among those rare girls whose innocence and tenderness could not endure the obscene heat of a man's desire and who would be crushed immediately upon falling into a man's embrace, forever losing her freshness, her scent (and what kind of barbaric man would imagine behaving in that manner with such a girl!). And despite all this, you wanted to crush her in your arms, to rip that veil of sadness from her eyes, and transform her into a vulgar, loose woman. Play dirty jokes with her, pierce your teeth into her white dove-neck, drink her sweet blood. All men are brutes at heart!

She was an exemplar of her beautiful nation, a real daughter of her race. Even though, going by Sheikh Kattar's information, she was enrolled in a local college, she was as yet untouched by the latest fashions. She still loved the floral cloaks of her ethnic community. A little nose-ring hung from her nose, stopping just above her small mouth, the same way it would have hung from the noses of her grandmother and great-grandmother. Her long, dark hair was plaited into two braids that I noticed reached her buttocks and ended in hair-ribbons (I noticed this again when she turned her back to us). I know I am repeating myself but I want to record these words: the daughter of Lee Market's butcher, this woman Razia, was the most beautiful woman I had ever seen. She threw a cursory glance at us and blushed when she saw me staring at her. (I cannot say if she blushed out of anger or embarrassment.) Nonplussed, she turned her back towards us once again (that's when I saw those braids I've mentioned above) and stood like that for a long time in the deepening twilight of the evening. Qurban Ali had now raised his eyes up from the *Oxford Dictionary* and I think for the first time, had dared to glance at his beloved. Looking at the back of your beloved is much safer than looking at her face because nothing about the reaction on the face could be predicted; but the back always remained the back of a kind and beautiful beloved. Someone called Razia from inside the house, 'Beti!' and she went inside.

Sheikh Kattar looked at me with proud and searching eyes. He was expecting me to pat his back for becoming the lover of such an exemplary lady. He looked utterly proud, as if he had a hand in Razia's beauty.

'What a wonderful creature!' I remarked. 'I congratulate you on your good taste, but frankly, the truth is, your success seems highly unlikely to me.'

'My success seems unlikely!' he exclaimed. 'Changezi, yaar, you always discourage me. I don't remember you ever encouraging me for anything. But this time I wish to tell you that my failure is impossible! And I cannot comprehend how my General Plan would not land me straight at my desired destination. The General Plan is complete and flawless.'

'Your General Plan,' I said, 'is admittedly praiseworthy but it is too bookish, and I have some doubts about the validity of some of your deductions. For instance, according to you, this girl has said somewhere that she would like to marry a professor. May I know who is the fount of this information?'

'All of my deductions are correct and based on research,' replied Qurban Ali Kattar. 'You already know that my respected uncle Haji Abdul Karim's daughter is Razia's friend and studies at the same girls' college with her. I have even seen her visiting her house often. I have learnt a number of things about Razia from her, and I believe I can count on my cousin for support and understanding in order to make the General Plan a success.'

'This is the first time you have mentioned that you are someone's nephew,' I said. 'Or, that you have a cousin who is also taking an interest in this affair and is backing you. Now I don't feel as cynical about your success, even though your General Plan completely overlooks the most critical factor. I don't remember if it contains anything about talking to Razia's father. I tried to make this clear to you in your previous love affairs as well that in this country it is far more important and vital to win over the girl's father than the girl herself. If the girl's father agrees, then obviously the whole matter stands resolved. On this crucial problem your General Plan is utterly silent.'

Qurban Ali Kattar's face drooped at the mention of Razia's father, and a sad, reflective look descended upon his eyes.

'In this particular affair I have already resolved to be successful without the old butcher,' he said bitterly. 'Don't mention that butcher.'

'But how is that possible, Kattar!' I tried to reason. 'You are eager to marry someone's daughter but you don't wish to deal with him – if this marriage is some kind of platonic, spiritual type of affair then forget about the girl's father, you can even overlook the girl herself. But if you want to marry the girl in the ordinary sense of the word – I mean, you understand what I'm saying, right? – then you will have to reveal your intentions to her father.'

I could understand his hesitation in bringing her father into the whole affair very well. Kattar was not the kind of man whom someone could consider accepting as their son-in-law. Apart from the hi-hello of everyday life, Kattar was utterly inept at the art of making room for himself in people's hearts. And then he did not have any family either, or a stable job for that matter. Only a lunatic would agree to marry his daughter off to such a man. And Razia's father was not an ordinary father (this I found out later), he was a frightfully angry and violent man like any true butcher. To ask for his girl's hand was synonymous with waving a crimson cape at a raging bull. Any young man who loves his life even a little would not even dream of such audacity. (This was probably why Razia was still unmarried!). It was undeniable, however, that without the butcher's consent Sheikh Qurban Ali Kattar's admirable General Plan was useless and unattainable.

'Look, Kattar,' I said. 'I am your true friend and I have resolved to help you in this matter because I feel that with Razia your life could completely change. For your sake, I will try to get myself acquainted with this butcher. You win over the girl, I will win over the father. As far as the General Plan is concerned, you may as well toss it to hell.'

'You are indeed my true friend!' Qurban Ali Kattar said. 'It's eight now. Let me walk you to the bakery and also take care of this nuisance of having dinner. I am starved; I didn't eat anything even in the afternoon. Come on, yaar Changezi, treat me to some chicken delicacy today ...'

And so we descended the stairs on that ashy evening, and began walking arm in arm towards the bakery. In that moment, there wasn't even a mote of displeasure in my heart against him, and if he had asked for my last remaining shirt, I would have happily taken it off and handed it to him.

7

Sheikh Qurban Ali Kattar, in the spirit of the General Plan, carried on as a 'professor' for the whole week. By the end of this period, he had developed such an emotional attachment with the gown and square cap that he had made that honourable robe of learning and wisdom his everyday attire. He kept it on from morning till night and (even though I have no evidence for claiming this) he even slept in it. In any other city, these masquerader's clothes would have resulted in its owner getting a certain kind of reputation and turning into a target of people's attention. But in Chakiwara, where even dressing and acting like a maniac could arouse only a superficial interest in people, the professor at first was perceived with mild curiosity, as some new kind of bird, but then was readily forgotten. Even then, I believe this attire brought a little excitement to his life. The children in the alleys ran after him clapping, thinking him to be a strange owl walking on its legs; some just stared at him with surprise and amazement; a few thought he was some sorcerer or djinn or some such and scampered into their houses. I remember one evening, while passing through Middleway Street, I saw a four-year-old holding the finger of a thin, pale man, asking him in a subdued tone, 'Uncle! This is that Count Dracula whose story you told me the other day, right?' And once on Corporation Street, the barbers and their customers rushed out of their shop to look at us. The barbers had razors in their hands and the customers' faces were lathered in foam: it was clear that they had come out running in the middle of getting a shave. (Those who had shaving lather on their faces couldn't help smiling at Kattar, due to which a little foam went into their mouths.)

To what extent did Sheikh Kattar's professorism assist him in improving his love prospects? Did it produce desired results? Was his ladylove suitably impressed by his scholarly attire, his bookwormish mannerisms, and did it kindle any interest or sympathy in her heart? But who can answer these questions. We have no way of knowing. It's possible that during the week, Sheikh Qurban Ali Kattar distinguished himself in her eyes as a hardworking professor; it's also possible that after the week, having observed well how 'certain' professors behave, she gave up on the very idea of marrying a professor, and being a professor's mate turned into a loathsome notion. Unfortunately, as I have written above, we have no way of knowing the state of her heart. As far as Sheikh Qurban Ali Kattar's professor-for-a-week part of the General Plan was concerned, its results were not entirely disappointing. The aims of this first step were just to convince the ladylove that:

a. Sheikh Kattar is a professor.
b. He is extremely fond of reading.
c. His lifestyle is somewhat different from that of other men.

And these aims had probably been met. Razia had seen him in gown and cap for the whole week. She had always found him fitting the sophisticated, feminine ideal of a man sitting in his room engrossed in a thick red book, and if any girl continuously sees a man in scholarly clothes, immersed in reading for a week, and if that man happens to be Qurban Ali Kattar, then it is quite probable that in her eyes he would assume a distinguished position and not remain an ordinary person any longer. While Qurban Ali did not make any claims about the success of the first stage of his plan, I must say that it cannot be termed as unsuccessful.

Despite this (forget the General Plan for a moment), the result was zero till now. Leaving aside the actual effects on ladylove – whether she started counting stars at night or seeing her sweetheart in her dreams (the sweetheart, in thick spectacles and gown, sitting with an *Oxford Dictionary* in front of him), leave all this aside – the lover and the beloved were as far from each other as they were at the beginning of this affair. The breadth of Middleway Street (about fifteen feet) stood in their way as before.

The only kind of love that's possible in certain parts of Chakiwara and all parts of Karachi is balcony love. I am referring to the kind of love in which the lover and his beloved carry out their loving while standing or sitting in their respective balconies. The techniques of this mode of love are different and more difficult than all other kinds of love and it's quite unfortunate that no expert of this art has bothered to write a book on it till now. American experts have penned many useful and convenient books for amateur lovers, such as *Do You Have a Beau?*, *Success in Love: Some Golden Rules*, *The Girl Standing at The End of the Alley Could Be Yours!*, *The Shortcut to Love.* Someone even told me that a number of institutes even offer distance-learning courses on this valuable subject and even guarantee a refund in case of failure. But American experts, who usually take a comprehensive and thorough view of things, have completely overlooked balcony love in their books. Perhaps that is just as well, by which I mean that in America, balcony love would be considered a dated form of love. Even in post-Victorian England, balcony love now stands more or less irrelevant and abandoned. By contrast, the only form of love possible in this country is balcony love (and it shall continue to be so for at least another half a century). But in the absence of proper guidance and instructions, the results of such love affairs are often ungratifying and in some cases even hazardous for the participants. Very few from among the participants have been able to cross the daunting width of the alley – some have ended up with broken arms and legs, while many others have ended up bald. These lovers, due to immaturity and inexperience, overlook the existence of the beloved's brothers and fathers, who are the mortal enemies of lovers and their biggest obstacles (some fathers wear spiked boots). Another huge problem with balcony love is that ninety out of a hundred times it is one-sided, and the beloved is either oblivious to it or indifferent or fervently antagonistic (in which case, he or she is with the rival's party – by which I mean her brothers and father). In such circumstances, therefore, in my humble opinion, there is an urgent and pressing need for an authoritative text on balcony love. It would be a national service. If some expert of the art could compose a distilled account of his experiences in lucid and crisp prose, the demand for such a book would run into hundreds of thousands (tentative title: *The Balcony Girl Could Be Yours!*).

In Qurban Ali's case, Razia did indeed visit her balcony once, and even threw a few distracted glances towards his flat with her gazelle eyes, and perhaps it's also true that her eyes did not betray an amused sneer (ah, those eyes were incapable of it), rather, what they contained was a mixture of interest and motherly compassion. In spite of all this, she had given no hint or signal that she was ready and willing, or that she had any special interest in the resident of the flat facing hers. Actually, she was the kind of chaste and modest girl who bides her time under her father's roof till the latter gets fed up of seeing her under his roof and gives her hand to some stranger husband. Like other girls of her age, she was certainly eager for romance. Surely her sad, doleful eyes hungered and searched for love. But the romance was in the hands of her father.

Perhaps we could have found out more about her thoughts and reactions from Qurban Ali's uncle's daughter, but it so happened that she left with Kattar's uncle for Multan to visit some relatives for a while. The truth is that Kattar was relying greatly on his cousin's help and understanding in the matter and her departure in the midst of his love affair without any rhyme or reason was absolutely against the General Plan. Resolving the whole situation with her help was an integral part of the Plan. If the plan were *Hamlet,* she would be Prince of Denmark. Through her untimely departure she had totally disrupted the Plan and now it was imperative to completely revise the next steps.

I remember those evenings in Qurban Ali Kattar's flat very well. I sat on a chair facing the window, and Kattar, on his armchair with his legs stretched on the table, looking at me through his spectacles. Between us, the *Oxford Dictionary* lay open in his lap and we would be discussing everything under the sun but the moment she came into the balcony our philosophical discussions would come to an abrupt end and silence would fall over us. Our pulse rate would shoot up and our hearts hammered against the walls of our chests. The dusk outside would gradually turn to darkness. Then Kattar and I would descend quietly from his flat and head towards the bakery to eat the chicken delicacies.

We were usually alone at the flat but sometimes we had a third creature with us as well. This third being was a tiny-legged, tawny dog. He was a little ball of wool with small round button eyes. His ears were too long for his body and seemed to have been ironed to the side of his face. He was the most innocent and the filthiest of all the dogs I had ever seen. His family history was unknown. No one knew about his ancestry or breed. In Sheikh Kattar's opinion, he was actually a respectable cocker spaniel whose master had died or had abandoned him to fate. Now he was forced to live off the leftovers he found in the alleys. Perhaps he was right, even though he sees a cocker spaniel in every dog (once near Lee Market he pointed to a big, frightening hairy Alsatian and said, 'Look, yaar Changezi, what a huge cocker spaniel!'). That woolly dog, which seemed to have escaped from some toy store, did not belong to Sheikh Kattar. In fact, its behaviour was too puzzling and mysterious for a dog. Quite often, to escape the sunlight and heat, and in search for human friendship, he would quietly sneak upstairs to Kattar's flat. He sat on his hind legs and wagged his tail, studied our faces, and after a while, silently disappeared. Sometimes Kattar and I would pet him lovingly, make him stand and dance on two legs by holding up his forelegs. Kattar even lifted him up and put him in his lap but he was extremely filthy. His acquaintance with Kattar was only a few months old. He had found him sitting on the stairs of his building, all alone and gloomy. When he gently crooned to the dog as he passed by, he began to followed Kattar.

Kattar used to call him: 'Musafir! Musafir!' Musafir – the traveller. To this day I have no idea why he foisted that particular name on the dog. Yes, he was certainly a traveller in the sense that no one knew of his comings or goings and he wasn't content with staying in one place for his meals (at Sheikh Kattar's flat there was no question of meals anyway).

(The conversations from those evenings are fully preserved in my diary. Like Samuel Pepys, I've kept a diary of the past four years. I hope that in the future when the historians of Chakiwara will write the social history of this town, they would find my diary – if it survives the batterings of time, that is – to be exceedingly valuable.)

But as the evening went by, I couldn't help but realize that our course of action was not leading us even a bit closer to our destination. His Makrani lady love, even now and despite all the toil, was as far from becoming his wife as she was on the first day, and there didn't seem to be any chance of Kattar's wishes getting fulfilled either. Therefore, it was necessary to proceed with even greater vigour and adopt more effective and concrete measures. The General Plan was now a piece of trash. Kattar himself admitted that due to the departure of his cousin, some of its components had become meaningless and irrelevant. Kattar and I discussed a number of new proposals but for one reason or another, due to present dangers or impracticalities, we had to abandon them. For instance, a suggestion that Kattar put forth was that a letter should be written through which it would have to be imparted that an ill-fated man was nearing his grave as he was suffering from love and separation, and his afflictions were increasing the more he attempted to cure them, et cetera, et cetera. My suggestion was that Musafir should be tamed and used as an emissary for conveying missives and messages from one side to the other. But the problem with both these proposals was that the message or letter headed for Razia could very well land into her father's hands. Sheikh Qurban Ali also put forth an extraordinarily bold scheme from one of his novels that unsettled and mesmerized us so much that before rejecting it we spent nearly two hours arguing about it. The scheme went something like this: when Razia left for college in the morning, I, in the garb of the Veiled Villain, would force myself into her carriage and pretend to grab her and hold her tight to my chest. At that moment, Qurban Ali Kattar, seeing an innocent girl being robbed of her honour, would jump into the carriage and land such a booming punch on my face that I'd come tumbling out. This scheme had to be rejected on certain technical grounds.

Now in my opinion there was just one way left for us, and it was that the butcher, Razia's father, should be approached directly with the proposal (even though the hazards of this approach were clear!).

And then one night, with great difficulty, by challenging his very manhood, I convinced Sheikh Qurban Ali Kattar that he must go to the butcher and tell him that he was eager to become his son-in-law. 'I can assure you,' I explained to him, 'that he won't refuse. Rather, he would consent happily. After all, it is impossible to find professor sons-in-law these days. Be a man, Kattar! Don't be a coward! Go up to him, look him in the eye and declare: "O Butcher!" – or whatever his name is – "I desire to marry your daughter. I am a professor. I am sure you will not have objections." If you utter these words with complete self-confidence, it would be impossible for him to deny you. People want sons-in-law who are self-confident – O yaar, why are you trembling? I will be by your side. And if something unexpected happens, you can rely on me.'

'This is not in the General Plan,' he said, protesting.

'The General Plan can go to hell!' I said. 'Tear it up! Toss it into the fire – I mean if you ever light a fire around here – where is the blueprint?' I yelled with my hand stretched toward him. 'Give it to me. I will make it the fuel for my bakery's furnace.'

'That's on my mind as well ...' he said, raising his hand to his head.

'My friend Kattar! I will help you,' I said boldly, even though my voice shivered as I said this. In my heart, I was thinking of myself as that noble and magnanimous person who was sacrificing an extraordinarily precious thing, which in fact was his own, for his good-for-nothing friend. 'I will make Razia's father's acquaintance, make him my friend and then gradually prompt him with the information that a novelist friend of mine is still a bachelor and is interested in his daughter ...'

Kattar went pale. 'For god's sake, don't do that!' he said. 'We should not bring Razia's father into all this.'

I tried to explain to him that the butcher would have to be involved in this, whether he liked it or not. And that the energies he was expending on his love affair with the butcher's daughter, he should use to convince the butcher instead. Even if the girl agreed, which was highly unlikely, her father's nod was still essential for their marriage. I assured him that Razia wasn't the kind of girl who would agree to run away from her father and guardian's house. And besides, Qurban Ali Kattar wasn't one of those Don Juan-esque lovers either who had the courage to abscond with a girl.

I think my arguments had some effect on him. If Razia's father was someone other than a frightening butcher, like, for instance, a benign, soft-demeanoured old man, he would have enthusiastically approved of my suggestion and proposal. But just the thought of a butcher was enough to scare him out of his wits. To try and win over the butcher seemed a horrifying prospect to him and in his mind it conjured an image of a sharp-horned, savage, rugged bull eyeing an excuse to run someone over – specifically Qurban Ali – and tear out his guts with its sharp horns.

If a young man harbours such unpleasant thoughts about the father of the girl he wishes to make his better half, then it's better that he shelves his plans and starts looking for a girl whose guardian is some gentle, obliging bearded old man or someone who doesn't exist at all. Perhaps Kattar understood very well that no prospective father-in-law could ever be persuaded to willingly accept someone like him as his son-in-law. He didn't have any quality that potential fathers-in-law usually desire. But yes, there was one thing that Kattar did have, even though he wasn't aware of it himself: he had a flat. As everyone knows, in present-day Karachi, a man who owns a flat is looked upon with enormous respect and admiration by society and he certainly deserves the esteem and regard he receives. Many examples could be cited of such Karachi fathers-in-law who gave their girl to a man simply because he owned a flat – and after giving him the girl, they descended upon their son-in-law's flat with their entire household. From a material perspective, this was the only point in Kattar's favour which could have attracted a potential father-in-law, but in the case of the butcher, this point did not carry much weight because he already owned a house of his own and sons-in-law who just owned flats had no appeal for him.

Perhaps here the dear reader might wonder why I, knowing Sheikh Qurban Ali's chances of success, embroiled myself to this extent in this love affair, especially when with similar past affairs I had been content to play the role of spectator. The reason was, this time I felt that Kattar's love was 'the real thing' and if it culminated in marital ties then it was very likely that Kattar's life would be transformed completely and he would once again resume his novel-writing career. Another reason was that Razia was a beautiful girl and it would have been a matter of immense pride to have a sister-in-law like her. Only Freud's disciples would be able to understand this – I mean, it is related to my subconscious, unconscious, or something like that. In any case, the dear reader must understand that now I had already descended into the arena with my sleeves rolled up and was ready to traverse hell and oceans for my friend.

By the time I was taking leave of Qurban Ali Kattar, I had already resolved to make friends with the butcher, somehow.

8

It was quite dark by the time I left Qurban Ali Kattar's flat and came out into the alley. There are street lamps on Middleway Street but I have never seen them lit. The bulbs of the lamps had had blown fuses for a long time and no one had thought of replacing them.

In the darkness of the alley, Hasan Ali's Soda-Lemon shop in front of me seemed an agreeable source of light, and the various cigarette brands in tin boxes felt warmly inviting. I went there for some cigarettes. In front of the store, a man stood chewing paan; he was a heavyset man, and was wearing a long shirt. He was balding from the top of his head and the shining yellow light of the store was falling on the bald part of his head to produce striking results. The man possessed a remarkably savage face and his stiff Hitleresque moustache only intensified that impression. But strangely enough, his eyes were bird-like, round and innocent like a child's. His jaw was strong and protruded aggressively from his face. It seemed as if this man had snatched his moustache from Hitler, his jaw from Mussolini and the naïve, tender sparkle in his eyes from President Truman. Despite all the frightfulness on his face, his complexion was dirty and floury. He was ill.

This was that butcher – Razia's father.

As soon as I saw him, I immediately dropped all plans of trying to form a bond with him and started sliding away after lighting my cigarette. But then as if someone called out from behind, 'Mister! O mister!' I ignored that 'mister' I continued on with my journey on Middleway Street planning to hit the first turn.

But the butcher leapt after me and with his long strides, caught up with me. Out of fear that he might grab me by the neck, I considered it wise to turn around immediately and address him. I tried producing a surprised smile on my face.

'Did you call me?'

'Mister! Are you deaf?' he said brashly. This wasn't an ideal start to a friendly conversation.

'No, I don't think so,' I replied. 'Yes, but my ears do get clogged up sometimes due to dandruff.'

'What's that? Dandruff?' he shouted. 'Even I have had the same problem for the past few days. I have many other problems as well, and this is just one of them. Whenever I have this problem I call one of those massage boys and tell them to scrape out the dandruff and pour some mustard-seed oil – that makes things better. What is your remedy?'

'Me? Me!' I replied, thinking hard. 'I don't do anything. I mean I fill up my cheeks with air – like this,' I showed him. 'And then I blow it out slowly through my ears. I can breathe through my ears if I want ...'

'That's amazing, mister! Amazing!' His bird-like eyes gleamed on his savage face. 'All right, I wanted to ask you something. That man in cloak and tassels, is he your friend?'

'Do you mean Sheikh Qurban Ali Kattar?'

'Whatever he may be – Kattar or Pattar! Tell him if he doesn't stop gazing at my house with his owl-like eyes, I'll chop him up with his cloak on and hang him upside down like a skinned goat.'

'Okay! Okay, I will go and alert him right away,' I assured him.

'Good, and by the way, what does that son of a crow do?'

'Do you mean Sheikh Qurban Ali Kattar?'

'Yes, by that I mean that dead goat.'

'He – he's a professor. Professor. You know those men who wear glasses and read thick books and when their eyes get tired of reading, they look out of their windows to refresh their eyes ...'

'I will strip that professor's hide and stuff it with straw! Bloody professor! Is my house the only place left for him to refresh his eyes?'

'I think that's just a coincidence,' I explained. 'The thing is that your house is right across his and the window of his flat opens onto your house...'

'This is not good, mister,' he said. 'We are honourable people. We have daughters and sisters ...'

'How many?' I blurted out. I am sure he heard me but he ignored it thinking it to be unrelated to our conversation.

'Tell him if wants to show his professorism he should do it somewhere else, and if I see him even raising an eye towards my house again – then – then – well ... tell me, what will I do?'

I told him what he should do.

'Yes, tell him that!' he instructed me. 'And you, you look like such a decent, reasonable fellow. I don't understand why you have kept up your acquaintance with such a wretched man.'

'I go to Professor Kattar for lessons.'

'Are you still a student?'

'I am appearing privately for exams,' I said. 'I am a businessman.'

'What kind of business? Dry fruit?'

'Bread!' I said and brought the business into focus. 'Where do you buy your bread? Our bread is the best in Karachi. Four aanas for the small ones, and eight aanas for large. Our man will deliver it to you. The place is Allah Tawakkul Bakery. I, I mean myself, am its err … Managing Director.'

'Oh, that Allah Tawakkul behind the bus stop, that's yours? I have passed by it several times.'

He switched to the polite 'you' from the informal one he had been using earlier. He was among those men who fully respected material successes and his glittering eyes showed that I had suddenly become important to him.

'Come on, Director sahib, have some paan or something.' In his savage mannerisms, there was now a sort of respect for me.

'Another time,' I said. 'I feel very happy to have met you. It's a rare kind of happiness. Your face resembles my father's a great deal …'

He laughed and I felt that he was chuckling with happiness.

'What kind of business are you in?'

'I am the chief butcher in Lee Market. Director sahib, where do you buy your meat?'

'From now on I shall buy it from you,' I replied. 'I also own a restaurant along with the bakery and we need some ten kilos of meat every day.'

'Oh you have a hotel as well? Jazakallah! Inshallah I will reserve the best of the best and tenderest of the tender meat for you and will also charge you less than the market rates. Please instruct your delivery man to deliver a loaf of bread here every morning. But I only have tea in the morning. Doctors tell me I have cancer in my stomach and that's why I completely avoid starchy food. Besides me, there are two other people in the house. My daughter and Mama, the maid. The girl's poor mother died.'

'Inna lillahi wa' inna illa'i hi raaji'oon,' I said.

'No, the poor woman's been dead twelve years now. Real good woman she was, a simple woman. I used to beat her a lot, and she never even uttered a word in protest. This girl is my only child. She is in a girl's college. If she gets married to a decent, well-earning boy then I'd be relieved of my burden. Director sahib, if you know any such boy, please let me know.'

'Qurban Ali Kattar is still unmarried,' I remarked casually.

'Who is he? What kind of boy is he?' he asked. He had already forgotten that Qurban Ali Kattar was the name of the man who he had wanted to skin and what not.

'He's a good, promising young man,' I said. 'I will bring him over to you sometime …'

'Sure, sure.' He wrapped his hands on his stomach, feeling a sudden surge of pain. 'This cancer is giving me more pain than usual. I should go now and get some poultice applied to it. All right, goodbye. We will be in touch from now on, Inshallah.'

He was in great pain; his dirty, bloodless face turned dirtier and paler. Putting my arm around his shoulder despite his protestation was for me like embracing a lion for the sake of friendship. Near the stairs of his house, he enthusiastically shook my hand. 'Thank you, Director sahib!' and panting, he climbed up the stairs. Now the butcher was my friend and despite the discouraging start to our conversation, the matter had resolved itself. For that I should've been thankful to Allah

Tawakkul Bakery, because the butcher respected success – like all men (however unpleasant and discouraging their exterior might be and however hard their hearts) who are fathers of unmarried daughters, and who do not have much time left due to cancer or some other fatal disease.

9

THREE DAYS AFTER MY CORDIAL AND AMIABLE CONVERSATION with Razia's father, Kattar and I, arm in arm, were passing by Lee Market. The central tower in Lee Market holds the same significance for Chakiwara as Eiffel tower does for Paris, and no matter which part of Chakiwara you are in, you can never escape it. This tower, forever imposed on the people of Chakiwara, is a kind of a centre around which the locals circumambulate like tiny bits of light. Without this tower, all these people would be lost: their lives would turn futile and they would drift away, and then who knows, these broken pieces of light might collide to produce dreadful results. That would be the end of an era, a civilization.

Penniless, despondent young men come to this tower to sit on its stairs and find a kind of solace and renewed courage to face the cruelties of life. Chakiwara's poets, artists and novelists come here to seek inspiration for their next poem or novel (for that they stand and gape at the tower clock for hours), and creditors, when they can't find their debtors anywhere, are blessed with their sight here and can then claim their debts. Chakiwarans, for all their needs, visit only Lee Market. Just below the tower is the world's most bizarre and beguiling bazaar where, among large colourful heaps of vegetables and fruits, you can find similarly lustrous and picturesque customers haggling, looking like animated cabbages, carrots and turnips, and so on. The charm of this bazaar can be experienced only by actually observing it. Besides the tower there is a small shrine complete with flags and signs, and the old man who sleeps in there is not Captain Lee who gifted this Bridge of Babel to Chakiwara but Pir Bhambo who is the main saint and benefactor of the people of this town. He bestows Chakiwarans with baby boys, brings prosperity to their businesses, relieves them of outstanding debts, and performs many other venerable tasks. Adjacent to the shrine is a covered market where the butcher shops are located and very few of the goats or sheep entering the market ever escape unscathed.

The subject of my conversation with Qurban Ali was the same heart-ravishing beauty of the balcony and Kattar was explaining to me how his novels' plots could help unravel his knotty love affair. I was paying little attention and not showing much interest in what he was saying because he was hell-bent on giving me the role of the Veiled Villain. Now, for a friend I am willing to cross seven oceans and take on djinns, etc., but towards this role of the Veiled Villain I had an aversion and my heart would not concede to it. Even his allegations of unfaithfulness and not helping a friend in need were not having any effect on me.

Suddenly from the shrine I saw the most learned conjurer, Professor Shahsawar Khan, emerging with his two friends, the cursed djinns. Seeing this inexorable calamity, I lost my wits and instinctively made a kind of nosedive and dragged a confused Kattar, who did not know what the matter was, through the crowd and finally took refuge inside the butchers' market. There I breathed a sigh of relief.

'What's the matter?' Qurban Ali said. 'Was it the milkman?' because he had hastily retreated in the same way on seeing the milkman earlier, and according to him, one scampers away like this only from a milkman.

'It was Shahsawar Khan,' I told him.

'Shahsawar Khan? You mean Professor Shahsawar Khan?'

'Yes, him.'

'Why did you have to run away from him?' Kattar said. 'He is an extremely useful and benevolent man. In fact, I have been looking for him for the past two weeks. He promised me a charm and I paid him an advance. Two rupees and eight aanas. I want to meet him,' he said, dragging me out of the covered market.

Suddenly I struck upon a bright idea. Razia's father must be in this very market and I had promised him that I would bring Qurban Ali Kattar to meet him – this was a golden opportunity! I scanned the butchers sitting on the stalls in front of us but I didn't see him. We moved towards the very last lane and I finally spotted him standing outside his stall: he was busy mincing a goat thigh with his long blade. He was wearing a vest. His dark forearms were swollen and with his gigantic body and savage face, he appeared ferocious.

'Look there, Kattar!' I said. 'There's your father-in-law-to-be.'

For a second, Kattar did not understand anything and when he did, he tried to leap towards the door but I blocked his way.

'Listen!' I said. 'I have not told you that Razia's father wanted to meet you. Even he's looking for a son-in-law urgently. I have chained the heavens to earth in your praise: I told him that you are a professor and a very worthy man. He was greatly impressed with what I said and promised that if he ever gave his girl to anyone it would be Qurban Ali Kattar or he would leave her sitting at home forever. He's asked me to tell you to approach him with a proposal for marriage – he would be delighted and his long-standing desire would be fulfilled.'

'I will meet him some other time,' Qurban Ali Kattar said, eyeing the escape route.

'Don't ruin a done deal, Kattar!' I said. 'Just for a moment, be as courageous as the heroes in your novels. This man has a heart of gold. He has seen you and knows you. You should approach him with courage and confidence and tell him that you want to marry his daughter. Come now, be bold.'

'He's busy right now,' Kattar said. 'He mincing meat.' (Skeikh Qurban Ali Kattar doesn't like to interrupt people when they are busy.)

'He's in his finest and most pleasant mood when he is mincing meat.'

I had to plead a great deal, taunt his manhood. Finally, he braced his heart: this was about to be the most heroic act of his life and I was responsible it. I walked with him till we were about five paces from the Makrani butcher's stall, after which he went forth all alone in an ambiguous state of self-confidence – a cowardly courage. He went and stood behind the butcher. Compared to the latter's size and stature, he looked like a little chick.

The butcher was busy with his work and oblivious to Kattar's presence. Kattar glanced at me. I encouraged him with a nod. With trembling hands, he clutched his gown in his hand, and said in a weak voice, 'Chief butcher sahib, I am Qurban Ali Kattar. Professor Qurban Ali Kattar.'

'Hunnh! Hunnh!' the butcher let out contented grunts, not upon the news of his visitor, whose voice probably didn't even reach him, but on successfully hacking off a stiff joint.

'Would you like to accept me into the fold of your son-in-lawship?' Qurban Ali said in a frightened, slightly raised voice.

'What?' the butcher turned around brandishing his blade in the air.

'One kilo meat I want!' Kattar said. 'From the thigh!'

'I don't have any meat. Get lost. If I see your face near my shop – or even in the market – I'll throw you on this chopping board and make mincemeat out of *you*. Didn't your friend tell you about my intentions for you?'

'I think you are mistaken,' Kattar said. 'I am Qurban Ali Kattar – Professor Qurban Ali Kattar.'

'Director sahib!' The butcher had spotted me and his manner tempered down considerably and became courteous. He turned to Kattar, 'Don't you have mothers and sisters in your house?'

'No,' Kattar replied innocently. 'My mother has passed away. No sisters to begin with. I am alone. Your daughter will not have any problem.'

'Get out of here!' the butcher thundered and because of the noise everyone in the market turned to look at us. 'I will yank off all your professorism – you bloody crow!'

I took Qurban Ali Kattar out of the market. Once we were outside, he turned around and blamed me for his insult, even though I tried to present my defence.

'I was called a bloody crow,' he said in a dejected tone. 'I had already told you that girls' fathers don't take to me and despite that you shoved me in his face. Suppose he had murdered me with his blade – what would you have done then?'

'That wasn't his intention,' I said. 'This is the way he speaks normally. His heart, I assure you, is of gold.'

'That man is ill-mannered – he's a beast,' Kattar said.

That incident caused an unnecessary rancour in Kattar's heart towards me. He alleged that I, despite knowing that the butcher's attitude towards him was hostile and antagonistic, had coerced him into asking for his daughter's hand, and by doing so, had put his life in grave danger. He was convinced that I had knowingly taken him inside the butchers' market, even though the butcher had never expressed any desire to meet him, that I had made all this up myself.

'And even if he did express the desire, I am sure it was so that he could dirty his hands with my blood. I am most astonished at the fact that I am still alive and walking.'

While agreeing with his assessment that the butcher's conduct was not quite friendly, I strongly repudiated his claim that my intention in arranging this meeting was malicious. Perhaps his interview, due to some misunderstanding, had not been too encouraging, but not even a word of doubt ought to be cast on my sincerity.

'It's quite possible,' I said, 'that the butcher adopted this demeanour simply to test his prospective son-in-law's courage and self-confidence?'

'But he was so respectful towards you,' Kattar said suspiciously. 'He called you Director sahib. You've probably told him that you're a film director.'

'I told him I am the director of Allah Tawakkul Bakery.'

'Director sahib! Director sahib!' He stopped in his tracks, trembling from head to toe. 'Changezi, you son of ... I've grasped your cunning! You are trying to overawe that butcher with your credentials to get closer to him. You wish to marry Razia yourself – I've suspected that for two or three days now. Ever since I asked you to play the Veiled Villain you have been dodging the request. Ah, the real reasons! Now, it would be much better if our friendship ended and we departed on the separate paths of our lives.'

'– and what would become of your food and shirt shortage? You'd be at a loss by terminating this friendship,' I said in a slightly heated tone myself ...

He acted as if he did not hear me.

'We are not friends anymore,' he said, looking at the Lee Market clock tower. 'Today, on the fifteenth of November at eleven forty-five, a historic friendship has come to an end because of one man's unfaithfulness and insincerity. Today Qurban Ali Kattar and Iqbal Husain Changezi depart on their separate paths.' Looking at the Iranian restaurant in front of us, he continued, 'We will drink one last cup of tea to mark this painful moment and after that Kattar will exit from one door of the restaurant and Changezi from the other and they will never meet again.'

'And who'll pay the bill?' I asked. 'You do know that there is a robust Iranian seated on the counter adjacent to the door and whichever one of us makes for the door, a voice would chase after that person: 'Four and a half aanas, Red Tie, four and a half aanas –!'

'You mean you don't even have four and a half aanas?' he said. 'Changezi! I have noticed that you are increasingly becoming more miserly and small-hearted. I've always thought of you as a man whose heart and pockets are open for his friends. Come, in that case, let's just go to the bakery. The significance of this moment is such that it is necessary to commemorate it. A poem is composing itself in my head; it's called "The Last Time While Drinking Tea".

Walking towards the bakery, Kattar told me that with our friendship was now over, I would have to tear out that page from my autograph book which Kattar had signed, and remove his photograph from my hotel wall and hand it to him. Imagining that now Kattar's photograph would not look down at the dining tables from between S. M. Jalal's and Nargis Baghdadi's, my eyes welled up. But I knew that so long as I harboured a passion for collecting authors and Qurban Ali Kattar remained in need of shirts, this historic friendship would not end ...

10

After that, I was unable to meet Qurban Ali Kattar for four or five days. The next day I had to go to Hyderabad for some important business. The clever Taj Ali had been insisting since last month that we should open a branch office of Allah Tawakkul Bakery in Hyderabad, where his nephew had managed to get a small shop allotted to him. I went to Hyderabad and took the necessary steps: met Taj Ali's nephew and inaugurated a joint bakery and restaurant modelled after the Chakiwara bakery. With that I returned to Karachi, feeling successful and like an actual managing director (now we even had a branch!), and conveyed the good news about the smooth inauguration of the Hyderabad branch to Taj Ali. We were making progress – excellent!

In the evening I visited Qurban Ali's flat on Middleway Street. He was not there, which was unusual for a man like him. I turned back and upon reaching Corporation Street, instead of going towards Lee Market and the bakery, I turned right for 'the Intersection of Pineapple Sherbet Sellers'. This is what I call the place; its actual name is something else. The most tireless pineapple-sherbet seller in Chakiwara – perhaps the most tireless pineapple-sherbet seller in the whole world – sells his most satisfying pineapple sherbet at this intersection.

Drink my friends! A glass for an aana!
Oye, a glass for an aana!
O come on, friends!

He cries very loudly, in a carping and infuriating tone. His litany doesn't cease even for a second; from dusk till dawn he carries on in his irritating voice. Even if his sherbet is refreshing (I have never tried it), his hoarse, nerve-wracking voice takes away all its succour and freshness. Earlier on, he had rivals on that intersection, other pineapple sherbet sellers, but they were soft-spoken, considerate men whose vocal cords were not that strong. He defeated them all by shouting incessantly and much louder and, eventually, unable to endure his voice, they all left. To achieve this end, he brought along a platoon of his boys, and those half-dozen boys – from the eldest to the youngest – were precise duplicates of their nonpareil father. Under his leadership, they became formidable players in that shouting match and defeated everyone else. Their father would cry: '*Drink, O friends: a glass for an aana!*' and then both father and sons would follow in unison, using their throats to full capacity: '*Drink, O friends: a glass for an aana!*' In the face of such an opposition their rivals were helpless. They could not tolerate it and left. That man now stands alone on that intersection like a victorious Napoleon who has trounced his enemy into fleeing. But despite this victory, he is not complacent. Due to the ever-present danger and possibility of his rivals' return, he keeps his voice as high and hoarse as ever, and does not soften it even for a bit. His platoon is still present and ready to come to his aid. For them, however, the refrain carries no joy and has turned into a doleful lament. If one of them is not shouting with all the force or if his heart is not in it, then his father scolds him with a sharp expletive and lands a blow or two on him as well. He is a cruel father. In this manner, day and night, this indefatigable team of father and sons hammers down the gloomy raga of 'A glass for an aana' onto the ears of Chakiwarans. There is much in this man's character that invites laughter, a lot that is pitiful, but some laudable qualities as well. On the strength of his vocal cords and through his passion – the passion for selling pineapple sherbet – he has routed his rivals. His victory is the victory of vocal cords and in that sense, no different from the triumph of a modern democratic politician ...

A little further on from this intersection there is a little 'garden': a patch of dried grass with a few miserable and shrivelled mulberry trees inside a rectangular iron railing. This is the Hyde Park of Chakiwara. Here, each evening, Chakiwara's conjurers, inventors of medicine, and other charitable men, assemble to inform Chakiwarans about their latest and most cutting-edge charms, formulas and other battle-ready inventions. And it cannot be denied that some gentlemen among others provide far more entertainment to their listeners than most political leaders do, and whether you buy their freakish remedies or not, just listening to them is a tremendous lesson in human psychology. Often in the evenings I wander into this garden for some recreation and relaxation. Here, I have heard the most fascinating speeches of my life, which, despite the fact that the speech-maker is using the same old tricks and techniques (for instance, the verse, 'Seed and soil unite to become blossom and garden') which have now become hackneyed, carry such captivating humour and eloquence, that while you may remain sceptical about the efficacy of the medicine, you are most certainly entertained. Here one must keep in mind that the art of speech for doctors and conjurers is quite different from other forms of public speaking and not easy to master. This is the art of fleecing people in broad daylight (not as straightforward as it seems), and to be adept at it one must be a babbler who can enchant his audience. These conjurers are a large fraternity. So when they hurl vile curses at their colleague-imitators and claim themselves distinct from their peers, you need not trust them. After delivering their speeches, they join the very same imitators for a meal in a small hotel and discuss their day's business. Perhaps they have a college somewhere – some institute where proper degrees are awarded, otherwise why would everyone use the same old tried and tested tricks that their old masters established, to attract customers? Each conjurer uses that 'paper flowers will never have a scent' verse and you can trust that if a conjurer is not using it in his speech, his authenticity is doubtful and he has no bona fide degree from the fraternal institute. Beware of such a conjurer!

A man with straight whiskers and a goatee stood on a box addressing the crowd. Ostensibly he seemed to be a professor at some college because he was wearing a square tasselled cap and a gown. It dawned on me a few moments later that the cap and gown were mine – the ones I had lent to Sheikh Kattar. (I recognized the small patch under the armpit.) But the man in the gown was definitely not Sheikh Qurban Ali Kattar. He was quite tall and broad and there was something familiar about his face and voice. At first I felt really angry at Kattar. Surely instead of returning my gown he had sold it to that man. I was about to cry: *This man is wearing my gown!* but then I gulped down my bitterness and kept quiet, thinking I'd make a spectacle of myself.

The man in the goatee was telling a rapt crowd about a magic ring that he held in his fingers in front of them. He claimed that this ring was the invention of his virtuous and deceased grandfather. Djinns used to visit his grandfather to acquire their religious education. One of them, a grateful djinn, of high pedigree and lineage – Noor Ahmad was his name – after completing his education and before returning to the Realm of Djinns, presented to the grandfather a strange and unique ring and apprised him of its wonders. With the help of that ring, his grandfather got two brick roofs laid upon his houses, defeated other claimants in a court case on his land, and in his old age just four years before his death, married again and had a child from the marriage as well, who was Goatee's own father. Just before he died, Goatee's respected father took off the ring from his index finger and presented it to his son and willed: 'My son, benefit from it and let the people of the world benefit from it as well and gain their blessings.' Goatee reflected later that there was some profound meaning in his father's wish – otherwise how was it possible to bring succour to the entire world with just one ring? Thinking hard and long, he came to the conclusion that there was nothing special about the ring itself, rather the wonders were the result of the words inscribed on a little piece of paper under the studded stone that even the sharpest human eye was incapable of reading. After much research and hard work, he extracted the piece of paper and read the text inscribed underneath with a microscope. They were the words of a charm, written in the djinni language. For days he practised writing those letters – first in big letters and then in small – and when he became adept at it, he resolved, in accordance with his father's will, to help the needy and the disadvantaged. Now he had many such rings which had the original charm inscribed by him on the back of the ring's stone. In terms of efficacy, there wasn't even a hair's breadth of a difference between his rings and the original. With just a little practice, adults could gain allegiance of the djinn and personal access to the court of the Shah of Djinns, Hazrat Suleiman, and find resolutions to their problems. If anyone among the audience is unable to win a court case, if your lover refuses to speak to you, if the husband is not divorcing the wife and the wife wants a divorce, if you have a headache – then by the wonders of this ring and the Orders of Prophet Suleiman, all problems will be resolved and all the desires of the desirous shall be met. Goatee told his audience that even though adults required ten days of practice before they could use the ring, any young innocent kid of less than ten years could use it anytime and have their heart's desire fulfilled by the Shah of Djinns.

And now he was going to exhibit the wonders of the magic ring in front of their eyes.

'Any young child may come forward – come, boy!'

A timid little boy stepped up. Goatee asked him his name and then told him to recite the kalima, the first article of the Muslim faith, and took off his ring and put it on the boy's finger.

'Boy, gaze into the stone on this ring.' He elaborately explained the proper way to hold the ring as if that was very important.

'Yes, boy! What's your name?' His hand was placed on the boy's shoulder.

'Abdul Shakoor,' the boy replied nervously.

'Yes, Abdul Shakoor! Do you see anything in the stone? Look carefully.'

'Nothing,' Abdul Shakoor replied with some trepidation as if he wasn't living up to Goatee's expectations.

'Nothing! Abdul Shakoor – are you really the child of your father?'

Abdul Shakoor did not deem it necessary to reply to this question. Some people from the audience laughed, thinking this to be a joke but Goatee threw an imperious glance at them, indicating that no illegitimate child would be able to benefit from this ring.

'So Abdul Shakoor,' said the goatee. 'Look carefully. Do you see anything? A grassy meadow?'

'Yes, I see it!' the boy immediately said, nodding his head and looking extremely pleased with himself. (Just for the record, I was absolutely sure he couldn't see a thing. When I was young, a conjurer made me see many things that I absolutely never saw.)

'What else? Just beside the grass, a golden throne – do you see it?'

'Yes, I do.' It was now very easy for the child.

'On the grassy ground a man, about half an inch, with two horns on his head and his back facing you – do you see it?'

'I do!'

'This is Faghfur djinn. Order him to call Saqqa the water-carrier, and have him spray the place.'

'Abdul Ghafur! Call Saqqa and have the area sprayed with water!'

'Has he left?'

'He's left.'

'Has Saqqa arrived?'

'Yes, he's arrived.'

'Has he sprayed?'

'He's doing it. He's spraying and coming towards me. Now he's gone.'

The same way Faghfur was made to call Furrash, who laid out a red carpet on the grass. When he left, four djinns appeared from beyond the meadow carrying a silver throne on their shoulders and placed it in a corner. The boy was bold now – not only would he say yes to everything Goatee told him, he would also add many details of his own to make him happy. Then the heralds called out: 'The Shah of Djinns, the Reliever of Difficulties, Hazrat Suleiman's carriage is about to enter!' following which King Suleiman, wearing his crown, entered the court and took his place on the throne.

The boy saw all this.

'Abdul Shakoor, greet Suleiman, Reliever of Difficulties!'

'Greetings, King Suleiman!' the boy said, lifting his hand to his forehead.

'Did he reply to your greeting?'

'He did!'

'Abdul Shakoor, beseech in front of the King of Djinns: O King! I have one wish, please fulfil it.' Abdul Shakoor repeated those very words.

'Yes, so did the King of Djinns say something?'

'He said it shall be fulfilled.' Abdul Shakoor, besides being able to see all this, now also started hearing things.

'Abdul Shakoor, beseech him: O great King, I want to know what my mother is doing at this moment.'

Surely, Abdul Shakoor must have been greatly disappointed with this statement! Instead of this pointless wish he must have had some other wish, like, for instance, that he could start flying in an airplane over everyone's heads, or be able to memorize his school lessons automatically without doing any work. Most of the spectators must have thought the same thing (at least I thought so) – that it is ridiculous to give so much trouble to Hazrat Suleiman for this senseless task. But most disappointed was Abdul Shakoor himself, who didn't seem to have any interest whatsoever in knowing about his house. Besides, what use was it to him to know what she was up to, or if she was up to anything at all? (I can relate to his emotions because once, I too, was an Abdul Shakoor.)

'I want to know what my mother is doing,' he told the ring.

'Now look! King Suleiman the Reliever of Difficulties has signalled Faghfur djinn to step forth.'

'Has he?'

'Abdul Shakoor! Shah Suleiman is giving him some orders! Now listen carefully to his.'

'He's ordered that ...' The boy was in some doubt and he glanced towards Goatee like a schoolboy stuttering while reciting a lesson to a frightening teacher. 'He's ordered that ...'

'Actually, it's very loud out here. One cannot hear the voice,' Goatee addressed the crowd. 'Yes, Abdul Shakoor, he has ordered the djinn to bring the interior of your house here on his back and place it in front of you ... Now look carefully. Those fairies carrying away the throne, can you see them?'

'Yes, they're taking it up with them.'

'And Faghfur djinn is preparing to bring in your house. Now look ... did he just land your house on the ground in front of you?'

'Yes, he did!'

'Now tell these men the details of your house.'

Abdul Shakoor told the crowd that that his house had these many rooms and so many windows; the stairs going up were made of wood. He had no difficulty in relating these details because it was his own house. Goatee glanced at the crowd triumphantly.

'Can you see your mother?'

'Yes,' said Abdul Shakoor.

'What is she doing?'

'She's sitting near the stove, cooking.'

'Who is with her?'

'A brown cat.'

'Good work, Abdul Shakoor!' The boy was very pleased and satisfied and went back to sit with his friends, from where he stared with astonished eyes at Goatee's awe-inspiring face.

After that, in a long speech, he assured the audience that with the magic ring every wish could be immediately fulfilled. With the help of Hazrat Suleiman, the Shah of Djinns, you could find a job, bring prosperity to your business, and no matter how unyielding a lover was, you could be united with them without even having to step out of your house. He told them that if they wanted to achieve something they must annihilate the 'self' because 'seed and soil unite to become blossom and garden', and clarified that 'paper flowers will never have a scent'. There was only one condition for using the ring: if it was a child, he could use it anytime, given he was not over eleven years. Anyone over eleven required some days of practice during which it was necessary that he refrained from sex – the purer and cleaner you were the sooner you would find success. There was no restriction on its use and it could be used by everyone: men, women, children. The procedure went like this: you needed to sit in a dark room every day for fifteen minutes and gaze into the ring and shun dirty thoughts from your mind. After ten to twelve days of practice, you would start seeing Faghfur djinn in the ring, through whom you'd be able to gain access to the court of Suleiman the Reliever of Difficulties, and present your plea. He assured the audience that he had absolutely no lust for money. With God's grace, he had enough to eat at home. He was only carrying out the orders of his late father (may he be blessed with a high station in Paradise) by handing out these rings. And his purpose was nothing other than serving God's creation, for which he would be rewarded by God in the Hereafter: two-and-a-half, three rupees was simply the manufacturing cost. By asking for a donation of one rupee he was bearing a loss of two rupees per ring. But he was offering the ring for a rupee only at that particular time and place. If purchased at his house on Chakiwara's Middleway Street, the donation would be five and a half rupees. He reminded the public that he had been present amongst them for the past ten years, commonly known as the Professor-Fakir of the World, the Inventor of the Magic Ring, a testament to the fact that he was not a fraudster. He had testimonials and certificates from India's famous rajas, kings, officers, insurance agents, and other big and important people, all of whom had highly praised the wonders of the ring. Some kings had even offered to make him Prime Minister of their states but he refused. He only wanted to spread the blessings of Suleiman, the Reliever of Difficulties.

'Look here, at this beard of mine,' he said. 'May God's curse be upon me if I lie with a beard like this! The whole world knows me. Professor-Fakir of the World is famous everywhere. I am not like other hakims or quacks who deceive and defraud the public and, after swindling the people of one town, disappear from it for years. I have been residing in Chakiwara for ten years. My address is flat no. 10, Middleway Street, the building adjacent to Ghareeb Muhammad's clinic. (Oh my Lord, the Knower of Secrets! This was Sheikh Qurban Ali Kattar's address!) So if I am deceiving you or if the ring does not meet its claims then come see me at my address. I am usually there. And in such a circumstance I guarantee that I will return your money.'

There was no doubt about the sincerity and earnestness of those words. He had even given out his address (which was in fact Sheikh Kattar's address). Even I started believing in the truth and miracles of the ring. His spell-binding eloquence and his powers to incite his audience were indeed in the finest tradition of true conjurers.

A soldier standing in the crowd took the initiative. He bought the Suleimani ring for one rupee and paid four aanas for a small bottle of Suleimani oil which was required for shining the ring. A navy man clad in a blue uniform, in order to one-up the army man, bought two rings (there is a healthy rivalry between the Army and the Navy and neither one allows the other to take a lead in anything). There was a look of pride on the navy man's face as if he had upheld the honour of the naval forces. Once the spell broke, requests piled in one after another, raised hands could be seen everywhere. Chakiwara's residents, with solutions to their financial, physical and sexual difficulties so close at hand, clambered over each other to present their rupees to Goatee. 'One ring here! Maulvi sahib! Pir sahib! Two Suleimani rings for me!'

'This opportunity won't repeat itself!' Goatee was saying, distributing the rings and bottles to his customers. 'At this venue, the donation is just one rupee. If you collect the ring from my house, it will be five and a half. Next month you won't find this for even a thousand. After this month I am not giving out any more rings because Faghfur djinn has persuaded me on trembling knees that he has become so preoccupied with fulfilling the needs of the needy that he doesn't even have the time to eat or sleep anymore ...'

The doleful faces of the Chakiwarans present lit up and their eyes glittered greedily. So far they had been unaware that the solution to all their problems lay in the magic ring. Now with just a little practice, they could fulfil their dearest desires and sweep up heaps of treasures, they could get palaces built, eat exquisite cuisines. Many licked their lips with hungry, salivating tongues.

Why did Goatee's face and voice look so familiar, I wondered. Where had I seen him and when? I thought of asking him once he was done with the customers, about how he got his hands on the gown and cap. I also meant to clarify to him that I had lent those items of clothing to Sheikh Qurban Ali Kattar just for a week or two ... but then it suddenly struck me: that man was Professor Shahsawar Khan!

The moment I realized this I leapt into the crowd and tried to run away. I had just turned around when I found Sheikh Qurban Ali Kattar standing behind me. He was without his gown and cap and it was not difficult to recognize him without them.

'How are you, yaar Changezi? Where had you disappeared?' he said. 'You heard the speech of the Venerable Fakir of the World?'

'Kattar,' I said, 'tell me why exactly you gave my gown and cap to him. I did not give them to you so you could go around handing them out to others. Tell him to take them off! I'm leaving –' and I made to go away.

'Wait, Changezi yaar! At least pay your respects to Fakir of the World sahib. I will introduce you to him.'

'No, I don't need any introductions. And this is no Fakir of the World but Professor Shahsawar Khan. He gave out your address to everyone; is he staying at your place?'

'Yes, he's been staying with me for two or three days,' Kattar admitted. 'But tonight he's leaving to do a tour of Punjab. There, people are struck by calamities due to floods and they urgently need his help. I requested him to stay longer but Shahsawar Khan declared, "Kattar! God's creation is calling out, Help! Help! And due to the floods it's a great opportunity to sell the rings."'

'And after the Punjab tour?'

'After the Punjab tour, he'll come to stay with me until another flood or some such calamity hits the country and the unfortunate mortals call out for his help ...'

'You mean he has assumed permanent residence with you?'

'Professor Shahsawar Khan loves me like his own nephew. He told me that I remind him of one of his nephews who has been missing for a long time.'

'Kattar! You are making a mistake,' I pleaded. 'Professor Shahsawar Khan is a leech! Your financial condition is not stable enough to keep him and his entourage, Mulla Huda, etc., with you. By taking on this disaster you have proved yourself to be a rank ass, and if you think that for the sake of eternal and never-ending friendship, Allah Tawakkul hotel will continue to provide pulao and halwa to you and those accursed djinns, then you are wrong!'

'Whatever. We'll see,' Kattar replied calmly. 'For now there is no question of my hosting the Professor. In a sense, *he's* hosting me. And I didn't give him the cap and gown just like that. I get a ten per cent commission from the sales of the rings.'

I had never thought Qurban Ali Kattar to be so astute businesswise and I felt a kind of surprise and a kind of happiness as well and, for a moment I forgot that this astuteness was being exercised through *my* cap and gown.

'And,' said Qurban Ali Kattar, 'he also sold me the ring for half the donation. You might have already heard from Professor Shahsawar Khan himself that this ring is about as useful as Alladin's lamp, and much lighter. You can wear it to any place – office, Shahzan Restaurant, Iranian Café or the cinema – anywhere. Imagine walking into the theatre with Alladin's lamp in your hand! You'd become a joke, everyone would turn around to laugh at you.'

Yes, I agreed, it was definitely better than Alladin's lamp. 'But, my dear Qurban Ali Kattar,' I said, 'tell me why Professor Shahsawar Khan has turned himself into Maulvi Fakir of the World and where he got his pointed whiskers!'

'There are some hazards in his profession,' Qurban Ali Kattar said. 'Certain people are baying for Professor's blood. Just yesterday a man on Middleway Street shouted abuses at him from his window and threw a water pot on his head. That's why he appears in public and in crowds under different names.'

Professor Shahsawar Khan answered my second question himself as he walked up to us. The crowd had now dispersed. Professor looked around and, removing his whiskers, slipped them into his bag. He then started talking to me as if donning and doffing whiskers was quite a normal activity.

'Iqbal Husain, my son. How are you?' he said in his flat voice that depressed me. 'You disappeared after that day I saw you in Lee Market with Sheikh Qurban Ali Kattar (may he be blessed with a long life). I tried looking for you but you disappeared so quickly I couldn't find you even though I looked for you for two hours. Tell me, do you also want a magic ring?' he said, thrusting his hand into his bag.

'No, no, Professor!' I said vehemently. 'I will tell you if I need one. These days, fortune has been smiling upon me. I don't have any difficulty for which the magic ring would be useful – I am not entangled in court cases, I do not wish to pass any exam, and nor am I in need of employment ...'

'My son!' he thundered. 'Union with the beloved! You have not been blessed with that, it shows on your face. Subdue Faghfur djinn and command him to open the doors – and if you don't find your beloved standing there with her arms folded then Professor Shahsawar Khan is not a man but a horse!'

'Professor, where are Mulla Huda, Miss Macy, the bear and the rest?' I said, changing the subject.

'They were among the accursed djinns who refused to obey Hazrat Suleiman, the Reliever of Difficulties. The last time I was in the Realm of Djinns, King Suleiman ordered me, "Shahsawar Khan, as a punishment, take them with you." Just the day before yesterday, they repented and swore allegiance to me. By swearing allegiance to a guardian saint, your previous sins are forgiven. Therefore, I sent a telegram to Suleiman –'

'Wait a second,' I said. 'Not so fast! You sent a telegram? Should we understand from this that you speak to King Suleiman over the telephone?'

'Guardian saints can speak to the Reliever of Difficulties whenever they please!' he said wrathfully. 'Just like you worldly people have telephones, we godly men also have our wirelesses.'

'All right, Professor, so did you send the message?'

'I sent this message: "Hello, this is Shahsawar Khan speaking. My Lord, all three djinns have repented and are imploring tearfully and humbly that their wrongs be forgiven." Suleiman ordered me to immediately appear at his court along with them, so I took them along to the Realm of Djinns.'

'How?' I asked. 'I mean, Professor, how did you go there? I mean, you didn't say if King Suleiman sent his djinn to fetch you?'

'One mustn't ask such questions, my son,' Shahsawar replied. 'All right, if you insist: this time I went on the back of Buraq.'

'And those penitent djinns were riding along with you on Buraq's back?'

This time he understood I was making fun of him. He gave me his wrathful look and turned to address Qurban Ali Kattar, 'My son, let's go and have tea somewhere.'

I tried slipping away quietly. The last misadventure to do with tea was still fresh in my mind. But Sheikh Qurban Ali Kattar is always hard at work trying to take advantage of my existence.

'Where are you going, Changezi yaar?' Kattar asked peevishly. 'Come, let's take Shahsawar Khan to tea at Shahzan hotel.'

'Shahzan?' I said, stuttering. 'I am a socialist,' I mumbled, 'and, on principle, I don't have tea at any hotel where the exploitative class goes to have its tea.'

'Let's go, son,' Shahsawar Khan said, suddenly belting his arm around my neck. 'Iqbal Husain! You don't find the company of holy persons every day. You mustn't stay away from me. Shahsawar Khan is a very resourceful man. I am leaving for my tour of Punjab today. I will return only after four or five months.'

'Via Pakistan Express?' I remarked, and then added quickly, 'Oh, it's about time. You'll miss the train which leaves in half an hour. Let's go straight to the station. Taxi! Taxi! O rickshaw!'

'No son, I am not going via Pakistan Express, and besides, due to the blessings of the saints, I can also catch the train from Hyderabad. And really, if I wish, I could make it wait here until I get on it – its tires would remain glued to the tracks. Actually, I will go on a flying bedstead.'

We hailed a Victoria to go to Shahzan hotel. I wanted to explain to Professor why it would be better for us to go there on the flying bedstead or on Faghfur's back. That would utterly stupefy Shahzan's bourgeoisie and leave them incredibly impressed. When they'd see a flying bedstead through the glass panes, landing next to their shining motorcars and Professor's proletarian friends emerging from it, they'd be shocked and envious. It would be a fitting blow to their decadent bourgeois mannerisms.

We sat in the carriage and, winding through the bazaars, reached Victoria Road via Bandar Road. Professor had taken off his square cap. His long henna-dyed hair was extremely filthy and bustling with lice. He stretched out his enormous body in a relaxed and leisurely manner and occupied the whole seat (I am sure Faghfur djinn didn't look too different.). Sheikh Qurban Ali Kattar and I sat on the little seat opposite him. Despite his ludicrous ideas, Professor did have a certain splendour on his face. And who knows, the wonders of the ring might actually be true. If guardian saints really existed, then Professor certainly was one.

I paid the taxi driver upon reaching Shahzan hotel. In front of the yellow box of a restaurant the lazy and the rich had parked their shiny cars (I am a socialist!), which were flaring their latest metallic nostrils at one another. I was a little afraid that Professor might be refused entry into the restaurant. However, even if such a thing had occurred to anyone, upon seeing Professor's splendour, they did not dare speak their mind. Our entry caused a sensation in the restaurant and many teacups paused on their way to bourgeois lips. Many others smiled – the same kind of smile that the bourgeois smile upon seeing a particularly miserable sampling of the proletariat. But really, there was such radiance in the professor's green-hued eyes that the bourgeois smiles withered at once when faced with them. And truth be told, Professor was feeling so at home and cheerful at Shahzan that even the wealthiest of the wealthy bourgeois was not able to match his composure. I was a little uneasy and panicked; Qurban Ali Kattar, of course, was beyond all such feelings. The prime cause of my embarassment and nervousness: the professor looked smug and victorious as if this restaurant was some garden in Chakiwara and the tea-slurping bourgeoisie merely a collection of bricks. Professor was among those people for whom 'proletariat' and 'bourgeois' mean the same thing. For him all of them were just men, just his audience, musical instruments which he could play for his entertainment, and whose chords he could strum to produce melodies. (Even then, I felt that it would have been much more dramatic had we arrived on the bedstead or on Faghfur; it would have been much more in line with our general appearance.)

In the restaurant everything was red. The walls were a light rose-red. The floor was wood-red and the furniture was red, too. Ostensibly, this restaurant had been built by some Red Collective with the intention to provide amusement to the bourgeoisie and filch their money. Even the waiters' uniforms were red. Under Professor's fiery leadership, wading across the plush carpet, we took a table in the dining hall. Professor placed his bag of rings, his baton and cap on the table and braced himself to relax on the sofa, but I grasped his intention and leapt onto the sofa so that he would have no place to fall asleep – the other seats were all single-sofas. In that huge hall, the atmosphere was calm and quiet and sad; you felt as if you were sitting in the harem of some Egyptian pharaoh. I have always imagined the colour red to be bright and cheery – the colour of youth, happiness and rebellion – but here in this hall it had turned into a solemn, grim, a mausoleum-esque colour – perhaps even black wouldn't have produced such a perfect effect. It was the kind of restaurant where you might have liked to be buried. From above, neon signs respectfully poured down divine light, and the swift, feline-footed, red-uniformed waiters roamed around like ethereal beings carrying dishes.

'That's a djinn,' Professor Shahsawar pointed to a little clown-like waiter. And to elaborate his pronouncement, he said, 'Often these djinns – just for fun – gain employment under the residents of the earth. They report the conditions here to the police department of the djinns. Actually, they spy on humans on behalf of King Suleiman.'

Upon discovering that there was a djinn in the restaurant, we naturally turned a bit anxious. Meanwhile, a waiter came to take our order – that same djinn waiter. He had an openly insolent smile on his face.

'How are you, Muhammad Deen? When did you come and for what reason?' Professor Shahsawar Khan asked him. The waiter's face showed signs of bewilderment, and he looked at Shahsawar Khan's face intently and with surprise, as if trying to recognize him.

'Maulvi Sahib, I cannot recall where we have met,' the waiter said, after some reflection. Apparently, he had never seen Shahsawar Khan before.

To my mind there was no reason why Shahsawar Khan would know the waiter already, but what was most astonishing – which was later confirmed – was that the waiter's name was indeed Muhammad Deen!

'All right, Muhammad Deen,' Shahsawar Khan was determined to call the lanky waiter by his name – like a good-natured master calls his servant – 'yes, how will you recognize us, after all. When did you arrive from King Suleiman's?'

'Oh that, sir, it's been about two months,' the waiter said. 'No news for two months. Now I'll go when he calls; life was good there.'

With some difficulty, I gulped something down my throat which wasn't really there. Professor gave me his triumphant, supercilious look.

'Sahib, should I get some chai?' the waiter asked. 'Cake? Some pastry?'

'Bhai Muhammad Deen, I won't have chai,' Professor said. 'Get me some pera lassi with ice.'

That was the first time I'd heard about this strange new drink; I did not know that there existed such people who drank lassi made out of peras. When I realized that the professor would never place the correct order if it was left to him and that the attention of several people was upon us, I quickly asked for milk and peras.

'And half kilo jalebis as well,' Professor Shahsawar Khan completed the order in his booming voice, and then turned to me 'We'll have them with milk.'

A condescending smile spread on the little waiter's face. Waiters of the bourgeois restaurants are also extremely bourgeois. He didn't deem it necessary to reply and left with the order. After a while, he appeared with the milk and peras and fled hastily after placing them on the table, as if he found it disagreeable to serve such tasteless men.

'Aray bhai, Muhammad Deen! Jalebis!' Professor called after him; however, despite his friendly and familiar manner, Muhammad Deen the djinn disappeared.

'He did not quite recognize me,' Shahsawar Khan said, turning his attention to the pastries.

The conversation suddenly ceased for some time due to an abrupt and intense bout of concentration: Professor and Kattar pounced on the eatables as if they had been starving for two days. To watch them eat was for me both incomprehensible and, for obvious reasons, traumatic. I was to pay the bill.

When all the plates on the table had been wiped clean and the milk glasses emptied, Professor Shahsawar Khan belched a lusty belch – quite possibly the lustiest belch that anyone had ever dared to belch in this elite restaurant. It drew all the bourgeois eyes in that restaurant in Professor's direction. I heard a bourgeois woman dressed in a flowery gharara drop the teacup from her hands to the floor out of shock. She'd probably thought that some raging beast had barged into Shahzan. Professor, however, was utterly unaffected and remained indifferent towards the tumult he had just caused.

'My son, Iqbal Husain, please call that Muhammad Deen,' Shahsawar Khan said to me loudly. 'Ask him to bring something else. These foreign pastries did not give me much pleasure; they are no match for the fresh jalebis of Mulla Husain Halwai in Lahore.'

Suddenly I looked up at the table in front of me and saw that my friend Colonel Saljauti was having tea with a beautiful lady, his newlywed wife. The last thing I wanted in the world was to be seen by my acquaintances in such freakish company. But Saljauti had certainly seen me. When I looked away in the other direction – oh Lord! There sat Muhammad Muneer Tanveer and some former directors of Allah Tawakkul Bakery, along with my former stenographer, smiling as they pointed in our direction.

Muhammad Tanveer, the Napoleon of the import-export business, called out, 'Mr Iqbal!'

Now I would have to go over to their table. Because they had seen me.

'Come, Iqbal,' Tanveer said. 'Where did you fetch that brute from?'

'What brute?' I said with apparent surprise. 'Keep your voice low. Do you even know who that man is?'

'Who?' Muhammad Tanveer inquired.

'He's the famous Polish vocalist – Professor Bernofsky.'

'Oh, whatever!'

'No, really. He's Professor Bernofsky. He's a bit superstitious and maintains a weird exterior, like prominent vocalists usually do; but let me tell you, he's a genius. He's been living in Bombay for seven years. He had to escape his country after the German attacks ...'

The interesting thing was that I managed to convince him that Professor Shahsawar Khan was Professor Bernofsky. Familiar with my reputation as a 'collector of geniuses', he started eyeing me enviously for having snapped up such an important vocalist. But right at that moment when my merit and worth were on the rise, a voice came from behind, 'Iqbal Husain! My son, see if you can find that Muhammad Deen. Ask him for the jalebis if you find him.'

'Professor Bernofsky seems to be very fond of jalebis,' Muhammad Tanveer said with a wily sparkle in his eyes.

I ran back and ordered another waiter to get milk and pastries to keep the professor quiet. (Muhammad Deen had disappeared for good.) As soon as the milk and pastries arrived, the same pouncing and plunging was re-enacted. After finishing the pastries and wiping his hands clean, Professor caressed his beard. Now he was in the mood for doling out knowledge.

'So, my son, Kattar,' he said (God knows from where he was drawing the thread of this conversation.), 'I was telling you that out of all my grandfather's disciples, two or three were djinns. But when my grandfather asked them if they were djinns, they would deny it outright and claim they were from the human race. Finally, to find out who the djinn was, my grandfather gathered all his disciples and pointed to his lota – his little water pot – and instructed, 'All right, who is brave enough to fit himself into this little lota?' Everyone remarked that this was not even possible. But that boy who was a djinn claimed self-importantly, 'I can do it!' And so, in front of everyone's eyes, he entered the lota and fitted himself in it. My grandfather immediately shut it with a lid and secured it with the seal of Surah Yasin. And that's how he punished that djinn for hiding the truth from his master.'

He provided Kattar and me with some fascinating details about djinns, and these should be of some interest to the dear reader: from Professor's conversation it was apparent that djinns were also Hindu, Muslim and Sikh, and he himself had re-proselytized many djinns who had deviated from Islam and had turned Sikh, and had brought them back on the correct path. Generally, people have misconceptions regarding their faces – and Professor is an authority on the matter. According to him, the common notions that djinns have horns or tails are mere conjectures. The faces of djinns are exactly like those of humans. They don't have horns. Those who do have horns are creatures of a different nation altogether, and many people, due to their lack of knowledge, confuse them with djinns, due to their lack of knowledge. Djinns are usually short. The tallest djinn is not more than three and a half feet. The main difference between men and djinns physically is that the eyes of djinns are raised a little upward and the length of their nose is directly proportional to their height.

'And how do they dress and so on?' Kattar asked enthusiastically.

'Dress? Dress is the same, just like the human dress. Yes, it's a luxurious dress. There are also poor djinns, just like there are poor men.'

In that case, I thought, those poor, lower-class djinns would visit the lower-class Irani restaurants, and the richer djinns would go to Shahzan Restaurant. Are even djinns bourgeois, and so on and so forth.

'And what's Faghfur's face like?' Kattar asked, beguiled.

'You'd start seeing him yourself after practising for ten, twelve days,' Professor said. 'Faghfur is a good, beautiful djinn, and well-mannered, and he is extremely short at just two feet.'

'And – and – if a man has a beloved, then with that ring can she pass through the door of the heart –?'

'The stubbornest of stubborn beloveds will walk right into your room automatically. If you're wearing the ring, Suleiman the Resolver of Difficulties will fulfil any wish you make.'

I am absolutely sure that such a brilliant and cerebral conversation must never have taken place at any table in that mournful and pompous hall. Neither would three such strange-looking men have ever walked in together to this restaurant. We sat there for a long time, even though I wanted to escape soon. Kattar had made Professor repeat the instructions for the ring's use some five or six times. Professor told him that he would not accompany us to Kattar's flat; rather, he'd take our leave at the restaurant itself. He had just remembered an important task: he wanted to see Hakim Allah Ditta Sanyasi before his departure to Punjab because he had to consult him over some matters about the current governments of this world.

It was very dark when I paid the bill and exited with my companions. Shahsawar Khan shook hands with us at the door of Shahzan Restaurant, and giving us the good news that he would meet us again within two months, he started off towards Saddar. After that day, we did not see his face – and neither did we see the gown and cap.

11

I HAVE HEARD FROM CERTAIN RIGHTEOUS MEN WHO HAVE read extensively in the fields of spirituality and hidden knowledge that our earthly matters are governed by a handful of guardian saints and divinely appointed men. The latter have been designated directly by the Divine Force and are accountable for the spiritual programmes of their districts. For instance, a guardian saint who is in charge of the Lahore Division cannot interfere in the affairs of the guardian saint of Rawalpindi Division; nor can he step out of his district without permission from higher authorities. Students of the spiritual realm state that just as in the Worldly System there are commissioners, superintendents, tax-collectors, patwaris, etc., and juniors take orders from seniors, in the same way, the Divine Force too has designated its own guardian saints and appointed men for the running and administration of the Spiritual System. Occasionally, a guardian saint might even be transferred from his own area. Some guardian saints are like inspectors; they tour other saints' territories and send performance reports to the higher-ups. 'Higher-up' signifies the next senior officer. I have heard this from my own cousin and brother, Sher Husain Changezi, who not only knows the guardian saints of his area, but his relations with them are also extremely cordial and intimate (one of them, in fact, is his chuddy-buddy). He told me that once he was out on a pleasure drive around his city in his car with his friend and guardian saint, Lala Musa, when Lala suddenly told him to stop the car and turn around. He said, 'My area ends after that tree and guardian saint Wali Muhammad's area starts. I cannot cross it without the requisite Warrant of Passage.'

It's very difficult to identify these guardian saints. Apparently they are in rags and patched up clothes and they herd sheep. They have their own means of communication and in the blink of an eye they can travel to another city two hundred miles away – even though they have sometimes been found travelling on motorcars and trains. They consider the railways to be their personal property and never buy tickets and no one even asks to see them. They possess supernatural powers and those who gain their blessings never lose a case, are never bossed around by their officers, nor do they ever taste defeat in love affairs. My personal view is that this is not a laughing matter, and it's not mere superstition either. Between heaven and earth, there are thousands of such incomprehensible and supernatural things which our imaginations cannot even begin to conceive. (Some time back, Hamlet said the same thing to his friend Horatio, and I don't consider it amiss to repeat it here because it is so true.)

Now, there was certainly a chance that Professor Shahsawar Khan was a guardian saint. I mean you couldn't say with certainty that he was *not* one. He had all the necessary traits and ingredients of a guardian saint – a tide of undulating splendour in his green-hued eyes, his mysterious arrivals and departures, his habit of testing people's sincerity by giving them a chance to serve him, his ability to consider himself the ruler of everything everywhere, even if it was Shahzan Restaurant. These were the out-and-out marked traits of a guardian saint. And besides, we had also experienced his secret powers first-hand when he called out the djinn-waiter in the hotel by his real name and the waiter admitted himself that he had been with King Suleiman sahib before becoming a waiter there. His ability to intuit human thoughts on so many occasions was also remarkable, especially when you started to have mean and miserly thoughts about paying for his tea ... No! He was indeed a guardian saint!

Sheikh Kattar was convinced of this, and never took his name without the prefix 'Hazrat'. He had no doubts about the heavenly properties of Professor's ring and he'd started taking Faghfur djinn's name with such affection and fondness that it seemed he and Faghfur were best friends in school. He had no need for General Plans anymore or for winning over Razia's butcher-father's consent for their marriage. And if previously he hadn't been keen on paying heed to my advice, he was now downright irritated, feeling no need for it at all. And frankly, I too had stopped giving him advice. My last recommendation almost proved disastrous for him and after that bitter experience he was not ready to take any more suggestions from me. While I am always ready to advise my friends (and my advice has changed many lives), I avoid counselling those who are incapable of appreciating the soundness of my word. Feeding mangoes to an ass is both pointless and useless.

The remarkable effects that the ring had on Kattar cannot be denied. It gave him immense self-confidence, the blemishes under his eyes also started disappearing, his ever-dejected and beaten face beamed with renewed vitality and optimism; even his gait became more upright and relaxed – it was as if he was stepping into a new spring of life. However, I did not like one thing about this change and it was his newly gained sense of independence and strong-headedness. I mean, he was being strong-headed with *me*! He acted as if he did not need me much anymore and he was utterly mistaken in feeling this, even though it was true that I did not have any more shirts to give him. He also stopped hinting at our historic and eternal friendship and treated me with the same superficial politeness that someone with an Alladin's lamp would use towards someone without an Alladin's lamp. The first couple of days I was afraid that he'd slip out of my hands – writers are unfaithful creatures, and I didn't want to lose him.

Still, I was happy for the change in him. He was like the slug who after years of captivity in the pitch-darkness of a shell, had finally succeeded in wiggling out into the shining light of day: his revitalized face and health left you happy and rejoicing.

I remember it was the third day after Professor's departure (a Saturday) – we were walking up and down Karachi's Elphinstone Street, watching the din and dazzle of bourgeois life, when he told me the plot of his novel which he had begun formulating the day before. I was surprised and delighted to watch him return to the creative act after years of barrenness. Now, I thought, Kattar is really at a turning point in his life. For so many years, he has been unable to write because he was stifled by spiritual and economic complications and failures. Now when he's actually found himself to be free and happy, he has finally resolved to write a novel. Now Urdu literature, without a doubt, is about to be introduced to a new, more mature phase of Sheikh Qurban Ali Kattar's novel-writing career. The thing is that he was not alone anymore in facing the future: he could ask Faghfur djinn to write a novel and with his help he could enhance his output enormously. The proof of this was the fact that his mental and cognitive powers were now at their zenith and the cobwebs entangled in his mind for the past four, five years were now disintegrating. His new under-construction novel, in its originality and avant-gardism, was a vastly different plot from his earlier novels. However, he had hit a snag while trying to resolve the ending and knotting together its various dangling threads. Assuming that two heads, after all, are better than one (no matter how shoddy the second head – mine – was), I concluded that he was, in fact, in need of my assistance and advice.

This novel was supposed to be a Sherlock Holmes-type, pure detective whodunnit, and love was implicated in it merely to add flavour. The main obstacle that Sheikh Qurban Ali Kattar faced was the same as all other whodunnit novelists face. In a nutshell, this novel was about the murderous and slaughterous exploits of the mysterious bandit Waliya, who carried out his horrific acts in broad daylight. After publicly proclaiming and informing the police in advance about the timing and location of the murder, he disappeared completely once it was done, leaving the police utterly stunned. Shahbaz Khan, a promising young inspector, is appointed to apprehend Waliya. Inspector Shahbaz Khan, as everyone knows, is Sherlock Holmes' class fellow, and he has brought to justice many hardened criminals involved in huge crimes. But in the face of Waliya's cunning, even Inspector Shahbaz Khan is rendered helpless and fails to discover how Waliya managed all these exploits. Once, before murdering his victim and looting his safe, he informs Inspector Shahbaz Khan via regular post, as a matter of polite routine, about the impending crime. This time Shahbaz Khan, to avoid giving the murdered the upper hand, locks himself up along with the candidate to be murdered, inside a windowless room in the latter's bungalow . Inspector Shahbaz Khan, to be doubly cautious, has a loaded pistol in each hand. Waliya had promised to dispatch his victim to the next world precisely at seven and Inspector Shahbaz Khan and the victim-to-be (a corporate-type boss) were looking expectantly and with some impatience, at the hands of the clock which were crawling with assurance towards the appointed time. Inspector Khan had also stationed a police cordon around the bungalow and had already claimed to his men that this time round, Waliya would not be able to deliver on his promise. Gradually the long hand of the clock crawled forward and the pendulum swayed, counting the seconds ... four minutes to seven, two minutes, one minute, half a minute, and the long hand is now about to touch seven, and the pendulum is swinging ...

Dhaz! Dhaz! The police standing outside the bungalow hear gunshots and storm the room where the victim-to-be and Inspector Shahbaz Khan are locked. They undo the lock, the key for which is with the head constable and enter the room which is filled with impenetrable smoke. When the smoke clears they see Inspector Shahbaz Khan's face, pistols in his hands, and beside him, the victim lying in a pool of blood. The window pane in front of them is smashed and Shahbaz Khan is shouting, 'That bastard has escaped through the window! Go after him, head constable! He had definitely hidden himself under the charpoy before we even came ...'

'Now Changezi, yaar,' Kattar said, 'my problem is that there should be a satisfactory explanation for Waliya's escape in the presence of police that would convince the readers. Think about it. If you were Waliya, how would *you* have escaped in broad daylight – right under the watchful eye of the law, blowing dust in everyone's eyes?'

'Blowing dust, hmm,' I said, reflectively.

'Stop joking, yaar Changezi. If a satisfactory explanation can be found, this novel could be a "smasher" – perhaps Urdu literature's best and most sensational detective novel ever.'

An idea struck me which, in my opinion, was an extremely bright one.

'Kattar, why don't you do this: in the end, show that Waliya, in fact, was Inspector Shahbaz Khan. You know, Inspector Shahbaz Khan wrote letters on behalf of Waliya and since he was always present at the scene of the crime and often he was the only one present with the victim-to-be, it would be extremely easy to pull this off. And besides, no one would suspect him because he's an inspector.'

'I swear to God!' Kattar cried. 'Iqbal Husain Changezi! You are a genius!'

And then suddenly, thinking that he had praised me more than necessary, he quickly added, 'Even I thought of this but I wanted to make Inspector Shahbaz Khan the hero. And making him the real murderer would ruin his past record. In my previous novels, I have shown him to be a sharp, upright and brave officer. I want to get him married in this novel.'

'Then – there is only one thing possible,' I said. 'Which is that Waliya has a magic ring and he's performing these murders through Faghfur djinn, who is invisible to the police, and being a djinn, can pass through walls.'

'This resolution is also good. Very good.' He didn't deem it necessary to praise me more but it was clear from his contented demeanour that this explanation had struck a chord with him and he had resolved to present this very denouement to his anxious readers.

The point of my writing all this is that Kattar's creative powers were reawakening, and after three or four years, he was once again full of hopes and dreams, and his fingers were itching to write once more. I should inform the dear reader that he would search in vain for the above-mentioned Great Cataclysmic Novel; Qurban Ali Kattar did not write more than thirty-two pages of this novel and never finished it. And there is no hope that he will finish it either because, dear reader, this spring of Sheikh Qurban Ali's life (alas! alas!) lasted for just a few days. The lotus of his heart started to wilt as soon as it bloomed. And ...

12

Since I came to reside in Chakiwara, I have kept a daily journal, like old Pepys, in which I inscribe the day's events, my musings about people and other important and trivial things that are somehow related to me. My daily journal, in a sense, is a winding chronicle (without head or tail) about Chakiwara, and I am certain that the future historian or novelist of this town would find a lot in here that would be of use to him. In it, I have made complete and comprehensive sketches of my acquaintances, friends and collected authors and other odd and bizarre characters. On many occasions I have even recorded lengthy and tedious conversations – as if the speakers were cabinet ministers or great philosophers and their conversations were of vital importance for the future of the world, or as if preserving each and every word they uttered was crucial for future generations.

The truth is, I am like the seasonal plague for many people. And since I believe that these people are Chakiwara itself, I consider it my duty as a memoirist to ensure that this neighbourhood and its characters appear as living, breathing people in the pages of my chronicle. As I write Sheikh Kattar's tragic story, my journal lies open in front of me and has allowed me to reproduce many conversations here. I am afraid I have not been scrupulous in my selection of the material – but let me admit: this was not an easy task. Going over the journal I now see that if I am to reproduce the events of the next twelve days (all our conversations, arguments, Kattar's anxieties and apprehensions), we would need an entire volume simply for that span, and I don't think that my kind reader, in spite of all his kindness, would be able to forbear those exasperating details (that is, if the dear reader has not already tired of this narrative and thrown it away, and hasn't already damned both Iqbal Husain Changezi and Qurban Ali Kattar). Therefore, I will state only in brief the events of the next ten, twelve days.

Sheikh Qurban Ali Kattar had started practising with the magic ring the same night Professor Shahsawar Khan had sold it to him, after which he was supposed to be able to recite the spell and see the grassy meadow and Faghfur and so on. Several evenings when I went to visit him, I had to wait outside his flat for ten, fifteen minutes. When he finally opened the door, his eyes glowed with a divine light and he explained apologetically that he had been busy practising with the ring and couldn't attend to the door in the middle of the exercise (as I have mentioned earlier).

At first this magic ring seemed to be making a new man of him, and he seemed absolutely certain and optimistic about the results. He also thought that he had Shahsawar Khan's special blessings and that the professor would never leave his side. He had some doubts regarding his method and wasn't sure if it was in line with the professor's instructions. He did not entirely understand the instruction that required him to gaze into the ring: did that also mean that you could not blink during the act? He could refrain from blinking for three minutes at most, after which tears started dripping from his eyes. Another one of Professor's instructions seemed questionable when put in practice. The professor had said that after exercising with the ring, there had to be an emptiness between the heart and mind and if any thoughts came to the mind at all, they had to be clean and pure. Qurban Ali Kattar told me that during the exercise, he often had thoughts which perhaps could not be considered chaste and clean. He did not tell me what those thoughts were, only that they weren't very chaste and clean; and by my speculation, these were certain particular thoughts about his beloved which are – from an ethical and moral point of view – commonly described as vulgar. I encouraged Qurban Ali Kattar that no matter how dirty his thoughts about his beloved, they are always pure and innocent, especially when the beloved herself is chaste and pure like snow and milk ... but not having read Freud, his sense of guilt was probably rather intense.

However, those slippages in the exercises didn't trouble Sheikh Qurban Ali Kattar too much; he had faith in Professor Shahsawar Khan's patronage and believed that despite his trivial errors, Professor would still lead him to the right destination.

13

I THINK IT WAS THE SEVENTH DAY OF KATTAR'S ADVENTURES with the ring. When I went to his flat in the evening, I found him in an utterly outlandish state. A terrified maniac opened the door for me and I was shocked when I saw him. On his face was the look of a corpse that had just met the two angels of death and been given the good news of his entry into Hell. For a moment I felt giddy, and my first reaction was that this was someone other than Kattar ... Actually, I had become accustomed to an optimistic, cheerful Kattar who whistled to himself and hummed film songs. My mind wasn't ready for the ghostly face I saw all at once that evening – it could hardly be called the face of a man: terrorized eyes, pale and distressed features, flustered hair ... and then a strange sound, *kat kat kat* ...

His teeth were clattering.

'What happened, Kattar? Is everything all right?' I asked, placing my hand on his shoulder. He could not bear the touch of human sympathy and he jerked my hand off.

He was throwing terrorized glances at the nooks and corners of the room and I once saw him looking beneath the charpoy.

'He's gone,' he said to himself, stammering.

'Who has gone, Kattar?' I asked. 'Who was here with you?' Now I felt really worried.

'Faghfur djinn!' he replied. 'He was here in this room before you came. Stood right here next to my chair.'

I thought either his nerves were giving up or he had really started seeing ghosts.

'Faghfur?' I said. 'But he was only supposed to appear in the stone on the ring. There's no reason for him to come into the room. And besides, it's just the seventh day of your exercise with the ring ...'

We sat on the chairs next to the open door. I noticed Kattar's condition improving in my presence and some colour gradually returned to his flattened cheeks. Even then it was clear from his trembling hands and clattering teeth that he had been severely jolted.

I took a cigarette out of my pocket and offered it to him, which just goes to show how flustered and pitiful his state was, because as far as Kattar was concerned, I had long quit the habit of offering him my cigarettes. He held the cigarette between his fingers and puffed out smoke (by doing this, his courage seemed to be returning to him), and said, 'Yes, Changezi my friend. Today when I finished my exercise, I glanced underneath the chair ... You won't believe what I saw. Next to my feet stood a little djinn – two feet tall and exactly how Professor Shahsawar Khan had described Faghfur: his eyes were a little raised and he had a small butcher-like beard. You understand that I do not expect to see Faghfur in this manner, and his presence here was surprising for me. He seemed friendly and was smiling somewhat foolishly at me. But I was seized by fear and my body broke into a sweat. I clenched the armrests of the chair and wanted to cry out loudly but no sound came out of my throat. I do know Changezi that there was no need for me to be so scared … Meanwhile, Faghfur turned around to look at me. He kept smiling and glancing back at me as he gradually went under the charpoy.'

'This is a product of your imagination,' I said, cheering him up. 'I think Professor Shahsawar Khan stated quite clearly that the djinn would appear inside the ring's stone. And let's suppose that it was indeed a djinn – in that case, his smiling and friendly demeanour shows that he's an innocent and benign djinn. I am sure that Faghfur is – *if* it was Faghfur – a sociable and benign djinn, and his entry into your room like this is a sign that he wants to be friends with you. It's quite possible that he came here to take orders from you in person. The fact that you unnecessarily felt harassed must have caused him immense trouble and embarrassment. And Kattar, as a friend and someone who holds your welfare and happiness dear, I think you should get used to djinns now, because after the fifteen-day exercise, when you start reciting spells for the ring, you will probably be acquainted with entire hordes of djinns.'

'But Faghfur had no right to barge into the room like this,' Kattar complained. 'If he or his companions had appeared inside the ring, I would have been much nicer to them.'

'At all events,' I said, 'even if Faghfur makes an intrusion despite your unwelcoming and irritable attitude – and I am not too optimistic about this – you must not let this opportunity slip. You should smooch him like he's your pet, talk to him, ask him, "How are you? What is King Suleiman up to these days?" I mean, make small talk which shows him that you really like him. This Faghfur, according to your story, sounds like an obliging man, or djinn, and he could be exceedingly useful to you – he could take your messages to Razia, fetch your meals from Allah

Tawakkul Bakery and bring them to your flat and, if he has a literary flair, he could be asked to work on your novels as well …'

'I don't know,' Kattar said, 'if you are serious or joking. But Changezi yaar, I beg you to sleep here tonight in my flat. It's quite possible that when you leave, Faghfur might again …'

Now I understood that the fear had entrenched itself in his heart and become something real for him. He truly believed that Faghfur, for some reason, was scared of me and avoided me and would not come into the flat in my presence. But in spite of our true friendship, to have to spend the night at Kattar's flat – sleeping with him in his bed, to be precise – was not a pleasant thought for me. And besides, it wasn't just a matter of one night. To keep Faghfur away I would have to spend many more nights at the flat while the djinn could be somewhere close…

Suddenly I saw Musafir's woolly body. He was giving me a clownish look, one eye shut, his pink tongue lolling out of his mouth. We did not know when he had come upstairs. This was Musafir's magic; he went in and out mysteriously. And all of a sudden you looked around and spotted him sitting next to your feet looking up at you with a funny face – even though you could swear that he wasn't there a second earlier.

Immediately I was struck by an idea.

'O Kattar!' I said. 'Why do I have to stay the night? Musafir is here. You know that djinns hate dogs and they don't come near places where there are dogs. I have read this myself in Professor G. P. Katuri's *Vanquishing Djinns,* which is the authoritative textbook on the subject. I think you should always keep Musafir in your flat. In fact, make him sleep next to you. He needs a master.'

From the looks of the long-eared, woolly Musafir, it appeared that he agreed with me. And even Qurban Ali Kattar was clearly affected by what I said. Generally speaking, he doesn't pay heed to anything I say without a reliable reference, but this particular idea had the endorsement of G. P. Katuri – you wouldn't be able to find a better expert on djinnism in this country no matter how hard you try.

We sat talking for a long time. Razia did not come out to the balcony and neither did the balcony door open. (It moved just a bit once – and a vertical slit of light appeared from between the curtains; we thought we heard some strange beast snorting and grunting, but then that slit of light got eclipsed into darkness.) I hadn't seen her on the balcony for two days now and was wondering where she could be (it was as if a light had been doused from my life as well). Qurban Ali Kattar and I debated the nature of the grunts and wondered what they could be: did the butcher have a pack of wild cats caged in his room? Were they fighting with each other? (And so on.) It did not occur to me at all that the creator of these sounds could be the butcher himself.

I left Kattar's flat around eleven; he had Musafir sitting in his lap. I told Kattar as I left that if Faghfur came in despite Musafir's presence, he could shout out to me from his window as I went down the alley. As I walked, I did not hear Kattar's voice and was assured that he was now safe and that Faghfur was as scared of Musafir as he was of me.

14

During the next three days, Sheikh Qurban Ali Kattar saw Faghfur just once or twice standing next to his legs – and that too when Musafir was out for a walk and a breather in the alley. But even his earlier meeting with Faghfur did nothing to lessen his fear of that social and noble djinn.

Those days Kattar rarely ventured outside; he turned into a recluse. Despite his closeness with Musafir, I noticed that his eyes seemed to be sinking. Sometimes a ferocious spark and a touch of madness danced in his eyes. Their redness indicated that he had not been sleeping well.

The trouble was that he did not know what time Faghfur might show up, and during those three days, he didn't even see Razia in the balcony. Sheikh Qurban Ali Kattar's spiritual barometer had plummeted and I felt very worried.

But once Faghfur djinn ignored even my presence. One Saturday, I goaded Sheikh Qurban Ali Kattar with great difficulty into going out to Elphinstone Street for a change of scene, hoping he would find some diversion in the bustle, din and glamour and the shiny motorcars there. Elphinstone Street usually buoyed him up. Not being a communist, he gets very excited looking at other people's motorcars. Other people's wives and girls also produced agreeable emotions in him. That evening we went around Elphinstone Street four or five times but he remained as sad and dejected as before. At one point, he tried to be funny and his comments made absolutely no sense to me. He stopped me as we were going past the alley near Paradise and asked me to read some words scrawled in charcoal on the wall in front of us. I started reading without suspecting anything: 'I am a fool! I am an ass! I am one hundred per cent an ass!'

'Changezi,' he said, 'I did not think so but now that you have admitted it yourself, I will have to agree with you. You are one hundred percent an ass.'

What an odd and awful sense of humour!

As we walked down Victoria Road towards Paradise Coffee House, I saw the famous Progressive writer Razm Hinai coming towards us. Razm Hinai is one of the top five members of the Progressives' Politburo and he is the only Progressive who doesn't allow even his clothes and body to deviate from his ideological colour. His hair and moustache are dyed red with henna and his face is red naturally and has turned even redder after he became a Progressive. He wears a red suit and brown boots. He's among those handful of men about whom you could say that they wear their hearts on their sleeves and whose interior and exterior are exactly the same. Razm Hinai is not his real name – he adopted this name last year after becoming a Progressive – his actual name is a dignified family name and it's extremely ordinary – Miyan Chiragh Deen Cheema. Last year, to quote the man himself, he was a conservative. But conservative or progressive, no one really cared much about him at the time, and even though some of his criticism and short stories were published in magazines, the editors of the magazines weren't convinced of his genius. And until last year, very few people had even heard his name. And then he saw that the editors of good magazines were returning his work to him. But there were some other magazines yet – for instance, Chaudhry Ma'iraj Deen's *Shaheen: The Falcon* and Maulana Muhammad Khan's *Khayal-e Fartut: Fancies of the Old Dotard* – that were ready to publish his stuff very obligingly. Especially Maulana Muhammad Khan, who, in the author's introduction, always praised him highly and informed his patrons that Urdu literature had immense expectations from Chiragh Deen Cheema.

'May God preserve him,' he wrote. 'Here he is once more: Miyan Chiragh Deen Cheema, illuminating our gathering. The short story that he has sent us this time round is such a masterpiece that in comparison even the great masters appear to be sweeping the trash at his door. This one short story is weightier than all the short stories published in Urdu all of last year.'

But Maulana Muhammad Khan's praise meant nothing. He praised everyone, and everything published in the *Dotard* was a masterpiece. If he praised some unlucky chap a few times, his literary career was certainly over, and it could be predicted that he would always remain a third-rate hack and never go much further. All the promising young men who were spotted by Maulana Muhammad Khan's trained eye and introduced to Urdu literature floundered immediately upon discovery. Maulana Muhammad Khan's distinguished pen sank many literary fortunes and his hyperbolic praise always proved to be the last eulogy on the unfortunate writers' literary lives. In the pages of the *Dotard* were buried many Urdu authors who had died before their birth, thanks to Maulana's messianic powers.

Chaudhry Ma'iraj Deen's *Falcon* was perhaps the oldest magazine of Urdu literature, besides *Bound.* It was as old as Chaudhry Ma'iraj Deen's ancestors; his great-grandfather had launched it. The most amazing thing about *Falcon* was that it hadn't changed its ways since its inception. *Shaheen*, since the time of the Mutiny, was like a dated, wretched, rich old man, still carrying on in his aristocratic ways and manners. Financially, no other Urdu magazine stood on such firm ground. This was the only Urdu magazine about which it could be said irrefutably that it has been published on time month after month and things will in all likelihood continue in the same way for the next one hundred years; and that the font used for its title, *The Falcon*, and that couplet right above it – All the nimble-footed ones caught up with the lovers / We were left spellbound by the bells of the caravan – will continue to agonize future generations. The special thing about *The Falcon* is its genteelness and blue-blooded attitude. You would never find anything in its pages that's 'uncivilized' – the heroes and heroines of its stories are utterly bereft of any bodily needs, they never curse, never take off their clothes or end up in bed together. All these things are uncivilized and *The Falcon* was a magazine that had not let go of civility. This seriousness, obstinacy, and these genteel attitudes had rendered *The Falcon* dry and unreadable for contemporary audiences. Not a single line in it depicted the tantalizations of life. It was like the embalmed mummy of a decrepit old man. Sometimes you desperately wanted the hero of one of its stories to seize the heroine, bite her neck and drag her out to the rice fields, but Chaudhry Ma'iraj Deen never allowed anyone to embark on such incivility and frivolousness.

While getting published in *Old Dotard* was synonymous with death at birth, having an article published in *Falcon* was like an act of admission by the author that he was an embalmed corpse that had been long dead, and was perhaps never born in the first place.

For Miyan Chiragh Deen, the pages of those two magazines were ever-ready to print him, but the top-flight modern literary magazines had all turned progressive. They were wary of his writings and tossed them out with the trash. Miyan Chiragh Deen, however, was a man of high ambition and wanted to establish a literary reputation for himself. With his natural perceptiveness and intelligence, he took stock of his circumstances and realized that if he continued on his old path and kept writing stories about drawing-room bourgeoisies, he would be buried comprehensively and comfortably in the pages of *The Falcon* and *Old Dotard*. He immediately decided that he would change from a conservative into a progressive. Earlier, he had published criticism against the Progressives for which they did not think well of him and they would have never forgiven him had he been even a little famous as a writer. Miyan Chiragh Deen was penitent and sought forgiveness. He visited the influential men of the Party, shed tears over the hideous crimes of his previous literary life and asked for pardon. He told them that the reality had finally dawned on him after he read a book of Maxim Gorky's short stories not too long ago, and that now whatever he wrote would be for the peasants and workers and against the bourgeois system.

Just as a snake sloughs off his old skin, Chaudhry Chiragh Deen Cheema shed his literary skin. At first, the Progressives weren't entirely convinced of his sincerity. To convince them of his earnestness he took some very extreme measures. His name still irked the Progressives as it was not a progressive name. He changed it to Razm Hinai. But he did not stop there. He adopted his new role with such enthusiasm and outward sincerity that gradually the fortress of mistrust that had risen against him in the hearts of the Progressives with his early essays, started to crumble. In their literary meetings, his speeches were the most cutting and vehement. During discussions, he offered acerbic criticisms of the 'bourgeoisness' of the essays that were read aloud. (There was never any doubt that he possessed a venomous tongue.) His essays, poems and stories started appearing in the Progressive magazines, and alongside would be his photos, where he was shown arm in arm with his comrades. He wrote satires on the bourgeois system – rambling caricatures that were silly and meaningless and which were not read by even the Progressives themselves. They were utterly bereft of a sense of humour. A famous Progressive once wrote a long essay in his own magazine, 'Razm Hinai – Our Greatest Satirist,' and Chaudhry Chiragh Deen Cheema finally felt that his struggles had not gone in vain and in the edifice of Urdu literature, he had found a permanent nook for himself.

Anyway, so when I saw this pioneer of the Progressives coming towards me, I quickly pulled Kattar in the other direction. I didn't want him to see Razm Hinai. Kattar's nerves are not well-disposed towards progressive writers. Upon their sight, his fists automatically clench, his face grows red, and all the symptoms of an epileptic fit suddenly make an appearance. As for me, I love progressives as much as I love conservatives or regressives. I collect all of them irrespective of their creed, looks or manners. In the palace of Muhammad Iqbal Changezi's heart, they are all equally near and dear.

Why the Progressives have this remarkable effect on Sheikh Qurban Ali Kattar, I don't know. As far as I know, Qurban Ali

Kattar, aside from a poem or two, has never read anything progressive. Despite this, a sense of rage and bigotry against them is rooted deep in his heart. He can sniff out a progressive like a hound sniffs out a rabbit. I think that beneath this hatred, the evil spirits of Qurban Ali Kattar's past and subconscious are at work. As I have suggested earlier, despite his tightfistedness and society's non-cooperation, he is a bourgeoisie at heart (and a ridiculous one at that). He has never given preference to any member of the proletariat over a bourgeois in anything. His experience has taught him that in times of need only the bourgeoisie can be of use, and only they can lend their shirts to someone.

Feeling nervous about the possibility of running into Razm Hinai again, I quickly took Qurban Ali Kattar to the upper floor of the coffee house in the corner. Due to an electricity failure, the coffee house people had placed a lit candle on each table and in the candlelight, the faces at the tables looked pale and ghostly, even though there was nothing ghostly about their voices. We sat at an empty table near a column and placed our order for coffee with the waiter named Muhammad Husain. Kattar was unusually quiet today and my attempts to engage him in conversation were in vain. Suddenly his face went pale and a trembling took over his fingers. I heard a faint clattering – *kat kat kat*. Looking straight at me, he said in a stammering voice, 'He – he has returned – Faghfur!'

'Where?' I said, a bit irritated. 'I don't see anything.'

'There …' he said, gesturing to his right with his eye. The moment I looked in that direction, my breath got stuck in my throat. To my right I found sitting that same progressive writer, Razm Hinai. I thought he had seen me and would now try to approach my table. But thanks to the dim candlelight he had not spotted me. I quickly snuffed out the candle at our table.

'What djinn, Kattar!' I shot at him. 'He's not a djinn. He's the famous progressive writer, Hinai.'

'No,' Kattar said. 'Not there. Look here, next to my foot, on the right.'

Next to his foot I found that dark black cat which was waiter Muhammad Husain's pet, and just about every patron of the coffee house had felt it purring and hugging his legs at one point or another. Sheikh Qurban Ali Kattar was seeing a djinn in this cat.

'That's a cat,' I said.

'Are you sure?' Kattar asked softly, his eyes fixed on me.

'Absolutely,' I said.

When the coffee came, Kattar, who usually took his time, slurped it up in a hurry and we went downstairs as soon as he was done. After that, we did not consider it safe or reasonable to roam around Elphinstone Street and took a Victoria straight to Kattar's flat on Corporation Street. I stayed with him till his senses were restored and Musafir joined us upstairs. And then I left him there and returned to Allah Tawakkul Bakery. I was greatly worried for my friend. God knows where that Professor Shahsawar Khan had disappeared. Only he could have shed light on Faghfur's bizarre modus operandi and remedy matters. 'In any case,' I thought, 'tomorrow I will discuss this case of neural disorder with Dr Ghareeb Muhammad.'

15

THE NEXT DAY AT THE HOTEL, I WAS DOWNSTAIRS, SITTING behind rows of bread loaves and cake jars; with my loincloth snug around my waist, I was getting an oil massage to the rhythms of a qawwali on Radio Pakistan. My heart was brimming with praise and gratitude for the performers on our radio station who had managed to transform poems by Iqbal into qawwalis – poems that no one could have ever imagined as qawwalis. If Iqbal was alive, I imagine this feat would certainly have pleased and gratified him. He probably wrote 'Pahar aur Gulahri' and 'Shikwa', 'Jawab-e Shikwa' and other masterpieces so that when he was dead, Bhalla Qawwal and companions could transform them into exhilarating qawwalis and broadcast them early in the morning on the radio. There are limits to human endurance and these radio people were testing one's patience and endurance to the utmost degree. It must be conceded though, that because of these qawwalis and na'ats, our country was now on its way to becoming the right kind of Islamic state, and that the radio management committee was vigorously laying the foundations for this, leaving no stone unturned in its devotion to the cause. As far as a certain man of this nation, Iqbal Husain Changezi, is concerned, he finds these qawwalis a fitting background music for his morning massages and physical exercise, and his heart is full of gratitude and praise for the radio performers.

A man entered. This man was Sheikh Qurban Ali Kattar. I was not expecting his visit because for the last three–four days his breakfast was being delivered to him at his flat in Corporation Street, and so Allah Tawakkul Bakery had been deprived of his sight. He was wearing my best shirt, a sight that sent knives hacking through my heart, and I signalled to the masseur to increase the vigour of the massage. But then, seeing his shrivelled face above the stiff collar and how sickly and ill he seemed, my anger dimmed. After all, he was no ordinary man. He was the author of *The Rogue Beauty* and *The Wretched Lover* and his creative capacities had not yet dried up: he still had to unveil his masterpiece, *Inspector Shahbaz Khan*, to the world (so I thought at the time).

With his emaciated body, and terror and madness lurking on his pale face, he seemed a lover in the grandest tradition of history's established lovers (Majnun, Farhad, etc.).

'Iqbal Changezi,' he said to me in a rueful voice. 'She has departed today.'

I was gripped with terror. We had not seen Razia for the past five–six days.

'What do you mean, Kattar!' I cried. 'She's not dead ...'

'Oh! No, no!' Kattar said. 'How could you even think such a thing? Even after reading so much literature, you don't know that she's eternal, indestructible, and cannot die? I meant she has left.'

I reflected for a while. 'So, you mean,' I asked eagerly, 'that she and her father have moved to some other house? That means their flat would be empty now. My friend Saljoti is very upset these days because he cannot find a flat. I think we should immediately take along three or four burly Makranis and raid the place ...' (In present-day Karachi, this is a tried and tested way of getting a house, and Chakiwara's Makranis have found a new profession ...)

'No, Iqbal Husain Changezi,' Kattar said in a subdued, alarmed manner. 'They have not left their house. Her father is still here. Only the girl, Razia, has been with her aunt in Hyderabad for the last four days. That is why we have not seen her, Changezi. I've heard that her aunt is extremely ill.'

'May she rest in peace.'

'No, she's only very ill. Her soul has not yet been released from its earthly abode, but hopefully soon ...'

'What has her aunt done to you??'

'Absolutely nothing,' he said. 'I have never seen that woman and perhaps, like all other aunts she's a very pious and God-fearing woman. But as you know, if Razia's aunt ... quickly – I mean if she stays ill for a long time, the desire of my forsaken heart – you know what I mean, right? She would not be able to return soon.'

'Where does her aunt live?' I asked.

'In Hyderabad, where else!' he replied as if it was the most obvious thing in the world. He probably thought he had already mentioned it. But with all that information, Sheikh Qurban Ali Kattar had astonished me: how did he find out all of a sudden that Razia had gone to her aunt in Hyderabad or that the aunt was extremely ill? It was quite possible that the first source of information, her cousin, had returned from Sukkur and told him. But then last night when I dropped him at his flat he did not know any of this.

'Did you dream this up? How did you find out all this?' I asked.

'Professor Shahsawar Khan mentioned it.'

'What! You mean he's returned from his tour?'

'Last night after you left, he met me in a dream,' Kattar said. 'You know he's a guardian saint and guardian saints often do this. He encouraged me in every way and delivered the good news that now my success is quite near and soon I shall be united with my beloved. The strangest thing was that he knew about the Faghfur episode and he said that he was surprised at Faghfur's inappropriate behaviour. He's assured me that he will speak to him personally and there is no reason for me to worry. Faghfur is a sociable kind of djinn. And then he told me that my beloved is visiting her aunt in Hyderabad for a few days, that the aunt is extremely ill, but Razia will return whenever I wish. After this he gave me his address and instructed me to immediately dispatch twenty-five rupees and eight aanas via money order to him. So one reason for my coming here is ...'

'I don't have twenty-five rupees,' I said quickly, sensing danger. 'You do know, Kattar, that there has been a sudden great slump in the bread business. Many major bakers in Karachi are committing suicide.'

'Really!' Kattar exclaimed cheerily. He is usually glad when he hears of other people's suicides.

'Yes!' I replied. 'Never before has such a horrific slump hit the bread market. Many people are simply refusing to eat bread and with all the bread being baked, the demand is for less than one-fourth of it. It's clearly an economic problem. The other day, when Haji Ali Muhammad Wali Muhammad, the most successful baker in Juna Bazaar, heard about the slump, he went down on his knees and crawled straight into his oven and was reduced to ashes.'

'Ohoo!' There was an element of understanding in Kattar's surprise.

'And the famous baker, Noor Husain Zahoor Husain, who is the President of Karachi's Association of Bakers, has gone insane due to shock. I saw him myself last afternoon on top of an electricity pole. In his hand he had the report of the Annual Conference of Bread Retailers and he was shouting to the passers-by, trying to convince them that the book has descended from the heavens.'

'Oh ho ho ho! It's definitely a horrific slump,' Kattar said, looking around the hotel. 'Thank God it hasn't affected you. Yes, so my friend Changezi, I'm sure you can spare twenty-five for charity. It doesn't seem reasonable to upset Professor Shahsawar Khan at such a crucial stage. The success of this venture depends largely upon his benevolence and goodwill.'

'What's his address?' I asked.

'Maulvi Abdul Samad the Most Learned, Spiritual Healer, Shikari Darwaza, Hyderabad.'

'Who is Maulvi Abdul Samad?'

'You know Professor Shahsawar Khan is Maulvi Abdul Samad in Hyderabad. Guardian saints change their names in different areas.'

'I didn't know that!' I said. 'So Professor is in Hyderabad these days. But yaar Kattar, if he needs the money why doesn't he ask Faghfur, etc. to arrange it for him?'

'Perhaps he wants to test me,' Kattar replied.

I reflected for a while. 'Are you sure he appeared in your dream?'

'Yes, Changezi yaar,' he said. 'He's a guardian saint.'

'Listen Kattar,' I explained to him. 'Give him a few more chances to appear in your dream. If you agree to his request the very first time, it's quite probable that he won't show his face again. Usually, the guardian-saint type of people appear three or four times in dreams.'

'Look Changezi,' he said. 'This matter is at its most delicate juncture. I fear that by doing this, we will ruin a matter that is decided and settled.'

'All right, I promise that if he instructs you again in your dream, I shall immediately arrange to have twenty-five rupees sent to him,' I said. 'Now tell me, how many days of practice have you had already?'

'Today is the last, that is the fifteenth day,' he said. 'From tomorrow I should be able to use the ring.'

'Meaning tomorrow your every wish will come true,' I said. 'Faghfur and his companions will be your slaves. Look, tomorrow when you start using the ring and when you plead in Hazrat Suleiman's court, your wish must be that your beloved be returned immediately from Hyderabad. That would help us find out if the magic ring is genuine, and if Professor Shahsawar Khan is a real guardian saint – if all this is true, Razia should return immediately. Even though, yaar Kattar, I am pretty sure that your beloved is not in Hyderabad.'

'How can you doubt it!' he said. 'It's a sin to doubt a guardian saint. Anyway, I will wait for you tomorrow at eight, and won't start using the ring until you come. I am a little scared of the thing.'

At around eleven, after Kattar had left, I was sitting in Allah Tawakkul Restaurant trying to win over a new literary personality. I had put myself in his service and was trying to ensure that his table didn't run short of the most delectable food and drink, and that this important literary personage's taste buds were satisfied to the maximum extent. This man was the famous revolutionary poet, Mr Shedad Pashmi (although he seemed more like a drenched cat yearning to be petted and caressed). I had found him an hour back standing next to the market's clock tower and brought him in with me when I recognized him from his photos in the Urdu magazines. Shedad Pashmi was a thin, timid man of little moustaches who appeared somewhat faint-hearted. He always had a silly and reluctant smile on his face. From his looks, you would never have guessed that he was the same writer whose fiery and caustic poems had caused a riot in Urdu literature between 1939 and 1945. Like Sheikh Qurban Ali Kattar, he too was now among the forgotten, although once upon a time he was the literary idol of young students and his name was on everyone's lips. Literature is an unfaithful and heartless patroness. Post 1946, after the British had departed, there wasn't much scope left for his type of passionate poetry and there was no one against whom he could use his razor-edged spears. That left him a little unhappy as a person. The only genre of poetry through which he could show off his talent and muscle with utter mastery was revolutionary poetry. Unlike Razm Hinai, he utterly lacked the ability to adapt himself to changing times and circumstances, and not only was Shedad Pashmi overlooked, he was also actively mocked. 'He writes nonsense,' it was said about him. But the fact is that he was quite talented and despite his dated ideas, there was true depth and poetic sensibility in some of his works. Some of his revolutionary poems as well as some of his love poems were far better than the modern 'streamlined' masterpieces, in terms of originality of content and narrative flow. But there was no doubt about the fact that Shedad Pashmi's name had been consigned to the forgotten shelves of Urdu literature and it was fast gathering cobwebs. His work was still featured occasionally in Maulana Muhammad Khan's *Fancies of the Old Dotard* and Maulana never showed meanness in bestowing praise, but most of the readers of *Dotard* were retired people. Maulana, instead of becoming the Grand Old Man of Urdu, had now become the Grand Old Clown of Urdu.

The life and times of Shedad Pashmi are beyond the scope of the present account, but still it could be said that he was one of those Urdu writers who never shied away even from the most menial jobs to eke out his living and who always earned his bread through sweat and blood. At the time he was writing his revolutionary poems and had become a renowned literary personality, he was often seen in a book-binding store in a nameless alley in Lahore. Whenever his more affluent friends patronizingly invited him for meals at a party or gathering, he always tried to excuse himself. And of course, as everybody knows, when his book-binding store flopped, he lugged bricks to earn his livelihood. He did this at a time when the literary world resounded with his name and he was considered among the top three poets of the era. He did not marry.

During the meal, the topic of our discussion was his golden days, and whenever he narrated a literary event from his life, he would start like this: 'When I used to run the book-binding shop on Qutb Road ...' or 'When I lifted the trunk at the station ...' He showed great interest in my restaurant and confided in me that once upon a time he had also planned to own a restaurant just like mine – calm and sparkling clean – but he was unable to do so due to lack of money. He did not exhibit even an iota of bitterness for being forgotten despite his literary prowess. When I mentioned Qurban Ali Kattar, his face lit up and he said, 'Kattar and Pashmi are two lions who died too soon.' He admitted to me that he had read almost all of Kattar's detective novels and had not still been able to shake off their spell. Later on, when he read the modern masterpieces by the progressives, he did not enjoy them even half as much as Kattar's detective novels. I promised him that I'd arrange a meeting between him and Kattar. Then he asked me a strange question: what does Kattar do for a living? It was strange because very few authors ask this question about another author as it is widely understood that they do nothing for a living and mostly depend upon the generosity of editors and the donations of their friends. I told him he was a clerk in an import office, but that now he was idle.

'Why don't you hire him for some job here in your hotel?' he asked plainly. And then, just as a by-the-by, he added, 'And since we are on the subject anyway, Mr Iqbal, do you require a table boy or someone who could wash dishes at the hotel? I have some experience in this line of work.'

When I finally understood what he meant, I was, in all honesty, utterly dumbfounded. Even though I myself am a strong advocate for respecting honest labour, I never expected that he, Shedad Pashmi, would offer to wash my plates. 'I am ready to join for thirty rupees a month and meals,' he said. 'I am fully trained in this profession.'

This idea was inconceivable for me. Shedad Pashmi washing plates in my hotel. His face showed signs of starvation and his request indicated that he had probably been in search of work for many days and had now reached the very limits of his forbearance. I argued with him that he could stay with me if he wanted and in the meanwhile look for work more suited to a man of his stature, like the editorship of some government literary magazine, and so on. But this was unacceptable to him. After the meal, he stood up, thanked me, and said he would pay the bill within a week when he found work. When I saw that he would agree to stay with me only on his own conditions, I reluctantly offered him to take charge of the kitchen. He said that even though he was a fine cook himself, he did not want another man fired so that a position could be made available for him. But when I explained that at this time we did not have a permanent cook, he agreed to take on the job and that too on his own terms: he would work for thirty-two rupees a month and meals.

Seeing his pale face glowing, I realized how intense his need must be. Then without preamble, he started gathering the plates and balancing them on his arms with an artistic ease, and said, 'Boss, you know, all this is the miracle of the ring!'

'Ring?' I exclaimed. 'What ring, Pashmi sahib? Professor Shahsawar's ring?'

'Yes,' he said. 'That's the one. It's been a month since I came to Karachi looking for a job. Fifteen days back when I had lost all hope, I saw a professor wearing a gown and selling that ring in one of the parks here in Chakiwara. Normally, I don't believe in such stuff but at that moment I was so wretchedly hopeless and Professor's words had so much truth in them that I bought the ring. Until now I have been practising with it for ten minutes every day and tomorrow is the day I should be able to use it. But the truth is that I was not expecting much from the ring and had gradually forgotten all about it when last night, while asleep on the MacLeod Road railway track, I saw that same man who sold me the ring. 'Go, son! Your difficulties are over,' he told me. 'Tomorrow, with Shahsawar Khan's blessings, you will find a job. And look, today, I have indeed found a job!'

You can imagine how befuddled I must have been after what Pashmi told me. Professor Shahsawar Khan did not strike me as a mere con-artist and swindler fakir anymore; he now seemed to be someone who possessed incredible supernatural powers. Pashmi was definitely speaking the truth because there was no reason for him to lie. But an even more amazing disclosure awaited me.

'Iqbal sahib,' Pashmi said, somewhat apologetically. 'I am sorry but I have a request which might seem unusual and illegitimate, but can you give me a month's salary in advance?'

'Yes, why not! You may take however much you want.'

'Actually, the thing is,' Pashmi continued, 'the professor also instructed me that as soon as I found a job, I should send him twenty rupees and eight aanas via money order to his address.'

'He said that to you as well!' I was stunned.

'You know, Iqbal sahib,' he said, 'I don't wish to upset him after all he has done for me.'

'No,' I said, reflecting upon something else now. I asked finally, 'What's the address he gave you?'

'He told me his address twice or thrice – I remember it well: Doctor of Spiritual Maladies, Maulvi Abdul Samad, adjacent to Shikari Darwaza, Hyderabad, Sindh.'

As I pulled out thirty rupees from the cash box to hand over to my anxious cook, I swear I did not know if I stood on my head or on my limbs. It was as if the world had flipped over and Professor Shahsawar Khan (or Maulvi Abdul Samad) was hovering in the air like a giant demon, amidst the constellation of his stars, Faghfur and company.

16

THAT EVENING WHEN I WENT TO SEE KATTAR ON Corporation Street, I saw a famous and familiar face standing at the stairs of the butcher's flat wearing a loose dark suit and an ancient pith helmet. This was Dr Ghareeb Muhammad. In his hand he held an attaché case that contained medicines and around his neck he wore a rubber tube like a necklace which, in medical terminology, is known as a stethoscope. Dr Ghareeb Muhammad is among my dearest friends and one could write an entire book about him. Chakiwara's medical history begins with the advent of Dr Ghareeb Muhammad. He's the grand messiah of Chakiwara. Dr Ghareeb Muhammad (many years before he descended upon Chakiwara) was a land registrar in a village in the state of Bahawalpur. That's where he gained his very first experiences in the field of medicine and his first patients were the peasants. How and under what circumstances he descended upon Chakiwara, that part of his life is somewhat shrouded in darkness. Dr Ghareeb Muhammad himself is a bit restrained about that part of his life (usually, when it comes to speech, the word 'restrained' does not apply to him).

In 1934 – he must have been a young man of twenty-eight then – he started his clinic, which he decorated with second-hand vials bought from junk-sellers, in which he kept his lizards, frogs and herbs. In those days you could find Sanda lizards crawling up the legs of his customers and many women used to faint from fear. He also had some luck with spiritual afflictions and was especially good at warding off djinns that would trouble women. (He used to charge two and a half rupees per djinn – but then, those were the easy days.) He was a smooth-talker and a smart man and quite well-versed in the art of subduing the uneducated, illiterate class of people. He made a name for himself as an expert on women's illnesses and made quite a lot of money. Many residents of Chakiwara came into this world through his hands. After the war of 1947, he bought a bigger and better shop on Middleway Street, one of Chakiwara's more gentrified areas. He kept revising his ways gradually to keep up with the changing times and circumstances and, while he had not lost his conviction in the effectiveness of lizards and Sandas, in order to satisfy his middle-class customers, he started keeping Western medicines as well. He put up a large board outside his shop:

Dr Ghareeb Muhammad

V. G. M. O. T

Expert in Diseases

Esp. Women's and Men's Sexual Health

Spiritual Illnesses are also treated here

No one ever felt the need to investigate what V. G. M. O. T stood for. Even now, very few in Chakiwara know whether Dr Ghareeb Muhammad really is a certified or qualified doctor. Chakiwara is a truly autonomous state where anyone can pass themselves off as anything. Dr Ghareeb Muhammad was lucky when it came to his wife (she has recently eloped with a Makrani and left him lonely and desolate), who, being a good and experienced nurse, proved extremely useful during the early days of his practice on Middleway Street.

Bringing in the new English medicines was good for the doctor financially but not so good for his patients – now their lives were in much greater danger. He confessed to me several times that he felt far more confident administering cures through lizards and frogs instead of these new patented medications. But the trouble was that the modern patient had become somewhat intolerant towards those old concoctions. I can demonstrate with figures and statistics that Dr Ghareeb Muhammad had no small role in populating the graveyard just across the promenade. It would happen often enough that he'd step out of his patient's house after administering his prescription and would be just turning the corner of the lane when the patient reached his Creator.

His stethoscope had its own history. He had bought it from a junk shop. The tube had two holes in it and the metal piece was half-rotten and rusty. He admitted to me that when he had first bought it he heard noises (*Shoon! Sharakh! Sharap!*) when he put it to his ears. Those noises stopped a long time ago, but since they did not mean anything to the doctor in the first place, it really made no difference to him. He confessed to me that personally he had no confidence in that thing but he had never found a better device to command the obedience of his patients.

Dr Ghareeb Muhammad has visited many homes in Chakiwara as the harbinger of the angel of death. Despite this,

Chakiwarans have a childlike faith in him and rather than take anyone else's tablets, they prefer to take their lives with Ghareeb Muhammad's pills.

I was struck when I saw Ghareeb Muhammad standing outside the butcher's flat because when a resident of Chakiwara agrees to call in a doctor – and if that doctor is Dr Ghareeb Muhammad – then it could be said with great certainty that the man is very badly off. Someone in the butcher's flat was extremely ill. Was it the butcher himself? I greeted the doctor.

'So, Doctor! How come you are here?'

'I was going upstairs to examine Umar the butcher. I stopped when I saw you.'

'Who is Umar the butcher?'

'That same guy, bhai, the Lee Market butcher! He seems a bit too ill. Just now one of his men came to summon me. But Iqbal sahib, the problem is that people call on Ghareeb Muhammad when the water has already risen over the head. Oh yes, Iqbal sahib, do you know the sub-inspector at the city police station?'

I thought he must have been in some trouble with the police for his self-awarded medical degrees. But the matter wasn't so serious. Last evening, some rogues had taken off with his buffalo from its stall (yes, it is still possible to keep a private buffalo in Chakiwara), and he wanted me to speak to the sub-inspector to retrieve his buffalo from the thieves. I promised him that I would try my best.

'The absence of the buffalo is causing me a lot of pain,' he said. 'With the state of Karachi's air, no man can maintain his manhood without pure buffalo milk – how is your throat now?'

When I met him four days back, my throat had been hurting due to excessive smoking and I had taken medicines at his insistence. I was forced to buy a dozen disgusting and suspicious-looking white tablets at the rate of four aanas per tablet. I told him it was perfectly all right. But he insisted that I should open my mouth and show him the throat. He shone a torch down my throat to examine it and then shook his head.

'It's not healed completely. It's still a bit swollen,' he said. 'Come to my shop tomorrow. I will give you another dozen Quinsy pills. All right, Iqbal sahib, I'll go check on Umar now.'

That is when it occurred to me that now that the butcher and I were friends, it was my obligation to go and ask after him. He could be very ill. Perhaps this way I might be able to glean some news of Razia as well, and if she was around I might get a glimpse of her, too. I told the doctor that I wanted to see Umar the butcher too and went upstairs with him.

A scrub-like relative of the butcher opened the door for us. In front of us, on the charpoy next to the wall, a fat, unconscious thing was lying flat on its back. It had a hideous, shiver-inducing face. I trembled. The face smelled of death. When I went near it, I saw the repulsive, horrific thing that the Makrani butcher had turned into. His face had mutilated him into a grotesque-looking thing. When I saw him in his shop in Lee Market the other day making mincemeat of some goat, I could not have imagined that just ten days later he'd be wrapped in blankets and bandages transformed into this thing lying in front of me.

He opened his eyes when we came near – he was conscious. His pale eyes glimmered with a hint of recognition and he tried to lift himself on his elbows but Dr Ghareeb Muhammad forced him to lie down again. His face and legs were all swollen, as if someone had pumped air into them, and his distended body was having an eerie effect on me. He continually moaned and smacked his head here and there. How pathetic he looked then, how dreadful!

While the doctor was busy placing the stethoscope on him and uttering meaningless reassurances, I looked around that room of death. There was a carpet on the floor and a little cupboard in the corner on which there was a radio. There were a few Urdu books in it as well. Two or three titles by S. M. Jalal, and one or two collections of romances by Maj. Rafiq Ahmad. Those days these two writers were the rage among girls, and educated girls everywhere found the fulfilment of their dreams in those pages. These were most certainly Razia's books. In the corner, a three-legged table was covered with a flower-embroidered tablecloth – on its edges, in between flowers and birds sat a little Taj Mahal. On the wall in front of us hung a framed painting by some Western artist, in which many imps frolicked among flowers in bloom. Razia's touch was everywhere, and this was clearly not a butcher's room; it could be the room of any good, well-to-do, educated family.

Umar was unable to speak. He would try to speak but soon he would begin pointing to his throat. Once he grabbed my hand and squeezed it to express his delight on seeing me. The scrub-looking relative took the doctor aside and I heard them speak to each other in low voices. At one point the relative said, 'His daughter Razia has gone to Hyderabad. Should I inform her via telegraph?' And once I heard Dr Ghareeb Muhammad say, 'It's a swelling. I am prescribing a balm, which you may apply to the affected area. If God wills, it shall be all right. There is nothing to worry about.' From this I gathered that the information about Razia's departure for Hyderabad was indeed correct and everything that Professor Shahsawar Khan had told

Kattar about his beloved was true as well. I started believing in the powers of guardian saints ...

In another half hour, Dr Ghareeb Muhammad and I left the butcher with his relative and went downstairs, and the first thing that the doctor uttered when we were out in the alley was, 'Iqbal sahib! Please do get that buffalo recovered from the thieves. I bought it last month for three hundred rupees. You have the influence and all ...' But while standing in the alley reassuring the doctor, a sound reached my ears – the sound of wings flapping in front of Umar's house – the Angel of Death was fluttering around his place.

A little disappointed and scared, I shot out from there, and without meeting Kattar, ran through the bazaar and went straight into the sanctuary of Allah Tawakkul Restaurant.

17

THE NEXT DAY WAS EXTREMELY BUSY FOR ME. I HAD TO PUT in the applications for raw sugar and flour permits at the Ration Office, and half of my day got spent there. In my absence, Sheikh Qurban Ali Kattar had dropped in at the bakery and left a message with Shedad Pashmi.

'Sheikh Qurban Ali Kattar called upon you in your absence,' he said in a completely diffident manner, placing food on my table. 'And he said that today was the day for putting it into action and that you should try to reach his residence a little early in the evening because he wants to discuss a few important things with you.'

'Good,' I said. I was happy that this era's two major pillars of Urdu had finally met, probably for the first time. To learn about Pashmi's first impressions, I asked, 'Did you two have a conversation?'

'I told him that I am Shedad Pashmi but he seemed utterly clueless. He hadn't even heard my name.'

'Sheikh Qurban Ali Kattar is a bit absent-minded these days. He is burdened by some serious matters.'

'It seemed to me that his liver was not all right,' he said with an affectionate curiosity.

I wanted to tell Pashmi that aside from his liver, there were many other things about Sheikh Qurban Ali that were utterly useless and rotten. But by then, a few customers had come into the restaurant and Pashmi excused himself to attend to them. He remained busy until evening. He seemed to be very thorough and competent at his new job, almost as if he had spent his life washing dishes and cooking food. My business partner said to me that we were fortunate to find such a man. Very few literary men are able to turn themselves into cooks.

In the evening around seven, I was on Middleway Street. The alley was drenched in twilight, almost deserted at this hour. There were moments when I was the only one walking on the flat brick surface; I shared the road with only a few skinny dogs. From the distance, Kattar's building, with its outstretched arm holding a lantern, and the three-storied building across from it, where Razia's father, the Lee Market butcher, lay dying, seemed ghostly, like enormous cubes of stone cutting each other obliquely at their bases while trying to conjoin at the peaks. An old woman in a flowery cloak passed by and threw me a malicious glance from the corner of her eyes. There was a cat was behind her. She was an evil witch or some kind of sorceress – who knows. On the stairs of the butcher's flat stood two or three men with long hair. Their faces looked yellow under the light of the shop and their manners were like those of vultures and phantoms.

Perhaps my dear reader is thinking that I am now trying to employ the cheap tricks used in ghost stories to create an air of suspense. I want to assure him that I have never had any such intention during the writing of this chronicle. I am merely trying to recreate that feeling that Middleway Street had on me – and many things could have played a part in this: the dying butcher, the first experiment with the magic ring, Professor

Shahsawar Khan's awesome and demonic powers – and I had a lot of evidence now that told me they were for real. But I still feel that on that evening, Middleway Street had an eerie atmosphere, something that I could not place my finger on. Often it happens that familiar things put on an invisible garb and cease to appear real anymore, and I am sure, dear reader, if you are the kind of person that I imagine you to be, you too must have experienced moments when objects shed their earthly, material clothes and stood stark naked before you.

Kattar opened the door when I knocked. I saw a certain unease and fear in his eyes. His face was even paler than before. But he looked so clean and dressed up – I had never seen him like that before. It seemed that he had taken a bath today, or at least washed his face and hair with soap. He had oiled and combed his hair too; there were also signs that he had attempted to part his hair. He had shaved, too. He was wearing my blue suit and my best American tie that had a woman's face printed on it. 'Stop!' is the word that could have been applied to him at that moment.

'Changezi, yaar! You're a little late,' he said, spreading himself on his armchair. 'What's the time now?'

'My watch is on your wrist,' I reminded him.

'It's eight-thirty,' he said, putting Musafir in his lap. 'I will start working on the ring at nine. I still haven't chosen the words I'll use to plead my case in Hazrat Suleiman's court. That's why I wanted you to come early; you are good at drafting and so on.'

In a moment of astonishing generosity, he took out a packet of King Start and presented me with a cigarette, after which he quickly put the packet back into his pocket. In our three years of friendship this was the first time Sheikh Qurban Ali Kattar had offered me a cigarette, and this last act of his showed how amenable he was feeling towards me and how desperate he was for my co-operation.

Another strange thing about Sheikh Kattar is that while he can write two- to three-hundred-page-long tumultuous romances without any difficulty or mental exertion, it is an onerous task for him to write a simple letter using correct and reasonable language. During such times, his face started to show signs of extreme pain, and the prolific machinery of his brain that has chiselled black-faced characters for Urdu literature like Imam Bakhsh and Noor Husain and constructed a vast and mind-boggling maze of tunnels for his readers, his flowing pen, which never ceased even for a moment while pursuing Pir Noor Husain's romantic exploits, absolutely refused to stir. He seldom wrote letters and the few times he was compelled to write them (when, for instance, he wrote a letter congratulating his uncle on the birth of a son, or twice or thrice when he wrote to various firms with job applications) I helped him prepare the text. He not only had problems choosing salutations for his various relatives and firm managers (he once began a letter like this: Your Holiness, Respected Sir, May the Most Exalted Allah protect you ...) but was also unable to select appropriate words to express himself. At such times, he was forced to seek help from Iqbal Husain Changezi.

We spent fifteen minutes debating just the form of the plea that Qurban Ali Kattar was going to present in Hazrat Suleiman's court. How would he address Hazrat Suleiman and what salutations would be suitable?

'For the address, I think, the English salutation, Your Gracious Majesty, would work well, because Hazrat

Suleiman is the emperor of djinns,' I suggested. Kattar seemed a bit sceptical.

'Changezi, yaar! I don't think Hazrat Suleiman or the djinns can understand English. It is quite plausible that they will take the English greeting badly and consider it insolent.'

'Pha! What are you talking about!' I said. 'Hazrat Suleiman can't understand English? He could even understand the language of the birds. And besides, English has now become a universal language. I am pretty sure that many djinns and their likes will have command over it. And it's quite possible that it is even the official language there.'

Like an intelligent man, Kattar accepted the soundness of my argument.

'But,' he said. 'I am not sure if he should be addressed as Your Majesty or Your Excellency.'

'Why Your Excellency?'

'It's quite possible that the Realm of Djinns is a democracy, a republic.'

'What do you mean?'

'Being a Muslim, Hazrat Suleiman's position would be that of President in a democracy, and for a president, 'Your Excellency' is the most appropriate salutation.'

This time I bowed to his argument.

After settling the manner of address, I immediately started drafting a letter consisting of the said plea on the flyleaf of the *Oxford Dictionary* in Urdu. Kattar's English was quite unreliable.

'Your Excellency,' I wrote and then started chewing the nib of my pen. Really, this wasn't an easy task. Then, I began to rapidly jot down whatever came to my mind:

'Your Excellency, if this worthless subject, Qurban Ali Kattar, is assured the safety of his life, he would like to present his heart's plea: as Your Excellency might already be aware, this humble man's beloved lives in the opposite flat, and he is wasting away due to this separation. Your Excellency might also know that she is the daughter of Umar the butcher and has recently gone to visit her aunt in Hyderabad. In these last six or seven days, the pining eyes of her humble lover haven't beheld her. At the moment, this menial servant has just this one request: please order Faghfur or some other suitable djinn in charge of this department to immediately make arrangements for Razia's return right away, at this very minute.'

Kattar wasn't sure if the plea was exactly as it ought to have been, but since he did not have anything better to offer, he accepted it. He only suggested one change that after Hyderabad we add the word 'Sindh' so that it could be distinguished from Hyderabad Deccan. He thought that some mischievous djinns, upon finding such loopholes in their orders, acted in ways that ostensibly fulfilled the order, but actually twisted the outcome. If Sindh wasn't mentioned, it was possible that some other Razia would return from Hyderabad Deccan. I added Sindh after Hyderabad.

It was almost nine now. Sheikh Qurban Ali went out of the room for his ablutions before prayers and I started staring out at the butcher's balcony. Behind the dark curtains, the butcher must have been rotting and groaning in his room as he ailed from that dreadful illness. His few scrub-like relatives would be hovering around him like vultures – I suddenly felt my head swimming. I immediately hushed away that scene of death from my eyes and thought about the ring. I could not laugh at it or its inventor anymore. Would Razia really return? Are these things even possible in the twentieth century? Spirituality is one thing that has always stupefied me and about which I have never been able to come to a decision ...

Kattar had returned after the ablutions. He cheerfully spread his bedsheet on the floor and sat down, humbly facing Mecca. I sat cross-legged in front of him and opened the *Oxford Dictionary* to the page of the petition so that he may read from it. Kattar, after signalling to me to be quiet, took out the magic ring from his pocket, wiped its stone with my tie and held it between his thumb and index finger in a way that the stone was about five inches from his eyes. He instructed me once again not to interrupt him and started gazing into the stone on the ring. The practice of the last fifteen days came good and his eyes, sunken and deep, bored into the stone like two drills. I confess I was in a restless state: I kept looking expectantly at Kattar's face. But five minutes passed and nothing happened.

Professor Shahsawar Khan was a wicked impostor after all. A fraudster, like all the rest of his brothers.

Sheikh Qurban Ali's lips were moving. He was beginning to see things inside the stone.

'Call in Khakrob,' he ordered someone inside the stone, most likely Faghfur. Then he – possibly for my benefit and to convince himself of his observations – started to rapidly narrate everything he saw in the stone. His commentary was a bit like Radio Pakistan's 'running commentary' in which the commentator rewards you with remarks like these: 'Now the Prime Minister has disembarked from the plane. General Dilawar Khan salutes the Prime Minister. Now the Prime Minister is leaving for the guard of honour, walking in between General Dilawar Khan and Governor Bahadur. He's dropped his baton. Now General Dilawar Khan is lifting it from the ground and giving it to him. General Dilawar Khan has bent down. He has succeeded in picking up the baton and is now presenting it to the Prime Minister with a salute. Now the Prime Minister along with five others, is moving towards the place where I am standing ...,' etcetera, etcetera.

Sheikh Qurban Ali Kattar's running commentary went something like this: 'Saqqay! Spray some water! Now Saqqa is spraying water. Now four chamberlains are walking in with carpets. Come on, spread the carpets, all of you, spread the carpets! Carpets are being spread. One chamberlain is looking at me. His face resembles that milkman's who delivers milk here. On the far corner a throne is being set up. A short djinn is placing a golden chair on the throne – Faghfur! That's definitely Faghfur. Now he's turned to look at me; he's smiling. A number of people in royal robes and holding staffs are gathering around the throne. There are some animals as well: a lion walking on his two hind legs is coming towards me; he's wiping his tears with his tail. Why, Lion? Why are you crying?' A couple of minutes later ... 'Baboons standing near the throne are exchanging their views on something ...'

Out of sheer bewilderment I got up and tried to look into the stone from over Kattar's shoulder. Sadly, it was just a stone to me.

'Someone is blowing the trumpet. People have taken their places. All the animals are in their respective positions. I am looking at the lion again who is now walking on all fours. There are birds too. A dove has turned to look at me. *Ghoo ghoo ghoo!* Little dovey! *Ghoo ghoo!* The mace-bearers in strange lustrous clothes are now coming in. Just behind the crowd is a man wearing a gold crown and a splendid robe. That man has now seated himself on the silver chair atop the silver throne with his face towards me. This is Hazrat Suleiman. The lion is once again standing on his hind legs and is wiping his tears with his tail. Looks like he's a condemned djinn. Hazrat Suleiman is looking towards me. Now I am about to present my plea. Raise the book a bit ...'

I lifted the book up to his line of vision and he began reading the plea in a trembling, shivering voice: 'Holiness – errr ... Your Excellency ...' and all the way to the end. Now he turned to look back into the stone. 'There's nothing here now! Your Excellency! Your Excellency!'

In the alley, we heard the clattering of hooves and the sound of a Victoria suddenly halting. Kattar also heard it. We looked at each other – we were thinking the same thing. Kattar stood up, pocketing the ring, and we dashed towards the balcony. Downstairs, a Victoria was parked right in front of the butcher's flat – one of Chakiwara's trashiest and most detested carriages. Its two burning lanterns were casting a ghostly yellow effect on the dark alley. Between the lanterns, inside the coach box, sat a short, extremely pale-faced man with swollen temples. His face reflected an unearthly green light and appeared twisted. For a moment, just for a moment, I felt his eyes were raised upwards. In a fit of fear and panic, Kattar brought his hand forward and firmly grabbed my arm. He wanted to tell me that the coach driver's eyes were raised, but terror (or nervousness) had robbed him of his powers of speech.

Two women in white burqas stepped out from the other side of the Victoria. One of them was exactly Razia's height and stature. The next moment she was standing in front of the lantern, her glowing white fingers drawing out the money from her purse; she lifted her veil and – ah, it was that white goddess! It was Razia!

The other woman was shorter and relatively broader. I found out later that this was the same Hyderabadi aunt of hers. Both the women climbed up the stairs and their scrub-like relative brought their luggage after them (the same relative I saw hovering around Umar the other day).

I could even recognize the Victoria driver now. I had seen him many times steering his rickety carriage around various places in Chakiwara for meaningless chores. He was a familiar face in Chakiwara but I had never dared to ride his broken carriage – partly due to the ghastly look of his car and partly due to the man's loathsome face. In such a carriage anything could happen to anybody – one's throat could be slit at the corner of the alley or one could get robbed. But I was thoroughly amazed by the miracle. The ring wasn't a hoax, Professor Shahsawar Khan wasn't a hoax. I was staggered by this immediate dramatic fulfilment of a desire.

The Victoria turned around to go back through the alley. Sheikh Qurban Ali Kattar gave me a triumphant and boastful look, which I did not appreciate. This was the look of a madman – of someone bewitched, a man not of this world anymore.

'She's returned! She's returned!' he cried. 'Didn't I tell you Shahsawar Khan's invention is going to solve all problems! He is the king of all real guardian saints. Tomorrow –'

All of a sudden we heard the bloodcurdling wails of women coming from the flat across the street – wails that confirmed someone's death in the house. My heart was jolted and an unknown voice chanted in my ears: 'The butcher is dead! The butcher is dead! The butcher is dead!' Human ears cannot falter when it comes to death. I went out to the balcony. They had opened their balcony door and I could see into the brightly lit room through the holes of the tattered curtain: a white-faced female on her knees, bent over a body lying on the charpoy. Ah, poor, poor Razia – all hiccups and sobs. In that room two or three other people were walking about, their gait deathly.

'What's all the crying for?' Sheikh Qurban Ali Kattar asked, coming up near me on the balcony. I had not told him anything about Razia's father's illness.

'Razia's father has passed away,' I told him.

He looked at me with a wrathful expression, as if I was joking. No matter how much he loathed her beloved's father, he could never have wished him dead.

'You are joking … but this wailing, it's coming from Razia's flat, right?'

I explained that I was not and clarified that her father had been suffering from stomach cancer for a long time now and yesterday when I had gone to ask after him, his condition was extremely sensitive and critical, and his relative was thinking about calling Razia back via telegram.

He turned quiet for a while and stood watching the rectangular room behind the tattered curtains.

'Razia must be greatly aggrieved, Changezi, yaar,' he said. 'What do you think? Should we do something?'

'We can participate in the funeral in the morning,' I said companionably. 'This is what we can do.' And then I turned back to go into the room. I was wiping the tears that had welled up in my eyes. I might be finnicky and sceptical but I have the heart of a delicate woman.

18

THAT NIGHT I DIDN'T SLEEP FOR A MOMENT. MAKRANI UMAR was nothing more than an ordinary acquaintance to me but his death caused me quite a lot of grief. I saw him standing near his shop in Lee Market – big, burly and gargantuan. And then I saw him on Middleway Street lying on his charpoy – swollen, inflated, disgusting human pulp. Tomorrow he will be lying in Chakiwara's graveyard ten feet below the ground. I will never see him again. And I found myself worrying about his financial state: did he leave behind enough money for Razia? Who would look after her now? That same sieve-faced, thief-like relative that I saw that evening next to Umar? Even that evening I did not find his looks and mannerisms particularly appealing. He seemed to be one of those relatives who never show their faces all your life but as soon as you are on your deathbed they are always by your side finding ways to accelerate your end. Razia must be saved from that man – but why was I so worried? After all, Umar was just a coincidental acquaintance of mine whom I'd met only three times.

The next morning I got ready before the first light and took along Shedad Pashmi to the deceased's house on Middleway Street. The mourners had not assembled yet; in fact, it was very early. I walked up and knocked on the door. That same relative opened the door. I said I was a friend of the deceased and had come to offer my help with the burial arrangements. He gave me a revolting look as if he did not understand what I meant. But then a female voice came from inside the house, 'Come in, son, come inside. Razia, my darling, please go in to the other room.' The relative still did not give us any room but we squeezed in from the side anyway. The dead butcher was lying on the charpoy. He was wrapped in a white sheet. A middle-aged woman who, despite being forty, still looked gracefully beautiful and whose sharp features reminded me of Razia, gave us a brief account of his death and said, crying, 'My son, when Umar was alive, my Razia lived like a queen. Umar also sent me fifty rupees every month in Hyderabad. Now we are destroyed.' But immediately she returned to the important matters that still needed to be resolved.

Razia was in the other room, behind the curtains. Once I did find her swollen eyes peeping in from behind the curtains, but when I looked again, I saw only the waving and rustling curtains. We took instructions from the old aunt. (Her practical sense was equal to fifty Sheikh Qurban Ali Kattars.) We left to make the burial arrangements. For the incoming mourners, we spread a straw mat in the verandah of the neighbouring house, and I instructed the sieve-faced relative to sit there with them. I sent Shedad Pashmi to the promenade graveyard to get a grave ready. (He told me he had also been a gravedigger for some time.) As for myself, I rushed to arrange for someone to bathe the corpse and stitch the shroud. The graveyard was four miles from here and funeral arrangements had to be made as well.

And then I made some astonishing discoveries. In this city, it is not easy to bury someone. In this city of two million there are neither washers for bodies nor tailors for shrouds – at the very least, it is impossible to find out where you could find them. However, there are a few co-operatives which make arrangements to dispatch the dead to their rightful place. For instance, there is Memon Funeral Society that is responsible for burying only Memons; Sheikh Mourners Society which makes arrangements only for Sheikhs; Bohri Mourners Society which washes and buries only the Bohris. There are many other societies, but they are for members only and they don't touch anyone except for their community members. I never knew these astonishing facts. Nonetheless, there was a lot of running around, but the general secretary of the Memon Funeral Society on being paid an advance of sixty rupees, sent along a truck, two maulvis and a washer with me. The secretary, however, clarified that the Society didn't allow such violations of its policies. (Their total bill of one hundred and thirty rupees was presented to me after the funeral.)

In short, we took the coffin of the deceased in our truck around eleven to the promenade graveyard, where we buried it forever. All the butchers of Lee Market participated in Umar's funeral and the number of mourners was quite large, and there were a few who actually looked sad as well, as if it was a personal loss for them.

It was a Friday when Razia's father left his lovely daughter all alone in the world and went away to settle in the promenade graveyard. That very night, Qurban Ali Kattar in his dream met Professor Shahsawar Khan on a white steed. He told Kattar that he (Shahsawar) was responsible for removing that thorn that was the butcher, which had been a hindrance in his path, and now (inshallah), there was no reason for him to not be united with his beloved. He also reminded Kattar that he still hadn't received the money order of twenty-five rupees and eight aanas.

19

In order to relate the events of the next twelve days, all of which are directly related to this romance, I'll have to shut my detailed chronicle, otherwise this story will never end. As long as that chronicle is on my writing desk, I cannot resist the temptation to refer to it (and copy its pages word for word). I lack any knack for selectivity. And personally speaking, I don't give a toss about W. Shakespeare's axiom that a narrative's vitality lies in its conciseness. But a friend of mine who has read these pages, is of the opinion that there are many dangers in this expansive manner of writing. He says it is poor art to write irrelevant details, and there is also a possibility of the romance's real aim getting obscured. Perhaps he's right. I don't know. Keeping his advice in mind (because he's an intelligent, refined man, and knows all about art), I will completely ignore the chronicle. I will write down a summary of the events of the next four days from memory alone, and will refer back to the chronicle only for the last chapter. That's why all that material which is spread over two hundred pages in my chronicle has been presented here in three or four – shutting a river in a jug, as the saying goes.

When Kattar asked again for a loan of twenty-five rupees and eight aanas so that he could carry out Professor's orders and dispatch him the money order, I convinced him with great difficulty to wait for the professor to appear a third time in his dream, and that if he still insisted on sending the money order then I would give him the money. Kattar, as usual, swore on our true friendship and pointed out that just for a few paltry pieces of silver I was obstinately putting off this matter which should have been all settled and done with. But I paid no heed to his complaint. The thing was that, at the time my own economic state wasn't too sound, and I was really unable to give him the money.

I don't claim to know what goes on in people's hearts but I think I was able to correctly guess the kind of ideas that took shape in Sheikh Qurban Ali's head, or rather, his subconscious. On the surface, he always expressed sorrow and distress at the death of Razia's father but in reality he felt in his heart a lively satisfaction and happiness at his demise. The butcher always seemed to him an enormous obstacle in his path to success, and just the thought of him was enough to give him cold shivers at night. Now that this major obstacle had been removed from his path (Professor Shahsawar Khan also felt the same way, that the butcher's existence was an impediment), the road (at whose end Razia could be seen standing) was now clear and comfortable for travelling. Due to the miracle of the ring he had become intrepid, and his self-confidence had increased. He also drew courage from the fact that he was not alone in this journey and that Professor Shahsawar Khan was personally striving for him too.

As far as the removal of the obstacle was concerned, in my view, things had not improved. After Umar's death, Razia's aunt had taken everything into her own hands. She was a wise, worldly and practical-minded woman and during those days I met her quite a few times (without Kattar's knowledge). She called me her son and felt affectionately towards me. When Razia was in the other room (curtains rustling and undulating like waves), she openly discussed the deceased man's financial and familial affairs like one would do with a close relative. It was during those discussions that I discovered that the sieve-faced relative was the son of the butcher's late brother who had earlier seized all of his dead father's family property and was now after the deceased butcher's Lee Market shop. And note his audacity: he had even asked the aunt for Razia's hand!

'I told him to go look at his face in the mirror – my Razia was not born for beasts like you.'

I helped Razia's aunt resolve the difficulties she was having at home. Umar the butcher, being a generous and open-fisted fellow, always ate and drank liberally. Whatever little he had saved had been spent on his treatment and in preparing Razia's dowry. (Here the aunt gave me a meaningful look.) She was having a lot of trouble meeting the household expenses. On her request I arranged to sell the deceased's shop at a reasonable price. I was at their house when that leech of a relative was shown the door for the last time.

The devotees of Freud will say that I showed such affectionate sympathy for that middle-aged woman and ran about to resolve their household problems because for me Razia held intense attraction – sexual attraction, in Freudian terminology – and they are probably correct. It's quite possible that I subconsciously harboured such a desire but was not aware of it. But yes, when I used to go and knock on her aunt's door, my heart would start pounding and a hot wave would begin to surge through my body. Often during discussions, when her aunt would mention Razia, I would blush and become confused.

Once it so happened that to amuse myself, I started browsing through the books in the corner cupboard. I did so partly because it was an old habit and also because I wanted to know what Razia's taste in reading was like. Among her books I found Kattar's 1941 novel, *The Exemplary Bat* – one of his less popular books, out of print these days. Razia must have bought it four years ago from some bookstall at a train station. The book's cover had a picture – one that was quite similar to all other covers of Kattar's books – that was extremely ugly and tasteless. I can use the word 'vulgar' to describe it, although it was not vulgar in the ordinary sense of the word. No, the beauty in the picture was not naked; yes, you could see the bulge of her breasts and her skirt was torn above her thighs – but no, she wasn't naked. She was a woman with rather plump and voluptuous features and she was sitting upon the boundary wall of a fountain in an artificial garden of extremely tacky colours, looking longingly upon an enormous bat suspended vertically in the air, above her head. This was the exemplary bat ...

All the covers of Kattar's novels are like that – tawdry and ugly and vulgar, and while the contents inside deserved such covers, Kattar did not have any hand in their design. Nonetheless, as far as I know, he has never taken any note of their tackiness and, in fact, has always found them attractive and artistic.

I have not read *The Exemplary Bat* but I don't think it would be too different from Kattar's fifty other novels. Dear reader, you probably think that Razia must be an ordinary, tasteless girl for reading Kattar's novels because any decent girl would never touch such books. You are right. Those days Kattar's novels were smuggled into houses and girls read them with immense interest and delight. But I don't think that these novels inflicted much damage on the girls. About any girl who read Kattar or S. M. Jalal's novels you could safely say that she was a romantic at heart and fed up with life. As far as the idea goes that she had to appease herself by reading Kattar or S. M. Jalal's novels: it's not her fault but a shortcoming of our own collective literature that there were no better novelists in this particular genre than Kattar and S. M. Jalal. And besides, in my view, the books that damage one morally – that could *really* damage one morally – would actually benefit our women greatly, and personally speaking, I would greatly prefer a girl who is an ardent admirer of Kattar to one who only reads Rashid ul Khairi and Deputy Nazir Ahmed. To my mind, the latter kind deserves immense sympathy; I mean, who could be more unfortunate than her whose ideas about life were shaped by these two venerable but insufferable bores?

'This book was written by my friend,' I told Razia's aunt in a loud voice. I was sure that Razia stood listening behind the rustling curtains.

'The picture is obscene. I don't even know where Razia got these books from. I will toss them in the fire – decent girls don't read such books!' was her aunt's reply.

Feeling embarrassed, I said, 'This is by my friend Sheikh Qurban Ali Kattar. He lives in the flat opposite yours. He's the friend I visit in the evenings.' I was addressing the invisible Razia.

'Who? Not that rotten, dreary man, is he? He sits stooped on his armchair stealing glances in this direction all the time.

I don't know what he's looking for. Iqbal, my son, tell him it's not right.'

If I understand a girl's psyche correctly, then, in my opinion, she develops an ardent devotion for her darling writer-man who populates the world of her romances. For instance, if I were a girl, I would have much preferred absconding with my darling writer than with any other man. In my view, if all the writers who are read by girls were courageous, they could easily whisk away countless girls willingly. They are wasting their time or frittering away these golden opportunities. Even their being middle-aged or balding is not an obstacle to their success. If they show half the courage and daring of their protagonists and heroes, their lives could be thrilling and full of romance.

After this incident Razia started taking a greater interest in the resident of flat number ten. Afterwards, the tattered curtains in her balcony slipped a little from the sides and the parting between them turned more generous. I persuaded myself that Razia's interest was only temporary. I also confess that I was a bit envious at Kattar's good fortune – I wish I had written *The Exemplary Bat*. I had kept my visits to Razia's house and my acquaintance with her aunt a secret from Kattar, although there is very little that I hide from anyone; but if he had not been so absent-minded and short-sighted he would have caught me going up and down Razia's flat himself.

The trajectory of his expectations had now climbed higher than ever before. Those days he was always in his coat and tie, and the *Oxford Dictionary* was always kept open in front of him (even though he did not consider it important anymore). The glances that he flung towards late Umar's flat during Razia's absences had a fervent and heart-piercing quality.

Despite all this, there had been no improvement in his physical appearance; he still seemed as ragged as ever, someone whose liver is dysfunctional and whose diet doesn't suit him.

I usually visited Kattar at six, sometimes even later. I found out from him that Razia rarely came out to the balcony after six. This was understandable because it gets dark after six, and besides, her aunt who must have been busy during the day, kept a strict watch on her.

When she was in the balcony and we became aware of her silky whiteness behind the tattered curtain, we would never look at her directly in case she felt embarrassed or startled. Kattar's eyes immediately dug into the dictionary and he would start looking oddly self-conscious and nervous. (It's quite possible that he still hasn't managed to get a good, satisfactory look at her.) I pretended as if I was not even aware of her presence behind the curtains. But once I did get a good, satisfactory look at her standing in the balcony. She was there in the evening twilight like a strangely tempting goddess, and her eyes were transfixed on us, and in them I saw immense yearning and love. I thought that she lowered her gaze when I looked up, and turned her face away. But she did not leave. On another occasion, when her balcony was bathed in moonlight (the moon shines in Chakiwara too), I saw her white face resting against the railing of the balcony. She was looking at us with sad and dreamy eyes. Her tender hand held her dark, silky head, her body resting against the wooden railing. How deliriously beautiful, how deathly beautiful she seemed that evening! (She reminded me of an Italian painting that had left a deep impression on me during my college days.)

If there was one thing Kattar was happy about it was that Faghfur had ceased his erratic visits to his room. After Professor

Shahsawar Khan's intercession, that stubborn djinn had desisted from repeating his misbehaviour. During that period, Kattar repeated his demand for twenty-five rupees and eight aanas, which I evaded by saying that we would talk about it if Professor demanded it again.

One evening when I reached Kattar's flat, I found him unusually restless, like a man who is at the edge of some bewildering event. To conceal his nervousness, he played and spoke with Musafir, while stealing glances in my direction with his dull eyes. Clearly he had some new idea in his head, some new plan ... and he was hesitating to discuss it with me.

Finally, overcoming his hesitation, he said, 'Changezi, yaar! I have decided I cannot wait any longer, and neither can she. Today in the afternoon, her aunt yelled at her for something; I heard her cry. Her aunt has made her a prisoner. Tomorrow I will bring her here forever.'

'Bring whom? Her aunt?' I asked.

'No, I meant my beloved, Razia. Even ten thousand cruel and malicious aunts can't stop her from coming here. She will be pulled towards me like iron towards a magnet, a honeybee towards flowers, and a flame towards a moth ...'

'You mean like a moth towards flame?'

'That's what I said. And even if I said it the other way around, you should know, Changezi, that right now I am speaking under great emotional strain.'

'How do you plan to execute this?'

'How!' he said. 'Changezi! Sometimes you behave so naïvely! Don't I have Professor Shahsawar's magic ring? I only have to ask Hazrat Suleiman and she will automatically come to me. Ten thousand aunts –'

'Yes, the ten thousand aunts idea might be okay,' I said. 'But in my view, even if she came here, how will you hide her? You could be taken to court for kidnapping ...'

'I have everything figured out,' Kattar said. 'Day after tomorrow we will leave for Lahore. Perhaps I didn't tell you. Four days ago, a film company there offered me a job. They want me to write stories and dialogues for their films. They also wish to adapt a novel of mine into a film – *The Exemplary Bat* – and they have sent me a cheque for two hundred and fifty rupees as an advance for its rights.'

'You did not mention this to me, Kattar!' I said in an admonitory tone.

'I avoided mentioning it deliberately because the kind of love and devotion you have for me, you'd feel extremely dejected at having to part with me. I kept this news for the very end. No, Changezi, yaar! Don't worry. Do forgive my mistakes – everyone makes mistakes. If you ever have a chance to visit me, you will be able to meet me at the studio of The Seasonal Partridges. In our bungalow, which will probably be in Model Town, Razia and I will always welcome you. And your framed photograph will always be on the mantelpiece in our drawing room. Our visitors will ask, "Whose photo is this?" and I will say, "This is the photo of my most trustworthy and eternal friend, I. H. Changezi, Director of Allah Tawakkul." Bring your framed photo with you when you visit tomorrow.'

He looked at me with a loving and sympathetic expression, which had the lustre of eternal friendship. That look gradually changed to another kind of look: I had seen that look many times before in Qurban Ali Kattar's eyes. It was the look of a man who was about to ask for money.

'That cheque which The Seasonal Partridges has sent me is post-dated and cannot be cashed for another fifteen days. I will hand it to you. Book two seats on the express train for me and Razia. Second class, and can you also lend me three hundred rupees? Meanwhile, you may take custody of this flat.'

But I wasn't thinking about lending him the money. I was thinking of having to part with him, that he was about to be taken away from me. And tomorrow or the day after, this Middleway Street flat would be devoid of his presence. I really felt as if it was happening already and that Kattar was already gone, having inflicted the wound of separation on me. I did not doubt his apparent conviction and decisive manner even a little bit. He was usually unable to contrive even the simplest of lies, and considering the windfall which he had mentioned, I concluded that he would indeed leave for Lahore the day after tomorrow and Razia would accompany him. I mean, he was so convinced that it was as if he knew for a fact that this was how things were going to play out.

Suddenly I woke up with a start. How could he say with such certainty that Razia and he would leave for Lahore on the Express the day after? The ring had yet to perform this particular feat. Professor Shahsawar Khan's wrathful face appeared in front of my eyes, 'You doubt again? All right, you'll see for yourself!'

Kattar was saying, 'Okay, Changezi, yaar, please prepare the draft of the petition. I will now memorize it. While using the ring, it is not possible to stare into it as well as read what's written below.'

'Yes,' I said, as though in a dream.

I prepared the petition once more, but my attention was elsewhere. God knows why my heart was sinking. I was confronted with Fate's inevitability. On the screen of my mind spun so many radiant and saintly faces – Professor Shahsawar, Razia's innocent, charming cheeks now pale, now burning – these images were racing past my eyes. A railway carriage passed. *Coo! Coo!* Qurban Ali Kattar stood in the second-class compartment waving his handkerchief. 'Keep writing to me!' he was saying. *Coo! Coo! Chak! Chak! Chak!!*

While I was wrenching out words for the petition, Kattar was saying something like, 'How strange that neither you nor I thought of this. Through the powers of this ring even an estranged beloved can be summoned to land at your feet, while this one is actually willing! Completely willing! Definitely get the seats booked tomorrow, first thing.'

I kept the petition brief this time round. Actually, my inventive and literary powers had gone dry. For the benefit of Hazrat Suleiman, I wrote a brief history of Kattar's love affair, and then the request in these words: 'Your Excellency! It is my desire that my beloved comes into my arms this very moment.'

Kattar liked it, even though I had feared that these words might violate Hazrat Suleiman's moral decorum. Kattar's appreciation for them was indeed strange. I did not think that he could've been associated with the kind of courage required to take a woman into one's arms. Such daring from that coward! The world was going awry.

Yes, we kept talking until one in the morning – about the golden days of our past – which cemented my impression that Kattar was indeed leaving. That evening Razia did not come to the balcony at all, which meant that either the watch had been made stricter or that she'd buried herself in some corner and was sobbing her heart out against the cruelties of her aunt. Kattar's opinion was that it was the latter.

When I asked for his leave, Kattar came downstairs to see me off. He does this very rarely but that evening we discovered those rivers of our friendship and fidelity that had been gurgling in our chests for a long time. The thought of separation had revitalized our true friendship, which due to past misunderstandings and borrowed money and so on, had worn out somewhat. Once we were in the alley, he reminded me yet again to book the seats.

20

You can imagine how restless I was the next morning, due to the fact that I had to call off even my light morning exercise and massage. I even forgot to book seats for Kattar. He came over for lunch and this time I welcomed him as warmly and gladly as I had on the day when he first came into my life. Allah Tawakkul's best dishes were placed in front of him and a special new tin pack of Black & White was unsealed especially for him. He seemed in very high spirits and discussed at length the comparative features of Studebaker and Packard with me and Shedad Pashmi; he wanted us to advise him which car would better suit his new status. Money was not a problem; he wanted the best and most exquisite thing. Since neither I nor Shedad Pashmi knew anything about cars, we couldn't advise him usefully on that matter. After that, he left. He told us that he had to collect his clothes from the laundry man. He borrowed thirty-two rupees from me. He repeated that he was going to give me the cheque from The Seasonal Partridges, as well as the flat. He said, 'If you want, you could send some stuff there right now for the sake of custody.'

When I visited Middleway Street in the evening, the sun's golden yolk was smeared on the stone houses and the street almost seemed beautiful and romantic. A certain sense of fear still lingered in the atmosphere but it was a different kind of fear. The buildings looked as if they were made of delicate flower petals. Restless, I'd left Allah Tawakkul a bit early. I paused in front of Kattar's mansion; through the window I could see him stretched out on his armchair. Why not pay Razia's aunt a short visit, I thought. It had been four days since I had last visited. And then I was also feeling anxious about a few things. This might be my last visit in Razia's presence. I climbed the stairs and knocked on the door. I didn't hear anyone for a long time. Then a nervous voice said, 'Who is it?'

'Is Aunt Rabia there?' I asked with a pounding heart. I knew who was addressing me from behind the door.

'No,' she said. 'She's gone to Malir to see a relative and will return sometime later in the evening.'

She had recognized me and did not ask who I was.

'You …' she began to speak but didn't finish her sentence.

'Yes, you were saying something?' I said.

'You … haven't visited for so many days,' she asked.

'Yes, I was occupied …'

'But every day you visit the flat opposite ours – Qurban Ali Kattar sahib's place.' She was opening up to me, and if I wanted I could have stood there talking to her for a long time, but the man in the ear cap and sleeping suit was peeping through the staircase railing trying to eavesdrop on our conversation.

'All right,' I said.

'You …' But I was already downstairs, cursing everyone in those flats (except Razia) and especially that outrageous man in the ear cap.

Her aunt was not to return before ten. Razia was alone. This fact went in favour of the magic ring inventor's word. Who could say what would happen …! Who could …

Kattar was silent and seemed a bit harassed as well. His fingers were trembling. He had his suitcase and other stuff ready in a corner. He was wearing my best suit. There was a large red rose in his suit's buttonhole.

He took the cheque out of his pocket and handed it to me. It was really a crossed cheque from The Seasonal Partridges, drawn at Imperial Bank Karachi, but it was indeed post-dated. Apparently, the money had not been transferred into Imperial Bank's Karachi account and they had put down the date by which they thought they would have the money in their account. And, by the way, it was a real cheque. Patrons of Qurban Ali Kattar, who understood his worth, were still out there. I presumed the director or producer of *The Seasonal Partridges* must have been Kattar's fan during his college days.

Kattar said, 'Here's the cheque. For two hundred and fifty rupees. Actually Changezi, all this is due to Professor Shahsawar Khan's blessings. That evening when I met Professor, I started sensing that a new phase of my life is about to begin and that the good days are not far away. Look here, two hundred and fifty rupees – I never saw a cheque for such an amount even during the most glorious days of my fame. I am getting an excellent job where I could work up to become a director, producer or something like that. Talent can never stay hidden for too long. And tonight I shall also be granted the union of my beloved. Professor Shahsawar Khan is really a guardian saint and holy man. Oh yes, Changezi, we still haven't sent the professor his twenty-five-rupee money order.'

I assured him that it would be good to wait another day. Tomorrow I would definitely dispatch the money via money order.

'As soon as she comes here,' Kattar said with the confidence of the almost-heroes of his novels, 'we will go to your hotel and board the Express tomorrow morning. I think it would be better to board from Karachi Cantonment.'

Looking out the window, I found Razia standing in the balcony and looking towards us with extreme attention. She did not have her dupatta on her head, her breasts swelling under her white kameez, and on her face there was a free-spirited look (so it seemed to me) – one that indicated that she'd risk her life for her lover. Nonplussed, I turned my gaze away. When I looked again she was no longer on the balcony and the door was shut.

Kattar and I sat looking at each other for a while. Finally, Kattar said, 'Did you see her?'

I still don't understand how Kattar managed to see her despite his shortsightedness – despite the myopia and despite the fact that he never looked up at her – even then, whenever she'd be in the balcony, Kattar would become aware of her presence, and this awareness revealed itself as a shifty nervousness and a reddening of the earlobes.

It was dark inside the room now. Kattar asked me to turn on the light. I switched on the light, but it was to no avail.

'What day is it today?' Kattar asked.

'Thursday.'

'Oh, today there will be no electricity before eleven.'

Everyone knows that due to the explosion of a boiler in the power plant (which was being repaired) six months ago, each week one area in Karachi has to languish in the dark. Today, it was Chakiwara's turn. It was one of those unalterable laws of nature against which you could do nothing but bow your head and surrender.

Kattar did not have candles. Usually he did not require much light in his flat and on Thursdays he stayed at Allah Tawakkul till the electricity was restored. Now he went to the window and checked the time on his wristwatch in the twilight outside.

'Four minutes to eight, Changezi yaar,' he said.

I did not reply and he went into the bathroom for his ablutions. Down below, the alley lay dark and deserted without even a hint of breathing. The doors of the balcony were shut tight and not a streak of light escaped from the cleft between the doors. After his ablutions, Kattar went outside for a while where he wiped the nameplate outside his flat with a wet handkerchief until the white letters began to glow again. Then he returned inside.

'See how God has expediently caused darkness today, so that a certain someone cannot not be seen coming or going.'

I knew who he was referring to by this 'someone'. However, even I found the disappearance of electricity today a bit mysterious. Fate was laying the groundwork.

At eight, Kattar sat on his chair facing Mecca and, holding the ring in his hand, gazed into the stone. I sat on the chair opposite him. His long, lean and half-drawn face appeared ghostly to me.

My God! Will she come! Will she come! Her aunt wasn't here. It was completely dark – and that bold I-don't-give-a-damn look of hers!

We sat in silence for ten minutes. I could hear my heart beating.

'Khakrob! Sweep the floor,' Kattar's quivering voice broke my thoughts – it was clear and airy, as if a ghost was speaking in that dark room.

'Lay the carpet!' the trembling voice arose once more through the silence like a muffled whisper echoing in the vast space of the room. The time between Khakrob's sweeping and King Suleiman's arrival seemed interminable, and as the requisite preparations for his arrival were made, my heartbeat grew more pronounced.

Qurban Ali Kattar's nervousness could be gauged from the fact that every command he uttered was more muffled than before, his whispers gradually getting softer, as if the speaker of the words had been seized by a delirium ... And finally that moment – it arrived.

After a short silence, during which I could hear the *tik tik* of Kattar's wristwatch, came Kattar's voice. Loud but heavy with feeling like Fate's own utterance and yet sputtering at the same time, 'Hazrat Suleiman the King! My beloved, by your command, must be in my arms!'

Silence. For half a minute we sat with bated breath. Then we actually heard the sounds of someone climbing up the stairs. She was coming! She was coming! Someone paused by the door behind me. The door opened – God knows why I had shut my eyes tight – someone was in the room.

That's when the electricity was restored. I opened my eyes as my heart pounded in my ears. Kattar was lying on the armchair like a drunkard, his eyes half closed. And in his arms was Musafir, standing upright on his hind legs!

Translator's Note

ALASTAIR REID, IN HIS PREFACE TO NERUDA'S *EXTRAVAGARIA* says, translation is a 'mysterious alchemy – some poems survive it to become poems in another language, but others refuse to live in any language but their own.' As a translator, I don't believe there is a royal road to translation. Every work of translation must negotiate its own preferences around which it can bear its losses. I have devoted these years to translating Muhammad Khalid Akhtar's work with primary attention to his narrative voice, which for me, as his reader and translator, embodies most fully his ironic, mischievous, sophisticated sensibility as a writer. I hope some of the delights of his work make their way across in English. In the final account, however, all imperfections, flaws, errors are my own.

Acknowledgements

THIS BOOK OWES ITSELF TO THE ENCOURAGEMENT AND guidance of Musharraf Ali Farooqi. Nearly seven years ago, I discovered Muhammad Khalid Akhtar's work when Musharraf urged me to read (and translate) *Chakiwara mein Visaal*. Later, he also instigated me to include other Chakiwara stories in this volume.

Many thanks to the PEN Translation Fund Grant for selecting this work for support in 2010.

I have been fortunate to have a line of readers who have improved the work with their feedback: Amna Chaudhry, Noor Habib, Aneeqa M. Wattoo and, most of all, Maryam Wasif Khan, whose immaculate ear and eye for English prose have helped me untangle the coils of meaning that my bilingual brain couldn't. I must also thank Professor Aamir R. Mufti for pointing out a crucial error of translation at the beginning of the book.

My thanks, as always, to Clare Alexander, for being ever-present with help, advice and guidance. Shruti Debi has been a marvellous champion for this book. It was in large part due to her efforts that this book was able to find a home at Picador India. Thanks to Diya Kar Hazra for believing in this book, and a very, very special thanks to Teesta Guha Sarkar for her meticulous editing. The book is much improved thanks to

Teesta's relentless attention to detail. I owe a special thanks to Haroon Khalid who has been exceptionally patient and generous with me over all the years I took while translating this work.

A book, although attributed to an individual is, in reality, the product of a community. I would like to give my utmost gratitude to all the people who sustain me through conversations, ideas, laughter and solidarity: Ali Raza, Ali Aftab Saeed, Ali Sethi, Ali Nobil, Manan Ahmed Asif, Umair Ibrahim, Azeen Khan and, most of all, Maryam Wasif Khan, who cannot be thanked enough for being everything and more.